"Chief, the body's this way."

Jess shivered. It was a sweltering dog day in August here in Alabama but she was wishing she had a sweater just now.

Techs were already on-site documenting the scene and gathering evidence. In Jess's experience when a cop or a cop's family was the target, the motive was often vengeance.

Lori headed in the opposite direction as Harper led Jess through the kitchen and down a few steps to a large room at the rear of the house that overlooked the backyard. Jess stalled in the entryway of the room and gave herself a few moments to absorb the details of the scene.

There was so much blood. The distinctive odor had permeated the room. The frigid air seemed to freeze in Jess's lungs as she stared at the word written on the wall in large sweeping strokes. The word written in blood.

Rage.

Praise for the Novels of Debra Webb

"*Impulse* solidly establishes the Faces of Evil as the 'must read' thriller series of the year! The characters you loved in *Obsession* are back in a chilling story that could only come from the inventive mind of Debra Webb."

—Peggy Webb, author of *The Tender Mercy of Roses* (as Anna Michaels)

"Compelling main characters and chilling villains elevate Debra Webb's Faces of Evil series into the realm of high-intensity thrillers that readers won't be able to resist."

—CJ Lyons, *New York Times* bestselling author

"Just when you think Debra Webb can't get any better, she does. *Obsession* is her best work yet. This gritty, edge-of-your-seat, white-knuckle thriller is peopled with tough, credible characters and a brilliant plot that will keep you guessing until the very end. Move over Jack Reacher—Jess Harris is comin' to town."

—Cindy Gerard, *New York Times* bestselling author

"Debra Webb has done it again with *Obsession*—which may well be her best book yet—a top-notch thriller that will keep you riveted to the page and wanting more. Webb is a writer's writer, who delivers the kinds of books we all wish we had written."

—Robert Browne, author of *Trial Junkies*

"*Obsession* is certain to please Debra Webb's existing fans and gain her a legion of new ones. An engaging, edgy thriller that's a one-sit read—with the lights on!"

—Vicki Hinze, author of
Beyond the Misty Shore

"Breathtaking romantic suspense that grabs the reader from the beginning and doesn't let up. Riveting."

—Allison Brennan, *New York Times*
bestselling author

"Webb keeps the suspense teasingly taut, dropping clues and red herrings one after another on her way to a chilling conclusion." —*Publishers Weekly*

"Bestselling author Debra Webb intrigues and tantalizes her readers from the first word." —SingleTitles.com

"Masterful edge-of-your seat suspense."

—ARomanceReview.com

"Romantic suspense at its best!"

—Erica Spindler, *New York Times*
bestselling author

"Fast-paced, action-packed suspense, the way romantic suspense is supposed to be. Webb crafts a tight plot, a kick-butt heroine, a sexy hero with a past and a mystery as dark as the black water at night." —*RT Book Reviews*

Also by Debra Webb

The Faces of Evil Series

Power

Impulse

Obsession

RAGE

FACES OF EVIL

DEBRA WEBB

FOREVER

NEW YORK BOSTON

PROM
Webb

Forever
Hachette Book Group
237 Park Avenue
New York, NY 10017

www.HachetteBookGroup.com

Printed in the United States of America

First Edition: April 2013
10 9 8 7 6 5 4 3 2 1
OPM

Forever is an imprint of Grand Central Publishing.

This book is dedicated to an amazing little boy named Amos. I am awed by your strength, courage, and resilience. May your future be filled with hope and happiness.

Acknowledgments

Being a cop is hard work. Whether you patrol the streets or investigate homicide scenes, the work takes dedication, courage and doggedness. I hope that my characters always portray the deep compassion and intense passion of those who serve our community.

A rage . . . that nothing can allay, nothing but blood.

—William Shakespeare

RAGE

Prologue

Birmingham, Alabama, Monday, August 2, midnight

A big flash of lightning streaked across the sky, making the room bright. Devon Chambers counted the seconds in his head. He didn't like storms. He hadn't wanted to come out of his house, but he'd heard the baby crying.

Six-one-thousand . . . seven-one-thousand . . . thunder clapped, almost drowning out the baby's wailing.

It was raining hard outside and Devon was dripping on the tile but the mommy wouldn't mind.

She was dead.

His stomach hurt even though he couldn't see the mommy now. It was too dark. But Devon understood dead. His mommy had died, too. He remembered watching her in the pink coffin and waiting for her to breathe. She never did. Not even once. No matter how long the preacher talked she still didn't breathe.

Devon hadn't liked it much when they closed the lid and put her in the ground where she couldn't get any air for sure. He'd worried about that until the next day at school when his teacher told him about being dead and going to heaven. He was glad about heaven. All the preacher had talked about was the angel taking Devon's mommy in his arms and giving her to God. Devon decided he didn't like angels much. But he guessed that was the only way to get to heaven. Couldn't hang around down here forever, his teacher said.

Lightning flashed again and he knelt on the floor and touched the blood. It was thick and sticky. He shuddered. Not because he was afraid. He wasn't afraid. Not for real. Rubbing the gooey stuff between his thumb and fingers he wished the lightning would come faster so he could see if the mommy had changed her mind about going to heaven and started to breathe again.

Maybe if he put her head back she would decide not to go with the angel. Patting the darkness until he touched her hair, he scooted the mommy's head back to where it was supposed to be. He couldn't figure out why the angel would cut it off like that. Wouldn't she need it in heaven?

He wondered if God would be mad about the bad words. They were written on her forehead. He could wipe 'em off, but the angel had written them there.

He didn't want to make the angel who took the dead people to heaven mad.

When the lightning had first shown him the angel taking the mommy, his throat got too tight and his heart had beat faster and faster. He'd had to go inside himself for a while. He tried not to, but he couldn't control it sometimes. Sometimes he just had to hide. The doctor said it was his safe place.

When he'd come out of his safe place, the baby had been

crying and he'd sneaked out of his house to see if it was okay. If anybody found out he'd come over here he would be in big trouble, especially with his sister. She would be really mad. But the baby was crying harder and louder, so he had to do something. The mommy wouldn't like her baby crying. She could probably hear it all the way in heaven.

He waited a minute for the lightning to come again so he could see where the glass was on the floor. The light flashed, blinkity-blink, and real carefully he walked around the broken glass and the blood and made his way through the house waving his arms around in front of him so he didn't bump into anything. He felt like a blind kid. He was glad the lightning came a little faster now, even though the thunder growled like a mean old bear faster and faster, too.

The baby's room was dark like the rest of the house. Devon thought about turning on the light but that might make the angel come back and he wasn't ready to go to heaven. He couldn't leave his sister all by herself. She would be sad. She pretended not to like him much but he knew she loved him. Working too much and trying to go to school made her grouchy. And he was a lot of trouble. When his mommy was sick Devon had heard her talking to his sister. She said that even though he was a lot of trouble, he was her brother and she should love and take care of him always.

Ever since then he tried not to be so much trouble, but always was a long time and sometimes he forgot.

He wiped his hands really good on his shirt, then he reached into the crib and touched the baby. It stopped crying but made funny sounds and flailed its arms.

What did he do now?

He thought about all the times he'd watched the mommy out by the pool with the baby. Sometimes when it cried she got a bottle and that made the baby happy.

He felt around in the crib until his fingers closed around a bottle and he smiled. The mommy must have put it there before the angel came. Mommies were smart like that.

Devon shook the bottle and he frowned. It was empty. Oh well. He gave it to the baby anyway. The baby sucked and sucked. Sounded kind of like when he got to the bottom of a milk shake and he just kept trying to get that last bit of foamy stuff through the straw.

The sucking stopped and the baby started to cry again. Devon didn't like the crying. Maybe he could take the bottle in the kitchen and put milk in it. Babies liked milk. He was pretty sure the daddy would be home soon. He would know what to do if the milk didn't help.

Devon took the bottle and felt his way down the hall and the stairs. He counted the steps so he would remember to go slower and to be careful. That was a rule. *Be careful on the stairs. Don't eat while I'm gone. And never call 911 unless the house is on fire or you're hurt. If you think someone's trying to get in the house, go out your window, climb down the trellis, and run to a neighbor's house.* His sister had a lot of rules. She was smart. Really smart. Not like him.

He held his breath as he opened the fridge door. The light made him squint. He blinked a couple of times, then got the milk. With the door open he could see to fill the bottle but he made a mess anyway. He cleaned it up and put the milk away. *Always clean up your mess.* That was another rule.

Finding his way back to the bedroom was easy. He

remembered the way even if it was dark. He hid in the dark a lot. It wasn't so bad. His sister told him being afraid of the dark was dumb. He didn't want to be dumb about that.

The baby was still crying real loud. He hoped the milk would make him happy. As soon as he put the bottle to its mouth it started trying to suck at it.

No more crying.

Devon smiled. He did good.

A door slammed somewhere in the house and he jumped. Was the angel back?

More lightning made the room as bright as the inside of the refrigerator. He didn't see anybody before the room went black again but he could hear someone bumping around in the house. Thunder rumbled and he shivered.

The bumpy noises sounded closer.

Someone was coming.

Devon hid in the baby's closet. His body shook so much he could barely stand up and the urge to hide inside himself was real strong. He couldn't see 'cause of the darkness, not even when he tilted his head to look through the slats in the door, but he smelled the angel. Smelled like flowers. The same as the angel that came and took his mommy to heaven.

Would the angel know he was hiding in here?

Angels could probably see through doors like this for sure.

His heart pounded so hard he could hear it in his ears. Tears burned his eyes and he squeezed them shut real tight. In his head, where no one would hear, he prayed for the baby.

Please, God, don't let your angel take the baby, too. The daddy will be so sad.

The angel left the room without taking the baby.

Wow. God heard him fast. Devon's knees felt like the Jell-O his sister made him eat when he was sick. He hated Jell-O. Especially the green kind.

He waited, listening for a while. The baby was happy. No more crying. The angel was gone. Devon should go home. The daddy would be coming soon. He might get mad if he found out Devon came into his house. He might blame Devon for the mess.

As quiet as a mouse he sneaked out of the closet and crept to the door. He didn't hear any more noises, so he hurried down the hall and all seven of the steps. He walked past the mommy, making sure he didn't step in the glass or the blood. The lightning let him see the way. It was still coming fast.

He stopped at the broken door. It was raining harder than before. He'd have to run across the yard in the rain and squeeze through the fence at the corner where it was sagging a little bit. He was almost too big to fit anymore.

Glass cracked behind him.

His heart bumped against his chest.

Run! the voice in his head told him.

He darted across the yard. Didn't look back. Skidded to a stop at the fence and squeezed between the boards. Something grabbed his arm. He jerked to get loose. Nails clawed him. He yanked and twisted. He hit the ground, then scrambled up to run. He didn't stop until he was on the other side of his house and under the floor, in the crawl space.

He hugged his scratched arm and hoped the angel couldn't find him here. And then he went inside himself.

1

Five Points, 7:35 a.m.

Hello Jess.

The appearance of those two words on the screen of her cell phone should not have stolen her breath or weakened her knees, but they managed to do both in the space of a single heartbeat, forcing her to wilt down onto the toilet seat.

Jess Harris shoved a handful of damp hair behind her ear, then hugged her knees to her chest. It wasn't really the words that had her crouched on the toilet seat of the cramped bathroom. It was the identity of the sender.

Tormenter.

Eric Spears . . . the *Player.*

Jess curled her fingers into her sweaty palm to stop their trembling. She pressed her fist to her lips and fought the trepidation howling inside her. *Answer him!* This might be the last time he reached out to her if she didn't do something.

She touched the text box on the screen and prepared to enter a response. Before she tapped a single letter another bubble of words appeared.

I watched you on the news last night. Your ex has impeccable timing. I can't wait to see who wins this round.

Pulse fluttering wildly with an infusion of anger, she considered telling Spears that, as he was no doubt aware, his current location could be tracked via this connection and that she intended to promptly inform the bureau.

But that would be a lie. Worse, he would recognize the lie. Spears knew her far too well.

Using the pad of her thumb she tapped one letter at a time until she'd filled the text box with the message she wanted to send the sociopath who had murdered dozens of women, maybe a hell of a lot more, in his sadistic career as a serial torturer-murderer. Jess smiled as she reread the words she hoped would prompt his need to grow ever closer to her.

One thing's for sure, it won't be you. I'm the one who got away, Spears. Guess that makes you a loser and a coward.

After hitting send, she reveled in the idea that her words would burrow under his skin and fester like boils until he just had to claw at the itch. Eric Spears's malignant narcissistic side wouldn't deal well with failure. Not only did he not like to lose, he hated the idea of being wrong about anything or anyone. He'd made several mistakes of late. Skating so very close to getting caught was one of them. Allowing Jess to live was another.

Whatever it took, she would get him.

Her cell clanged that old-fashioned tone, announcing an incoming call. She jumped. Nearly dropped the damned thing. Spears wouldn't dare…

Harper calling appeared on the screen, banishing the stream of conversation between her and Spears.

"Jess, you are truly pathetic." She swallowed back the lump of undeniable fear that had risen into her throat and forced herself to breathe normally. "Harris."

"We have a homicide, Chief. Shady Creek Drive off Columbiana Road."

Jess dropped her feet to the floor and banished thoughts of Spears. "How many victims, Sergeant?"

"Just one . . . but . . ."

The silence that filled the air for several endless seconds had Jess's pulse revving with the surge of adrenaline charging through her veins.

"It's bad, Chief. Really bad. It's the wife of one of our own. Lieutenant Lawrence Grayson's wife, Gabrielle."

Oh damn. "Crimes Against Persons isn't working this one?" No need to start the week off like the last one, in a pissing contest with Deputy Chief Harold Black, bless his ornery heart. Today's staff meeting was supposed to clarify some ground rules and cement the team spirit to ensure better cohesion as they moved forward. That meeting likely wouldn't happen now. Couldn't be helped. Justice was the last thing the dead should have to wait for.

"I got the call since the first officers on the scene felt the murder might be connected to the Lopez situation," Sergeant Chet Harper explained. "The wife was decapitated and there's a message including some of the buzz words from this weekend's hit on your place."

"Jesus Christ." Jess scrubbed at her eyes with her free hand. Images from the destruction that had been her room at the Howard Johnson Inn flickered through her mind. They had to get a handle on this escalating gang situation.

It was turning into a blood bath and resurrecting the ugly memories of the city's violent, racially unjust past.

The MS-13 clique operating in Birmingham, once lorded over by Salvadore Lopez, was at war with a faction that had split off to follow his younger sister, Nina. The sister was currently in custody for kidnapping Jess, among other charges. Salvadore had gone into protective custody with the promise of rolling over on his infamous father, Leonardo. The elder Lopez was the messiah-like leader of the West Coast's rampant and ruthless MS-13 activities. Every three-letter agency in the country wanted him to go down, and now they had their chance.

Squaring her shoulders, Jess began the process of tuning out her personal frustrations with the whole damned Lopez family and the regret for the loss of life—particularly an innocent life—that would only get in the way. "Is Captain Allen on the scene?" Allen headed up Birmingham PD's Gang Task Force. His insights would be invaluable if a gang connection was substantiated.

"En route as we speak."

"I'll be there shortly, Sergeant. You know what to do."

Jess ended the call as she pushed to her feet and headed for the door. She caught her reflection in the mirror over the pedestal sink and paused mid-stride. Her damp hair would just have to dry on its own. She shoved her phone into her robe pocket so she could pile her blond locks into a manageable mass that was annoyingly curly when wet and snapped a claw clip in place. Makeup she could take care of en route. A flick of mascara and a dab of lip gloss would do.

She silently repeated the mantra she'd clung to for the past thirty-six hours or so. *I'll be okay.* It would take more than being kidnapped by some ditzy, power-hungry teeny-bopper and having her place and her things destroyed to knock Jess off her game.

The tone that accompanied an incoming text had her rummaging for her cell.

I'm deeply wounded, Jess. I thought by now you would miss me as much as I miss you. See you soon.

"The sooner, the better," she grumbled. Jess Harris was not afraid of anything. Except maybe the possibility of failing to get Spears before he added more victims to his heinous résumé.

With renewed purpose she deleted the conversation and emerged from the bathroom to find Lori, on her cell, probably getting the news about the murder. Jess grabbed the one suit that had survived last night's kill-the-deputy-chief's-stuff episode and ripped it free of the dry cleaner's plastic. She'd failed to pick it up from the dry cleaner on Friday, which was the only reason it had been spared from the carnage.

Since her Audi had been at the lab for processing related to her abduction—and still was, damn it—the car and this one suit were about all that remained of the belongings she'd rolled into Birmingham with. Well, except for the dress and the turquoise pumps she'd been wearing last night. The pumps would just have to do until she had time to shop.

"You need a cup of coffee to go?" Lori asked as she headed for the kitchen with her own mug. Her Five Points studio was one big room with a small bath and closet carved out of the already-tight floor space. Any level of privacy was basically impossible.

"That'd be great." Jess stepped into her pumps while

she picked through the bag of undergarments, cosmetics, and necessities she'd purchased at Walmart late last night. Living out of a plastic bag was no fun, and though Lori insisted she was happy to have her as a guest, Jess was anxious to get a place of her own. She liked Lori a lot, and was proud to have the detective on her team, but staying on Lori's couch was going to get old, fast. Maybe it had something to do with being in her forties and set in her ways, but having alone time felt immensely important, especially when she hadn't had any in about forty-eight hours. She needed her space. Along with a new wardrobe and almost everything else a woman required to operate on a day-to-day basis.

Unfortunately, all of that would have to wait.

She had a homicide to get to.

Shady Creek Drive, 8:30 a.m.

"Whoa." Lori surveyed the crowd gathered as she turned off Columbiana Road. "This is going to be complicated and"—she blew out a big breath—"messy."

News vans cluttered the intersection of Columbiana and Shady Creek. Birmingham Police Department cruisers lined the street on either side of where they needed to turn. This tragedy had befallen one of their own and a show of strength was expected. The gesture was heartfelt, but there was no place for crowds at a homicide scene. At least not until after complete scene documentation and thorough evidence collection. The potential for contamination and/or loss was far too great with every warm body that entered a crime scene.

"Do you know Lieutenant Grayson?" His name sounded familiar but Jess couldn't recall meeting him. She'd been introduced to so many of Birmingham's finest since her arrival scarcely three weeks ago that she couldn't say for sure whether she'd met him or not.

"I've seen him around but I don't really know him." Lori powered down her window and showed her badge to the uniform controlling access to the block. When he'd waved her through, she went on, "Grayson is with Field Operations, South Precinct."

Still didn't click for Jess.

"What kind of reputation does he have?" As wrong as it seemed, close family members were always the prime suspects in a case like this until evidence and alibis proved otherwise. Lawrence, aka Larry, Grayson was a cop, so the fundamental steps in a homicide investigation would be no surprise to him.

"A good one as far as I know. I've heard his name a few times when accommodations were handed out." She glanced at Jess. "If you're asking me if he would kill his wife, I don't know him that well, Chief."

"I guess that's something we'll need to learn." They were on duty now. Jess was the deputy chief of SPU, Special Problems Unit, and Lori Wells was one of her detectives. Their ability to be friends and step back from those roles as needed fascinated Jess. After nearly two decades doing investigative work, this was her first time to have friends, in the true sense of the word, on the job. She'd certainly never been the houseguest of a coworker.

Maybe an old dog could learn a new trick.

The houses along Shady Creek were modest *Brady Bunch*–style ranches and split-levels, circa the seventies;

it was a typical blue-collar neighborhood. Good folks who were forever stuck on the low end of middle class while being overworked and underpaid.

Crime scene tape circled the yard, using trees and shrubs for support and announcing that bad things had happened to those who called this address home. Outside that gruesome yellow line a host of cops had surrounded an emotionally distraught man and were struggling to get him into the passenger seat of a sedan.

"That must be him." He looked vaguely familiar, but Jess still couldn't say for sure if she'd met him.

"Yeah. Damn." Lori shook her head. "Looks like he's lost it."

Jess grimaced at the emotionally charged scene. "Who wouldn't?" She steeled herself in preparation for what was to come. No matter how experienced the investigator, when murder hit this close to home—a fellow cop—it was difficult to take in stride.

"You see any sign of the coroner's wagon?" Between the cruisers and all the other vehicles crowding the street, not to mention what looked like a brigade of cops and no shortage of neighbors, it was difficult to see beyond the driveway.

Lori guided her Mustang as far to one side as possible considering the middle of the street was about all that was left in the way of unoccupied pavement and shut off the engine. "It's the van right behind that Camry riding my bumper."

Jess craned her neck to see. There appeared to be a male passenger but, with the sun glinting on the other side of the windshield, she couldn't see the driver. Opting to jerk to a stop in the middle of the street, whoever was at the wheel of the van didn't seem to care if more of a bottleneck was created.

Jess climbed out of the low-slung Mustang. Instantly the heat crushed around her. The humid air was as thick as molasses. Last night's storm had ensured a sweltering morning and that little or no viable evidence would be found outside the home.

With one more glance behind her, she checked to see if the ME had climbed out of the van yet. She probably wouldn't be lucky enough to get Schrader again. For all she knew Dr. Harlan Schrader could be on his way to the job offer at the Mayo Clinic by now. They'd worked a case together last week and not having to go through that awkward *first time* business again so soon would be nice.

The driver's side door of the van opened and a female emerged. Shoulder-length brown hair, pale complexion. No one Jess had met so far, that she recalled anyway. The woman wore a lavender wrap dress with matching strappy stilettoes. Her sophisticated—scratch that—arrogant body language confirmed they had not met. Jess was one hundred percent certain she would remember that cocky stride, not to mention the haughty tilt of the woman's chin.

"This should be interesting," Lori murmured as she moved up to the front of the Mustang, where Jess waited.

"What's that?" At the scene perimeter, Jess showed her badge to the uniform.

"That's the associate coroner, Dr. Sylvia Baron. She's the lieutenant's ex-wife." Lori ducked under the crime scene tape and Jess followed. "She's a little pushy. No one likes getting stuck on a case with her."

Pushy or not, sounded like a conflict of interest to Jess.

An older man had gotten out on the passenger side of

the van and joined the woman's purposeful movement toward the house as Jess and Lori made their way up the sidewalk. He looked vaguely familiar. Sixty maybe. Tall. Broad-shouldered. Blond and tanned. All he needed was a diamond stud in one ear and he'd have the whole Harrison Ford thing going on.

At the front door she and Lori stopped long enough to drag on shoe covers and gloves. "Who's the man with her?"

"That's Dr. Leeds."

That was Martin Leeds, the Jefferson County chief coroner? Jess really had to find some time to get to know the various chains of command in Birmingham. She was woefully uninformed. In her own defense, she'd held the position for only two weeks and she'd been embroiled in murder and mayhem all fourteen or so of those days. Well, maybe she'd had a small break here and there. The unbidden memory of steamy, stolen hours spent between the sheets with Daniel Burnett the weekend before last had butterflies taking flight in her belly.

Those frantic and breathless minutes in his fancy Mercedes just last night wouldn't exactly be dismissed any time soon either. Particularly since he was her boss.

"I don't want that bitch anywhere near my wife!"

Jess's attention snapped back to the street as Lieutenant Grayson's angrily shouted words reverberated in the impossibly thick air. Those closest to Grayson were trying to calm him, but he was having no part of it.

Jess decided that an introduction to Leeds and the former Mrs. Grayson could wait until they were inside and had surveyed the crime scene. The situation outside was a ticking bomb and it wasn't going to get any calmer until Lieutenant Grayson had been removed from the scene.

The man's wife had been murdered. The ability to think clearly or to reason was long gone.

Inside the house the atmosphere was somber and *cold.* Jess shivered. It was a sweltering dog day in August here in Alabama but she was wishing she had a sweater just now. Her nose twitched. Even the frosty temperature couldn't completely conceal the distinct odor of coagulated blood hanging in the air as if she'd stepped into a meat locker rather than a home where a family lived.

Techs were already on-site documenting the scene and gathering evidence. Jess's first step and top priority was to find the motive, in part based on what she observed here this morning. Had the wife been murdered during the commission of a robbery? Were drugs, money, or both the reason she was dead? There was always a slim chance the killing was a random act of violence. Slim because this was the home of a cop and the neighborhood was not exactly a prime target location for thieves. These weren't rich folks with a treasure trove of readily sellable goods for the taking.

In Jess's experience, when a cop or a cop's family was the target the motive was often vengeance. There was always jealousy, of course, if one or the other had a problem with fidelity. Whatever evidence Jess discovered here, final assessments and conclusions could not be reached until all witnesses or persons with knowledge were found and interviewed. Every hour that passed before all those steps happened lessened the likelihood of success in solving the case.

Harper spotted their arrival and made his way through the main living area and into the foyer. "Chief, the body's this way."

"Detective Wells"—Jess hesitated before following

Harper—"why don't you find the officers whose duty it is to protect the scene and explain how that concept works." She surveyed the number of warm bodies milling around inside the house and shook her head. "I want anyone who's not a witness or who doesn't belong to the Crime Scene Unit or the coroner's office out of here *now*."

"Yes, ma'am."

Lori headed in the opposite direction as Harper led Jess through the kitchen and down a few steps to a large room at the rear of the house. Jess stalled in the entryway of the room and gave herself a few moments to absorb the details of the scene.

There was so much blood.

Words were scrawled in blood around the walls.

Pig. Whore. Kill the bitch. Kill the pigs. One by one.

The chilly air seemed to freeze in Jess's lungs as she stared at the other word written in large, sweeping strokes.

Rage.

She blinked away the images from her motel room that attempted to transpose themselves over those currently burning her retinas. Shaking off the eerie sensation of déjà vu, she visually inventoried the rest of the room.

A massive flat panel television hung over the stacked-stone fireplace. A local morning talk show filled the screen but the sound had been muted. Beefy, well-worn leather sofas stood like sentinels on either side of the fireplace waiting for the family to gather. Windows, blinds tightly closed, spanned the walls. The only natural light breaching the space was from the broken sliding door, its two panels of glass lying in pieces on the tile floor. Beyond the broken door, a wood privacy fence surrounded the backyard and swimming pool.

Jess shivered again. "What's going on with the air-conditioning, Sergeant?"

"The thermostat was adjusted as low as it would go," he explained. "It's about sixty-two degrees in here."

"Seems our killer took the time to think things through before taking his leave." And he or she obviously knew a little something about skewing attempts at determining time of death. Just another reason to hate all those *CSI* shows.

"I believe the murder was carried out right here," Harper said as they moved across the room. "The child, a six-month-old boy, was left in his crib in a bedroom. Nothing in the house, as far as we can tell, was disturbed beyond the damaged patio doors. The standard grab-and-run items like laptops and jewelry are still here."

"Where's the child now?" Jess hoped he wasn't out there amid the chaos on the street. Grayson was in no condition to care for himself, much less a child.

"The lieutenant's partner, Sergeant Jack Riley, called his wife and she took the baby home with her as soon as a paramedic confirmed the child was unharmed."

After fishing for her glasses, Jess shoved them into place and moved closer to study the placement of the body. Dressed in a yellow spaghetti-strapped nightgown, the victim lay supine on the tile floor, a pool of coagulated blood around her, her head severed from her body but left right next to the stump of her neck. Tissue was torn in a jagged manner as if the perp had had a hard time getting started with a sawtooth-type tool. Multiple stab wounds along the torso had dotted the pale yellow gown with ugly rusty spots. Her arms were outstretched at her sides, crucifixion style. Legs were straight and together.

Across the victim's forehead, written in what appeared to be her own blood, were the words *PIG WHORE*.

Jess stepped nearer and eased into a crouch. She pointed to the victim's upper arms. "Looks like our killer had a good grip on her at some point." There was bruising on the chest, just above her breasts. Jess passed a gloved hand over the area. "He held her down while he committed this final atrocity. Judging by the bruise pattern I'd say he was right-handed."

Harper nodded. "I counted ten stabs to her torso. All postmortem, like the beheading. Didn't see any indication she had been sexually assaulted."

"I agree, Sergeant." The coroner's office would check for sexual assault, that was SOP. As for the rest, there wasn't nearly enough blood for the visible damage to have been inflicted while her heart was still beating. No arterial spray from the decapitation. A little castoff from the saw, but that was about it, other than the blood that gravity drained out of the body. In fact, seemed as if the killer waited until livor mortis was well under way before bothering to play psycho surgeon.

Harper pointed to the victim's hands. "No defensive wounds on her hands or forearms to indicate she fought her attacker. No ligature marks to indicate she was restrained."

Very strange. Lividity indicated she had been in this position since her death or very quickly thereafter. But why here and like this? Had the victim been watching television when her attacker crashed into the room? Had she fallen asleep on the sofa? Or did she hear the breaking glass and come to check it out? How had he disabled her?

"Could be damage to the back of the head," Jess suggested. There didn't appear to be any to the temple areas or the forehead.

"I don't see any blood matted in her hair close to the skull." Harper pointed to the long hair fanned around her head.

That was true. Jess rubbed at the wrinkle furrowing her brow with the back of a gloved hand. "Once he'd killed her, what distracted him for so long before he did the rest?" She glanced around the room. Had someone come to the door and interrupted his work? Had the baby started crying and thrown him off balance? The latter wasn't likely, since the baby was still alive.

"Reminds me of the Manson murders," Harper said. "I watched a documentary the other night. The anniversary is coming up this weekend."

Jess had noted that similarity, too, but she wasn't about to say it out loud. Not with so many ears around. All they needed was the media bringing that kind of connection into this. She scrutinized the tile floor around the victim. Not a single footprint. The perp had been exceptionally careful. "No blood anywhere else in the house?"

"Nothing we've found so far. Looks like someone showered recently in the hall bath. The shower floor is damp and so's the rug in front of it. There's a faint smell of shampoo, gardenias."

Surprised, Jess said, "The shampoo should be logged into evidence. We need to be sure the techs check the drain as well. What about a towel?"

Harper grunted a negative sound. "Not in the bathroom or laundry room. If the perp was the one who took the shower, he took the towel with him. Already took care of the rest."

Jess lifted the victim's arm. "We have full rigor. She's been dead nine or ten hours anyway. Maybe longer."

The manner of the decapitation was primitive. As if the perpetrator hadn't been able to get the job done on his first attempt, he'd started over a couple of times, mutilating tissue and making one heck of a mess. "No murder or mutilation weapon lying around?"

"No, ma'am. Whatever the perp used, he took that with him as well."

With no weapon and no ready signs the perp had been careless, the odds of nailing him were stacked against them. "Who discovered the body?"

"Johnny Trenton," Harper said. "The pool guy."

Jess made a face. "They have a pool guy?" She'd noticed the pool out back, but this wasn't exactly the kind of neighborhood where one expected to encounter a cabana boy.

"He arrived at six this morning, as scheduled, to clean the pool. He has a key to the garage and the door that leads out of the garage into the backyard." Harper gestured to the patio and sparkling pool beyond the broken sliding door. "He made the nine-one-one call. Says he didn't come inside for fear of stepping in the blood or otherwise damaging the scene. Since it was obvious Mrs. Grayson was dead, he figured there was nothing he could do anyway."

"He didn't come in the house to check on the child or the husband?" If he knew the family, he had to know there was a kid and a husband.

"He says the place was as quiet as a tomb when he arrived, so he assumed anyone else in the house was dead, too."

More likely he hadn't wanted to risk suspicion by entering the scene and leaving behind a footprint or fingerprint. "Where is this pool guy?"

"In the dining room. I didn't see any blood on him and his hair definitely doesn't smell like gardenias."

"Well, that certainly rules him out," Jess mused.

Harper cast a somber look at the victim and shook his head. "I don't think he did this, Chief. This involved some serious rage and a good chunk of time. Trenton doesn't seem like the type to invest that much emotion, if you know what I mean."

"Have him transported downtown. I'd like to question him in a more formal setting." Being driven downtown in the back of a police cruiser should have him eager to cooperate if he knew anything at all. And Jess did understand what Harper meant. Like a crop of choking crabgrass the I-don't-care-about-my-neighbors attitude had taken root among Southern folks, too. No one wanted to get involved anymore.

She pushed to her feet and walked to the now useless slider and stared across the yard. The lawn was thick and lush. No sign of mud, which meant no footprints out here either. Only the tops of neighboring homes were visible above the fence but one, at the farthest end of the yard, was a two-story like the Grayson home. A pair of side-by-side windows overlooked the Grayson's backyard.

"Have the neighbors been canvassed?" Jess strained to see any movement beyond the windows across the way. Anyone looking out those windows at just the right time would have had a clear view of the murder.

"Yes, ma'am." Harper pointed to the house with the windows that had captured Jess's attention. "We checked that one first. Looks abandoned. Yard's all grown up. The utility meter has been pulled. No answer and no vehicle in the drive."

"Damn." She turned her attention back to the victim, Gabrielle Grayson. Dark hair and olive skin. Thirty or thirty-two. "Latino?" she asked Harper.

"Mrs. Grayson was born in this country but her parents moved here from Spain. Lieutenant Grayson's partner told me she was a nurse until her son was born and she opted to become a full-time mother."

"We need to know if she has any connections whatsoever to the gang world." This was the fifth decapitation Jess had encountered in the last week. The other four ritual killings had been carried out by members of the MS-13 against those they deemed traitors. The major difference was those decapitations had been accomplished while the victims were still alive. This one looked wrong. The words scrawled on the walls were unfocused. The whole scene, including the possibility the perp had showered, was way off when compared to an MS-13 assassination scene.

"There's no connection that we know of, ma'am."

Another of those aggravating frowns tugged across her brow. "Where is Captain Allen? I thought he was en route."

Harper looked away and cleared his throat. "He... ah...dropped by. Took a quick look and said he'd let us know if he heard any rumblings about this. He knows Grayson. Said the lieutenant and his partner have been helping out with GTF but neither has been involved on a level that would ignite something like this. He doesn't think there's a connection."

"He couldn't hang around until I arrived?" Jess understood the guy had it in for her since she'd barged her way into the Lopez case and stolen the big takedown Allen had had planned, but this was a homicide for Christ's sake. A cop's wife.

Jess took a breath, brought her voice down an octave or two. "Stay on Allen, Sergeant, and find out from Grayson's division chief if he's worked a case, past or present, within the division that may have landed him on someone's hate list."

"Yes, ma'am."

Jess was as sure as anyone could be that this murder didn't have anything to do with the MS-13. It was way too neat and there were too many discrepancies. But she couldn't rule out that possibility just yet any more than Allen could. "We also need cause of death ASAP," she said, more to herself than to the detective next to her. "The media will have a field day with this. We need something to give them before they start making up stuff."

In the past forty-eight hours a Lopez hangout had been blown up and three clashes in the streets of downtown Birmingham had barely been defused without bloodshed. A couple of fires had been started in abandoned houses. No matter that the Lopez clique was falling apart all on its own, there were some in the community who were looking for an excuse to take matters into their own hands. The murder of a cop's wife—the mother of a small child—would fuel that fire into a raging inferno.

"There was another clash in Druid Hills just before daylight," Harper mentioned. "Another house burned after being hit by Molotov cocktails, but no one was injured."

Damn. Druid Hills was the neighborhood where this

war had started. Jess had lived there for a while as a kid. Not much had changed in all this time. Harper's news just confirmed what she already knew. They needed damage control on this one. "What the devil is taking Leeds and his colleague so long?"

She hated waiting. Worse, Jess's attention settled on the victim; she hated for this woman to lie here like this any longer than necessary. She hoped Grayson and his ex hadn't gotten into a war outside.

"I'll check on that," Harper offered.

"Do that, Sergeant, and make sure—"

"If you'll get out of the way," a haughty female voice announced, "we'll try to make up the time we lost due to BPD's incompetence at securing the scene and preventing the flash mob outside."

Jess turned and came face-to-face with the tall brunette in the lavender dress who appeared determined to live up to her reputation of being pushy. *Sylvia Baron.*

"Somebody adjust that damned thermostat," she shouted at no one in particular. "Are we trying to turn this vic into a Popsicle or what?"

"I'll take care of that," Harper said as he made himself scarce.

Jess thrust out her hand. "I'm Deputy Chief Harris. I'll be investigating this case."

"Dr. Sylvia Baron, associate coroner and medical examiner. This is Dr. Martin Leeds, Jefferson County's chief coroner. As I said, if you will get out of the way, we'll attend to our responsibility in this matter."

As true as it was that the coroner had jurisdiction over the body, Jess was king of the hill when it came to the scene. "Dr. Baron, I'm certain this is an awkward and perhaps difficult time for you. Be that as it may, considering your ties to the victim's husband, I have strong reservations about your ability to maintain objectivity under the circumstances. Your being here obviously represents a conflict of interest."

Baron didn't look surprised that Jess had already heard about who she was. In fact, the ME laughed. "Like I care about your reservations. Now step aside or I'll call Chief Burnett and have you removed from this case."

A bad, bad feeling struck Jess. Was this woman another of Burnett's fancy private-school cronies? Or maybe Sylvia Baron was a former lover or another ex-wife? The man had at least two exes Jess hadn't met. Either way, she wasn't running this investigation. Jess was.

Big breath. Stay calm. She stepped around the body and moved closer to Baron. "I think that's a very good idea. Calling Chief Burnett, I mean." Jess kept her smile in place as she reached into her bag and retrieved her phone, then offered it to the other woman. "Why don't you use my phone? Burnett's at the top of my contact list."

The woman matched Jess's fake smile with one of her own. "No need." She whipped out her iPhone and made the call with scarcely more than a swipe and a tap. "He's at the top of mine as well."

2

Birmingham Police Department, 11:30 a.m.

Sandy-haired, golden-eyed, and well-tanned, Johnny Trenton was thirty-two years old and, judging by his rap sheet, a former male prostitute who had discovered a better way to earn a living amid the wealthy and prominent in Birmingham by cleaning their pools and offering private swimming lessons to the kiddies.

Or maybe he'd just assumed a better cover for work in one of society's oldest professions. At the moment, seated at the interview table and with murder on her plate, unless his occupation was relevant to the case, Jess didn't particularly care.

Problem was, to her knowledge, the Graysons were neither wealthy nor prominent.

Jess surveyed the file Detective Wells had prepared on Trenton. She reminded herself not to rest her right arm too heavily on the table, since it had one leg shorter than the other three, which was inordinately annoying.

"This is your second summer working for the Grayson family?"

Trenton's boredom with the proceedings loud and clear, he remained slouched in his chair on the other side of the table, barely bothering to lift his gaze to meet Jess's. "You got it."

"Who hired you? Mr. Grayson or his wife?"

"Mrs. Grayson." A smirk twisted his lips. "She said her old man was never home and she needed someone to take care of the stuff he neglected."

Do tell. "What sort of *stuff*, besides the pool, was her husband neglecting?"

Trenton hunched his shoulders in a shrug, a lackluster gesture at best. "No clue. She hired me to take care of the pool and that's what I did."

"Did Mrs. Grayson seem worried about anything lately that you're aware of?"

Jess would ask the husband that question as well. She hadn't gotten to interview him at the scene, which was understandable. He had followed the coroner's vehicle back to Cooper Green. He was most unhappy that his ex-wife had not been instructed to back off. In fact, according to what Jess had overheard the other cops outside saying, Grayson and Baron had carried on quite the screaming match outside the murder scene. Dr. Leeds, the official coroner of record on the case, had stood his ground on having her at his side and that was that.

"She never mentioned anything to me." Trenton made a face that suggested he'd just remembered something. "She did complain that since her husband was never home and she got no breaks that the kid was driving her nuts. I didn't pay much attention though. That's what I hear from most of the wives. Sometimes it's a come on," he added bluntly, "but not with Mrs. Grayson. She wasn't interested."

"Interested in what exactly?" Jess closed the file and waited for his response. The man had no shame. She agreed with Harper. Trenton was far too shallow to have invested enough emotion to murder a victim the way Gabrielle Grayson had been murdered.

"In sex." He lifted his shoulders and let them drop in another lackadaisical shrug. "Some are lonely, others just need a little excitement in their lives. It's one of the perks that comes with the job, you know. A *fringe* benefit."

"Do the wives pay you for these additional services? We do have laws against that sort of transaction, Mr. Trenton. But then you're aware of that, aren't you?"

His posture tensed just the slightest bit. "I don't get paid for sex anymore, Chief Harris. That was a past life I don't care to revisit. I maintain very expensive pools for very wealthy people. If I provide an extra service here and there or just a little intimate companionship I get a better tip, that's all."

Jess resisted the urge to roll her eyes. "But Mrs. Grayson is not wealthy, correct? And she didn't live in one of the mansions you typically cater to."

He exhaled a big breath. "All right. You got me. Mrs. Grayson's pool wasn't on my regular billing plan. She paid me what she could afford. But I would have done it for free for the rest of my life if she'd let me. But she wouldn't. This year, she even insisted on paying me the same as everyone else since her finances were better."

"Why is that, Mr. Trenton?" Guys like Trenton rarely did anything nice for anyone other than themselves. The comment about Grayson's improved finances she would follow up on soon enough. "Why would you have worked for free for Mrs. Grayson?"

"Three years ago I did a stint in rehab." He puffed out a big breath. "Gabrielle was the head nurse. She helped me through it. I would never've gotten my act together again without her help, and I didn't make it easy for her to help me, trust me. I owe her my life."

The seconds ticked off as his admission elbowed its way into what Jess had surmised about him. She hadn't expected honesty or compassion and it felt as if she'd just gotten both. She suspected there was more behind that peacockish facade he paraded. "Thank you, Mr. Trenton." She scooted back her chair and stood. "If we have additional questions we know where to find you. Be advised that you'll need to remain available until this investigation is closed."

"You got a pool, Chief Harris?" he asked, his gaze blatantly roving over her as he got to his feet. "My rates are reasonable and I've never had a dissatisfied customer."

Jess laughed. "No, Mr. Trenton, I do not have a pool." In fact, she didn't even have a roof to call her own. She had to do something about that. Soon. "I'll see that someone takes you back to your SUV."

Outside the interview room, Sergeant Harper waited. "Trenton ready to go?"

"He is and, unfortunately, if he knows anything he's not ready to share just yet. Has Lieutenant Grayson arrived?"

"He and his attorney are waiting for you in Chief Burnett's office."

It wasn't surprising that Grayson would have an attorney already. As an experienced cop he would understand his position in the investigation. Husbands always had to be cleared when wives were murdered. And he was likely still furious that his ex-wife was involved in the case on any level. That decision had legal trouble painted all over it. Who wouldn't want legal representation considering all that?

"I just spoke to Chief Waters over at the South Precinct," Harper went on. "He wanted to be sure we understood that Grayson is one of the best BPD has and we'd better take care of him. I let him know the case is in good hands."

"Thank you, Sergeant." Chief Waters's assurances were exactly the accolades she expected. Grayson was a highly decorated veteran detective. Waters and his division couldn't be involved with the investigation but his input as regards Grayson was duly noted.

Jess's senior detective gave her a nod. "Waters is reviewing the cases assigned to Grayson over the past two years but he doesn't recall anything that would have earned him this brand of enemy. He believes the trouble came from his work with Captain Allen's team."

Just another reason for her to want to wring Allen's neck. Was it too much to ask for a little professional courtesy? "Whatever he's been doing for Allen, we need full disclosure."

"Already on it, ma'am."

"Keep me posted, Sergeant, and please escort Mr. Trenton back to his vehicle at the Grayson home." She leaned in a little. "See if you can learn anything more about his time in rehab. The victim was the head nurse when he was there."

"Yes, ma'am."

Burnett's office was on the fourth floor and Jess opted

for the elevator. Not that she was opposed to climbing the two flights of stairs, but these were her only shoes at the moment. Snapping a heel would be a problem. And the truth was she hadn't gotten into a fitness routine since her move south. Even two flights of stairs would probably kick her butt at this point. No need to go into an interview out of breath.

Tomorrow, she promised herself. She would get into some sort of normal workout routine tomorrow. Next week at the latest.

Detective Wells was back in the SPU office gathering the latest financials on the Graysons, along with Gabrielle's family and employment history. Officer Cook, another member of Jess's small unit, was tasked with going over the information in Grayson's official personnel jacket. Jess had scanned his as well as his partner's as soon as she arrived back at her office. Unless Grayson had changed his mind since bringing in his attorney, he had given carte blanche to this investigation.

As much as Jess wanted to assume the husband was completely innocent, it was her job to vet him the same as she did all other persons of interest and potential suspects.

Tara, Burnett's receptionist, greeted Jess as she entered the cozy and richly appointed lobby of Birmingham's chief of police.

"Chief Burnett's expecting me."

"Yes, ma'am. Sheila's still at lunch so you should just go right on in."

Jess thanked Tara and made the short journey down the hall to Burnett's private office. His personal secretary's desk stood in a more intimate waiting area just outside his door. Jess gave the door a rap as she opened it.

At the head of his conference table, Chief of Police Daniel Burnett stood and motioned for her to come in. His gaze swept over her as if he needed to ensure she was in one piece. Or maybe he was remembering those frantic minutes in his SUV last night before all hell had broken loose.

Lieutenant Grayson and his attorney rose, joining Burnett and yanking Jess back to attention. She didn't recognize the attorney and Grayson looked as if he'd barely tacked himself back together for this meeting.

"Gentlemen, this is Deputy Chief Jess Harris, head of our SPU and the lady we've been talking about for the past *fifteen minutes*." Burnett underscored the last with a pointed look at her.

Jess paused at the chair directly across the table from Grayson. "I apologize for keeping you waiting, Lieutenant. I assure you it was in the interest of this case." She extended her hand toward him. "I am so sorry for your loss."

Grayson accepted her offered hand and gave it a feeble shake. "I'm grateful that Chief Burnett put your team on this. I'm aware of your reputation, Chief Harris, and I want whoever did this found as quickly as possible. My wife"—he visibly struggled to maintain his composure—"deserves speedy justice." A single tear slid down his stony jaw.

Jess studied his face and eyes. The agony was genuine. She'd bet her scrawny savings on it. "I appreciate your confidence, sir."

The attorney offered his hand next. "Marcus Davenport. I'll be representing the interests of Lieutenant Grayson and his family during these grim proceedings."

Made sense. Davenport was the city attorney. Jess

hadn't met him before but she knew the name. Davenport would want his thumb on the pulse of this investigation.

"Of course." She shook his hand. "It's a shame we have to meet under these circumstances."

They settled in their seats and Burnett started the conversation. "Lieutenant, you've been in the department far too long for me or anyone else to presume to enlighten you on how this investigation will proceed. Why don't you offer whatever suggestions or questions you have and we'll go from there?"

"I've tried all morning to think if anything was different... but the truth is, nothing comes to mind." More of those tears glittered in his eyes.

"What about your work with Captain Allen?" Jess prodded. The gang-related avenue was one she'd like to close as quickly as possible, since her instincts were pointing her in a different direction.

Grayson blinked as if just waking up. "I only started working with the Gang Task Force a week ago." He dragged in a shaky breath. "I've had no run-ins with any gang members. Nothing. I can't imagine how any of them even know I exist. And yet, somehow..." His face crumpled. "How could this happen?"

"Mrs. Grayson hadn't mentioned any strangers in your neighborhood? No encounters at the supermarket?" Jess asked.

Grayson cleared his throat and took a breath. "Nothing. We talked every day at lunch and if I worked late, I always dropped by in time to help tuck in our son." His voice cracked on the words. "There just wasn't any warning. And absolutely nothing in the house appears to be missing. It doesn't make any sense."

Jess reached for her notepad and pencil, then settled her eyeglasses in place. She had resigned herself to the fact that without them she was blind when it came to reading. "Lieutenant, do you work the night shift often?" According to the report made by the first officers on the scene Grayson had been on duty until the call came in about his wife's murder a few hours ago.

"I hadn't worked nights in years until I volunteered to support the GTF," he explained. He lapsed into silence for a long moment. "I should have been at home last night."

"As you said, there was no warning or reasonable expectation of danger. You couldn't possibly have known your family was a target."

Grayson was fifty. Fit and more than a little vain, judging by the lack of gray in his blond hair and the contacts his personnel file indicated he wore. Nothing wrong with that. But he had a small child at home and a wife nearly twenty years his junior. Why volunteer for extra duty? Especially dangerous duty?

"What made you decide to give Captain Allen a hand with GTF?"

Obvious frustration crept into his expression. "My partner, Jack Riley, has been picking up extra shifts with the GTF for months. He believes Captain Allen's efforts are making a hell of a difference in the mounting wave of gang activities washing over this city. Jack's conviction made me want to do my part, too. I have a son, Chief. I need to help put these bastards out of business. That's the only reason I wasn't home with my wife and child last night," he said with a notable hint of anger in his tone now. "If that makes me a suspect in your eyes there's nothing I can do about that except pray you won't waste valuable time."

Jess accepted the lieutenant's not so subtle rebuke with a nod. "A more than worthy cause, Lieutenant. I hope you understand that every question I ask is essential to getting to the bottom of this awful business. I'm not in the habit of wasting time."

He scrubbed his hands over his face, the platinum wedding band glistening on his left ring finger. "It's hard as hell to sit here and answer your questions" he admitted, "but I recognize we have to do this. Ask your questions so we can move on."

"All right. Beyond your recent support of the GTF, have you worked any cases that could have somehow put you on someone's revenge list? Think carefully, Lieutenant. Sometimes trouble can come from the last place we expect. Could be something that happened in your personal life."

Grayson shook his head. "I've gone over and over the cases in my head, frontward and backward. Not one comes to mind. My partner and I have been pulling surveillance for GTF, nothing more. Most of the time the field ops are reserved for those trained specifically for drug and gang enforcement. Jack and I have been involved in only one field operation. You might not remember but I was on the scene at your recovery Saturday night."

That was where she'd seen him. "I appreciate the backup, Lieutenant." The reality that his wife had been so gruesomely murdered scarcely more than forty-eight hours after he'd come to Jess's rescue made keeping her emotions at bay more difficult. She cleared her mind of the sickening images of the scene at his home and steadied her full attention on the man and the case. Even regret was a distraction she couldn't afford on this case.

"Nothing in your personal life comes to mind either? No problems between you and your wife? Sometimes the birth of a child can change things. Drive a wedge between a couple."

Fury lit in Grayson's eyes. His jaw hardened as if holding back his initial response took enormous effort. "My wife and I could not be happier. Our marriage is..." His expression turned haunted. "Our marriage was as close to perfect as any couple could hope for."

Jess held his gaze when she felt confident he would have looked away. "Even with you away from home so much? Some women might not have been so understanding. There are, after all, husbandly duties around the house and in the bedroom."

Burnett sent her a warning look. The attorney shifted in his chair. No one wanted her to go down that path, but the question had to be asked.

"I took care of my family, Chief. Always," Grayson promised. "If you can find anyone who'll say otherwise I'll be shocked."

The man was sure of himself. He'd thrown down that gauntlet without hesitation. Maybe Trenton was wrong about Gabrielle feeling overwhelmed...or maybe Grayson didn't know his wife as well as he thought.

"I'm not making any accusations," Jess reminded him. "Just asking the necessary questions. To your knowledge Gabrielle was having no regrets over giving up her work to be a full-time mother? No depression issues?"

"None." The snapped word echoed in the room.

"There were no problems when you last saw her around eight last night?" Jess pressed. "She wasn't upset or feeling bad or ignored?"

"Hell no."

"But you were there only ten minutes or so"—Jess glanced at her notes—"according to your statement to the first officers at the scene. You didn't have coffee or anything with your wife. How can you be so certain of her state of mind?"

"I know my wife." He ground out the words from between clenched teeth.

He was angry at Jess right now and she couldn't blame him. She made a note or two on her pad before settling her full attention on him once more. "So you and Gabrielle hadn't argued recently? Neither was mad at the other? No frustrations or grudges at all?"

"No, no. and no," he said flatly, anger still simmering in his eyes.

"All right then. You have my word, Lieutenant, that my team and I will do everything we can to find the person or persons responsible for this tragedy. I hope you'll call me with any questions or with anything you recall that might be useful to our investigation."

Grayson's only response was a steady glare.

"This has been a terrible morning for you, Lieutenant," Burnett said, breaking the awkward silence. "I would urge you to stay with extended family or friends and allow yourself to grieve this loss. As Chief Harris said, it's imperative that you keep her informed of any relevant information." Burnett pointed his attention in her direction. "As I am sure she will keep you fully informed as well."

Jess flashed him a smile as she dug around in her bag for a business card. "I absolutely will," she said to Grayson as she passed a slightly dog-eared card to him. She'd crossed out the bureau logo. At some point she needed new business cards. Along with a new apartment and clothes...and her car back. The list of all that needed doing was overwhelming.

Grayson accepted the card and tucked it into his interior jacket pocket. "Thank you, Chief." He pushed to his feet. His attorney did the same. "My partner insists my son and I stay with him and his family for now. So that's where I'll be." He seemed to lose his train of thought for a moment. "I have people to call and...arrangements to make."

Jess stood. "Lieutenant, just one last question." She didn't have to look at him to know Burnett would be aiming another of those warning stares at her.

Grayson said nothing but waited for her to go on.

"Your ex-wife, Dr. Sylvia Baron, remains adamant about being involved with this case when I feel strongly that she should step aside. Her superior, Dr. Leeds, has backed her up. In any event, are you and Dr. Baron still friends? That wasn't the impression I got this morning, but there must be some reason she refuses to budge on the issue."

"Chief Harris," Davenport offered, "as Chief Burnett pointed out, my client has suffered a great deal today—"

"No," Grayson cut him off. "I'll answer the question. That crazy woman"—he spoke through gritted teeth—"is likely reveling in my pain. She refused to be a real wife to me or to have children in the ten years that we were married. Her career was too important. And now..." His voice cracked and trailed off. He shook his head. "We are not friends. I don't trust her motives. I can't believe she's getting away with this." He closed his eyes a moment.

"The idea of her touching my wife pains me more than you can imagine."

"I understand your reservations," Burnett put in. "Unfortunately the decision belongs to Dr. Leeds. We spoke just before you arrived. He is aware of the department's objections and has assured me that he will be personally responsible for your wife. Dr. Baron will be an observer and nothing more."

That was news to Jess. A few hours ago Burnett had basically told her to back off on the Sylvia Baron issue. Sylvia Baron had reveled in setting her iPhone to speaker so Jess could hear the words straight from the horse's mouth. So far there hadn't been time in Jess's day to demand an explanation from Burnett. But she'd get around to it.

"I've lodged my objections with Leeds as well," Davenport added. "I suspect we haven't heard the last on that issue."

Burnett assured Grayson and Davenport that he would stay on top of the matter. Jess waited until Grayson and his attorney were gone before turning to Burnett. Here they were, just the two of them, with a few minutes on their hands. She decided now was as good a time as any to question him about Sylvia Baron.

But she'd have to tread carefully or he would see right through her motives. No one wore jealousy well. And as much as Jess would love to say that distasteful emotion had nothing to do with her curiosity, she tried not to lie to herself too frequently.

"This is going to be a tough one," Burnett said before she could launch her interrogation. He plowed his hand through his hair. "Grayson's holding up a hell of a lot better than I would, I can tell you that. The guilt over not being there to protect his family has to be eating him alive."

"It's the kind of nightmare no one ever wants to face," Jess agreed. "And speaking of which, I should get to my office so we can begin building a case board." She could ask him about the haughty ME later. Right now she had far more important things to do than whine about the women in his life, past or present. Besides, Wells or Harper could get the skinny on Sylvia Baron. Being armed with a little more info before questioning Burnett would be a good thing. To bring it up right now would simply look petty.

As Jess gathered her notes, he moved closer, making a deep breath ridiculously burdensome. Damn it. She hated that she had absolutely no control on her most basic reactions when it came to him. But after nineteen days back in Birmingham she had no choice but to admit defeat on some level.

There was still something between them, even after two decades apart. She could deny that until the day she died and it would be a lie. It had been there ten years ago when they'd run into each other in that damned Publix the night before Christmas and it was there now.

And, much to her dismay, she had learned that every cotton-picking southernism she'd ever heard as a child still lived somewhere in the far recesses of her brain. Evidently changing latitude and longitude had somehow propelled her vocabulary into some sort of time warp.

"You okay? You need anything?" he asked softly.

And Burnett knew just how to make her squirm. His simple question wouldn't have carried nearly as much impact had he not moved in close enough for her to smell that subtle yet sexy aftershave he wore. "I'm fine. Thank you." She hefted her bag onto her shoulder and scooted away a few inches. "I should be prepared to brief you by the end of the day. Say five thirty?"

"We'll need a statement for the press before the department briefing at six. I'll need time to prepare. So how about five?"

"Why don't I just give you a statement for the press now?" She gifted him with a big old smile. "We are doing all we can to solve this heinous crime," she said in her most authoritative and somber tone. "Any information that might facilitate that effort would be deeply appreciated. Otherwise, stay out of the way and keep your innuendoes and unsubstantiated claims to yourselves." She flashed another fake smile. "How's that?"

He ignored her question. "Whatever you do, be careful. I'm not happy with you moving forward as if Saturday night didn't happen. You're still a target, Jess. Your face has been all over the news. You really should be lying low for a while."

She made a derisive sound. "And let Chief Black hijack *my* case? I don't think so. Besides, you know you want me on this one. Grayson mentioned this was your idea."

"I need you on it," he corrected. "There's a difference. I want Wells or Harper with you at all times. You can keep your head down and still work this case. Stay out of the limelight. Don't piss off any reporters and have them hounding you more than they do already. Their focus on you adds to your visibility as a potential target."

"As long as they stay out of my way we won't have a problem." She absolutely did not need Burnett telling her how to play nice with the reporters or how to take care of herself. They had been over this before.

Instead of arguing with him as he spouted all the reasons he was right and she was wrong, she used the most ridiculous observations to distract herself. He was wearing the navy suit today. The one she really liked. With the pale blue shirt and the red tie. The suit with its narrow lapels and sleek cut accentuated his broad shoulders and the color did amazing things for those blue eyes of his. None of which she wanted to notice, but she had no more will power where he was concerned than she did with a bag of peanut M&M'S.

The abrupt silence made her blink. He had stopped talking and was watching her stare at him. "You shouldn't wear that suit." She made an unpleasant face for emphasis. And to think just the other day she'd almost told him it was her favorite.

He looked down at his jacket, smoothed a broad, long-fingered hand over the trim lapel to the one button fastened at his lean waist. "I like this suit. What's wrong with it?"

Her shoulders poked up then fell. "Don't know. Maybe it's the color." She backed toward the door. "Or the cut. Something is"—she held up a hand and moved it back and forth as if she couldn't excavate the precise words—"just not right with that one."

He waved her off and headed for his desk. "I want a proper sound bite by five o'clock."

There was something else he did exceedingly well. Tick her off. "Maybe then you can brief me on Sylvia Baron and why she thought you would take her side over mine." The demand was out of her mouth before she could stop it.

Her insecurities notwithstanding, Burnett was supposed to have *her* back at moments like the one that occurred today between her and Baron. And he'd fallen down on the job.

"She's Senator Robert Baron's daughter. The Baron family believes they still run Birmingham the way they did in the old days." He shrugged. "She's throwing his office around, that's all. It's what she does."

A senator's daughter. Well, well. Jess remembered something about him and a senator's daughter. "Weren't you married to a senator's daughter the first or second time?"

Burnett glowered at her from behind his desk. "I was not married to Sylvia." He shuffled a stack of messages.

Oh my God, that was it. If he hadn't been married to her it had to have been someone close to her. "Her sister then."

"Yes," Burnett confessed as he reluctantly met her gaze once more. "I was married to her younger sister. It was a long time ago but Sylvia doesn't seem to notice. When it suits her, she uses that ancient history to her benefit."

Right there, in a nutshell, was the number-one reason Jess disliked small-town life. Everyone knew everyone else and made it a point to know his or her business. Furthermore, most people were related by blood or marriage, or both. The whole small-town mentality was as pervasive as it was invasive. It made her crazy.

"Do you have any other ex-wives or ex-sisters-in-law running around here that I'm likely to lock horns with?" Might as well get all the cards on the table. Burnett had married the first time less than a year after his and Jess's breakup. Just like that, she did a mental finger snap. Six years together and he was over it in less than one.

But, like he said, that was ancient history. And yet, she couldn't put it fully behind her.

"That is none of your business, *Chief* Harris." Burnett

faked a smile. "By the way, I almost forgot to ask. How's Agent Duvall?"

Chief Harris? "Don't even go there. Wesley is my only—*only*—ex. Everyone's entitled to one." Jess promptly turned her back. "I have a case to solve."

"See you at five," he called after her.

"Five thirty," she tossed back on her way out the door.

That was the thing about exes. Whether it was the other half of her one failed marriage or her twenty-year-old love affair with Burnett, an ex was like a bad penny, they just kept showing up again.

And these days a penny was pretty much worthless.

3

Lieutenant Grayson saw his wife at eight last night when he stopped by to tuck his son into bed. When he left Mrs. Grayson was watching a movie." Harper added the movie title to the timeline he had created on the white board in the SPU offices. "The DVD was lying on the coffee table at the scene this morning."

"Can anyone else corroborate the times he gave for returning to work last night and leaving for home this morning?" Jess leaned against the front of her desk. According to Grayson, he and his partner, Sergeant Jack Riley, had been providing support to BPD's Gang Task Force in their off-duty time. As head of the GTF, Captain Ted Allen was drawing as much manpower from the other divisions as he could in an attempt to get a handle on Birmingham's escalating gang problem.

"Sergeant Riley and Lieutenant Prescott have confirmed that Grayson left for home just before eight last night and returned shortly before nine." Harper noted the times on the board. "He pulled an all-nighter and didn't return home until he got the call about the murder this morning."

Prescott belonged to SPU but she, too, was on loan to the GTF. Considering she was not happy at all that an outsider like Jess had gotten the newest deputy chief position, she wasn't likely in any hurry to be taken off that detail. Or to assist Jess in this case or any other. No matter that Birmingham was her hometown, Jess had spent more than two decades away. Most of that time she had worked with the Federal Bureau of Investigation. That made her an outsider to those who'd served locally for their entire careers.

That she'd been offered this position by her former fiancé, Chief of Police Daniel Burnett, ensured that most failed to consider her qualifications for the job before assuming the worst. Jess had a long, uphill journey when it came to fitting in and gaining the respect of her peers and subordinates.

No problem. She'd been climbing hills since the age of ten.

"Nothing from Dr. Leeds on the time of death?" she asked Officer Chad Cook, the youngest and least experienced member of their unit.

"Not yet, ma'am," he piped up. "Dr. Leeds's assistant expects they'll have some preliminary information around two."

Jess hoped so. She had to give Burnett something by five thirty. The BPD's division chiefs and the mayor would likely be at the six o'clock briefing. All involved would want assurances that the investigation was well under way. Getting some estimate on time of death and narrowing down cause of death would be helpful.

Detective Wells turned in her chair to face Jess and the others, hopefully with an update on the Grayson family financials.

"Lieutenant Grayson's finances have changed in the past year. He inherited a handsome sum from a rich uncle. In addition," Lori went on, "to the home on Shady Creek Drive, and the pool guy, he recently purchased a beach house just outside Mobile along with a boat and two Jet Skis as well as a vintage Corvette. We're not talking millions here, but a tidy sum nonetheless."

"A vintage Corvette," Cook noted. "Nice. We young guys can never afford that. It's always the old geezers driving a sweet ride like that."

"That's what Trenton meant," Jess rationalized, ignoring their youngest member, "when he said Gabrielle's finances had changed this last year." Tied up that loose end.

"Gabrielle Marquez Grayson came into the marriage with no savings or assets that I can find," Lori added, "but she had a good job. Charge nurse at New Life Rehabilitation Center. She worked there for five years before leaving to become a full-time wife and mother about the same time the lieutenant got his inheritance."

"What about the divorce from Sylvia, the senator's daughter?" Jess ventured. "Did money change hands other than what went to the lawyers?" Probably wasn't pertinent, but Jess wanted to know for her own selfish reasons. She wanted to know more about Sylvia and her sister.

"Not anything documented. But" —Lori shot her a look—"in case you wondered, Sylvia Baron was born very rich and her tax bracket doesn't appear to have changed."

Jess wasn't surprised. "I take it she didn't remarry?"

Wells shook her head. "No other spouses, no children."

Jess pushed off her desk and walked to the case board. She scooted her glasses up her nose and viewed the photos of the Grayson family, the partner, and the pool guy that Harper had posted. The timeline started at eight last night, since Gabrielle was alive at that time according to the husband. There was more to this woman's life than they knew, far more. And a whole lot more to her death.

"Add Sylvia Baron and MS-13 to the board," she told Harper.

"You really think this is gang-related?" he asked as he complied with her request. "Seemed way too personal to me, and Captain Allen says no one is claiming responsibility or issuing warnings of more to come."

Jess agreed with the way too personal part. "No, Sergeant, I do *not* believe this is gang related. But if anyone asks or drops by and looks at our case board"—she turned to the board, which would be impossible to conceal from anyone who popped into their office—"they won't know that until I'm ready for them to know."

Some things were better left unsaid, she had learned, until theories were proven. Like the scenario that the ugly words written in Gabrielle's blood were nothing more than an attempt to mislead the investigation. To distract from the true evil.

"We have a gruesome murder in a bedroom neighborhood that hasn't seen any criminal activity beyond the occasional robbery around the Christmas holidays in its forty-year history." Jess paced the length of the case board as she thought out loud. "Working-class folks. Most have lived in the neighborhood for a decade or longer. They go to church on Sundays and take pride in their homes and yards. It's picture perfect."

"Until now," Harper countered. "Last night's murder put a black spot on their clean record."

"Let's consider the scenarios. *All the scenarios.*" Jess grabbed a dry erase marker and uncapped it. "If this is gang related, which I doubt, what's our motive?"

Harper peeled off his jacket and hung it on the back of his chair. His and Lori's desks were stationed face-to-face. Lori's gaze followed Harper's move to get comfortable before turning back to Jess. Lori's hardcore independent woman attitude was slipping just a bit. Jess wondered if she realized how hard she was falling.

"If," Harper suggested, "this was an MS-13 grudge or revenge killing, then the motive would be related to something Mrs. Grayson or Lieutenant Grayson had done, either on purpose or unknowingly." Hands bracketed at his waist, the senior detective strode over to stand by Jess. "Since Grayson has been helping out with the GTF, we could assume he's crossed someone or gotten his name on the wrong list. He doesn't believe so, but he could be wrong. He may have been in the wrong place at the wrong time and not realized it. All white guys look alike to some people." Harper smirked.

"Except," Lori chimed in, "Gabrielle Grayson was decapitated, marking *her* as a traitor, in gang terms. We know she worked as a nurse at a rehab center for several years, maybe she provided medical care or drugs to the wrong people. And now it's come back to haunt her."

"And they waited more than a year to kill her?" Harper challenged.

"Unless," Jess interjected, "she never stopped." She

listed the scenario on the case board. *Medical/drug connection.* "Maybe she liked having money of her own. She was a career woman before, earning a nice salary. Maybe motherhood and financial dependency wasn't exactly how she'd seen her life playing out." And maybe Jess was infusing a little too much of her own personal concerns into the scenario.

Lori got out of her chair and strode to the board. "What if she finally said no? After all, she was a mother. She had the child to think of. And there was always the worry that her husband would find out—assuming he had no idea about her extracurricular activities. Maybe she decided to do the right thing and refused to aid this unknown perp and he got pissed."

Jess passed her the marker. Lori sent the two males in the room a cocky smile before adding motives to the medical/drug connection. *Money and fear*, then *revenge.*

Harper held out his hand. "If we're tossing out fictional plot points," he said flatly, "what if this make-believe person she provided with drugs and medical care is really the father of her child and threatened to take him. When she wouldn't cooperate, he killed her."

Lori harrumphed. "Did you get that from Lifetime's movie of the week?" She passed him the marker and he added his scenario without acknowledging her jab. "Not to mention, if that were the motive, why didn't he take the child?"

"Maybe someone interrupted him," Harper argued. "He had no choice but to flee the scene without the child."

Officer Cook joined them at the case board. "Other than the broken slider, there wasn't the first sign of a struggle or an attempt to get away from her attacker inside the house. Don't things usually get turned over or broken? Besides the glass and the blood where the victim was found, the place was neat as a pin. Did the intruder have a gun and that prevented her from fighting or"—he looked from Harper to Jess—"did she know her attacker? Maybe an old lover, like Sergeant Harper said. Did the broken slider have anything to do with the murder? Maybe that happened before the killer arrived or when he was leaving. Or maybe the killer just wanted it to look as if someone broke into the house."

"You going for brownie points, Cook?" Lori teased.

"Valid scenario, Cook," Jess said with a chastising glance at Lori.

Cook added his two cents' worth to the board. *Did vic know her assailant?*

"The pool guy said the kid was driving her nuts," Lori reminded them. "Maybe she was bored and lonely and had gotten involved with the wrong people. Could be a recent lifestyle change. Bored housewife and all that jazz. The reality TV industry is making a killing on what America's housewives are up to."

Jess nodded. Another credible scenario. "We need to know if Mrs. Grayson was suffering from depression or anxiety related to motherhood or to her marriage. Was her husband not paying attention to her needs and worries as her old pal Trenton suggested? And what had she done about that?"

Harper reached for the marker and added *husband's lack of attention* to the growing list.

Jess turned to Lori. "Detective, track down Gabrielle's girlfriends or coworkers from her nursing days. Find out who she was and what she did when she wasn't busy being a wife and mother. See if anyone is aware of her ever skating on the dark side with a bad guy like Lopez."

"I could also dig around to see if she'd joined any support groups," Lori offered. "If there was anything going on from the new mother perspective, she may have felt more comfortable seeking advice from strangers."

"That, too," Jess agreed. "Officer Cook, spend some time with any academy buddies you have in the South Precinct or in the GTF. See if anyone's talking about Lieutenant Grayson. We've been a little focused on the wife, but she may not have been the one living dangerously. This new money may have gone to his head. Maybe volunteering with Allen's task force was about getting away from the house." Jess pressed Cook with a warning look. "Tread carefully. We don't want anyone thinking we're trying to build a case against an innocent man, especially one who carries a shield."

"Yes, ma'am, I'll be very careful," he promised.

Harper waited patiently for his orders. "Talk to your contacts in gangland and find out if one clique or the other is taking responsibility for this murder. Maybe Captain Allen isn't sharing all he knows. Though I can't imagine why, unless it would somehow put us at odds over jurisdiction again. We have to determine if someone had a grudge against Grayson or Gabrielle. Did she have friends in that world that her husband might not know about?"

"And you?" Harper inquired.

Jess's gaze narrowed. "I'll be following up with the crime scene techs and the ME. Translation," she stated for emphasis, "I'll be fine without a babysitter." If Burnett didn't stop whispering in her detectives' ears she was going to give him what for. She was a grown woman, a highly trained one at that.

Of course that hadn't protected her Saturday night. She'd gotten snatched right off the street like an unsuspecting child. Not her proudest moment.

"Yes, ma'am," Harper acknowledged. "Just trying to keep the big boss happy."

The big boss. Ha! Jess motioned for them to go. "Shoo... go find witnesses and motives."

Harper grabbed his jacket. Wells got her purse and Cook just smiled and followed the crew. Jess watched them go and felt relieved. She felt good, actually. *This*, her new job and her new life, was going to work out better than she'd expected. There would be more bumps along the way but she could see a future here.

The door opened and Jess looked up to see who had forgotten what.

Sergeant Jack Riley, Grayson's partner, wandered in. "Chief Harris." He gave her a nod. "I made sure my LT got home okay. My wife, Sarah, is seeing after him and little Gary. I thought I'd check in with you. See what I can do to help."

The reality that all their notes were in plain sight had Jess rushing across the room to meet him. "Thank you for stopping by, Sergeant." She snagged him by the arm and directed him to the small conference table, which would put his back to the case board. He favored his right leg. Had a bit of a limp. There had been some mention of medical leave in his file. "I was hoping for the opportunity to speak with you today."

"I want to help any way I can," the younger man assured her.

Jess settled in the chair across the table from him and didn't waste any time on idle chitchat. "How long have you worked with Lieutenant Grayson?"

Riley was considerably younger than his fifty-year-old partner. At thirty-three he was a ten-year veteran of the department. Married with two children. His wife was also a former nurse and now a stay-at-home mom.

"Five years. It was his guidance that got me promoted to sergeant a year ago. The LT is the best. You won't find a better cop, friend, husband, father." He turned his hands up. "He's a model human being."

"The two of you have never had any problems?" Two years ago, shortly after returning from his medical leave, Riley had requested a transfer out of his division but then he'd withdrawn the request.

He moved his head side to side. "I've had problems with Chief Waters, but never with my partner."

"What sort of problems? Chief Waters has been your superior most of your career as a detective. What suddenly went wrong?"

His brow creased into a deep frown. "Am I a suspect, Chief?"

Jess laughed. "You know the answer to that, Sergeant. Until I clear them, everyone who was a part of Gabrielle Grayson's life is a suspect. Including you and her husband."

He jerked his head in acknowledgment. "Yeah." He heaved a big breath. "I know the drill. It just feels weird being on this side of the table."

She definitely understood. Not so long ago she had been on the wrong side of an interview. Eric Spears, the Player, had tried and succeeded in destroying her career at the bureau. But she had bounced back. Funny, she hadn't expected a journey to her past to turn into her future.

"Chief Waters didn't see me as up to the job after my accident," Riley explained. "I was in an automobile accident. Left me with a limp, but I'm as good as I ever was."

"So you had to prove yourself to Waters," she suggested.

He nodded. "Ticked me off at first, but I got over it. Leaving the precinct wasn't a problem but losing Larry Grayson as a partner was out of the question."

"Did you and your wife spend a lot of time with the lieutenant and his wife?"

"Yes, ma'am. My Sarah and Gabrielle are... were best friends. We were just there for a cookout yesterday before Larry and I went on shift with the GTF."

"You've been supporting the GTF longer than Lieutenant Grayson. Was that a financial decision, Sergeant?" The man didn't have finances nearly as solid as his partner's. Then again, he was younger and hadn't inherited a tidy sum from his rich uncle either.

"At first it was purely a financial decision. I got two kids, Chief, and a wife who's a stay-at-home mom. The extra money came in handy. But when I saw what an impact Captain Allen's people are having on the gang situation I would've kept doing it regardless of the money."

"Can you tell me if Lieutenant Grayson and his wife were having any sort of trouble? Sometimes parenthood throws a kink in the best marriages."

Riley took some time before answering. "I've been a part of their lives since they met and married. They never fought, at least not publicly. And they seemed genuinely in love. But she was lonely, I guess, like most of the wives. And bored maybe. She had a high-octane career as a nurse before and I think she felt a little sad that she'd given it all up. Sarah went through the same thing after our first was born. Otherwise, Larry and Gabrielle were the perfect couple."

Jess could sympathize. She couldn't imagine her life without her career. That wasn't necessarily a good thing, but it was what it was. "No marital issues at all, huh?"

"If there were any, I didn't know about them and I probably spent more time with the family than any other person on the planet."

"Did your wife know Gabrielle when she was a nurse?"

"Oh yeah. They worked together for a couple of years. They knew and respected each other. My wife introduced Gabrielle and Larry at a cookout at our house."

"Wasn't Grayson still married to Sylvia when he met Gabrielle?"

"That would be an affirmative." Riley whistled a long, low sound. "Now that was hairy."

"What do you mean by that?"

"Sylvia Baron wanted a husband just so no one could call her an old maid. That Larry was a decorated cop—a hero—made him suitable, I guess. She was never home and she refused to have children." He shrugged. "To be honest, she's one of those women who's self-sufficient. She doesn't need a man for money or anything else."

"You mean, she's independent and ambitious?" Jess shouldn't have taken offense, but she did.

Riley hesitated but then nodded. "Guess so. No offense intended to independent, ambitious women. She's just a little cold-hearted. I guess you have to know her."

"Maybe so." That was the thing with Southern men.

If a woman was ambitious and independent and had no desire to breed she was cold-hearted and probably a bitch. Jess supposed she was in real trouble. "Were there any problems between Sylvia and Gabrielle?" It was doubtful Sylvia would have set out to murder the other woman years after Gabrielle had stolen her husband, but stranger things happened.

Riley was shaking his head. "None to my knowledge. I never heard Larry or Gabrielle mention Sylvia. Not in the last year or so anyway. Like I said, things were a little sticky at first but everybody moved on."

"No marital problems. No financial problems." Jess tapped the file she had been reviewing earlier. "I guess if Gabrielle's murder wasn't related to their personal lives or Grayson's work, it was a random act of violence."

"Had to be." Riley turned his palms up. "We know all the same people. Same friends—all cops, by the way. And Gabrielle was a saint. She had no enemies. Everyone who ever met her loved her."

Unfortunately, most saints died as martyrs. "If you think of anything else that might prove useful, please call me immediately, Sergeant. You have my number already." She'd given him a card at the scene.

"For sure."

Jess showed him to the door, mostly to ensure he didn't turn around and get a good look at her case board. The less he knew, the fewer questions Grayson would ask.

When he was gone, she marched over to the board and considered what she could do to protect the privacy of their timeline and notes. The board stood on legs but didn't rotate as some did. Maybe this one was too long for that. It did have wheels though.

It took some finagling but she got it turned around so that the side with their timeline, photos, and notes faced the wall.

That worked. For now.

She grabbed her bag. A set of keys lying next to the phone on her desk snagged her attention. She picked up the keys and the note beneath them.

Jess, use this Taurus until your Audi is released. You'll find it in the garage, 2nd level, slot 32. It belongs to the department so take it easy. DB.

PS: I took care of your parking ticket.

"God, I hope it's not beige." Department vehicles were purposely nondescript. At least she had transportation at her disposal without having to visit the department carpool. It annoyed her that her Audi was still in the print shed. They knew who had abducted her. Why did they still need her car? And that parking ticket was beyond ridiculous. If she hadn't been distracted by that damned thing she might have noticed trouble was about to swoop in on her. Right now, all she wanted was her car.

Maybe she could give someone at the lab a nudge and get her car back by tomorrow. Jess dropped the Taurus keys into her bag and headed for the door, checking her watch as she went. Two fifteen. The coroner's office had had better than four hours to have a look at the victim's body. Under normal circumstances that would mean nothing. But Jess felt certain that Dr. Sylvia Baron would permit Dr. Leeds to waste no time doing a preliminary examination. Jess wanted to know what, if anything, they had found. She wished she hadn't ticked off the woman at the scene, but

Jess had done what she always did. She'd spoken her mind, putting herself at odds with the highbrow ME.

She'd have to find a way back into her good graces. In this line of work, good contacts were vital.

The door opened just as Jess reached it. A tall, undeniably handsome man blocked her path.

Wesley. Her ex. Supervisory Special Agent Wesley Duvall, who had come all the way from Southern California to help with a case... and to see that she was safe.

"Jess." He smiled. She liked his smile. Always had. "I was about to go for a late lunch." He chuckled. "I'm still on West Coast time it seems. Anyway, I thought maybe you'd like to join me. I remember how often you forget to eat, so I'm guessing you haven't had lunch either."

"That's so sweet." Her stomach sent a signal of its own confirming his conjecture. She hadn't eaten. "I was just on my way to check on the progress at the coroner's office."

"I have nothing scheduled this afternoon." He held up his hands. "We could have a quick lunch and then make your stop."

She hadn't heard from Leeds or Baron. There might very well be no news at this point. Why not take Wesley up on his offer? "That works. Sure." She pushed a smile into place. "I'll drive." She could pick his brain about how the Lopez situation might relate to the Grayson case. Not that she really believed it did, but it was one of those avenues that had to be fully investigated.

They were barely out the door when Jess's cell clanged. She dug in the bottom of her bag while ensuring she kept Wesley marching toward the elevator. What she really wanted to do was get out of the building before Burnett saw them together. He would drive her nuts about it.

...Drive her nuts.

People tossed that phrase around all the time. Had Gabrielle Grayson meant it literally or was she just using a common expression when she made the statement in front of the pool guy about her child?

Jess managed to get her cell to her ear and said, "Harris," at the same time she paused at the elevator and hit the down button. *Hurry. Hurry. Hurry.*

"Chief Harris, this is Dr. Sylvia Baron."

The elevator doors slid open but Jess ignored them. "You have news?" She couldn't imagine any other reason for the call. The woman already disliked her immensely. She certainly wasn't looking for a lunch partner.

"Before you get excited, Harris, understand that we've completed only a very preliminary exam, but we have narrowed time of death to a smaller window and we have a few other details confirmed."

The elevator doors had closed with Jess too caught up in the conversation to act. She stabbed the button again. "I was actually just about to have a quick lunch and then drop by your office but, please, don't keep me in suspense, Dr. Baron."

Jess turned the phone away from her face and to Wesley whispered, "It's the medical examiner about my case."

Wesley made an "oh" face and gave her an understanding nod.

The elevator doors glided open once more and Jess started to step inside, determined not to let it get away this time. She stopped just in time to prevent running into Burnett on his way out.

As he looked from her to Wesley and back, Jess silently swore at her bad timing.

"Gabrielle died between nine and midnight," Dr. Baron said, dragging Jess's attention back to the phone conversation. "That's as close as we can narrow the window with any real accuracy at this stage and considering the fact that she was lying on a cold tile floor. Be that as it may, I suspect what you're going to find the most interesting, Chief Harris, is cause of death."

One hand held up for Burnett to give her a second, Jess's full attention zeroed in on the conversation. She tuned out the sound of the elevator doors trying to close with Burnett blocking their path. Every instinct warned that whatever Baron was about to tell her, it was pivotal to the case and finding Gabrielle Grayson's killer.

"First, we found no evidence of sexual assault."

Jess was thankful to hear that.

"The beheading, which I believe was accomplished with a saw, something with *teeth*, was done postmortem. The stab wounds were postmortem as well, but I'm sure you surmised that much already," the associate coroner announced. "Ironically, cause of death was manual asphyxiation. Now, my question to you, Chief, is, unless the killer was trying out for a part in the next *Saw* movie, what was the point of all the theatrics?"

That was a damned good question with only one clear answer.

Distraction.

4

Jefferson County Coroner's Office, Cooper Green Hospital, 2:45 p.m.

Dr. Sylvia Baron waited next to the stainless-steel table where the body, along with the detached head, of Gabrielle Grayson waited for the next step in the final act of her time on this earth. Jess hoped the wounds that told the story of her horrifying death would guide them to some answers about her killer or his motive.

Dr. Martin Leeds stood next to his protégée like a beaming father about to introduce his one and only debutante to society.

Weird. Just weird. Why would the ex-wife of the victim's husband want anything to do with this? Was she that elated over the woman's death? Had the two been friends? Seemed a stretch considering the victim stole her husband.

Sergeant Harper waited next to Jess. She'd called him en route and asked him to meet her here. Two sets of eyes and ears were always better than one. On the way in they had talked about how odd this particular aspect of the situation was. Jess opted not to mention the awkward moments in the elevator when she'd smiled and informed both Wesley and Burnett that she would catch up with them later. She'd left them in BPD's lobby with the suggestion that they have lunch together. Just because she couldn't join them was no reason the two shouldn't get to know each other better.

Now *that* was weird.

Jess wished she could be a fly on the table wherever Burnett and Wesley ended up sharing a meal, assuming they took her advice. As far as she was concerned, about the only difference between that scenario and this one with Sylvia and Gabrielle was that both men were still breathing. Maybe that fact made the situation even stranger.

Maybe she and the snobbish Dr. Baron had more in common than either one would want to admit. The primary example was the nontraditional track they had both taken. Here they were in their forties with no husbands and no babies. Not to mention some sort of abnormal connection with an ex.

"Due to the sensitive nature of this case, we're giving Mrs. Grayson top priority," Leeds announced, kicking things off and promptly evicting from Jess's head thoughts of her two exes and her life's wonky pattern. "I'll be performing the autopsy at eight tomorrow morning. Based on our preliminary examination we, Dr. Baron and I, concur that the manner of death was, of course, homicide, and the most probable cause of death appears to be manual asphyxiation."

Like a well-choreographed dance routine, Baron stepped in next. "Note the slight bulging of the eyes and the petechial hemorrhaging." She gestured, Vanna White style, with a gloved hand. "The lips are swollen and we found traces of blood in the mouth and nostrils, despite the absence of tissue injury in those areas. Based on that evidence, we anticipate that when we have a look at the lungs in the autopsy, we'll find them gorged with blood and darker in color, confirming the assessment of manual asphyxiation."

Jess was impressed. She hadn't expected such a thorough call this quickly. "That certainly adds a new twist to our investigation." It definitely pushed Gabrielle's murder even farther from the possibility of being related to the Lopez war. Jess felt confident there was no connection whatsoever. Yet someone had gone to a lot of trouble to make it look related. A *distraction.* A cunning killer worked extra hard to throw an investigation off his trail.

"We will notify you as soon as the final report is available," Leeds assured Jess. "For now that's the best we can give you."

That was actually more than she had expected this early in the process.

"I appreciate your assistance in our efforts to move swiftly on this one," Jess said to Leeds. She acknowledged his colleague with a nod. "As you say, due to the sensitive nature of the case, time is more of an enemy than ever. The media will pounce on the idea that if the police can't protect their own who can they protect? We don't need another reason for folks to take the Stand Your Ground law the wrong way." God knew national headlines had shown the bad end that resulted far too often from that misguided choice.

"Chief Burnett conveyed that sentiment earlier today,"

Leeds said. "Unfortunately, some of the toxicology can't be rushed and will require time, which will, in turn, delay issuing the official final report." He held up both gloved hands to halt the protest she'd started to launch. "But we'll do everything possible to have a preliminary report on our physical examination findings late tomorrow."

"I can't ask for more than that." Jess felt relieved. She hadn't expected this level of cooperation after last week's Chandler case and the head butting between her and Deputy Chief Black. With Black's seniority in the department, the coroner's office had leaned in his direction when it came to choosing sides.

Sylvia Baron peeled off her gloves. "Since I intercepted you on your way to lunch, Chief Harris, why don't I make it up to you by taking you to my favorite sandwich shop down the street?" She produced a credible smile. "I'm certain you're as famished as I am."

Under the circumstances Jess wasn't sure her appetite would return anytime today and she did have that briefing with Burnett at five thirty. She shouldn't take the time... Burnett hated waiting as badly as she did. But she couldn't resist the opportunity to learn why Baron had barged her way into this case. "You have a deal, Dr. Baron." Jess turned to Harper. "Sergeant, why don't you carry on and I'll meet you back at the office at five or so."

Harper gave her a nod. He'd been on his way to talk to his gang contacts when she'd diverted him here.

Before he could be on his way, Jess snagged him by the sleeve of his jacket. "And, Sergeant, don't forget what we talked about."

"Yes, ma'am."

Daniel Burnett was Birmingham's chief of police but

he had no business checking up on her via her detectives. She'd warned him about that already. Since giving Burnett what for hadn't done any good, she'd spoken to both Lori and Harper about her feelings on the situation. She made a mental note to ensure Officer Cook got the same lecture. She had her own way of doing things. Having Burnett all up in her business cramped her style.

Jess tucked her glasses into her bag as she followed Dr. Baron to her office. The room was smaller than she'd expected. Seemed to Jess it should have been considerably larger to house such an enormous ego.

Small or not, the lady had her prestigious diplomas and awards adorning the walls. Each was framed in rich wood and surrounded by regal matting. Her desk sported a nameplate, a crystal vase with a single long-stemmed white rose, and the surface was totally free of any clutter whatsoever. Reminded Jess of Burnett's desk. Maybe they taught neatness skills at that fancy private school he and all his pals had attended.

Jess sure never got classes like that at her school. Not that she would have paid attention anyway. Her sister had always been the studious one.

The doctor's wall of pride had Jess wondering why a woman of such means would go into the business of dissecting the dead. Jess spent most of her time studying the dead as well, but that was different. Since she had never been rich or the daughter of a senator her options had been somewhat limited.

Dr. Baron removed her lab coat and turned to Jess as if she'd read her mind and realized her mistake. "I don't actually have time for lunch, Harris. I wanted a moment of your time in private."

Well, well. Seemed Jess wasn't the only one who had a nosy boss.

"And here we are." She propped a smile in place. "What's on your mind?" So much for lunch. Or manners, for that matter. The doctor couldn't have talked and eaten at the same time?

"Yesterday Gabrielle Grayson called me."

Now there was a revelation Jess hadn't expected. "Were the two of you friends?"

Baron laughed. "Hardly. I hadn't spoken to her since the day she tried to apologize for fucking my husband."

There was that. "If you hadn't spoken in all that time, what was her reason for suddenly calling you, after what"—Jess shrugged—"two years?"

Baron leaned against her desk and crossed her arms over her chest. "I made it a point not to get to know anything about the *other* woman. For the first year or so I hated her. Then I decided she wasn't worth the emotional expenditure. I put it behind me and moved on."

"Ten years was quite an investment to just put behind you," Jess countered. Sylvia Baron and the lieutenant had been married for a whole decade. Seemed to Jess that would be about like her trying to pretend the relationship she and Burnett had shared was dead and buried.

"Touché, Chief," Ms. Hoity-Toity confessed rather than going off on Jess as she'd expected. "It wasn't exactly the easiest thing I've ever done but I managed."

"Have you spoken to your ex-husband since the divorce?"

"Not once." She laughed, the sound deep and rich yet tinged with a hint of self-deprecation. "That's what lawyers are for."

"You were saying that Gabrielle called you yesterday." They'd gone off course there for a moment.

"She did. I was frankly"—she turned her palms up—"stunned when she identified herself. I almost hung up on her." Baron shook her head. "But there was something in her voice." She paused, appeared thoughtful. "Gabrielle was worried. Afraid even. Whatever it was about, it involved Larry and she wanted to talk to me. I think you'll agree that for her to take that step required considerable desperation and no small amount of courage."

Certainly explained why the associate coroner had insisted on showing up at the scene. "I take it you didn't learn what *it* was."

"She wanted to meet and talk last night. She said she couldn't discuss it over the phone and since Larry was working last night it would be a good time, but I had other plans and..." Baron looked straight at Jess, defeat in her eyes. "That's not true. I didn't have any plans. I didn't want to see her." She looked away then. "Really, how was I supposed to react to that kind of abrupt call? I needed time to come to terms with her request so I put her off until lunch today." She lifted her chin higher as if in defiance of the guilt she clearly felt. "I wasn't going to jump just because she called."

So much for having moved on. "But you sensed that she was worried and afraid and it was related to her husband?"

"Gabrielle said as much." Her shoulders sagged. "And now she's dead."

Jess reminded herself to choose her words carefully, but that just never worked for her. "You said you'd moved on but two years is hardly any time at all on the cheating-spouse scale. You surely understand that it's necessary for me to determine whether you're passing along this information out of concern or as some sort of payback against your ex-husband."

Sylvia started to object but Jess held up a hand so she could say the rest. "You also stated that you haven't spoken to your ex-husband in all this time. It's quite convenient that the day after his wife is murdered you announce that she called you about a possible problem with him. I'm not accusing you of misstating the truth, Dr. Baron," Jess pointed out, "however, I do need you to see this the way others will. Before I go forward with this information, is there anything at all you'd like to revise about what you've just told me?"

The other woman stood. She adopted that arrogant posture she pulled off so well and leveled a challenging gaze on Jess. "*Before* you waste time trying to round up a bevy of suspects from gangland, I would urge you to take a long hard look at Lieutenant Lawrence Grayson. His wife was worried and it was about him and now she's dead. That's all I have to say."

"Count on it," Jess assured her. "Thank you for your time, Doctor."

As Jess made her way back to the lobby, she put a call through to Lori. She'd already waylaid Harper once, so this time she'd snag Lori. Not that she felt she needed someone with her at all times as Burnett had suggested. No, sir. What she needed was that second pair of eyes again. A trip back to the crime scene without all the distractions of evidence techs and concerned cops was in order.

She needed more of the story only the scene could give her. As soon as the techs had done their final sweep, cleaners—whether professionals or friends—would wash away all traces of the unspeakable act that had taken place in the Grayson home.

One more good review was essential before that happened.

Same friends—all cops, by the way.

Especially if that killer was a cop.

In the parking lot Jess climbed into the Taurus and jammed the key into the ignition. What she needed was a list of all who kept up with Lieutenant Grayson's activities, friends, coworkers. She twisted the key. Nothing happened.

Jess glared at the dash. "What in the world?" She tried to start the vehicle again.

Nothing. Not even a *click, click, click.* Dash didn't light up. Radio didn't work. Dead battery.

"For the love of..." She snatched up her cell and called Lori again. "Can you pick me up? This stupid car is dead."

"Heading your way now," Lori assured her.

Jess tossed her phone into her bag. "Damn it." She hated wasting time.

The idea that Gabrielle's killer had waited so long to stage the body with all those stab wounds and the decapitation filtered into Jess's thoughts. What had the killer been doing all that time? Why the backtracking? Jess at first thought the killer had methodically staged the scene to appear as if the crime was just another gang hit.

But she had been wrong.

There was one surefire way to try to disguise manual asphyxiation—a botched beheading job. The killer had been forced to step back and change his strategy. To stage a distraction.

And that meant just one thing, in Jess's opinion. The murder *hadn't* been planned. Whoever showed up at the Grayson home had come with another agenda that had evolved into murder.

Someone Gabrielle Grayson knew and maybe even trusted.

And that trust had cost the poor woman her life.

Shady Creek Drive, 4:05 p.m.

The officer left in charge of the crime scene's security unlocked the Grayson home for Jess and Lori. He reported that a second team of evidence techs had come and gone. No one wanted to miss a single speck of evidence on this one.

After donning shoe covers and gloves, Jess spent the first half hour on scene going through the master bedroom. Lori reviewed the mail and any other papers scattered around the house. Jess had summoned Officer Cook to join them. She'd tasked him with sifting through the files in the small home office. Most appeared to be the usual receipts, tax and medical records, but Jess wanted to be sure.

As she had noted that morning, the house was clean and well organized. The bed in the master bedroom was unmade. Gabrielle had apparently already been in bed when the perpetrator either knocked on the door or forced his way inside through the sliding glass doors. It appeared she had received no phone calls on the home's landline or her cell after seven forty-five last night when her husband called to say he was stopping by to tuck in their son. Since calls could be erased from caller ID lists the records for both lines had been ordered.

It could prove useful to see who else Gabrielle had called yesterday. If she had another friend with whom she might have talked about her concerns regarding her husband, Jess needed to know ASAP. And if she had in fact called Sylvia Baron, Jess wanted that confirmation before she questioned the husband again.

Why would Gabrielle have called the ex-wife? Didn't make sense. Jess moved on to the baby's room. Smelled like powders and lotion. The scents caused a little cramp in her chest. There was a good possibility she would never have children. Not that she actually wanted any. Her work was too demanding. Besides, she had no mothering instincts. None. No child deserved that.

The sensation in her chest was probably an allergy to the powders.

Dismissing the foolish thoughts, she crossed to the crib and touched the stuffed bear that lay tangled with a blue blanket. An empty bottle had been cast aside. The blinds on the window over the crib were closed. Hand-painted ABCs in vivid colors adorned the sunny yellow walls. It was a damned shame this little boy would have to grow up without his mother. Thank God the killer hadn't come in here.

Or had he? Jess considered the length of time the perpetrator had been in the house. He'd showered. The evidence techs had confirmed there were traces of blood in the drain. No prints on the shampoo bottle, not even the vic's, which likely meant it had been wiped. The bathroom was right across the hall from the baby's room. If a light was turned on or noises made, the baby might have awakened.

Jess stared at the empty bottle in the crib and a new theory jumped ahead of all the others. "It's possible," she considered as she reached for the bottle. Grasping the nipple between her thumb and forefinger she went in search of an evidence bag. She carried necessary stuff like that in her car but her car hadn't been returned to her just yet.

In the hall that separated the bedrooms, she called out, "Officer Cook!"

Cook popped out of the home office. "Yes, ma'am?"

"I need an evidence bag."

He looked from Jess to the bottle and back. "I'll grab one from my car."

Jess followed the path Cook had taken, down the few steps that led to the main living area of the house, to wait in the entry hall. Lori joined her there. "You find anything interesting?" Jess asked hopefully.

"Nothing but the usual bills and to-do lists." Lori sent a skeptical look at the bottle. "You discover something in the kid's room?"

"It occurred to me that if the perp was in the house for a while the baby might have awakened and started to cry. Most everyone, even me, knows the fastest way to stop a baby from crying is to give it a bottle."

"Very good." Lori grinned. "I think you know more about this baby business than you let on."

"Yeah, right," Jess muttered. Thankfully Cook reappeared with an evidence bag, banishing that touchy subject. Jess dropped the bottle inside. "I'd like you to run that to the lab, please. Detective Wells and I will finish up here."

"I completed reviewing the last of the files in the office, ma'am." He shook his head. "Didn't find anything out of the ordinary. Receipts. Copies of tax documents and insurance policies—I didn't find one on the victim but there are several on the lieutenant."

Jess hadn't anticipated that an insurance payoff was the motive for this murder. The family's finances were better than average and the heavy-duty death benefits all leaned in Gabrielle's favor. Sometimes though, at this stage, it was difficult to tell what was ordinary and what was not. A thorough review was the best they could do. Better to be prepared than scrambling for answers later.

"I guess you can call it a day after you make that delivery for me." She beamed him a smile of appreciation.

"Yes, ma'am."

When he'd gone, Jess turned to Lori. "Let's have another look in the family room."

"Officer Tierney, the uniform outside, said someone would be here to board up the slider before dark." Lori headed in the direction of the family room. "I suppose a cleanup detail will show up by tomorrow."

"Probably so." As important as it was to keep a crime scene untouched as long as possible, it was also imperative to ensure it was secure. At this point they had likely found all they were going to. No need to drag out the nightmare these images resurrected.

In the family room the television had been turned off. Other than the removal of the body, nothing else had been touched by anyone other than evidence techs—at least not once Jess had arrived on the scene.

Beyond the evidence that a heinous crime had taken place here, the home gave all the earmarks of a loving, normal family. Framed photos of happy times served as reminders most everywhere one looked. In this morning's interview Lawrence Grayson had appeared every bit the devastated and grieving husband.

Still, Sylvia Baron's revelation nagged at Jess. Having been a cop for so many years made Grayson very good at presenting himself in whatever way he chose. Detectives often had to be actors, confidants, and straight-up liars.

It was the nature of the beast.

Jess moved around the room and studied the words written in Gabrielle Grayson's blood. If this murder, as she suspected, was not related to the war between Lopez's former followers and the Black Brotherhood—the group that had claimed responsibility for blowing up one of Lopez's hangouts—the perp was obviously attempting to make it appear so. There was nothing here in terms of crime scene similarities that hadn't been released by the media in last night's late-breaking news except the reference to *pigs* and *pig whore.*

In the dealings she'd had with Lopez's people they had used plenty of unflattering references to the police but not once had she heard them use *pig.* Like Harper, she had noticed the mentions of TV specials focused on the anniversary of the Manson murders. Maybe that buzz had resurrected the term *pig.*

Jess couldn't think of Charles Manson without thinking of drugs. Nothing but Tylenol and Aleve in this house. If either of the Graysons used drugs they kept all signs out of their home. Every little thing was in its place and immaculate.

Her gaze drifted down to the family room's tile floor. Except for the blood.

Why had the perpetrator brought her in here to butcher her body? Had Gabrielle already been in this room? But she was wearing her nightgown and the bed covers were tousled as if she'd gotten out of bed.

"Why did you come in here, Gabrielle?" To have coffee, tea, or wine with a friend? To discuss whatever was bothering you about your husband?

Jess surveyed the room again, more slowly this time. "Did you have unexpected company?" Two coasters, the cork kind, sat on the coffee table between the two sofas. Four others were stacked neatly in the center of the table.

"Detective Wells, how about checking the dishwasher for glasses or cups. Maybe Gabrielle had a visitor, other than her husband, last night." The visitor may have been a neighbor, but then again it could have been their perpetrator. *Or Dr. Sylvia Baron.*

"Dishwasher's empty. The entire kitchen is spotless." Lori made a face that reflected her frustration. "It's almost like the place was thoroughly cleaned except for the blood and glass in this room."

The idea wasn't outside the realm of possibility. "Check the coffeemaker, too," Jess suggested. "If she had a visitor after the lieutenant had come and gone, she may have made coffee for her unexpected company."

"Or opened a bottle of wine," Lori suggested. "I'll check the trash again as well."

Having two detectives who understood exactly where she was going with a theory without her having to explain still amazed Jess. Usually it took months, at least, to develop this kind of working relationship.

While Lori went off to check the kitchen, Jess crouched down next to where Gabrielle's body had been discovered. Judging by the saw's castoff, the perp had been right-handed and had knelt on the victim's left side. Jess got into position. She looked left at the door leading back to the kitchen and the rest of the house. Then she looked right and considered the backyard and pool beyond the disabled doors.

"Why right here in front of the doors where someone might see?"

It had stormed last night but there hadn't been any reports of power outages.

Maybe the perp had positioned the body and then turned out the lights to do his dirty work. Nothing to fear from the dark. Maybe the darkness had caused him to have to start over a couple of times with his saw. Cutting off a head wasn't as easy as one might think. Then again, more likely he'd been attempting to disguise the way he'd strangled her.

Had he brought the saw he used or gotten it from the garage? Jess's money was on the garage. A good question for Grayson. She was well on her way to being utterly convinced that the killer had done all this to cover up what he had done and that there hadn't really been a plan.

Still. Why here? In this room? Maybe the perp thought the tile floor would help with skewing the time of death. With the frosty temperature, the tile floor would have been damned cold. Like lying on a refrigerated slab. Had that been the point? To skew time of death.

Jess pushed to her feet and walked around the glass to go out the damaged door. And if the perp was someone the vic knew, why break the door? Though the set of sliding doors were old, the glass was still a safety type that was much harder to break and crumbled rather than shattered.

It would have been easier to break a window. Had that move been yet another to throw off the investigation? And how did the perp break the door? The impact had come from outside, sending the glass inward.

Jess looked around the patio, her attention settling on the wrought-iron table and four chairs. She lifted one of the chairs. Definitely heavy enough to do the job. The set was old. A little chipped paint and rust here and there.

According to the initial report from the first officer on the scene, Grayson had stopped by only long enough to kiss his wife and baby good night. He hadn't stayed for coffee or anything else and all had seemed fine.

But someone had been here. Whether a stranger or a friend someone had come into this house and murdered a mother while her child slept in his crib.

Outside, even as the sun descended lower and lower behind the trees, the heat was suffocating. Last night had been hot like this. The rain torrential. Thunder and lightning like a fireworks display in the black sky.

Jess turned back to look at the broken door she'd exited. Even with the lights out, the flashes of lightning would have provided an occasional view of the murder scene. Several minutes had been required to do the job. Several streaks of lightning to spotlight the gruesome work.

The dog-eared wood fence provided some amount of privacy from a ground-level view, but it had seen better days. Jess's gaze moved to the second floor of the neighboring home. "Except from right there." The windows provided a bird's-eye view like a box seat at a stadium.

Only the neighboring two-story was run down. Probably abandoned, Harper had said. A foreclosure maybe. God knew there were plenty of those around, even in the better neighborhoods. When the neighborhood had been canvassed today, not once but twice, there had been no answer at the home. Which was not surprising, since the utility meter had been pulled.

That someone actually did live there and might have witnessed the murder was wishful thinking.

The knowledge that the house was abandoned could have been the reason the killer hadn't worried about anyone seeing him. He knew no one would be home. Just another reason to believe Gabrielle knew her killer.

Jess lifted her gaze once more to those second-story windows. A face appeared beyond the glass. Her breath stalled. She blinked. Stared harder. Was that a . . . child?

The face vanished as abruptly as it appeared. Someone did live there, or at least was in there now. *Right now.* Whoever it was she definitely wanted to talk to them.

There was no gate to exit the backyard. Her heart pumping in anticipation, she eased back through the shattered door, moved carefully around the blood and glass, and flat-out ran for the front door—at least as fast as she could run in heels and shoe covers.

"We going somewhere?" Lori intercepted her in the kitchen.

"There's someone in the house across the backyard." When Lori didn't look as though she understood, Jess added, "The one with the windows that overlook the pool." She hitched her head in the direction from which she'd come. "When the neighbors were canvassed this morning that was the one no-answer with the pulled utility meter."

"I thought the house was empty," Lori said, joining Jess's rush to the entry hall.

"That's what we all thought."

Outside the front door, they tore off the gloves and shoe covers. "We'll be right back," Jess assured the officer guarding the scene. Since the Grayson house was the next to the last on the block, it took only a minute to go around to the street running parallel behind it.

"There's a green minivan in the drive," Lori said, spotting the vehicle a split second before Jess.

The minivan was a Ford and looked to be as used up as the house it sat beside. The gutters of the house sagged from last night's rains and months of neglect. A pile of rolled up newspapers lay disintegrating in the overgrown grass.

They took the few steps up to a small stoop, where Lori rapped at the door and Jess struggled with the urge to kick it in. She needed to talk to whoever was here. She needed to talk to them now.

"Pretty quiet in there," Jess noted, her nerves jangling. "But I saw someone in the window. A child, I think. Whoever it was, they're in there." Surely they hadn't gotten away so quickly.

Lori rapped again. "We'll just keep knocking until they invite us in."

Jess swiped the back of her hand over her damp forehead. Damn it was hot. "Just breathing is exhausting in this heat."

"Give it a week or two," Lori promised. "You'll be wishing for these temps again."

Jess could feel her clothes wilting to her skin. "God, I'd forgotten how hot it gets down here in the summer."

"And we've got at least six more weeks of this to come." Lori pounded on the door a little louder, then rubbed her knuckles. "If they didn't hear that they're either deaf or dead."

"Or gone already." Jess fanned herself. She hoped like hell they weren't too late.

5

Devon huddled at his bedroom door. If the two ladies didn't stop making all that noise his sister would wake up and she would be mad. Really mad.

The two ladies from the dead mommy's house pounded on the front door some more.

Why did they come here? Police people had been over there all day. Bunches of them. They had taken the mommy away. The daddy had been real upset. Devon saw him crying. The baby had cried, too.

Devon still felt those funny butterfly things in his stomach when he thought about how scared he had been in that closet. And then when the angel had chased him he thought he was going away for sure. His arm hurt from the scratches. He'd crawled under his house and then he'd finally come inside when he was sure the angel hadn't followed him home.

It was daytime when he woke up and police people were everywhere.

The police had come to his house this morning, but he

didn't answer. His sister told him over and over to never answer the door.

Why were the two ladies here now? They banged on his front door again.

Devon held his breath.

His sister's bedroom door opened.

She was gonna be so mad.

As if she had heard him talking in his head, she shook her finger at him. "You stay right there. Don't make a sound."

His sister didn't like for people to see him. She said they would take him away if they found out she couldn't afford a real babysitter. He didn't want to go away. Not with people or with angels. This was his home. Since his mom died it was just him and his sister. He couldn't go away and leave her all alone. And he didn't need a babysitter.

She answered the door and he tried to hear what the ladies said but he couldn't. Crawling on his belly, he sneaked down the hall and closer to the stairs so he could hear the words. He had to be careful. If he got too close they would see him. That would be bad.

"I'm Deputy Chief Harris and this is Detective Wells," one of the ladies said. "Were you aware that your neighbor, Gabrielle Grayson, was murdered in her home last night?"

"What? No!" his sister cried. "That's awful."

Murder. Devon knew that word. He saw murders in some of the movies his sister watched. She didn't know he watched them while she was at work. Murder was when a bad person killed a good person. Devon was pretty sure the angel took the mommy next door. Angels weren't bad.

There was a mistake, he decided. The police didn't know about the angel. Maybe it was supposed to be a secret.

"Were you home last night, Miss Chambers?"

"I work the graveyard shift at Steward Machine Company. Then I have classes at Lawson State. I just got home a couple of hours ago. I was sleeping."

"I'm sorry we had to bother you today," the same lady who was doing all the talking said. "Do you live here alone?"

"It's just my brother and me."

Devon couldn't help himself. He eased a little closer so he could see past the railing.

"Was your brother home last night?" the lady with the blond hair asked. She was the one asking all the questions. He liked her voice. She sounded nice. He'd seen her in the dead mommy's backyard.

His sister shook her head. "He's only eight. He stays with a sitter when I'm at work or school."

Devon didn't like when his sister lied, but she said it was the only way they could stay a family.

"Miss Chambers, how long have you been living here without electricity? We thought the house was vacant since the utility meter has been pulled."

His sister stared at the floor a second like she was embarrassed. "I didn't get paid until today. They're supposed to turn it back on sometime this evening." She shrugged. "I'm late with the payment sometimes. It's no big deal."

The blond lady and the dark-haired lady looked at each other as if they didn't believe his sister. She was telling the truth. Devon pressed his lips together so he wouldn't say anything. His sister didn't tell lies except about him staying at home alone so much.

"So no one was home last night?" the blond lady asked.

His sister shook her head. “I’m really sorry about Mrs. Grayson.”

“May we speak to your brother?”

The air stuck in Devon’s chest and swelled up like a big rock.

The blond lady looked up as if she’d heard him. He scooted back. His heart started that funny flapping it did when he was scared.

Had she seen him? Was he in trouble? His sister was gonna be mad!

“He might be asleep.”

“Miss Chambers,” the blond woman said—he couldn’t see her but he knew her voice now—“it’s very important that we speak to everyone who lives near the Graysons. You and your brother are the only people we haven’t interviewed. I’m certain you want to help us find Mrs. Grayson’s killer.”

“My brother is . . . autistic. I doubt he can be any help.”

His sister said the word! He hated that word. The urge to hide inside himself started pulling at him. No! He had to stay. He had to hear what they said next. His sister needed him!

“Can he communicate at all?” the lady asked.

What a silly question. He was autistic, not a dummy. He could talk and he could hear. He could see real good, too. He did lots of things real good.

“He can but he’s very shy.”

That bad feeling in his tummy started again. What if they found out the truth and tried to take him away? He should never have sneaked out of his house. He shouldn’t’ve been watching next door. This was his fault!

“With your permission,” the blond lady said, “we’d like

to try to speak to him. Maybe he's seen someone new in the neighborhood or heard something. I noticed some of your windows are open. In this heat, most of your neighbors keep their houses shut up tight. You and your brother may be the only people who might've heard any trouble in the neighborhood."

"I explained that we weren't home last night," his sister repeated. "But I'll go up and get Devon if that's what you want."

The blond lady said something else and then he heard footsteps on the stairs.

His sister was coming!

Devon scrambled back into his room. He jumped in his bed and covered himself. *Don't take me away. Don't take me away.*

"Devon." His sister jerked the cover off him. "The police are here. They want to talk to you. You have to—"

His sister made a sound with her mouth like he did a little bit ago. Like she sucked in a big breath that would turn into a rock in her chest.

He looked up at her but she was staring at his T-shirt. Why did she look so funny? Was he wearing it inside out? Devon looked down to see. There was lots of dried blood on his T-shirt. He'd forgotten about wiping his fingers on the shirt after he touched the dead mommy's blood. Uh-oh.

His sister clamped her hand over her mouth and fell to her knees next to his bed. "Oh my God, Devon," she said behind her hand. "What've you done?"

His sister's eyes were big and round like she was scared…

"I scratched my arm under the house." He held out his hurt arm for her to see. Much as he didn't like telling stories to his sister, he couldn't tell her about going into the neighbor's house and he couldn't tell her about the angel. No one could know.

Leslie stopped being afraid and got mad. "You shouldn't be going under there. How many times have I told you to stay in the house?"

He shrugged. "Sorry."

She helped him change his shirt and then she held out her hand. "Come on. The police want to ask you some questions. Remember, Dev, we have to keep our secret."

He bobbed his head up and down again and then reached out and took his sister's hand. Telling lies was bad, but he didn't want to get taken away. If he'd listened to his sister he wouldn't have to tell any lies.

He tugged at her when she started toward the door. When she looked back at him, he dared to ask, "Do angels take live people too?"

His sister looked like she didn't understand or was too tired to answer silly questions. "What?"

Devon shrugged. "They take the dead people. Like they did mommy. What about the live people?"

She squatted down to put her face close to his. "Devon, angels don't hurt people. They protect them. They take dead people to heaven like they did mom but they don't hurt anyone, especially not live people. Okay?"

He nodded. "Okay."

She hugged him real hard. "We'll be fine, Dev." She looked at his eyes then. "I promise."

Devon smiled. He wasn't gonna worry about that angel anymore. Leslie would make everything okay. She always did.

Besides, she just told him that angels didn't hurt people.

6

5:30 p.m.

Jess ignored the vibrating in her jacket pocket. It was Burnett calling. She didn't have to look. She was supposed to have briefed him by now. And the BPD staff meeting was only half an hour away.

Unfortunately, geographically speaking, she was twenty minutes away—if they left now, drove like a bat out of hell, and somehow managed to avoid the worst of rush hour traffic, they might make it. But she couldn't leave now.

"Chief Burnett's going to have our heads," Lori muttered as she glanced at her cell phone. She turned to Jess. "That's Harper calling."

"Step outside and let him know we may be on to something here and that we'll be on our way soon."

"Will do."

The door closed behind Lori and Jess's attention shifted to the top of the staircase. The home was a split-level sadly in need of an update on the inside and major

TLC on the outside. The front door opened to a small entry hall where two short staircases waited. One went up seven or eight steps to what she presumed were the bedrooms, the other went down the same number of steps to the main living area.

Jess had a feeling about Leslie Chambers. The girl wasn't more than twenty or twenty-one and she was hiding something. Drug use? Maybe. She seemed awfully busy to be involved in anything she shouldn't be but what she said and what she actually did might be two very different stories. Between her job and school she sounded like she had a full schedule. Who watched after her eight-year-old autistic brother while she slept? No one was taking care of the home, that was for sure.

Was the room with the windows overlooking the Graysons' pool and this end of their home the brother's? Jess's instincts were on full alert. There was something here. Maybe they hadn't seen anything last night, but that didn't mean the two didn't know something relevant about the Grayson murder. Leslie appeared at the top of the stairs, her younger brother at her side. He was small for eight. Had the same red hair as his sister. As they descended the stairs, coming closer, Jess noted the freckles and the blue eyes. The two could be twins if not for the age difference.

When Leslie reached the final step, her brother sat down right there, not wanting to come any closer and consciously avoiding eye contact with Jess. He had his arms wrapped around his waist, one resting on top of the other.

"He's really shy."

"I understand." Jess joined him on the bottom step. She offered her hand. "Devon, I'm Deputy Chief Harris of the Birmingham Police Department."

He didn't look at her and he certainly didn't take her hand.

Angry scratches marred the arm he tried to cover. "What happened to your arm?"

He didn't answer.

"He's always climbing trees and getting stuck in places," Leslie assured her. "That's a boy for you. What they don't try to climb they try to take apart." She sounded really nervous now.

"Did you get stuck, Devon?" Jess asked him. "I've fallen out of a few trees myself. Did you climb too high and get stuck there?"

Not a blink.

"I'm sorry," Leslie repeated. "He's that way sometimes."

"That's okay. Maybe he'll want to talk another time." Jess got up and dug for one of her business cards. "This has my cell number. Please"—she squeezed the girl's hand when she took the card—"call if either of you remember anything at all that happened in your neighborhood recently, particularly involving the Graysons. It could be as simple as a stranger you saw lurking about. We really need to find the person who did this. To do that we can use all the help we can get." Jess glanced over at Devon. "Until we find that person you and your brother won't really be safe in your own home. Especially with the windows unlocked."

Obviously a little shaken by Jess's warnings, Leslie put the card on the hall table by her keys. "We'll call if we think of anything." She squared her shoulders and cleared the emotion from her face. "But like I said we weren't home last night so..." She shrugged. "I wish we could help. Mrs. Grayson was a nice lady."

"Your complete honesty is all we can ask for." Jess gave her and her brother a smile. "Thank you for your time."

As she left, Jess glanced back at the little boy once more. This time he was watching her but he quickly looked away.

He'd been listening and she would wager he understood every word.

These two were hiding something. Could be a mountain of debt, could be drugs or another crime. She doubted the latter. But there was definitely an element of fear or trepidation in those matching blue eyes.

Lori looked up from her position on the sidewalk, well away from the front door. "We're almost there," she lied, most likely to Harper. "Thanks." She ended the call and made an uh-oh face.

Jess descended the front steps and joined her. "Let me guess, they're waiting for us."

"Burnett started without us but he assured Mayor Pratt and the others that you were five minutes away."

"Great." Jess headed for the corner of the block. "I want you to find out everything you can about Leslie and Devon Chambers. Where are the parents? How many times in the past year have the utilities been disconnected?" Lori was busily typing notes into her phone as Jess listed off her questions. "Is Devon high-functioning autistic? Where does he go to school? Does he have a psychologist or other specialist keeping tabs on him?" Jess had a feeling about those two. "There's an issue but maybe not one of a criminal nature. Maybe just a sad one. They may need help that they either don't know how to ask for or are afraid to ask for."

She paused to meet her friend and colleague's gaze. "My instincts are screaming at me that they might almost need us more than we need them."

Lori tapped the screen of her smart phone. "I'll get on this list right away."

One of these days Jess was going to have to learn to do that. She was still dragging around pad and pencil. Truth be told, she preferred it. Since she was old enough to go to school, she'd always loved the smell of freshly sharpened pencils, even if she'd disliked using one in the classroom.

Her cell clanged. She should've left it on vibrate. At the end of the Graysons' driveway she checked the screen. *Lily.* Her sister.

The call went to voice mail to join the other four Lily had left since midnight last night.

"The chief?" Lori asked as they resumed their trek toward her car.

"My sister." Her phone started clanging again. "Damn it, Lily, I don't have time to chat." Jess heaved a frustrated breath and dragged out her phone. "Hey, Lily. What's up?"

"That odd old man called," Lily announced.

A wrinkle-inducing scowl tugged at Jess's face. She rubbed at it with her free hand. "What odd man, Lily?"

"The one from church who called my house in the middle of the night last night and told me he'd seen you on the news and offered a garage apartment for you to rent."

Jess held her tongue to the count of five. "Lily, I have no idea what you're talking about."

"You didn't listen to my voice mails?"

Busted. "No. I've been investigating a murder all day. I haven't listened to any voice mails." That was the God's truth. She had six others since eight this morning.

"Anyway," Lily griped, "Mr. Louis belongs to my church. He's a widower I think and about a hundred years old. He doesn't talk to anyone, ever. I almost fainted when he called my house last night."

"Lil, get to the point, please." Burnett was going to kill her for sure.

"He lives in Forest Park in one of those beautiful old Craftsman-style homes but he's odd, Jess. I can't vouch for him but my minister says he's fine."

Oh my God. "You talked to your minister about my living arrangements?"

"You're my sister. Of course I talked to my minister. I talk to him about everything. You need a place to stay and I added you to the prayer chain. Someone contacted Mr. Louis and he called me. He has a place to offer. But I don't really *know* him. I mean, really know him."

"Just give me his address and number, Lil. I spent nearly two decades in the bureau, I'm deputy chief, for goodness sakes. I think I can vet my own landlords." Jess grabbed back control just in time. Her voice had already climbed two octaves.

"You are so hardheaded," Lily complained. "Nine-nine-one-one Conroy Road."

Jess repeated the address and then the phone number so Lori could add it to her nifty electronic list.

"I don't know why you're even considering this, Jess. You should be staying with me. Your only sister in the whole world."

"Thank you, Lil. Love you!" Jess ended the call. She had to do something soon. Between her sister and Burnett, this whole home search business was turning into a nightmare.

"Lori, I need you to do me a huge favor."

"As long as I have my job afterward, I'm game."

Jess hoped she still felt that way after she heard the favor. "Drop me off downtown and then go to the address I gave you. If this Mr. Louis is not a total freak and if the apartment is okay, rent it for me. See if I can move in tonight."

"I'll be glad to, but you know you're welcome at my place for as long as you need."

"I appreciate that but as long as I'm staying with you, my sister is going to ask why I'm not staying with her. Trust me, that would be bad for all of us. You wouldn't like me very much if I lived with my sister. God love her."

"I get the picture," Lori acknowledged. "Forest Park's a swanky, old money neighborhood. Should be a nice place."

"If it is"—Jess prayed it was—"I'll move in immediately." She unearthed her wallet from the bottomless pit that was her bag and signed a blank check. "Give him this for the rent and deposit. Since he knows my sister surely the rate's reasonable and he'll take a check."

"But you don't have any furniture. No dishes or linens," Lori pointed out. "No bed."

"True." Jess's hopes deflated. "You know, I'm never home. All I need is a bed. Maybe the place comes with a bed."

Lori checked the time. "If not, some of the super stores will still be open. I could grab Harper and we could get you one. He's a guy. Surely he has a friend with a truck." She looked hopeful. "It could be kind of a housewarming gift."

Jess raised her eyebrows. "There are two things you

should never offer to give me as a gift, Detective. Shoes and a mattress. When it comes to furniture, a good bed is all that matters to me. King-size. Air-cooled memory foam. Money is no object as long as my credit limit holds out." She picked through her credit cards. "This one should handle it." She passed it to Lori. "Just pretend you're me. And don't be embarrassed if they tell you it's declined. Beg for mercy."

Lori grinned. "Do I get to boss Harper around while I'm pretending to be you?"

"Absolutely." Jess checked the time again and groaned. "We are so far beyond late." She managed a pitiful laugh; there was nothing else to do. "Does this Mustang of yours have wings?"

"Nope." Lori jingled the keys in her hand. "But that doesn't mean she won't fly."

7

Birmingham Police Department, 6:28 p.m.

Where the devil was she?

Chief of Police Daniel Burnett sat at the end of the conference table with the deputy chiefs of every division in his department as well as Mayor Joseph Pratt seated around him. All waited for one woman, Jess Harris.

Just as he had held off the members of the press whom he had promised a briefing at five thirty, he had dragged out this meeting for twenty-eight minutes by rehashing what everyone seated at the table already knew.

Jess had given him nothing new and she wasn't answering her phone. According to Sergeant Harper, Jess and Detective Wells had been five minutes away for the past fifteen.

Mayor Pratt cleared his throat, breaking the silence that had descended. "Are we still waiting for Harris?"

Dan appreciated the fact that he hadn't asked the questions that were likely actually on his mind. *Doesn't your*

new deputy chief keep you informed? Didn't she meet with Dr. Leeds at the coroner's office this very afternoon? She promised you an update at five thirty, didn't she?

"We are waiting for Deputy Chief Harris." Dan resisted the urge to stretch his neck. Then everyone in the room would know he felt choked by the tie cinched around his throat as well as the tension and frustration thickening in the room. "She's been delayed by—"

The conference door opened and Jess walked in looking for all the world like she was right on time and that everyone in the room should be glad she'd showed up at all. "I apologize for keeping you waiting, gentlemen, but we can't control the unexpected, can we?"

Dan was torn between sagging in gratitude and exploding in frustration. "Chief Harris." He stood as she approached the conference table in those sassy shoes she'd been wearing last night. The brown suit fit her body like a glove and made her brown eyes look darker and those full, soft lips richer.

That was perfect. Just perfect. For the past hour he'd been ready to claw the finish off the conference table and when she finally shows up all he can do is fixate on how much he'd like to rip off that conservative suit and...

The others at the table belatedly got to their feet, as Jess dropped her bag next to a vacant chair and sat. "Let me just get settled here and we'll get started."

"Actually," Pratt announced, "we started half an hour ago, Harris. What was your delay?"

Jess tucked her glasses in place and smiled for the mayor, not intimidated in the least. "I was interviewing two potential witnesses that we were unaware of until just over an hour ago. I assume everyone here"—she glanced around the table—"wants the most up-to-date and accurate information available."

"Get on with it then," Pratt growled, annoyed that his highhanded tactics didn't work on Jess.

Dan loved it. But it would have been nice to get a call or even a text about this new development before she announced it to everyone else at the table. He was the chief of police after all.

She retrieved a file folder from her bag and spread it on the table in front of her. "You'll all forgive me for not having any handouts available. There's been no time to get that organized."

Dan ordered himself to relax in hopes of lowering his blood pressure. In another three years he would reach the prime age range for greater heart attack risk. The way it was going, Jess would likely shove him past that boundary a few years early.

"Gabrielle Grayson was murdered between nine and midnight last night," she began. "Dr. Leeds and his associate will perform a full autopsy tomorrow morning. Both feel confident that their preliminary assessment of manual asphyxiation as the cause of death will be confirmed. The beheading and the stab wounds were postmortem. Since, at this time, we have absolutely no evidence of a gang-related connection beyond the staging of the scene, we are pursuing other avenues. We believe that the person or persons who committed this atrocity wanted us to focus our investigation into Gabrielle's murder on the gang troubles the city has been experiencing. But our killer isn't nearly as smart as he thinks."

Jess looked up from her notes, cleared her throat, and waited for questions.

"These new potential witnesses," Dan inquired, getting his focus back on task, "have they provided additional insight?" She'd left him hanging here, damn it. The idea of just how little concern she had for the chain of command exasperated him all over again.

Jess Harris didn't like answering to him or anyone else until she was good and ready.

"I'm not sure yet," she told him, "but I believe this turn of events may develop into a viable lead."

"How are we presenting this to the press?" Pratt wanted to know.

Jess braced her elbows on the table, laced her fingers, and rested her chin atop them as she considered the mayor's question. Or pretended to. "I believe we should release a statement to the press advising that we have ruled out any gang involvement and that we are closing in on a suspect."

Deputy Chief Black, Crimes Against Persons, spoke up. "Chief Harris, do you think it's wise to mislead the public that way? We don't want the department to end up looking inept when we can't close this case in a timely manner."

"That's an excellent point, Harold," Pratt said sagely. "Birmingham has some very savvy reporters. Look at Gina Coleman. If she or any of the others of her caliber got the impression that we were bluffing, the entire business would be a media fiasco. Already today there have been two more incidents between the MS-13 and the Black Brotherhood. Our luck neutralizing these situations without bloodshed is going to run out and then Birmingham will be back in the national news for all the wrong reasons."

As annoyed as Dan was at Jess for showing up late and failing to keep him briefed, this reaction sent his frustration level to a whole new zone. At some point, the deputy chiefs seated around this table were going to have to accept Jess as one of their own rather than finding fault with her every step. Dan had already encouraged Harold Black to be the one to set the example, particularly after what Jess had gone through last week to solve not one murder case but two. Her numerous accomplishments in such a short time should have earned their respect already, yet they were quick to stand against her even now. The staff meeting he'd planned to address that very issue had had to be postponed.

Dan ignored Pratt's and Black's comments about savvy reporters and gave Jess his full attention. "How do you see that route playing out, Chief Harris?" She was way too good at her job to suggest a wrong move. Her colleagues should recognize this already. At the very least they should give her the benefit of the doubt just because she was one of them.

"First," she explained, "if any gang or brotherhood or whatever is responsible for this murder, they aren't going to want their work to be denied or credited elsewhere. As soon as we put it out there, if we're wrong, they're going to speak up. That's a given. If a gang hit goes down, brag tags show up. No one's bragging yet. If that's still the case by this time tomorrow, then we can likely check off any potential gang involvement."

She surveyed the table and seemed to hesitate before saying the rest. "We've all been at this business for long enough to know that when a killer goes beyond simply murdering his victim, there's more to the motive than ending a life. We can assume the beheading was to throw us off track but the stab wounds were totally unnecessary and irrelevant to any other high profile cases we're working. Those wounds, I believe, were an act of emotion. Whoever killed Gabrielle hated her or envied her in some way that defied rational behavior. The need to ravage her body was uncontrollable. The killer was clearly enraged."

She paused, letting the others stew a moment. "Yet our perp left numerous signs of attempting a cover-up. The words written on the walls. The beheading. The use of gloves, since we found no prints in any of that work. As careful as our killer was, he couldn't control the need to ravage the victim over and over with a knife and that, gentlemen, will be his downfall."

"The killer did all this," Chief Waters, head of the South Precinct, Lieutenant Grayson's boss, spoke up, "with a six-month-old baby asleep only a few feet away. It's a miracle the baby didn't wake up and end up a victim as well."

"The baby wasn't the killer's target," Jess countered. "We suspect the killer showered after mutilating Gabrielle's body. The baby was literally right across the hall. If he had wanted to murder the baby, the baby would be dead. But this wasn't about the baby. This was about Gabrielle. This murder was intensely personal."

"That the killer felt no rush to leave the scene," Black put in, "and even went so far as to shower tells us that he knew Lieutenant Grayson would not be coming home any time soon, wouldn't you say, Chief Harris?"

Now that was what Dan was talking about. Despite getting off on the wrong foot, Black was showing his support now.

"No question. And," Jess added, "since working the night shift was out of the ordinary for Grayson, it's probable that he knows the killer more than just in passing. Perhaps the victim did as well. With that fact staring us in the face, we cannot rule out the possibility that this murder was not only committed by someone Lieutenant Grayson knew but maybe even by someone with whom he works currently or has worked with in the past."

"Are you suggesting a cop murdered Gabrielle Grayson?" Waters demanded.

Jess held up her hands to quiet the defiant remarks flying around the table. "I'm saying that we cannot dismiss the possibility. This sort of intense emotion in an act of violence doesn't typically come from a stranger. No one at this table can deny that sad fact, as hard as the idea is to swallow. And, so far, most of Lieutenant Grayson's friends appear to be cops."

The briefing lost ground from there. No one wanted to leave the possibility that a cop killed Gabrielle on the table.

Dan stood and the fiery conversation settled down. "This is SPU's case," he reminded all in attendance. "We will proceed as Chief Harris deems appropriate until evidence guides us in a different direction. Anyone who has a problem with that can see me in my office when we're finished here."

The boys played nice after that. Chief Waters agreed that Lieutenant Grayson would be on paid leave for a couple of weeks despite his determination to return to work as quickly as possible. His partner, Sergeant Riley, would remain on duty. Satisfied that there was nothing else he could complain about, Mayor Pratt took his leave.

A few minutes later the conference room had cleared except for Dan and Jess.

There was a lot he wanted to say to her as the chief of police... and plenty he wanted to ask as Dan Burnett, the man who had made love with her less than twenty-four hours ago.

"I rescheduled the press briefing for ten tomorrow morning." She wasn't getting off the hook with the press so easily. When she sent him a questioning look, he explained, "I gave them what I could but they all want to hear from you. *Directly from you.* You've become quite the celebrity."

She stuffed the file folder back into her bag. He'd gotten used to the huge black leather bag she dragged around. The thing held everything she deemed important, and pretty much everything she had left since her motel room was totaled.

"How am I supposed to get any work done if I'm always preparing for one briefing or another? Good Lord. Can't the department's public relations liaison handle this?"

"Our PR man is on parental leave. He and his wife just welcomed their first child. A beautiful baby girl. He'll be back next week."

Jess rolled her eyes. "Congratulations to him. But his personal life is making my professional one more complicated."

Dan laughed. "Welcome to my world." He spent more time appeasing the press and the mayor than he did overseeing his department. Even when his PR liaison was on duty.

"I don't like that part of your world," she said bluntly. That was Jess. Never sugarcoated anything.

"You look exhausted." She'd returned to the motel with Detective Wells in the wee hours of the morning to dig through her things at the motel to see if anything was salvageable. He'd wanted so badly to hold her and promise her nothing like that would ever happen to her again. But her motel room had been an official crime scene and he'd had a duty to act as chief of police.

Then her ex-husband had appeared out of nowhere.

What man flies across the country in the middle of the night to check on his ex-wife?

Dan didn't want to know the answer to that question.

Jess shot him a sour look. "I beg your pardon?"

"I just meant it's been a long day and you've been through a lot the past seventy or so hours. You're exhausted, I'm certain."

"I can't argue with that but you said I *look* exhausted." She cocked her head and waited for a better explanation. "Is there something wrong with the way I look?"

"Absolutely not. You look amazing." He needed a subject change. Fast. "Did you ever manage lunch?" Talk about an awkward hour and a half. Taking Jess's ex to lunch had bordered on masochism. Sure gave him a better grasp on how she felt having his former wife and former sort of girlfriend popping in and out of their lives. Not that he would admit any of that to Jess. Not in a million years. She would find far too many ways to use it against him.

"Didn't have time for lunch." Mischief glinted in her eyes. "What about you? Did you and Wesley have a nice lunch?" She draped that enormous bag over her shoulder. "He's a really interesting man once you get to know him. He graduated from Princeton with honors. He interned on

President Clinton's staff during his last term. He has a law degree and a—"

Dan held up his hands. He could do without hearing all that *again*. He'd done his homework on the guy. He knew all about Supervisory Special Agent Wesley Duvall and how smart he was. "Oh yeah. We got to know all about each other." Actually, they had discussed just one subject. Jess. The guy had done nothing but ask question after question about her. Made Dan want to climb the walls of that ritzy restaurant he'd taken him to.

"That's nice." She heaved a sigh. "I have to go. I have a lot of notes to review and I'm starving. Plus I may have found a new place and I need a whole new wardrobe. Unless you want me wearing the same thing every day."

Like he cared what she wore. He'd take her without clothes any day of the week—or night for that matter. The thought had a completely unprofessional tension spiraling inside him.

He cleared his head of the images of her naked body nestled against him amid tangled sheets. "What new place?"

"Some older gentleman Lil goes to church with has offered his garage apartment until I can find something else. Apparently he saw the news last night and called her."

"Lily can vouch for this guy?" Sounded a little dubious to Dan.

"He goes to her church. How bad can he be?" Jess frowned. "By the way, the Taurus died on me. It's at the coroner's office."

"What do you mean it died?" The carpool sergeant had assured him that car was in tiptop condition.

Jess shrugged. "How do I know? It does nothing when I turn the key. No clicking, no nothing. Lori had to pick me up. I need my car back, Dan." She gave him an I-mean-it look. "A...S...A...P."

"Okay, okay. I'll take care of it." So much for that plan. All carpool vehicles were equipped with GPS, making pinpointing their locations a simple matter. He couldn't exactly have a device added to Jess's personal vehicle just because he worried about her. In any event, she wanted her car back and he had no choice but to have it released to her.

Trying to keep tabs on her was a full-time job.

His first order of business was getting the details on this new landlord and checking him out. "It's too late to pick up your car now," he countered. "I'll call in the morning, I swear. So what's the address of this new place of yours?"

She rolled her eyes and rattled off the location of this Good Samaritan.

Dan made a mental note of the info, then took her by the elbow. "Why don't I take you to dinner? I'll call a friend of mine who has a great little boutique in Homewood. I bet she'd open up after dinner just for you."

Jess scoffed. "What makes you think I can afford your friend's boutique? I've met several of your friends, Dan. I'm only a deputy chief, you know."

Damn. She really was tired. Calling him by his first name was reserved for when they were far away from work and, more often than not, naked. "Don't worry, I'll make sure she gives you the public servant discount." Jess wouldn't ever have to know that discount went on his American Express. Whatever she needed, he wanted her to have.

"Wait." She scrutinized him, her eyes narrowed in suspicion. "She's not one of your ex-girlfriends or wives is she?"

"No, Jess. She is not. She's a friend of my mother's."

Her face fell. "That's even worse."

8

10:15 p.m.

Turn here."

"Are you sure?" Dan asked.

Jess leaned forward. She felt like a kid at Christmas. It was only a temporary apartment but she couldn't wait to see it. "This is it. Lori said to turn just past the house. The driveway goes around behind it to a detached garage. The key'll be under the mat at the top of the stairs."

Dan turned onto the narrow drive. "Your sister says this guy's a recluse?"

He wasn't happy that Jess had taken the apartment, but she was desperate. She needed her space. She needed her sister off her back and she needed out of the temporary limbo she'd been in since returning to her hometown. It was time. Time to move on with her life.

"He goes to church every Sunday. Her preacher suspects he's the person who leaves a wad of cash in the collection box, but he can't prove it."

"Should we offer our lab services?" Dan shifted into park. "We can check for prints. Nail down the perpetrator."

"Funny." The garage looked fairly large with a staircase going up one side. It was hard to see with nothing but the moonlight, but there seemed to be a lot of trees. "Looks well maintained." Lori had told her the place was immaculate. The man, Mr. Louis, seemed a little shy but well-mannered and normal looking.

But then so were a lot of monsters... like Eric Spears. Ha ha. Jess wasn't even going there.

"It's not too late to change your mind," Dan suggested, as if he'd read hers.

"Stop." Jess opened the door and climbed out. She snagged her bag and went to the rear hatch door to grab an armload of packages from Doree. She was now one hundred percent certain she had no limit left on any of her credit cards. If her house in Virginia didn't sell quickly she was going to be cash poor and eyeball deep in debt.

The thought was beyond depressing. "You know." She watched while Dan gathered the rest of the bags. "I may need a raise."

He laughed. "We can't talk about work right now." He hit the key fob and the door closed. "I'm officially off duty, which means I'm your friend, not your boss."

"What a cop-out, pun totally intended." Jess glanced at the back of her new landlord's house. The windows were all dark. "I hope he won't have a problem with my coming and going all hours of the night." She hadn't thought of that. Tomorrow she would need to have a heart-to-heart with her kindly benefactor. He might not realize what he'd gotten himself into.

At the stairs, Dan insisted, "I'll go first."

Was he never going to get over this whole protective thing? "Suit yourself."

Out of habit, Jess counted the steps as she climbed. Sixteen. Wide treads with a comfortable rise. Iron so there was no worry about rotten boards since they were exposed to the weather.

Dan moved the welcome mat, used his cell phone to light the landing so he could spot the key. "Here we go."

It was foolish but she felt a little giddy as he unlocked the door. He reached inside and flipped a switch. Jess squeezed past him. Her bags hit the floor.

The apartment was one big open space. Hardwood floors. Soft sandy-colored walls. Clean white ceiling. There were windows on all sides, which she liked. The kitchen was small. Just a few cabinets, a sink, fridge, and stove filling one corner. An old-fashioned table, the metal and red Formica kind with the matching metal and red vinyl chairs, stood nearby.

On the far side of the room near the only other door was her brand-new bed. It was massive. She walked straight over to it, hopped on, and dropped onto her back. "Heavenly. Air-cooled memory foam." She smoothed her hands over the lush comforter.

"There's a card." Dan sat down on the end of the bed and tossed her a large white envelope.

Her name was scrawled on the front. Jess tore it open. "It's from Lori and Harper." She laughed. "The linens and comforter are housewarming gifts. There're towels in the bathroom. I never even thought about that." She closed her eyes and sighed. "Just the bed."

"Speaking of bathrooms." The mattress scarcely moved as he got up and walked over to the door and opened it. "Not bad."

She had to see it. Jess rolled off the bed, groaning at the loss of the glorious support to her weary muscles. She joined him at the bathroom door. There was a claw-foot tub, a century-old pedestal sink, black-and-white-tiled floor, and a big leaded glass window. There was even a small linen closet.

Marvelous... except... "Where's the other closet?" Jess turned and went back out into the main room. The bathroom was actually a square that had been carved out of the space. The matching square next to the bathroom made for a kind of L-shape in the big room. A curtain hung there. She drew it back and gasped.

Shelves and rods lined the walls, along with a nice row of built-in drawers, and at the back was a massive triple mirror. "Now this is a closet."

Next she checked out the kitchen. The cabinets were clean. She would need dishes, pots, and pans and most everything else.

Mostly she would eat out. Not a big deal. Whatever minor details remained outstanding, she was just glad to have a place. She owed Lori and Harper big time. She turned back to admire her luxurious king-size bed. How the heck had they gotten that thing here from the store much less up the stairs?

"I could help you put away your stuff."

She jumped at the sound of Dan's voice. She'd been totally lost in thought. And she was really tired. "That can wait until tomorrow."

"You sure about that?' He glanced over at the half

dozen bags. "We wouldn't want those snazzy outfits to wrinkle."

That was a point she couldn't deny. "You just want to see the underwear I picked out. I know you." She skirted around him and went to gather a couple of the bags.

"Actually," he picked up a few bags himself and followed her to the closet space. "I don't like the idea of leaving you here without more information on this guy."

"Stop being paranoid." Jess pulled the first of her four new outfits from the bag. She was glad Doree had included the silk-encased hangers with each outfit, otherwise she wouldn't be hanging anything. Just another item she would need. Not necessarily silk-encased.

"Wells is picking you up in the morning?"

"She is." Jess sent him a scowl. "You need to remember to call whoever's in charge over there at the lab and tell them I need my car back by lunch."

"I'll call," he promised. "Have you charged your phone?"

Jess hung the ivory two-piece suit. She loved the belted jacket. "I will. There's a bag over by the bed that Lori brought from her place. It has all the stuff I bought last night. The charger's in there somewhere."

While she took care of her fledgling wardrobe, he plugged in her phone. Evidently he intended to make sure she was reachable.

The fridge door opened with a squeak. "You want me to run out and get you some bottled water or something?"

"Go home, Dan." She reached into the last bag and removed the shoes. The first pair were gorgeous Mary Jane pumps in a sleek ivory with four-inch heels. The second pair, black stilettoes, the kind of shoes every woman needed. Perfect for any occasion. "I've got this under control."

She opened the first drawer and sniffed. Surprisingly, there was a floral liner that smelled faintly of peony. Took all of two minutes to store her new, silky undergarments there. The few cosmetics she'd picked up at Walmart, and the shampoo and body wash went to the bathroom next and she was done.

"If you're sure you're okay," he said finally.

Setting her hands on her hips she turned to face him. Just then, with nothing but a historic light fixture providing the room's ambience, Dan could have been twenty years younger. He looked so sweet standing there all worried and reluctant to leave her alone in a strange place with a strange old man right next door.

But she wasn't twenty anymore and all that reluctance was getting on her nerves. "Go home!" She strode straight up to him and took him by the arm. She ushered him to the door. "I'll see you in the morning and we'll go observe the autopsy or something."

"Okay, okay. I'll call you when I get home."

"And I won't answer. I'm about to try out that shower."

Reluctantly, he walked out the door and hustled down the stairs.

Leaning against the door frame, Jess watched until he was in his fancy Mercedes and backing away. Once his headlights disappeared, she closed the door and locked it. The dead bolt, too.

Shedding her shoes and clothes as she went, she made her way to the bathroom. She turned on the shower spigot and climbed into the claw-foot tub. With a whoosh of metal on metal, she drew the curtain around her and lifted her face up to the gloriously warm water. Turning her back, she let the water soothe her weary muscles. She stood beneath it until she felt ready to melt. The fluffy new towel made fast work of drying. She dabbed on a little moisturizer and opted not to dry her hair. She could fight with it in the morning.

With teeth brushed and the borrowed robe Lori had sent along, she claimed the Grayson file from her bag and climbed onto her new lush bed.

She spread out the crime scene photos and studied the images. "Who was this angry with you, Gabrielle?"

The woman had no living siblings. Her brother had died as a teenager. Her father had passed away two years ago and her mother was vacationing in the Mediterranean. She wouldn't be back to Birmingham until late tomorrow. No cousins, no extended family here at all.

Maybe Lori would find something during her interviews with the friends.

Jess stared at the photo she had borrowed from the house that showed Larry and Gabrielle Grayson with their brand-new baby boy just a few short months ago. They looked so happy. How had this happened to two people who seemed so much in love?

Could Sylvia Baron be right about the problem being related to the husband? "Why in the world did you want to talk to your husband's ex?" Jess asked the image of the lovely woman who was now lying on a cold hard slab at the morgue.

What would make a woman call upon her husband's ex-wife—the ex-wife she had stolen him from? A snob, frankly, who obviously thought she was way better than Gabrielle.

Her cell clanged. Jess swung her feet over the side of the bed and hopped off. She strode to the kitchen counter and checked her screen.

Burnett.

She shouldn't answer. But knowing him, if she didn't he would drive back over here just to see if she was okay. "You woke me up," she lied.

"Blake just called. Lily's in the hospital. I'm on my way to pick you up now."

The blood seemed to drain from her body, pooling around her feet. "What happened? Why the hell didn't Blake call me?"

"Lily told him to call me," Dan explained. "She didn't want you rushing over there alone. Blake said she hasn't been herself lately. Tired and achy all the time. No appetite. Tonight she passed out in the shower and he rushed her to UAB. They're running tests now."

"'kay." Jess blinked as her mind ran the possible medical scenarios. "How long until you're here?"

"Ten minutes tops."

"I'll get dressed."

Jess ended the call. Anxiety tightened around her chest. What if Lil was really sick? What if Dan hadn't been home and here she was without a car?

She needed her damned car.

And her sister could not be that kind of sick. *Impossible.* Lily was as healthy as a horse. She wasn't the one who took risks, not even with her diet. She ate all the right foods. Went to the gym. All that stuff Jess put off.

Where the hell was the bag of clothes she'd gotten from Walmart? She needed the sweats she'd bought for the workouts she wouldn't do.

"Aha." She snagged the sweats and a tee. Flip-flops, too. Lil would chastise her for not dressing better. She always said that going to the doctor was one of the times when you wanted to look your best. The first time she had passed along that advice Jess demanded to know why the heck it mattered. If you were sick, who cared how you looked? Lil had promptly explained that looking respectable was important so the doctor would think you were worth saving.

Fear closed Jess's throat, making a decent breath impossible. She stalled at the foot of her bed. *Please let Lily be okay.* She could not lose her sister. Jess had too much lost time to make up for.

"Get ahold of yourself." She evicted as much of the fear as possible. Her sister needed her to be strong and optimistic.

It was likely nothing. For that matter, Lil could be pregnant again.

"Better her than me," Jess mumbled.

Sweats and flip-flops dragged on, Jess grabbed a clip for her hair. She was out the door and waiting at the street five minutes before Dan arrived.

UAB Hospital, Tuesday, August 3, 12:55 a.m.

By the time the ER physician returned to Lily's room, Jess was ready to take the roof off the place. She had been sitting on this hard exam table with her sister for an hour at least. According to Blake, the test results were supposed to be back way before now.

Jess leaned close to Lil and muttered, "Good thing

you weren't bleeding about the head or neck." Their second foster mother used to send them outside on Saturday mornings while she did her weekly housecleaning. She always warned that they'd better not bother her unless one or the other was bleeding about the head or neck.

Lil elbowed her.

Jess pinched her lips together to prevent a giggle. And people wondered why she didn't want kids. Truth was, after their parents died, no one wanted her or Lil. Jess wondered how her sister had put that aside to have her own children. Maybe Jess was just a coward.

"What'd you find, Dr. Young?" Blake asked as he straightened out of the one not-made-for-comfort chair in the small room.

Dan was kind of stuck behind the door the doctor had left partially open.

The doctor's name was a perfect fit. He was *really* young. "Why's she been feeling so tired?" Jess demanded before the doctor could answer Blake's question. She made a face at her sister. "And why didn't *she* tell me?"

Lil waved her off. "You have enough to worry about."

Blake cleared his throat.

"Sorry," Jess offered.

"Your family medical history is a little vague," Young said, rifling through the file he held. "Your parents are both deceased?" He looked up at Lil. "Car accident?"

Lil nodded. "We were just kids. Our parents were in their thirties, if either one had any health problems I don't remember."

Jess shook her head. "None I ever heard about."

"No grandparents or other close family members?" the doctor asked.

Lil turned to Jess.

"There's a maternal aunt," Jess admitted. "We haven't seen her since we were kids." This was not sounding good. "What's going on, Doctor?"

"Maybe nothing," he said with obvious hesitation. "Lily's liver enzymes are a little off." To Lily he added, "Considering the other symptoms, tremors, achiness, and fatigue, you'll need to follow up with your family physician for additional testing." He closed the file. "Could be stress or depression related but it's always best to take the extra steps to be certain."

Blake's gaze connected with his wife's. Jess knew instantly what they were thinking.

"Are you suggesting this could be something serious?" she asked the question neither Lil nor Blake had the nerve to present. Her heart felt as if it had stopped completely as Jess waited for his answer. Potential problems that affected the liver raced through her brain. Hepatitis. *Cancer.*

Young shrugged. "Unfortunately, I can't give you any specific answers. I can tell you that your health isn't something you want to ignore. See a doctor you trust and check on your family's medical history. Whatever you're dealing with here, having that medical history is far more important than you realize. Especially as you get older."

Between Blake and Lil arguing over who said a year ago that they should get physicals and Dan stepping out of the room to take a call, Jess's head was spinning from trying to read between the lines of what the doctor didn't say.

When Young had given the release order and they were back in the lobby, Jess gave an order of her own. "You see your doctor this very day, Lil, do you hear me? And I'll see what I can get from *her*." Their aunt. Wanda Newsom. A woman Jess hadn't seen or spoken to in better than thirty years. But she knew exactly where to find her.

"Don't worry," Lil griped. "I'll see my doctor. I want to live to see my grandkids."

Oh God. *Grandkids.* "We aren't that old," Jess complained, no matter what that baby-doctor said. When had a guy old enough to have graduated medical school suddenly become so young? He looked thirteen, for heaven's sake!

"I'll make sure she does exactly that," Blake promised Jess.

Jess hugged her sister and then her brother-in-law. God almighty, her sister couldn't be that kind of sick. Not Lil.

At the lobby exit, Jess watched Blake hold Lil close as they made their way across the parking lot. Seemed like just last year that Lil and Blake were going to the prom. Jess had pretended not to like Blake. He'd been a total nerd. Deep down she'd actually been a little jealous of how they made everything about being a couple look so easy. Lil had known from the first kiss that he was the one and the two had been together ever since.

Jess had never been that absolutely certain of anything other than getting out of this town.

And here she was, back home...not quite at square one but close.

"You ready to go?"

She looked up at Dan. "Yes." The weight of the day settled on her shoulders and the urge to cry came out of nowhere. Damn that too young Dr. Young. He was right. They were getting older. Falling apart, one vital element at a time. Jess already had to wear glasses.

Dan gestured for her to precede him out the door. It

was late and she was tired. Otherwise she wouldn't be wallowing in this stinking pity party.

"You'll let me know the second you hear from Lil what's going on?" He adjusted his stride to hers as they headed for his SUV.

"Course."

"Chief Hogan called." Dan opened the passenger-side door of his SUV for her. "There was another demonstration at midnight. Downtown at Linn Park."

"Any injuries?" So far no casualties had come of the clashes between the Black Brotherhood and the MS-13, or during the former's anti-gang rallies. Since busting up Lopez's little sister's party, the only homicides had been the executions carried out by the MS-13 against their own members who had been deemed traitors. But that could change any second.

The image of Gabrielle Grayson filled her head. Jess was convinced that her murder had nothing to do with the MS-13 insanity. Harper was right about the emotions that had driven the motive of Gabrielle's killer. But someone sure wanted them to think there was a connection.

Whoever had murdered her, Jess would get him. Soon, she hoped.

She leaned back in the leather seat and closed her eyes. This night couldn't be over fast enough to suit her. Somehow coming back here had made her far more keenly aware of her own mortality. Or maybe it was just that she had to look at all the past decisions she'd made—right, wrong, or indifferent.

Like allowing what she and Dan once had to fall apart. And spending most of her adult life far away from her only family.

So much lost time and no way to get a single second of it back.

How did she make sure she didn't lose any more?

The answer was way too complicated to figure out when she was this tired. She just wanted to watch the lights go by and not think so hard. She'd always loved riding through town at night. The streetlights and the blanket of stars overhead…the endless possibilities. As a teenager she'd been a dreamer. She'd had so many plans. A lot of those plans and dreams she had attained.

But not all…not by a long shot. And tonight the stars hadn't come out. Maybe that was a sign. Her attention settled on the driver's profile. She had been so in love with him and they'd fallen apart. Maybe some dreams just weren't meant to be.

And yet, there was still something smoldering between them. Try as she might, there was no way to ignore it. Maybe it was just a kind of friendship that came with knowing someone so intimately for so many years. Or maybe it was the real thing and they were both too preoccupied to notice.

Great. Just what she needed, another mystery.

The downtown buildings gave way to the neighborhood streets of Forest Park and her new home. Her new, luxurious bed waited inside. There was a lot upside down in her life right now, but today she had taken her first step toward righting things.

Dan was out of the SUV before she had a chance to tell him good night. He walked with her up those sixteen steps. Jess stalled at the door and faced him. There was no way she could trust herself with letting him come inside. No way.

"I still have reservations about this place," he admitted. "You sure you'll be okay tonight?"

He wanted to stay. The offer was tempting. Standing this close it was impossible not to feel the tension in his body. He wanted to be with her. To deny she wanted the same thing would be a lie, and lying to herself was not a smart move.

This was just another of those upside down things she needed to right. To do that, she needed a little distance and more time to understand where they needed to go from here.

"Dan, I can't do this when I'm on a case." That sounded so very lame, but it was true. She shook her head. "I have to keep that *us* and this *us* separate." She wished she could find the words to better articulate her feelings. "I know what I'm saying doesn't make sense. But I just can't be your lover and focus on being your deputy chief at the same time. When the case is over... we'll see."

She doubted her explanation made a lick of sense, but she felt what she felt. As foolish as it sounded, somehow when she had no pressing case hanging over her head and they were off duty it was different. Maybe the bottom line was that too much had changed in the past three weeks. She needed to regain her footing before she could feel right about much of anything.

"I understand," he relented, letting her off the hook. "You're right. We need to take this slow." He backed up a step. "Night, Jess."

Letting him go was the hardest thing she'd done since making the decision to come back here. She was exhausted and worried and there was this gruesome case... but letting him go was the right thing to do.

For now.

When he'd driven away, she turned to unlock the door. As soon as she touched it, it swung inward with a low aching creak. The fight or flight instinct kicked in. She jammed her hand into her bag and claimed her Glock.

Beyond the door it was dark as a cave.

But if anyone were in there and wanted to shoot her or charge at her, they'd already had a prime opportunity.

With her free hand she felt for the light switch just inside the door. The glow from the ancient fixture spilled over the room.

Clear.

Relief flooding her, Jess exhaled a jagged breath.

The Grayson file was scattered over the bed and floor. She checked the bathroom and the closet. *Clear.* Nothing tampered with except the file as far as she could tell. Even if there'd been a breeze outside, she hadn't left any windows up. The ceiling fan above the bed was off.

The papers hadn't gotten scattered by a draft.

Back at the door, she examined the locks. Had she forgotten to engage the dead bolt? Evidently. In her rush to get to Lily she hadn't been thinking. Jess crouched down to visually examine the knob and lock. She shook her head. Telltale scratches warned that someone had picked the lock.

"Damn it." She slammed the door and set the dead bolt. Getting the locks changed to a newer, less simple system would be the first item on her agenda tomorrow morning. *Before* that damned press briefing.

The Glock in one hand, she surveyed her new bed. She hoped the bastard hadn't left her a message beneath the comforter. Jess started that way but the photo of Grayson and his wife lying on the floor amid the pages from the file snagged her attention.

Scrawled across the photo in what looked like blood were three words: *You are next.*

Fear trickled inside her but the outrage quickly drowned it. "Son of a..." She retrieved her cell phone from her bag and put through a call to Harper. She didn't bother with a greeting. She was too damned angry. "I need you and an evidence tech at my new place. And, Harper, I want this kept just between us for now."

Guilt wormed its way alongside the waning outrage. Dan would be furious if he discovered she'd kept this from him. Problem was, if she told him, he'd start smothering her again—not that he'd actually stopped completely. She couldn't have him treating her differently from his other deputy chiefs just because they had this *thing.*

Harper assured her he would be there ASAP.

Phone in one hand, Glock in the other, Jess sat down at her vintage table to wait.

That was when she started to shake.

9

2:30 a.m.

Devon could hear the angel moving around inside his house.

The angel was back to take him away.

Leslie said angels didn't hurt live people but Devon was afraid to find out. And he knew it was the angel because no one else ever came to their house. The police ladies did, but that was about the dead mommy.

Maybe the angel was here because Devon wasn't supposed to see the stuff he saw.

When he told Leslie about the angel that came to the Grayson house she got all upset. Good thing he didn't tell her about the angel chasing him. That woulda been bad.

He hugged himself more tightly in his sleeping bag. He hadn't hardly slept in two days. Yesterday night because of the crying baby then all day and night today because he kept worrying the angel would come back for him. That funny feeling that warned trouble was close had bugged him all day. But all day had passed and the angel didn't come. He got mad when his sister made him go to old Mrs. Nicholson's before she went to work. Mrs. Nicholson didn't even like kids. The last time Leslie made him go there she asked a bunch of questions and called him a dummy for not answering. When he told Leslie she said he didn't have to go back there anymore. Leslie must've been really worried to ask the old lady to keep him again.

Soon as Mrs. Nicholson was asleep, Devon just came on home. The angel hadn't come back all day and all night.

Until now.

Leslie was right. He shouldn't've gone to see about the baby or the dead mommy. Now he was in trouble with the angel. The cops didn't know about him going over there but the angel did.

The lie he told Leslie made him feel bad in his stomach. He'd told her that he scratched his arm under the house. He was afraid to tell her about the angel trying to catch him. Maybe people weren't supposed to get so close to an angel without going to heaven. He didn't know for sure. But his sister had too much to worry about already.

What if the angel tried to take Leslie? He didn't know if there were rules about that or not. But that wouldn't be fair. Leslie didn't do anything wrong. He was the one who caused trouble. Specially for his sister.

A loud crash above him made him jump. His heart tried to pop out of his chest. He was glad he was down here and not up there. As soon as he'd heard someone at the front door he'd sneaked out his window and down the trellis. He'd crept around to the back of the house and through the little door to his hiding place. No one ever looked under the house.

Since he made this his special place he had found all kinds of neat stuff under the house. He wasn't scared of nothing under here. It was dark but he had flashlights. His sister was always complaining that the flashlights went missing. There were about ten under here with him but only one with good batteries. Pretty soon he would need another one.

He had a sleeping bag, bottles of water, and little cans of potted meat and a pack of crackers. His sister hated potted meat but he loved it. She made funny faces every time he opened it in front of her. Made good camping stuff. He could stay down here for days and days and just eat potted meat like he was camping. Leslie said their mom used to take them camping, that's why they had sleeping bags and stuff, but he couldn't remember.

He listened at the place where the silver stuff was loose from the vent in the floor. Made hearing things in the house easy. The angel was going upstairs. Probably to his room to look for him. He shivered at the sound of footsteps. He wondered how come the angel didn't fly instead of walking up the stairs. Maybe there were rules about angels flying inside houses. Something could get broken. The scratches on his arm burned a little. Maybe the angel being close could make the scratches burn. He might have seen that in a movie. What if his skin fell off?

He shuddered. Hoped the angel couldn't see him down here in the dark all zipped up in his sleeping bag. It was real hot outside but it stayed kind of cool under here. Smelled like dirt but he didn't care. Not much anyway.

His breath stopped in his throat, making that loud sound in his mouth he didn't mean to make. What if he forgot to close his bedroom window? He couldn't remember if he did or not. If he left his window open the angel would know he had sneaked out of his room. He always closed his window, even when it was hot, if he climbed down the trellis. That way no one would notice the trellis sticking up to his window with smushed leaves and broken limbs where his hands and feet went as he climbed on it.

All day police people had been next door. They had walked all around the dead mommy's house and the neighbor houses. He wished the police people were back, specially those two lady cops who came to his house. The angel had stayed away while the police were next door.

He wondered if that meant this was a bad angel. He just didn't know enough about angels.

If the angel was looking for his bloody T-shirt it was gone. The dead mommy's blood was on it and that was bad. Maybe that was why the angel had come back. He should've stayed in the house last night like his sister said. Then he wouldn't be hiding under here with that dead people angel in his house looking for him.

He wished he could see what the angel was doing. Seemed like a long time before he heard moving around again. Devon held real still and listened hard. He heard the front door open and then close.

Was the angel leaving? Seemed funny for an angel to go out the front door.

He waited a really long time and then he unzipped his sleeping bag. The flashlight blinked. The battery was running out. He turned it off and left it next to his potted meat and stuff. Crawling on his hands and knees he went back to the little door and moved it just enough to peek outside. It was too dark to see anything. No lightning and not much moon. Sometimes the moon and stars liked to hide. Sort of like him, he guessed.

He was getting a little sleepy now. It was so quiet outside. The angel must have decided to fly away. That was good. Maybe he could go to bed.

A few more minutes and he would climb back up to his room. The front door was supposed to be locked but the angel had come on in anyway. Maybe locks didn't stop angels. He wished he knew all the angel rules.

He probably should read the Bible. The preacher where he used to go to church read about angels from the Bible. Devon could read better than anyone else his age. His teacher said he was way ahead of his age group in reading. He didn't always know what the words meant but he could take them apart in his head and understand how to say them.

His eyelids didn't want to stay open. He was getting real sleepy. Maybe he'd just sleep under here tonight. But then his sister would yell at him for crawling around under the house like a bug. That's what she said when he told her about this special hiding place.

"Under the house is for spiders and bugs," she'd told him. *"Maybe even snakes. You shouldn't go under there."*

He'd never seen any snakes. Just bugs and spiders. They didn't like the flashlight.

He was really tired. The angel had to be gone by now. Everyone else in the whole neighborhood was asleep except him.

Devon sneaked out the little door. He put it back over the hole like it belonged. He would need a bath. He smelled like the dirt. Maybe in the morning. He was too tired for a bath. He walked through the dark to the trellis. Seemed like a long way up to his window. He was tired.

He reached up to grab the trellis but a sound made him stop. He looked hard to try to see through the darkness. The moon and stars were hiding behind the clouds tonight.

Even though it was really dark he would swear that something moved close to the front corner of the house. Like something came from the front yard and then just stopped to stare at him.

Could angels see in the dark?

His chest got real tight and the hair on his arms stood up.

He knew what that meant... *Run!*

Devon ran. He reached the hole. Pushed the little door aside. He dove under the house.

Hurry! Crawl faster!

His heart was running in his chest. He had to hurry! All he had to do was get to his special place behind that big shiny silver thing. Nothing could get him there!

Hands grabbed his leg. Jerked him back.

He kicked at the hands. They wouldn't let go!

He opened his mouth to scream but no sound came out.

The hands pulled him closer. Pressed over his mouth.

"Got you, you little shit!" a mean voice growled.

Devon went inside himself.

10

Caldwell Avenue, 4:00 a.m.

Sergeant Jack Riley waited outside his south side townhouse in the darkness like a goddamned criminal. Where the hell was she?

If she didn't get here in the next thirty seconds he was going after her. To hell with the consequences. He'd called her cell. She hadn't answered. Finally he'd left her a voice mail and told her he was waiting.

He didn't have to say more. That was enough to have her scared shitless, he'd bet his next paycheck. He didn't like being the last to know anything and he damned sure didn't like her sneaking around behind his back. She had gone too far this time. He'd let her ridiculous little mistakes go in the past. Overlooked all her annoying faults. And she had plenty.

Not this time.

This was serious shit and he wasn't about to allow her to screw up all that he had worked for. No way. If anyone went down for this it would be her. This was her fuckup.

He spotted headlights up the street. Fury roiled in his gut. The stupid bitch rolled to a stop at the curb and shut off the lights and the engine. He didn't wait for her to get out. Too many neighbors with nose trouble to stand around out here and have a discussion. And they damned sure couldn't go in the house. Not with Larry and his kid here.

He walked up to the passenger side of the Corolla he was stuck paying three-sixty a month on and rapped on the glass. The automatic door lock clicked to the unlock position. She didn't say a word as he settled into the seat. Wasn't any need for her to say a damned thing. He knew what she'd done.

He just didn't know the precise details. The devil was always in the details.

He let another ten or so seconds elapse just to make her sweat, then he demanded an answer. "You ready to tell me what the fuck is going on?" He clamped his mouth shut to keep from screaming at her. Same went for his hands. Squeezed his fingers into fists to prevent slapping the living daylights out of her. He knew better than to do that. Cops couldn't be knocking their wives around—even if they deserved it. He worked double shifts three, four days a week and she couldn't even keep her shit together for one fucking night.

"I had to check on something."

Her voice trembled like a frightened child's. The sound made his dick hard. Her fear was like a drug. It gave him a hell of a rush. Hell yeah. That's what he should do. Take her in the woods somewhere and break her down like a shotgun and give it to her like she'd never had it before. Teach her who the hell was boss once and for all.

"Like what?" He stared across the darkness at his idiot wife. Seeing her eyes wasn't necessary. He could smell her fear.

"I was just being paranoid. I couldn't remember if I put the glasses in the right place after I cleaned up."

He'd been a cop too long to buy that load of bull. Every nuance of her tone screamed *liar, liar, liar.*

"Are you lying to me?" He allowed the question to echo in the darkness for a bit. "You said you took care of everything. That was supposed to be the end of it." He shook his head. Damn, he wanted to teach this dumb bitch a lesson. "You had one thing to do." His mouth tightened in fury. "Just one. How could you screw up that one thing?"

She said nothing but her breathing told him she was growing more terrified by the second. She drew in short little shaky puffs of air. "I'm sorry. I was trying to help. I made a mistake."

He was the one who'd made a mistake. "If I come home just one more time and find you unaccounted for," he warned, "I will make sure it's the last time. Do you understand me?"

"Yes. I swear this was the only time. I just had to—"

He thrust his fingers into her hair and jerked her face close to his. "Don't lie to me, Sarah. Old man Haines told me you were out a second time that night. The babies' crying woke him up. He said next time he was calling nine-one-one instead of me. Can you even fathom what would happen if he told anyone about that?"

"I needed milk," she whimpered. "Chloe wouldn't

have had any milk for breakfast so I ran out before I went to bed."

Did she really think she could fool him? "You just gonna keep lying?"

"I won't do it again. I swear."

"Good." He twisted his fingers in her hair. She made a desperate sound. "You try to take me down with this, I will make sure they know it was you."

She somehow managed to hold back the sobs he could feel quaking her body.

"That's right," he promised. "I'll tell 'em all the things you've done and then you'll wish you were the one dead instead of poor Gabrielle. Too bad your friend didn't realize when you first met that you would be the death of her."

11

Linn Park, 10:45 a.m.

Jess hated this part of her job.

The reporters were shouting questions at her before she'd gotten the cursory *thank you* out after giving her statement regarding the Grayson case. The whole crowd had nearly gone to sleep during the mayor's opening remarks. Jess had spent that time mulling over what the evidence tech had found at her place—nothing. The note left on the photo had been written in blood but it wasn't human. No hits on any of the prints yet. Officer Cook was at her place now overseeing the installation of new locks while she was stuck here doing *this.*

The shouts drew her attention back to the present.

No matter that she'd given a detailed, admittedly brief, statement, now she had to do the rest. Take questions.

Okay, Jess, just pick somebody.

Gina Coleman, Channel 6, stood out amid the clutch of reporters. She had been the first to find and report

Jess's abandoned car to Burnett only moments after Jess had gone missing on Friday evening. The entire concept of Lopez's younger and seriously twisted sister sending two of her goons downtown to snatch Jess off the street scarcely a block from the police department still blew her mind. It wasn't exactly the way Jess had planned to rescue DeShawn Simmons, but she'd managed to accomplish that goal just the same.

And though it pained her to admit it, she owed the reporter one. "Ms. Coleman, Channel Six."

"Thank you, Chief Harris," Coleman said as the others backed off.

How could the woman look this good on a regular basis? A white sheath gloved her thin figure and showed off her perfect tan, which in turn made an amazing backdrop for her dazzling smile. Not a single, lovely hair was out of place. Makeup was exactly right. Jess could spend days prepping and never look that good.

"You stated," Coleman said, dragging Jess's wayward attention back to the reason they were all gathered on this muggy August morning, "that Gabrielle Grayson's murder is not related to the MS-13 violence we've seen escalate this past week. How can you be so certain of that conclusion? Are there any details about where you're taking this investigation that you can share with us at this time? A suspect, perhaps?"

Jess smiled politely. "Let me clarify, Ms. Coleman. I did not say that Gabrielle Grayson's murder is unequivocally not related to the MS-13 activities," she corrected. "I stated that we found no link and, for now, we're moving on to other scenarios."

"Point taken," Coleman acknowledged.

Grumbling and mumbling rolled through the crowd of newshounds and citizens curious enough to come out in the heat.

"We have gathered considerable evidence," Jess went on, "and we do have a list of persons of interest we're narrowing down." Let them make what they would of that. "We will find Gabrielle's killer."

"Are you giving your personal guarantee?" Coleman challenged.

"What about you, sir?" Jess said to the gentleman from the *Birmingham News* standing behind Coleman. She'd gotten her question. Time to move on.

Before the reporter could ask his question an African American man pushed through the gaggle of reporters. "What about me?" he demanded. "Are you going to call on white reporters all morning?"

More of that grumbling churned around the crowd of onlookers. Just what she needed at her first open press conference. *Someone drawing the race card.*

"I'm new here, sir," Jess acquiesced. "I didn't recognize your affiliate, but, please, go ahead with your question."

"No one in the BPD," he said, his tone mildly accusing, "ever explained why it took almost seventy-two hours to start investigating DeShawn Simmons's case. Or why police protection was removed from his friend, Jerome Frazier, ensuring he lost his life to the devils who call themselves the MS-13!"

A crowd of angry folks who apparently wanted answers to those same questions seemed to come out of nowhere and everywhere at once. The small group of reporters and curiosity seekers were suddenly flooded with a mob of people who had no real interest in the life or death of

Gabrielle Grayson. Uniforms filtered into the throng but they were vastly outnumbered.

This just got better and better. Jess moistened her lips and braced for whatever came next.

The man who had asked the questions shouted over the rumbling. "Do you have any answers, Deputy Chief Harris?"

Burnett moved up next to her and whispered for her ears only, "Let's get you out of here."

Jess ignored him. "Yes, sir. I have answers." She surveyed the disgruntled crowd of new arrivals. "If anyone is interested in listening. Y'all need to settle down so no one gets the wrong impression of why you're here. You're here," she suggested, "because you want justice. You want to feel safe in your own homes and on the streets of your city."

The crowd relaxed a bit. "As to your first question, sir," Jess began, "there was a communication drop between the North Precinct and my office, which created the delay you spoke of. The moment we were made aware of DeShawn's case, we launched an investigation that ultimately saved his life."

Several in the crowd started chanting Jerome's name. The man asking the questions held up his hands until they quieted. Then he repeated his other question. "Why was police protection dropped for Jerome?"

Burnett's hand settled at the small of her back. She understood the signal. *Don't answer. Walk away.*

"That was my decision, sir," she announced. "And mine alone." Jess rode out the angry cries of outrage. Her heart stepped up its pace. This could get ugly, but the man had asked her a question and there was no need to give him anything less than the truth. Jerome Frazier deserved no less.

The man, who she had decided was about mid-sixties, and definitely the leader of this citizen group, raised his hands again. Silence fell over the park. "Will you explain to us why you did this?"

"I will." Knots of regret twisted in her belly. "I dismissed his surveillance because he asked me to. Jerome—"

The crowd hurled accusations at her for five or six seconds, until their leader raised his hands again.

Jess cleared her throat. "As soon as I became aware of how close DeShawn and Jerome were and the possibility that he might have some knowledge of certain things that could endanger him, I put him under protective surveillance. Jerome confronted me about this and demanded that I cancel the surveillance because he feared that being followed by a cop was going to make a target out of him far more so than anything he knew. I honored his request, sir. I wish I could have made a different decision but I had no choice but to do as he asked under the circumstances."

More of those vicious remarks were shouted at her. A chant calling for equal treatment started out with one voice then grew into a roar. Jess focused on keeping her respiration steady and her attention on the crowd. Burnett tugged at her arm. She wanted to say something more... but what? That the law didn't always make their job easy? Or that a passionate young man had made a mistake that almost cost him his life and did cost his best friend his life?

As if her internal struggle had summoned him, DeShawn Simmons elbowed his way through the crowd.

He stared at Jess for a moment and a certainty passed between them. He broke free of the crowd and came to stand beside her.

Silence fell over those assembled.

DeShawn pointed at her. "This lady saved my life." He took a deep breath and tried to compose himself before going on. "We were both hostages. I was one"—he poked his chest with his thumb—"because I was a fool. Chief Harris was one because she was trying to save me. She had a chance to get away before we were both almost killed. But she didn't. Instead, she told me to run . . . to save myself. She was willing to sacrifice herself for me. A kid she had never even met before that night." He shook his head. "Whatever beef you got, it's not with this lady."

He hugged Jess and that was just about her undoing.

Silence fell over the crowd again and Jess turned to see what was going on.

Burnett had walked into the crowd and offered his hand to the man who had been asking all the questions.

Cameras were snapping and rolling. What was this?

"Mr. Jones, you are welcome in my office any time you have questions or would like to offer any suggestions for how I might better serve our entire community."

Several of the younger, angrier men huddled around Burnett and started making demands of their own. Jess's pulse reacted. Uniforms pushed forward. This could turn into serious trouble. What the hell was Burnett doing?

Jones held up a hand. "I believe it's time we allowed the newer blood in the police department to fight our battle with their badges rather than our brothers fighting with their blood in the streets. We"—he surveyed the crowd that had arrived with him—"would be best served to take our efforts back to our neighborhoods and our churches and expend them there." His gaze settled on Burnett. "We've all learned a great lesson these last weeks."

Burnett nodded. "Yes, sir, we have. The Birmingham Police Department protects and serves *all* our citizens. We won't be repeating the past under my watch."

While the crowd dispersed and the reporters reluctantly followed, Jess watched Burnett and this Mr. Jones shake hands again. She had to hand it to Burnett. He had turned into quite the man on the street. Mayor Pratt had better watch his back.

"I gotta go, Chief Harris," DeShawn said. "If my grandmamma sees me on the news, she'll skin my hide."

"Thank you, DeShawn." Jess gave him another hug. "For coming to *my* rescue this time."

"Chief Harris."

She turned toward Burnett's voice. He and the man, Mr. Jones, were striding toward her.

"This is Wendell Jones," Burnett told her. "He's the current president of the Black Brotherhood."

"Mr. Jones." Jess offered her hand. "I'm pleased to meet you."

He gave her hand a firm shake. "I've been working with Chief Black and Captain Allen. It seems my followers have been blamed for certain black on brown activities that we absolutely did not do and do not condone. Despite what you saw here this morning, we are a peaceful group. Fierce but peaceful."

Fierce was a good description. "With the Grayson investigation, I'm afraid I'm a little behind on where we are with the Lopez situation. But I'm very pleased our Gang Task Force is seeing results and working closely with folks like you to sort out the needs of the community."

"It is my singular goal to see that our community leaders become completely color-blind," Jones said. "I've been watching you. Your briefing this morning allowed the opportunity for my people to see you and our good chief of police say those things with such heartfelt determination. We've had too many broken promises in the past, Chief Harris."

So the angry crowd was a setup. Judging by his reaction, Jess was confident Burnett had been as in the dark about it as she was. "Mr. Jones, I'd like to make you a proposition."

The older man smiled. "It's been a while, but I think I can handle whatever you throw my way, young lady."

A sense of humor, too. "I am in charge of the BPD's new Special Problems Unit." She wished she had a proper card to give him. "I'd like to invite you to breakfast the first Monday of each month so that we might discuss any issues you feel need to be hashed out."

"I'll join you," Burnett offered, "when possible."

Jones shook Jess's hand again. "I look forward to the opportunity, Chief Harris."

Jess realized something very important about herself at that moment. "I grew up in Birmingham, Mr. Jones. I've been gone for more than twenty years, but now I'm back and I'm here to move forward."

Whatever enemies she'd made here in the past or in the last three weeks, Jess wasn't afraid to face a single one of them. Whatever happened with her and Burnett, she wasn't running away. She might not have a long-term relationship or children to show for her forty-two years on this earth but she had other assets, like the ability to ferret out evil. Birmingham needed her. Her sister needed her. Maybe even Burnett needed her.

Jess was here to stay. That was what *she* needed.

Noon

After surviving her first official BPD press conference, Jess was starved but there was no time for lunch. Officer Cook had kindly thought to pick up a little something for the crew. Burgers and colas in the office wasn't Jess's favorite kind of lunch but it beat nothing.

Harper was at the case board adding new developments. These kinds of brainstorming sessions were an important part of any investigation.

"There were four distinct sets of prints on the baby bottle. Our victim's, the mother. And the baby's." He scrawled this information on the white board. "And two others we haven't identified."

"Why do most men have such lousy penmanship?" Lori asked.

Jess almost choked on her Pepsi.

Harper shot both of them a look over one broad shoulder.

"Is that harassment?" Officer Cook rallied to the defense of the males in the room.

"No, it is not," Jess said for the record. "It's merely a statement of fact. Carry on, Sergeant."

Lori smirked.

"One set is clearly a child's, but not the baby's."

The little boy next door, Devon Chambers, came immediately to mind. "We need to ask Lieutenant Grayson if the Chambers boy who lives next door ever came over to play or visit. If he visited earlier on Sunday, the prints might be his." The more accurately they could pinpoint who had access to the home in the hours before Gabrielle's murder, the better the understanding of the events leading up to her death.

Lori stood and strolled over to the board. She took the dry erase marker from Harper. He straightened his tie and went back to his desk.

"Dr. Baron has determined," Lori began, "that cause of death was manual asphyxiation. Since some results haven't come back yet, the official autopsy report won't be available for a few more days. But one screening has shown that the victim had at least one glass of wine and either consumed or was administered a rather large dose of OC, OxyContin. According to her husband and her medical records, which I was able to have a look at this morning, Gabrielle was not on any prescription medications. He wasn't aware of her taking anything beyond an Aleve for the occasional headache. And, to his knowledge, she had not consumed any wine when he visited around eight that evening."

"The OC explains the lack of defense wounds," Harper noted. "With a heavy dose like that, if she wasn't a regular user, she was probably unconscious."

Lori jotted down his comment. "And it suggests intent on the part of the perp. He didn't drug the vic for nothing. He had a goal. But was it murder?"

"If murder was his intent," Jess argued, "why the disorganized methods? What was the motive? Did Gabrielle have something he wanted? Did she make him angry? Did he kill her because he hated her or was this an unplanned act of rage?"

Lori jotted down *jealousy* and *rage* as possible motives.

Harper pointed out, "This new development confirms we're not dealing with a gang hit."

"Definitely not," Jess agreed. "If any one of the MS-13 cliques operating in Birmingham had wanted her dead, they wouldn't have bothered with all the foreplay. She'd be dead." She thought about that for a moment, then added, "If one of the anti-gang groups wanted to make her murder look like a gang hit, someone somewhere would be bragging."

"Still no tagging about this one," Harper confirmed.

Gangs always tagged their threats, accomplishments—anything they wanted to brag about would be scrawled on walls somewhere for the world to see.

"I spoke with the administrator at the rehab center this morning as well."

Lori had been very busy this morning. "Anything interesting come of that?"

"Unlike the pool guy's assessment"—Lori tapped Trenton's name on the case board—"Gabrielle's former supervisor said she loved being a housewife and mother. The patients loved her, and her coworkers, subordinates, and supervisors all adored her. She was above reproach. A *true saint* was the term used."

"And yet," Jess offered, "Gabrielle Grayson is dead. The victim of a brutal homicide that is not related to a burglary or any other criminal activity we have found thus far." Didn't add up, that was for sure. Honestly, the only real credibility she gave to Trenton's statement was that he had spent time with the victim more recently. Still didn't make his remarks the gospel.

"I got the same reaction about the husband." Cook

joined Lori at the case board. "The guys and gals in the South Precinct think he's some kind of god. He adores his wife. Talks about her and the kid all the time. Carries tons of photos in his wallet. His friends call him a *saint*."

"Seems to me," Jess countered, "that somewhere between these two saints there's a little splinter of evil." Somehow that splinter had sliced right through their lives like a machete laying down sugar cane. "And we have to find that tiny splinter."

A somber silence held the room for a moment. No one wanted to believe evil could lurk so close to home. Yet there was no escaping the facts. Gabrielle Grayson had almost surely known her killer.

"Detective Wells, dig deeper into Gabrielle's work and social life. Find someone, besides our less than credible pool guy, who knows the dirt. It's there. Maybe only a speck, but it's there. Something or someone that worked its way into the Graysons' lives. We need to find it." Jess wadded her burger wrapper and tossed it into the trash. "Sergeant Harper, set the lieutenant down and go over everything again. Maybe he's remembered something else."

"His mother-in-law is arriving today," Harper reminded her. "I may have to catch him around that schedule."

For the moment, Gabrielle's mother would need her son-in-law for emotional support far more than Jess needed him for questioning. "Don't push the issue, Sergeant. See when he's available. We can work with the family's schedule for now."

Cook looked at Jess expectantly.

"Officer Cook, check in with Captain Allen and verify that he's found no connecting threads between recent

MS-13 activities or enemies and this case." Jess couldn't completely close that avenue of the investigation just yet. Particularly after last night's warning that *she* was next. That note put a slightly different spin on the investigation. There were two common denominators shared by Jess and Gabrielle Grayson. They were both involved with cops and each had a connection, however remote, to this out-of-control gang business.

"Yes, ma'am."

"And while you're there, get a feel for how Lieutenant Grayson and his partner were fitting in with the GTF." Maybe he could get more from Allen's people than Harper had. Most in the department knew that Jess and Harper were friends as well as colleagues. If anyone was holding back on account of their dislike for Jess, sending in a new face could help.

Cook grabbed his jacket. "On my way."

When Cook was out the door, Harper cleared his throat.

Jess turned to him. "You have something you want to say, Sergeant?" She hadn't told Lori about the business at her newly rented apartment. Harper might have beaten her to the punch.

"I saw your press briefing," Harper announced.

"*We* saw your briefing." Lori nodded to the flat panel TV on the wall.

Jess looked from one to the other. "And?"

The two shared a look. He said, "I had to break out my handkerchief for her."

"You did not," Lori argued. "You did good," she told Jess. "You looked very professional." She gave Jess a nod of approval. "Love the new suit."

Jess had worn the ivory one today. She liked it, too. "Thank you. I'm curious to see how the community reacts to what I'm doing." Working under the public microscope was a little different. At the bureau she had been just a small cog buried deep in the big machine. There were people who handled interaction with the media in all but very rare situations. Like when the media stalked her after the Spears case went to hell in a handbasket.

Harper stood and reached for his jacket. "You got nothing to worry about, Chief. They love you already." He grinned. "They have since you sent a cold-blooded killer the message to man up and come get you."

God, Jess didn't want to think about that. Especially since a twinge of guilt accompanied the idea that Eric Spears had contacted her just yesterday and she hadn't told a soul.

She didn't have time to worry about him right now.

The other message, the one delivered to her new place, however, was a different story. That one she had to worry about. At least a little.

"I'm working on getting an interview with Grayson's partner's wife," Jess said, focusing her attention back on their homicide case. "I didn't want to push since she and her husband have been so involved with helping Grayson. But I think it's time. The grandmother will be here to help with the baby. No need to cut Sarah Riley any more slack."

"I'd like to go with you on that one," Lori said.

"That's a good idea," Harper remarked with a knowing look in Jess's direction.

Before Jess could admonish him, Lori said, "He told me about the break-in." She shook her head when Jess would have griped. "Harper and I think whoever it is in the department that has it in for you is using this case to reach out. It had to be someone close to know your new address."

"And"—Harper moved a step closer as if he feared being overheard—"since no one has claimed responsibility for tearing apart your old place and now this... I'm thinking this has something to do with Lopez and the GTF."

Jess was thinking along those same lines. She had to keep that theory under wraps until they had a hell of a lot more than supposition. Particularly, as Lori pointed out, whoever sent the note last night had to be close. Too close. "We can't go accusing anyone until we have evidence." She held her hands palms up. "If someone in the department has it in for me, we don't know how deep or how high it goes."

"High enough," Harper said, prodding a memory she'd just as soon forget, "that Salvadore Lopez warned Chief Burnett about it. Why do you think the chief wants someone with you all the time?"

"Let's just get on with the job of investigating this homicide," Jess suggested. She wasn't debating her ability to take care of herself with Harper too. "I'm thinking of having a security system, complete with cameras, installed anyway."

"Good idea," Lori agreed.

"So," Jess steered the conversation back to work, "we'll shoot for this evening or first thing in the morning for interviewing Sarah Riley. Unless I get my car back today, I'll need a ride anyway." Jess had a feeling her car wasn't ready for pickup yet because Burnett didn't want her to have that much freedom. Knowing him, he'd had a GPS tracker put on the Taurus. Fat lot of good that had done him.

"Sounds good." Lori pulled out her smartphone and tapped the screen a few times. "On the Chambers family, I don't have much yet, but there are no parents. The mother died a year ago and the father doesn't appear to have been in the picture for quite some time. I confirmed what Leslie told us about school and work. I haven't tracked down Devon's school yet. Must be a private one."

"So it is just the two of them." Damn it. Jess had a bad feeling about those two. Her cell vibrated against her desk and she reached for it. "Harris."

"This is Leslie Chambers."

That bad feeling crept deeper into her bones. "Hey, Miss Chambers." She and Lori exchanged a questioning look. "How can I help you?" Judging by her voice, she needed something. She sounded as if she were in tears.

"It's my brother. He's missing. I think he might be in real trouble." She burst into outright sobs. "I think he might know something about Mrs. Grayson's murder."

"Where are you, Leslie?"

"At my house. I've looked everywhere and I can't find him."

"Stay right there. I'm on my way."

Whispering Stream Lane, 2:05 p.m.

"He said he heard the baby crying."

Seated at the Chamberses' well-used kitchen table, Jess readied her pad and pencil. Leslie had explained how her brother had come clean with her after they left yesterday. "What did he do about the baby crying?"

As Leslie Chambers told her story, Lori was outside calling in the All Points Bulletin on eight-year-old Devon. He had been at a neighbor's home when his sister left for work last night. When he wasn't up at breakfast this morning the neighbor, eighty-year-old Earlene Nicholson, assumed he had gone home to be with his sister. At eleven Leslie had gone across the street to pick him up and he wasn't there. She hadn't freaked out until she searched their house, including the crawl space, and cruised the neighboring streets. Her brother was nowhere to be found.

Lori was also to get someone over here from Alabama Power to reinstall the utility meter. The idea that this young woman and her brother had suffered so much ripped at Jess's heart.

"He said he climbed out the window in his room and went over to see if the baby was okay." Leslie wrung her hands. "There's an old iron trellis outside his window. He climbs up and down it like a ladder."

"This was the night of the murder, Sunday night," Jess clarified, "during the storm?"

Leslie nodded. "When the lightning would flash, he said he could see Mrs. Grayson lying on the floor in the family room. She was dead—like our mother at her funeral. You know, not moving or breathing and there was blood everywhere—that part he's seen in movies." She shook herself as if her thoughts were all running together. "He understands dead but not the difference between natural causes and murder, I don't think. Anyway, he touched the blood and that's how he got blood on his T-shirt."

She stared at her hands. "I shouldn't have thrown

the shirt away. But I was worried for him. I didn't want him to be in trouble. And he said he didn't see anyone in the house other than Mrs. Grayson and the baby, so I didn't figure he could be of any help. Mrs. Nicholson had already agreed to keep him last night. I planned to talk to him some more about what happened this morning. By the time he told me I had to get to work and..." She made a desperate sound. "I should have called you."

"Let's not worry about that right now." Jess tapped her pencil on her pad. "Did he remember the time when he heard the baby crying?"

Leslie shook her head. "Time is irrelevant to him except for the things he knows should happen at a certain time. Like breakfast by ten. The sun rising or setting around a certain time frame. He's very schedule oriented when it comes to the routine of his day, but when he's doing something or watching something he's totally oblivious to the passage of time."

"Where does he go to school, Leslie?"

"Our mother tried several different schools but he seemed to do best at the Gateway Academy. It's really expensive. By the time our mother died she had used up her savings. But the school let me keep bringing him this last year. They're looking for scholarship money for next term. I'm hoping he'll still be able to go."

"I know this is hard," Jess said carefully, "but where is your father?"

Leslie shrugged. "He left after Devon was diagnosed. He didn't want to deal with it."

That kind of cowardice was all too common. Made Jess want to hunt the guy down and kick him right in the... *focus, Jess.* "Your mother died nearly a year ago and you haven't asked for any assistance?" Good grief, this poor girl was working herself into the ground. "You're entitled to numerous benefits, Leslie. Social Security benefits for your brother. Probably food assistance and help with your utilities."

"I was afraid they'd take him away from me if they found out I was trying to take care of him alone. I promised my mother that I wouldn't let that happen."

"So you've been working nights at this factory while he stays here by himself? And while you're at school three days a week?"

She nodded, her expression one of shame. "He's done really well. This is the first time anything like this has happened."

Jess suppressed the urge to lecture the girl. Now wasn't the time. "First, we're going to find your brother. Then we're going to make sure the two of you get all the help you're entitled to. And no one," she promised, "is going to take your brother away from you." Jess would never forget those first few days when she and Lil went into foster care. They weren't sure if anyone would take the both of them or if they would have to be split up. "You have my word on that."

"Thank you." Leslie swiped at her tears.

"So." Jess readied to take notes. "Let's go over this again. Devon climbed down the trellis."

"He checked on Mrs. Grayson first. He recognized that she was dead. Then he went to see about the baby. The baby wouldn't stop crying, so he filled his bottle with milk and that made the baby happy. Once the baby was happy, he was coming back here to watch from his window until Mr. Grayson came home." She licked her dry lips. "I've drilled it into his head for so long that he shouldn't let anyone find out he's staying here alone while I work that he was afraid to call the police. And he knows Mr. Grayson is a policeman and that he would take care of everything when he got home." She closed her eyes and shook her head. "But that's no excuse. This is my fault."

"There was nothing anyone could have done for Mrs. Grayson," Jess reminded her. "The fact that he didn't call the police didn't cause further harm." She could see how it made sense to the boy to wait for the father to come home.

"But," Leslie said with obvious hesitation, "someone was still in the house."

The news interrupted the rhythm of Jess's heart. "Did Devon see this person?"

Leslie shook her head. "It was too dark. He just kept saying it was probably the angel who takes the dead people to heaven. One of his teachers tried to explain about angels and heaven after our mother died. Whatever he heard that night, I don't think he knew whether it was a man or woman even. Or real, for that matter. He swore to me that he didn't see anyone. He heard a noise and thought it was the angel coming for Mrs. Grayson and he ran home." Her lips started to tremble again. "I should have asked him more questions."

Jess reached across the table and squeezed her hand. "We'll find him." Now for the most important question. "Is there any chance that Devon would leave out part of the story? That maybe he did see someone and that someone saw him?" Jess found herself holding her breath in anticipation of the answer.

Leslie shrugged her slumped shoulders. "He said no

but he might not tell me that part if he thought it would make me worry. He worries about me as much as I worry about him." Her face furrowed with worry. "But he had scratches on one arm. Like someone grabbed him and their nails dug into his skin as he pulled away. I asked him about the scratches and he said it was from when he plays under the house. He calls it his secret hiding place." Tears streamed down her cheeks. "But I'm scared to death that the angel he thinks he saw may have been a person... the killer, and maybe the killer saw Devon and he barely escaped being murdered."

That was exactly what Jess feared as well. "We can't rule out that possibility," she confessed. "But Devon could be hiding because he thinks he's in trouble. He sounds like a very bright and resilient young man. What about his school or your work? Would he know how to get to either one from here?"

Leslie shook her head. "He's never been to my work and his school is in Mountain Brook. I don't think he would remember all the turns."

Leslie had already confirmed the boy wasn't on any medication. That was one worry they wouldn't have to deal with. Depending on the health issue, missed medication could create a deadly scenario. Beyond being taken by the killer or some other sick bastard, the next big worry was water. There were no bodies of water nearby other than a few pools, all of which had been checked already.

The most likely scenario was that the killer had seen him and had returned to tie up that loose end. Jess hoped that wasn't the case but, based on what she had just learned, the odds were not in the child's favor.

"Has Devon ever run away before?" The sister had said

nothing like this had ever happened before but it never hurt to rephrase the question.

"Never."

"When you came home did anything look out of place? Was the door locked? Anything unusual at all?"

"The door was locked and everything was exactly as it always is except Devon wasn't here." Tears welled in her eyes. "This is my fault."

The front door didn't have a dead bolt and like the old one on Jess's apartment the lock would be simple to pick. That safety issue needed to be addressed immediately. She made a mental note to have her locksmith change the locks on the house and add dead bolts. What was a couple more hundred on her already hefty credit card balance?

"You can't blame yourself, Leslie," Jess urged. She shifted uncomfortably in her chair. Considered that the girl probably needed a hug or something. She reached across the table once more and patted her arm. "You've been doing the best you could. Now, until we find Devon, I'm sure you want to stay here in case he comes back, and I think that's wise."

Leslie nodded adamantly. "I don't want to leave. This is the only place he really knows."

"I'm assigning surveillance, so you'll see an officer in an unmarked car parked in the street in front of your house. I'll just feel better knowing you're safe until we get Devon home." On the slim chance Devon had wandered off on his own or decided to run away for some reason, there was still the risk that Gabrielle Grayson's killer had seen him and would be looking for him here.

Leslie nodded her understanding. "What happens now?"

"Let's make a list of anyone he might try to contact or places he might try to go. Is there a favorite toy store or bookstore? A doctor he's visited enough times to remember the location?"

Leslie gave the name and address of his physicians. The name of the mall they usually shopped at, though those occasions were rare. The names of their few friends, all of whom they hadn't seen in ages. Leslie had no time for a social life.

When they had exhausted the young woman's ideas on the subject, Jess moved on to the one other detail she needed to cover. "One last question, Leslie." Jess dreaded asking but, until they knew more, no rock could be left uncovered. Every possibility had to be explored.

Leslie waited expectantly.

"Did anything happen between the two of you that might make Devon want to run away?" More tears spilled down the girl's cheeks. Jess felt like a wicked old witch for making her feel worse.

"I complain every day about how much trouble he is. Every single day. Yesterday was no different. So, yeah, he had every reason to want to run away. But he never did. He always stayed right here as if he were the one protecting me instead of the other way around."

Urgency welled in Jess. She wondered if Leslie understood that she had just made the situation crystal clear.

Devon Chambers hadn't left his sister because he was angry or afraid or for any other reason. He would never leave Leslie willingly. Devon was victim number two in this grisly case.

Dear God, would they be able to find him before it was too late?

12

7:00 p.m.

Jess stood next to her Audi in the city's parking garage. Burnett had promised it was waiting for her, keys under the mat, and here it was. She should get in the car and start the engine so the air-conditioning could begin the struggle of cooling down the interior. Or at least she should turn around and thank Burnett. Somehow she just couldn't work up the enthusiasm. Instead, she stood here melting in the heat.

A woman was dead and the one possible witness to her murder, a child who'd already seen more than his fair share of pain and loss, was missing. Vanished. No one had seen him. No one had reported a small boy wandering around.

He was just gone. And his sister was terrified.

Jess was terrified.

She had to find that child...alive. If anything happened to him, his sister would never forgive herself.

Jess knew a little something about that. She had ignored Lil a million times. Like the voice mail she had left two hours ago. Jess had been busy, that was true. But she hadn't wanted to talk to her sister just then. She'd wanted to hear the latest update from a distance...via voice mail. It was easier that way.

Lil's personal physician, Dr. Collins, was concerned with her test results. He had mentioned potential problems ranging from clinical depression to various forms of cancer. There were numerous other possibilities in between and lots more testing to be done. He agreed with last night's ER physician, that relevant family history would be helpful.

That was one problem Jess wasn't looking forward to solving. It wasn't that she minded going to see their one known living relative and demanding answers. She didn't. Jess would do anything for her sister. It was the idea that two doctors had insisted on the importance of this step. Made Jess wonder if both men were leaning toward the worst and just didn't want to suggest as much until they had evidence. Jess did that all the time in her work.

She didn't want her sister to be that sick.

"We can do this another time."

Jess shook off the disturbing worries and turned to Burnett—Dan, they were off duty now. She'd almost forgotten he was right behind her. "I need to do it now. I might not have time later." With the Grayson case and little Devon missing...she really didn't have time now. But she had to do this for her sister.

Dan moved up beside her. "Let me take care of this. I can do this for you and Lil."

She wished he wouldn't get so close. Especially right

now. She was weak. Really weak. And that deep, familiar voice made her want to lean into him and squall her eyes out. "This is something *I* have to do." She took a breath and reached for the car door but then hesitated. "I'm glad you're going with me."

"You're exhausted. Why don't you let me drive you?"

Before she could argue he was guiding her toward his SUV. He hit the remote and the vehicle started well ahead of their arrival at his reserved parking slot.

"Your fancy Mercedes is going to stick out like a rose in a patch of weeds."

He opened her door and motioned for her to climb in. "I don't think this will be the first high-end vehicle they've seen in that neighborhood considering what the pimps and drug dealers are driving these days."

He had a point there. Jess settled into the passenger seat. The air-conditioning vents were already blowing out cool air. Now there was a good reason to have keyless start. She'd have to think about that when she got around to buying a new ride. In about ten more years.

Rush hour was over. Rush hour... what a misleading concept. Both the morning and the evening rush hour traffic issues lasted two hours at least. That didn't even include road construction. As far back as she could remember one street or the other in Birmingham was always under construction, causing bottlenecks or detours.

Dan slowed for a turn and Jess dragged her thoughts back to their destination. Wanda Newsom lived in the Druid Hills neighborhood—the same one where much of the city's gang troubles were taking place. Jess hadn't discussed her drive-by of her aunt's home the other day with Dan or anyone else. Last week's case had drawn her to the neighborhood and she'd ended up going by Wanda's house. Jess had no idea why she'd bothered. Temporary insanity maybe. Morbid curiosity mostly.

Nope, she hadn't said a word to Dan but he clearly knew the way. He'd done his research. That was the kind of guy he was. She was learning that side of this older version of Dan. He was far more grounded and steady than he'd been two decades ago. He was strong and brave. And incredibly handsome and a generous and ambitious lover.

Not the path to go down just now, Jess.

She wondered if Wanda had changed in all these years. She considered the idea that according to DMV records, her aunt had never remarried and never moved. She'd married young, before her older sister, Jess and Lil's mom. But her husband had gotten killed on a military operation in the Middle East. After that, Wanda had turned to drugs and eventually prostitution. She never had any children. She was alone.

Jess supposed she lived on Social Security these days or maybe a VA check. She was a widow after all. How else was a sixty-plus-year-old prostitute going to make a living?

Why hadn't she ever gotten help? Why hadn't her only sister helped her? Giving her mom credit, you couldn't help someone who didn't want help. If a person was determined to commit the same mistakes over and over again, there was no diverting their path. Jess and Lil had been too young to know or understand whatever had been going on between the two sisters.

Jess wondered if she would end up alone like Wanda.

"Do you think," she asked, breaking the silence that

had settled inside the car, "we become more and more like our parents as we get older?" Or like any other close blood relations, she kept to herself.

"I think," Dan said as he made the final turn onto the street where her aunt resided, "that we exhibit characteristics related to how and where we grew up. If you're asking me if your aunt being old and alone is a path you'll follow, the answer is no. I won't let you take that path."

Jess laughed. "I have your word on that, do I?"

"Unconditionally." He parked at the curb.

Jess unfastened her seat belt and turned to him. "Let's make a pact right now, Dan. Like we used to." This was crazy. She knew it was crazy but she couldn't stop herself.

He turned to her, those blue eyes as familiar to her as her own. "All right. Shoot."

"When we reach sixty, if we're both still single, we'll get married and live together just so we're not old and alone." She'd said it. By God, she'd said it. She held her breath and waited for his answer.

A frown of confusion claimed his face even as humor sparkled in his eyes. "Are you proposing, Jess?"

"I'm proposing that we not spend our sixth decade of life, and onward, alone. That's what I'm proposing."

He reached across the console, offering his hand. "Well then, you have a deal."

Jess closed her hand around his and gave it a shake. "Good. No need to worry about that anymore."

She was out of the SUV by the time he came around the hood. Jess squared her shoulders and headed for the unknown. Dan stayed right beside her. She would not end up like this. Wanda's ancient Toyota sat in the drive. The yard was overgrown and two pots with dead geraniums sat on either side of the steps. Dan knocked for the third time before a female voice demanded, "Who is it?"

"Chief of Police Daniel Burnett," he said before Jess could respond.

The door opened just far enough for the woman to view the credentials Dan flashed. Then she opened it the rest of the way.

"Whatever happened, I don't know anything about it. I stay in the house," she was saying, "except..." Her voice trailed off as she looked at Jess, really looked at her, for the first time. "Jessie Lee?"

"Yes...ma'am. It's me." Jess's mouth had gone so dry the words scarcely squeezed out. "I apologize for arriving unannounced, but I have some questions for you if you have a few minutes."

For one long moment Wanda stared at Jess as if she'd seen a ghost. Jess kind of felt the same way. Wanda, though her lifestyle showed in her face, looked so very much like Jess's mother, Helen. If Helen were still alive she would be sixty-five now. Wanda would be sixty-three in October, according to the DMV. Her blond hair was gray. Her brown eyes a little faded. She was too thin. Jess couldn't remember her mother being that thin.

"Come in." Wanda backed up and opened the door wider. "You'll have to look over the mess. I wasn't expecting company."

The place looked the same as it had three decades ago. Tattered sofa and chairs. Magazines and newspapers piled about. The whole house smelled of Lysol. Her aunt might have been a lady of the night, but she'd been almost phobic about cleanliness.

Dan waited until Jess had taken a seat on the sofa, then he settled next to her. "I appreciate your time."

"I usually have Bible study on Tuesday nights," Wanda said, breaking the tension. She sounded a little nervous, excited almost. "But so many people are trying to get in that last vacation before school starts."

Bible study? Maybe Wanda had changed. Better late than never. "I wanted to ask you a few questions about my mother and father."

Wanda blinked. "Okay."

There was a distinct loss of enthusiasm in her voice. Even with that one word Jess heard it, saw it on her face. "Can you tell me if either one had any health issues or maybe if my grandparents on either side had any"—she shrugged—"heart issues, cancers, anything like that?"

"Helen and Lee were completely healthy as far as I know," she said, her attention wandering all over the room. "Our parents, yours and Lily's grandparents, died young. Your grandfather died in a work accident. He was an ironworker over at Sloss."

Jess didn't remember having heard that story. All those times she'd been to that old place she'd had no idea her grandfather had worked there back in the day. That he'd died there gave her a chill.

"Your grandmother died in childbirth having our little brother, who didn't make it either. If either one of 'em had any health problems I didn't know about it. We were poor. Medical attention was something generally reserved for life and death situations."

She hadn't known any of that either. "What about aunts, uncles, or cousins?" Jess pressed.

Wanda shook her head. "My mother was an only child and I never knew any of my father's family."

"What about *my* father?" Jess was named after her father, Jessie *Lee*. "Any health problems on his side that you know of?"

"Your father never spoke of his family. He moved to Birmingham for college from down around Mobile and, to my knowledge, Helen never met a single member of his family."

What kind of people didn't know their own family? Jesus Christ. Jess wanted to scream her frustration. But she wouldn't show it to this woman for anything. No matter that she usually had Bible study on Tuesday nights, she was still the same woman who had chosen her life of drugs and crime over two little girls when they needed her most.

"What about you, Ms. Newsom," Dan asked the question Jess was too mad to ask. "Have you been diagnosed with any health issues that you would be willing to talk about? We realize we're invading your privacy a bit, but any information would be appreciated."

God, he was a born politician. Jess wasn't showing any appreciation for a thing this woman said or did. Tuesday night Bible study, for heaven's sake. Wait until she told Lil.

"The usual," Wanda said. "Arthritis. Found out I have a cataract last week. That's about it." She turned to Jess. "Is something wrong with you or your sister?"

The fake sincerity in her voice made Jess want to puke. "We don't know yet. Lily is having some testing done. The doctors suggested we get as much family history as possible."

"I hate to hear that," Wanda responded. "Tell her I'll be praying for her."

Jess shot to her feet. "Well, I have to be going now." She had to get out of here. Right now. Or she was going to say something Dan would likely regret.

Dan stood. "Thank you for your time, Ms. Newsom."

Wanda followed them to the door but Jess didn't get a word of what she said to Dan. Jess had to get out of here. Her heart was pounding. Her stomach was churning. Her throat kept closing, blocking her ability to get air into her lungs.

Jess stormed the length of the cracked sidewalk and straight up to the waiting SUV. From somewhere behind her Dan started it. She climbed in and faced forward, absolutely refused to glance back at the woman or the house.

"Take me to my car," she ordered. "I don't want to talk about this. I just want to go away from here."

"I understand."

Thankfully he proved as good as his word. He didn't argue with her or ask any questions. He drove her to the Audi and gave her a hug before walking away.

Jess got into her faithful old car and drove to her new home. Dan followed her. She'd expected he would. At her door she'd disengaged the new locks, stuck one hand in her bag to get a grip on her Glock, and then gone inside. She hadn't managed a decent breath until she'd confirmed the place was clear.

When she closed and locked the door, Dan had driven off. She watched from the window until his headlights disappeared. This day had been too long.

After stripping off her clothes she climbed into the shower and scrubbed her body. Her stomach roiled each time the remembered smell of Lysol revisited her senses.

Memories from that awful year she and Lil had spent with Wanda swirled in her head over and over like a bad movie. That was one part of her past she'd just as soon never think of again.

After she'd practically skinned herself, Jess let the evidence and facts of the Grayson case fill her head. A sense of calmness settled over her.

Call her a coward, but that was the one place she felt most comfortable…deep inside a case. It was funny how she felt more at home immersed in the elements of a homicide than she did with the people who were part of her personal life.

10:00 p.m.

This was exactly what she'd needed.

Jess taped a note onto the section of wall between the two windows on the east side of her apartment that overlooked the main house. She quickly scribbled another observation about Devon Chambers and his sister, Leslie, tore it out of her notepad, and taped it on the wall.

She stood back then, took off her glasses, and considered the duplicate case board for the Grayson investigation she had created on the wall of her place.

"That's perfect." She could put a desk right there. She considered the floor space beneath where the biggest dry erase board that would fit, maybe a six-footer, would hang. As soon as she had some free time during normal business hours, she needed to round up those items and maybe a small sofa.

The stuff she had in Virginia was being sold with her

old house there. None of it would work in this place anyway. Besides, she wanted a fresh start. This was a new beginning for her professionally and personally. Nothing about her old life would fit.

Which was exactly why she had been ignoring calls from Wesley all evening. And two from Dan. The one conversation she hadn't avoided was the one with her sister. Lil was feeling a little better. She wasn't surprised that dear old Aunt Wanda didn't know jack.

Speaking of Jack. Jess moved back to her makeshift board. She needed more in-depth info on Sergeant Jack Riley and his wife. They were closer to the Graysons than anyone else. Since Jess hadn't been able to meet with the wife, Sarah, today, she was hoping that would happen tomorrow. Since Grayson's mother-in-law had finally arrived in the city, he and his son would be staying with her rather than the Rileys. Made setting up interviews simpler. Jess also needed to talk to Grayson about his neighbors, Leslie and Devon.

Jess's attention shifted down to the picture of the little boy Leslie had given her. An AMBER Alert had been issued and flyers sent out all over the city along with media blasts. Devon Chambers's cute little freckled face was all over the place. Hopefully someone had seen him and would call the hotline.

As much as she wanted to nail Gabrielle Grayson's killer, that little boy was Jess's top priority.

She turned away from the case board. Enough for tonight. She tightened the sash of her borrowed robe. Lori had been happy to part with it. Jess loved the well-worn cotton. She didn't care that it was now more white than pink. It suited her.

This place, she decided, suited her. Particularly now that she had better locks. There was no way anyone could reach one of the many windows without a ladder. Breaking in now wouldn't be such a simple matter.

Her cell vibrated against the countertop. She walked over to the phone. Her pulse rate climbed at the idea that it could be Spears texting again.

But it wasn't.

Did you have dinner?

Jess rolled her eyes. Dan worried over her like a mother hen. Y…e…s.

She couldn't remember when she'd enjoyed going to the market. But after she'd had a shower, she had driven to the closest grocery store and forced herself to shop. As if walking into the store and smelling the scents emanating from the deli had somehow tripped some you-need-to-eat trigger, she had shopped like a maniac. Her fridge and cupboards were now crammed full of stuff.

She had eaten half a banana and two chocolate bars on her way home.

And she had a nifty new single-cup coffeemaker and all sorts of coffee and tea selections in a very cool lazy Susan–style rack. She might never visit a Starbucks again. What she didn't have was pots and pans and dishes. Or silverware. She'd grabbed a pack of disposable coffee cups.

Good was Dan's response. She decided to put on a cup of French vanilla–flavored coffee and put him out of his misery. Every time they were alone together she could feel the way he wanted to touch her. That caring hug he'd given her in the parking garage after the pointless trip to Wanda's house had been filled with barely restrained need. But even more telling was the obvious and innate urge he clearly felt to protect her. Those were facts she could no longer deny. However painful their past, she could trust Dan.

The vow to be there for each other when they were old...every look, every touch, all of it tugged at a place so deep down inside her that it scared the hell out of her. She wasn't sure what it meant or where it was going but she could no longer pretend the journey wasn't real. The trick now was to find some sort of balance.

While her cup of coffee brewed, she sent him a text saying she'd bought out the Fresh Market and had a kitchen full of food now. She bit her lip and waffled on how to word the next text. "What the hell?" She typed the message and hit send before she lost her nerve.

Phone in hand, she paced the floor while she waited for his response. Yes. I would love to come to dinner on Saturday night.

She smiled. She would need dishes, cookware, and a sofa before then. And she needed curtains for all these windows if she expected to have any privacy. When this case was closed, if she and Dan had even five minutes alone she suspected they would need some serious privacy.

Her heart thumping with foolish anticipation, Jess walked around the room and tried to distract herself from thoughts of sex with Dan. She needed a few rugs here and there. Maybe a side table for her bed. She paused at the window that gave her a view of the city lights in the distance and got lost in the undeniable beauty. She could get used to this place. It wasn't too much to take care of. No yard or exterior maintenance. If something broke she would call her landlord.

All she needed was a maid and it would be like she was back at the Howard Johnson, only with a way better bed and neighborhood.

Snagging her coffee and her Glock, just in case, she went out onto the deck and leaned against the railing. She needed a glider for out here. She could sit and enjoy the cooler temps at night. When fall came, it would be really nice.

Not that she was sure she would still be here in the fall. Mr. Louis had offered her the place until she could get back on her feet. He might not want a permanent tenant. She glanced toward his house. There were lights on in his house but she hadn't seen any sign of him at any of the windows.

In fact, she hadn't seen him at all. She hadn't even met him. But there hadn't been time really. Admittedly, the situation was a little strange, living over the garage belonging to a man she'd never laid eyes on.

Jess sipped her coffee. "Mmm." She should have had one of these convenient gadgets ages ago. Movement on the patio behind the house drew her attention there. Her pulse skittered. She wasn't sure if it was a person or an animal. She squinted and tried to see if anyone was down there. Last night's message—*you're next*—had ice slipping through her veins.

She went back inside and engaged the new locks, then wandered to the sink to leave her cup there. After turning out the lights, she peeled off her robe and climbed onto the bed. A sigh escaped her as she sank into the pillows.

"Where have you been all my life?"

Her cell vibrated and she felt around in the dark. It was caught between the pillows. She stared at the text message on the screen and all those soft, sweet sensations vanished.

Pleasant dreams.

She sat up and surveyed the darkness. The idea that she'd thought someone was outside resurrected old fears.

Spears couldn't be here...he wouldn't dare. He was assuming she was in bed. That's all. Wherever he was he would know it was bedtime here. She thought about that night at Dan's when Spears had sent her the same kind of text message. He had been there...watching.

Jess scrambled out of bed and got her Glock. She tucked it under her pillow and laid her head there. If he showed up again he was a dead man.

She didn't know how much time passed before she drifted off, felt like hours. One mantra kept playing over and over in her head and followed her to sleep.

I'll get you, Spears. Just you wait and see.

But first I have to find a little red-haired boy who believes in angels.

13

Devon didn't mind the dark. It was almost like being home. But it wasn't. It smelled different. Like dirt, but somebody else's dirt.

The angel had put tape over his mouth and his hands and feet. His wrists hurt. His ankles, too. The tape was too tight and he couldn't move around. He really needed to go to the bathroom. He'd already done number one in his pajamas. He tried to hold it as long as he could, but when he went to sleep he forgot to hold it. Felt yucky. His sister would be mad when she found out.

He wondered if she was looking for him. She'd probably be mad about him leaving Mrs. Nicholson's house too.

His stomach growled. It would be nice to have some potted meat. Seemed liked a bunch of hours since he ate. Maybe days. He couldn't tell.

The angel had put him under here and hadn't come back. Maybe this was where he would be living now. He kinda thought heaven was in the clouds, not under somebody's house. He could hear moving around in the house. He wondered if his mommy was under someone's house? Once or twice he even heard some kids crying and hollering.

Maybe the angel had brought them here too. This might be just a hiding place before they went to heaven.

But he wasn't dead. He didn't want to get dead.

Devon wished he could be up there with the other kids. They might know what the angel was gonna do to them.

Mostly he wished he could go home and be with his sister. Leslie would be all worried.

If he could get loose he might be able to find his way home. He wished he hadn't gotten scared when the angel caught him. His sister told him that angels didn't hurt live people. But he went inside himself anyway and he didn't get to see which way they came.

He twisted his hands but it didn't work too good. The tape covered his fingers, so he couldn't work them. Made it hard to move even a little bit.

Maybe if the angel came back he could ask to have some water. He wished he could go home and get his own water and potted meat. He wished he had his backpack and flashlight too.

Angels probably didn't let you have wishes.

A man shouted mean words at somebody. Devon jumped. He stared up through the darkness. There was a man in the house with the crying kids. He was mad or just mean. He kept hollering. A woman was screaming and crying.

Something crashed. Somebody was real mad. He didn't like all that hollering.

It got all quiet.

Devon held real still and listened hard.

Something scraped and dragged underneath the house... not far from where he was stuck.

A bright light shined in his eyes. He squinted against it.

His heart started jumping as the light came closer and closer. His body shook and he went number one some more.

The light stopped real close to him but he couldn't open his eyes 'cept a crack 'cause the light was so bright. Was it the angel's light?

Devon closed his eyes and tried to remember how to pray.

Please, God, tell your angel to take me back home. I promise to do better.

14

Dunbrooke Drive, 11:00 p.m.

Dan stared at his cell. He'd been resisting calling Jess for nearly an hour now. He just wanted to ensure she was okay but that would only annoy her. She didn't like him checking up on her. She'd invited him to dinner on Saturday. What else did he want?

He exhaled a big breath. Everything. No point pretending. He wanted to explore every inch of her as if he hadn't already touched every part of her. He wanted her with him at night when he closed his eyes. He wanted to see her face first thing each morning when he opened them once more.

Slow down, pal. The one thing he understood with complete certainty was that Jess would not be pushed. He had to let this happen in its own time.

The late news droned on in the background. The highlights from their press conference had been replayed a dozen times on every local channel. Jess was quickly becoming Birmingham's new hero. He wondered if she had any idea how that was going to change her life.

He had to be careful of the advice he offered her these days. She'd given it to him straight when he'd taken her home from the hospital. Balancing the work relationship and the personal stuff was giving her a hard time. He hadn't meant for that to happen. He had hoped they could find a way. But not at the expense of her peace of mind. Or her happiness.

That aside, *he* wasn't happy with her new living arrangements. He would have much preferred she move into a normal apartment building or home. This over-the-garage place popping up out of the blue from someone she or Lily didn't really know didn't sit well with him.

He'd run a background search on George Louis. Lily had been wrong about the widower part. The man had never been married. He'd lived with his invalid sister until she died ten years ago. She had never married either. The two had moved to Birmingham thirty-four years ago. No records whatsoever, not even a parking ticket. Louis had worked with one of the city's top architectural firms until nine years ago, when he retired shortly after his sister's death.

There was absolutely no reason to suspect anything untoward. But this was Jess, and Dan couldn't not worry about her safety.

Not with Eric Spears still out there somewhere. Jess's old boss at Quantico kept Dan apprised of any updates. They had nothing. No idea where Spears was at this point. There was no record of him coming back into the country but that meant nothing—not when a man like Spears was involved. He had endless resources.

Bottom line, Dan needed to have a talk with Mr. Louis

just to make sure he understood Jess's situation. Maybe that was all he needed to get comfortable with her new living arrangements.

The thing was, as much as he wanted to be with her every chance he got, he wanted to protect her. For him, the problem with balance was that one ultra-sensitive issue. Jess was a strong, independent woman. He cramped her style on and off the job. Pushing her away with his need to protect was not his intent.

He tossed his phone onto the coffee table and puffed out a weary breath. Well, it had taken them two decades to get to this place. He shouldn't be surprised that it was going to take some time for them to reach the next level.

The doorbell rang. Dan shoved off the couch and considered that he was shirtless and in his pajama pants but whoever was at his door needed to consider the hour and appreciate the fact that he was even answering. Could be Jess. Not too many others would have the nerve to show up at his door at this hour. If there was a department issue, he'd get a call.

He checked the security peephole. *Sylvia?* He drew back, puzzled. Maybe she'd learned something new from Gabrielle Grayson's lab results. But they'd had this conversation already. She could not act in an official capacity on this case under any circumstances. He couldn't prevent Leeds from allowing her to be involved as an observer, but that was as much leeway as the law would allow. Anything beyond that and the investigation would be jeopardized.

He opened the door. "Sylvia? Is everything all right?"

She surveyed his bare chest and lifted a skeptical eyebrow. "Make yourself decent. We have to talk."

"Come on in." He tried to be patient with Sylvia. He really did. But she went too far any time they were forced to interact. He gestured toward the living room. "Have a seat and I'll go make myself decent."

Dan refused to let his frustration get the better of him. There was no use fighting a battle he couldn't win. The Baron family was by far the wealthiest in the city and her father carried the weight of a Senate seat. What was the chief of police to do except be accommodating, as long as it didn't break the law? Truth was, they had a personal connection that he couldn't pretend never existed. More of that baggage he carried around after three ex-wives.

He rummaged through his bureau and grabbed a tee. That was the best she was going to get. He dragged it on as he made his way back down the hall. She paced the living room. Whatever she had on her mind, she was worked up. Not unusual. The Barons were never satisfied with the status quo.

"Would you like coffee? Water? Bourbon?" If he recalled correctly, her favorite drink was bourbon.

"No thanks." She stalled in the middle of the room and leveled her full attention on him. "Gabrielle called me the day before she was murdered. She wanted to talk but I didn't have time. I told this to Harris but she doesn't seem to have followed up."

Dan set his hands on his hips. "Why did Gabrielle call you?" He hated that the question came out with a little more disbelief than he'd intended but it was done.

"Like I told Harris, she wanted to talk about Larry. Evidently there was trouble in paradise."

"But you don't know exactly what she wanted to talk about," he countered.

Sylvia folded her arms over her chest and hiked up her chin. "God, you sound like Harris. I just told you she wanted to talk about Larry. *To me.* There was a problem. She was worried and now she's dead. Do you get that?" she demanded. "You should be looking more closely at Larry and whatever problem he has or is involved in."

Dan plowed his fingers through his hair. "Do you know how this sounds?" Surely she did. Sylvia was an extremely intelligent woman. "You're the scorned ex-wife. You would love to see him go down for this. That's what everyone will think."

Sylvia laughed. "I don't care what anyone thinks. But I do care that no one, not even the woman who stole my husband, deserved to die like this. You and Harris need to get your acts together. This murder had something to do with Larry. I heard the fear in her voice, Dan. Do you have any idea how much courage it must have taken for her to call me?"

That part he got. "Jess *is* investigating Larry. Anyone close to Gabrielle is a person of interest. You know how this works. She's not going to ignore the possibility that Larry was involved. Coming here all worked up about this doesn't lend any more credibility to your claim, Sylvia. You have to know that, too."

She dropped into the nearest chair. "Maybe that was an excuse."

Dan went on alert. "Is there something going on with Nina?" Just saying her name out loud resurrected memories he'd just as soon leave dead and buried.

Sylvia shook her head. "She's not responding to the treatments the way we'd hoped. I'm not so sure she's going to come around this time."

Nina had been such a fun-loving, warm person. Or so it seemed. Dan had run into her at a fund-raiser. It had been nearly a decade since he and Jess ended their relationship. He'd decided it was time to settle down. Somehow he was always trying to find a way to get over Jess. Nina had presented the exact opportunity. She had been adventurous and his parents had fawned over her. She was a senator's daughter after all. Only the senator's family had been keeping a deep, dark secret. And Dan had almost paid the ultimate price for their vanity.

He forced away the memories that didn't need revisiting. For years he had worked vigilantly to prevent himself from recalling those horrors whenever he thought of Nina.

"We're considering moving her to a clinic in New York where they're seeing better results with this intense therapy that has failed so miserably here."

"How's the senator handling this?" Dan could just imagine. Nina was his baby girl.

"Exactly like you think," Sylvia admitted.

Nina suffered from paranoid schizophrenia. She'd shown the signs for years. The family had ignored them. Then, six months after she and Dan married, she went over the edge. How she'd made it through law school and started her own practice by the age of twenty-eight he would never fully understand. She'd tried to kill Dan with his own service revolver and he'd had no choice but to admit he couldn't handle the situation. The family had resumed her care and the divorce was hastened along. Irreconcilable differences. That was all the world would ever know.

Dan had visited her every month for a while. But his presence only seemed to agitate her, so eventually he'd stopped going.

Then he'd stopped thinking about that side of her. He chose to remember the intelligent, vivacious woman he'd first fallen for.

"Is there anything I can do?"

Sylvia shook her head. "Afraid not, Chief. The demons in her head don't want to let go and we just can't seem to find a way to oust them."

"I truly am sorry, Sylvia. I wish there was something someone could do to bring her back."

"Me, too." Sylvia straightened her shoulders and shoved her hair behind her ears. "So tell me about you and Harris. How long have you been in love with her?"

Dan held up his hands stop-sign fashion. "I'm afraid that topic is off limits." He smiled in spite of himself. "Besides, I'm certain she would tell you that she doesn't have time for that kind of stuff."

"She's the one from high school, isn't she? The one you followed to Boston?"

Why bother lying? She'd only dig up the answers later. "Yes. Yes, she is."

"So did she break your heart or did you break hers?"

He shrugged. "I think there was mutual damage."

"I see." Sylvia stood. "I hope you know what you're doing this time."

Dan frowned as he pushed to his feet. "We're lucky to have her in the department. I'm damned glad she accepted the offer."

Sylvia stopped at the door and turned back to him. "I wasn't talking about the job. I was talking about the falling in love again." She lifted one shoulder in a half shrug. "Or maybe you never really fell out of love."

"Good night, Dr. Baron."

"Make sure she follows up on this Larry thing," Sylvia urged.

"You have my word."

She searched his face a moment. "That means a lot, Dan. There are few men on this planet who are as good as their word, but you're one of them and I appreciate that. I hope Harris does as well."

And with that off-handed compliment, the senator's elder daughter was gone. Dan watched her back her Lexus onto the street and drive away.

He closed the door and locked it.

The ego-driven male side of him wanted to argue that Sylvia was going overboard in her assessment, but he couldn't do that. There was some part of how he had felt about Jess at seventeen that he had never gotten over. Through three marriages and countless relationships she had always been there, haunting him.

How she felt was far more difficult to measure. What her ex, Duvall, wanted was as clear as a bell. He hadn't sent one of his underlings here to look into the Lopez family situation. He had come personally. Dan suspected the man was having second thoughts about having left Jess in the lurch.

If Jess was really smart, she'd tell them both to go to hell.

Dan chuckled. What a mess they had made of that aspect of their lives.

He checked the time. Almost midnight. Maybe he'd do a drive-by. If her lights were on, he'd call to see how she was doing.

He should probably just go to bed and forget the whole thing. Jess was, as she reminded him quite often, a grown woman who was highly trained in the art of self-defense.

But if he didn't go he'd never get any sleep.

His cell chimed to alert him to an incoming text.

He grabbed it from the coffee table and checked the screen.

Night Burnett.

Jess. He smiled as he sent her a good night.

She was okay. Now maybe he could get some sleep.

15

Five Points, Wednesday, August 4, Midnight

It was almost time.

Lori didn't want him to go. She trailed her fingers along his bare torso. He shivered. She loved when her touch did that to him.

"You know what you're doing?" Chet murmured.

"Umm-hmm." She made circles around his navel with the tip of her finger and then moved downward. He gasped. Her fingers curled around him and the rock-hard feel of him was her cue. She rolled atop him, pushed up to a sitting position. "I know exactly what I'm doing." She rocked her pelvis gently against his.

He groaned. "It's late. What about that no spending the night rule?"

She ground fully against his erection, making him growl. "Rules are made to be broken."

He reached up, wrapped his arms around her, and rolled her onto her back. She gasped.

"Don't toy with me, Lori," he whispered against her lips. "You know what I want."

She did. Oh man, she did. Determined to maintain her independence, she had fought him for all these months. He wanted a real relationship. One with commitments. She had fully believed she wasn't ready for that. That level of commitment hadn't been in her five-year plan.

Two weeks ago her life had changed. That sick bastard Matthew Reed, Eric Spears's protégé, had kidnapped and tortured her and two other women. He'd murdered one right in front of her. During those seventy or so hours one thing remained steady on her mind: this man. If she survived, she promised herself that she would not take him for granted ever again. She would take nothing for granted. Not her mother and her sister or her friends. Not one second of her life from this moment forward was going to be a throwaway moment.

She wanted to live every minute of it to the fullest.

"I want the same thing," she confessed. "I really do." She caressed his jaw. "It's time." She slid her hands over his back.

He rolled off her. Before she could ask what was wrong, he'd dragged on his boxers and walked away.

What the hell? She pulled on her abandoned tee and joined him at the kitchen sink. "Okay, so what did I say wrong?" Jesus Christ this relationship thing was as frustrating as hell.

"I know why you're doing this and it's a mistake."

"I thought I was doing what you wanted."

Disappointment flared in his dark eyes and she instantly recognized her mistake.

"What *we* want," she amended.

"When you skate that close to death, it makes you afraid of what the next hour will bring. You grab on to everything you can as fast as you can so you don't miss anything."

So maybe she was more transparent than she realized. He'd zeroed in on exactly how she felt. "What's wrong with choosing not to take life for granted?"

He shook his head. "Nothing. But this ferocity you feel will wear off in time. And then what happens to us?" He reached out, twirled a wisp of her hair around his finger. "I love you, Lori. I want you to want this because you love me, not because you're afraid of what might come next. There are no guarantees when it comes to life. But I can guarantee that I will love you with all I've got for the rest of my life, whatever else happens. If that's not enough, there's nothing more I can say or do."

"It's enough."

Chet pulled her into his arms. "If that's really how you feel, what would you like to do about that?"

Her heart was thundering. Was she really going to do this? Yes. Yes, she was. "I think we should try out living together." She laughed at how embarrassed she felt at saying the words out loud. "See if we can do it without killing each other or having it interfere with work."

"There are more rules about that," he warned. "I'm senior to you and we're assigned to the same team. There could be career consequences."

That was the only part that worried her. "I know." She wasn't looking forward to dealing with those issues. "I'll talk to Jess. See what she thinks." Lori looked him straight in the eye. "Jess's friendship beyond the job means a great deal to me. I don't want to lie to her. Ever."

"Same here. I respect the chief too much to do that."

Had they really made this decision? "So, what do we do next?"

He grinned. "We pick the place. Yours or mine?"

She backed out of his arms and walked to the middle of the room. "There's no privacy here." She turned back to him. "And when you have Chester he probably wouldn't be comfortable here."

A big grin spread across Chet's face. "Do you have any idea how happy that makes me?"

Confusion had her making a face. "Your son being uncomfortable?" The kid was cute—for a kid. And he was the light of his father's life. Lori recognized this was a package deal. She would adjust. Hopefully.

"No." He was really grinning like a jackass now. "The idea that you would think about his comfort makes me extremely happy."

She decided to say the rest of what was on her mind. There should never be any misunderstandings between them. "I wasn't expecting to have children in my life at this point. I had that penciled in a few years down the road." She tried to smile but her lips trembled with the effort. "But I love you. Chester is your son, and that makes me love him too. I want to be a part of his life because he's a part of yours." She took the few steps to the bed and plopped down on the foot of it. "After my father died my mother wouldn't even think about another man, much less look at one." Even as a teenager she'd recognized her mother's loneliness. "I remember thinking how much she and my father must have loved each other for her to feel as if no one else could ever take his place."

Lori pulled her knees to her chest and hugged herself.

"But I was wrong about that. I mean, they did love each other that way. But years and years later, after my sister went off to college, Mom and I were talking and she said something I totally didn't see before. She told me that at first the idea of another man was unthinkable. But eventually she got lonely, even with two girls to keep her running. But she never dared consider having anyone else in her life because she was terrified that she would be forced to choose, on some level, between him and us." Lori blinked back the tears. "My mother sacrificed her own happiness because she was afraid. I don't want to live in fear like that and that's what that son of a bitch did to me. He made me afraid."

Chet sat down beside her, wrapped his arms around her, and held her tight. "He did make you afraid. You would've been a fool not to be afraid. But you can't let that fear rule you, the way your mother did. That's the part that you have to get past." He drew back, searched her eyes. "I don't want to be a part of your fear, Lori. And if you're afraid that refusing to move to the next level with me is going to make me give up"—he laughed—"that ain't happening."

For a long time they just held each other. No talking required. But she knew what she wanted. And he needed to know that, too.

"I vote for your place. Chester has his own room. There's a backyard." Not that she was looking forward to using a lawnmower. "As long as I get to do a little redecorating."

He nodded. "You drive a hard bargain, Wells, but I can live with that." He glanced around. "What about your place?"

"I'll be keeping this place for a while. Just in case I find out all your man secrets and decide I can't handle the real you."

He laughed. "That might be a smart move."

They held on to each other, and a comfortable silence settled around them. It felt good. Right.

"I'm worried about the Chambers kid," Chet said eventually. "He's only a few years older than Chester and the thought of what may have happened tears me apart."

Lori hugged him closer. "I know. That's the hardest part of this job. When a child is hurt or missing, it's tough to take. I can't imagine being a parent and having something like that happen."

"I was just thinking about that, too." He turned his face to hers. "If we have the time this week, we'll pick Chester up for a few hours," he said. "I think the two of you should spend a little time together. See how it goes."

Lori prayed he didn't spot the fear in her eyes. "Sure. Sounds good." The thought sent another wave of terror roaring through her veins. She had met Chester briefly. She had looked at photo albums with Chet. But she had never sat through dinner with the child or played a game with him. Talking about him and planning for his being a part of their relationship was simple. Having the concept become a reality—this week—was way, way complicated.

What if he hated her?

16

8:00 a.m.

The weatherman on the radio warned that the heat wave would continue through the rest of the week. Birmingham was expected to sizzle.

"Lucky us," Jess grumbled. People in general grew exceedingly more impatient and short-tempered when the temperature lingered in the triple digits. As it was, drivers turned utterly stupid between the hours of seven and nine every damned morning and then again around four in the afternoon. Dog days did not help.

Maybe she'd take First Avenue and go all the way to Twenty-fourth Street and then double back on side streets to get to the station. She knew better than to leave for work after seven. Some days it just couldn't be helped. Her hair had totally refused to cooperate this morning. And the outlet in her bathroom wasn't working, so she'd had to plug in her blow-dryer by the bed and dry her hair there. One of the charms of an older home. Historic, she reminded herself, a historic home. She hated for her first meeting with Mr. Louis to be a complaint about a faulty outlet. Maybe she'd just Google it and see if she could figure out the fix herself.

Why not? She was qualified with numerous weapons; how hard could it be to replace a single electrical outlet?

As she made another turn and discovered her plan had been a good one, Jess relaxed a little. There was no traffic on Twenty-fourth. Thank God. As she reached Marconi Park and the left she wanted to take, a car whipped around her.

She stamped on the brakes. "Idiot!" The sound of revving engines had her checking her mirrors. A black SUV was right on her bumper. Another roared up beside her and the imbecile who had barreled around her had now come to a near stop in front of her. She slammed on her brakes again. Her cell flew off the console onto the passenger side floor board.

"Damn it." Adrenaline slid through her veins. She reached into her bag for her Glock. She had no choice but to stop. She couldn't risk ducking down for her phone.

Damn. Damn. Damn.

Stay calm. Her fingers wrapped around the butt of her weapon.

A man approached her window. He leaned down and came face-to-face with the business end of her Glock, which she had leveled on him.

"May I help you, sir?" she said loud enough for him to hear through the glass.

He ignored the gun. "My name is Hector Debarros. I am unarmed, Chief Harris."

As if to prove his words, he backed up a couple of

steps, held his arms up surrender-style, and then turned all the way around. Jess knew the Debarros family from the first case she had worked after returning to Birmingham. Hector had helped Burnett find Jess when Leonardo Lopez's twisted offspring kidnapped her. So maybe she wasn't about to get dead.

Which was a really good thing considering she had a little boy to find, a murder case to solve, and her sister needed her.

Jess checked to see if any other traffic had come along. Nope. Just her luck. See if she took the back streets again. She cracked her window a few inches. "Let's see some ID. Slowly," she reminded him when he reached for his back pocket.

He removed his wallet and stepped closer to her window, a driver's license in his hand.

Damn it. Her glasses were in her bag. "Closer," she ordered. God, how ridiculous was this! She squinted at the photo and then the name. Then she shifted her attention back to the man's face. "What do you want, Mr. Debarros?"

"Mr. Lopez would like to speak with you."

"Which Mr. Lopez?" She flicked a glance at each mirror to make sure no one else was approaching her car.

"Leonardo."

A shot of adrenaline fired through her veins. Looked as if Wesley wasn't the only West Coaster who had decided to pay the Magic City a visit. Leonardo was the father of Salvadore and his crazy sister. Seemed daddy had come to do some housekeeping. Unfortunately he was a little too late. And he wanted to talk to the wrong cop.

"Tell him to call my secretary and make an appointment," Jess suggested through the glass, which she had no intention of lowering any farther. Not that it would stop a bullet, but it made her feel better. She didn't have a secretary but that was irrelevant at the moment.

Hector glanced toward the SUV behind her. "You have my word," he assured her, but he was obviously growing nervous, there was an urgency in his voice and on his face, "that you will be safe, Chief Harris."

Well, gee. That made her feel *way* better. "Tell Mr. Lopez that if he wants to talk he can join me on the bleachers over in the park. *You and him.* No one else."

Before he could respond, Jess cut the wheel of her Audi sharply to the right and bounded over the curb and sidewalk. The frame of the car dragged—at least she hoped that was all that scraped the concrete. She drove straight across the ball field and to the first set of bleachers, ensuring the driver's side door faced away from her pursuers.

She snatched up her cell and hit Harper's number, set it for speaker and slid it into the pocket of her new dress jacket. As much as she liked this snazzy tangerine suit she didn't want to die in it. Moving quickly, she climbed out and turned to face the two black SUVs that roared to a stop on the other side of her Audi, blocking her in. The rear doors opened. Jess prepared to defend herself, feet wide apart, both hands firm on her Glock and ready to swing into a firing position.

Hector and a man who looked to be in his late forties approached her position.

The two walked right past her car and to the bleachers. Jess tracked their movements. When the older man had taken a seat on the bottom row and Hector had climbed to the top so he could see Twenty-fourth, Jess decided it was safe enough to join the man who had gone to so much trouble to have a meeting with her.

Satisfied the others were staying put in their vehicles, Jess strode over to the bleachers. She sat down next to the man who was an older version of Salvadore, but not so much older. Leonardo was younger than she had expected. The surveillance shots she had seen hadn't done him justice. Good looking. No visible tattoos. The elegant suit would likely pay her salary for a month. She kept her Glock palmed as she settled her hands in her lap.

The man's dark eyes studied her for a long moment. "Hector tells me that you are a very persuasive and trustworthy woman."

Jess lifted a skeptical eyebrow. "He tells me you're Leonardo Lopez." There was always the chance this could be a body double. Guys like him sometimes had numerous look-alikes for security purposes.

"As much as I would prefer not to be who I am just now, unfortunately that is beyond my power to change."

Seemed even badass gang leaders weren't happy when their children misbehaved.

"What would you like to talk about, Mr. Lopez?"

"Straight to the point. I admire that in a woman."

That was probably intended as a compliment. "I also admire that trait in a man." Where most things were concerned anyway. There was a time for foreplay but this was not it.

Acknowledging her pointed comment with a dip of his head, he said, "There are many things I can offer in exchange for leniency where my daughter's charges are concerned."

Jess would just bet there were. "I'm afraid you'll need

to speak with Supervisory Special Agent Duvall and Chief of Police Burnett about that. I just catch the bad guys. I don't make deals."

"I'm certain you can see how speaking with your friends would be quite impossible."

There was that. "Getting your *followers* under control might help your case," Jess offered. "You make that happen and I'll put in a good word for you." Sounded fair to her.

"Perhaps that step has already been taken," he suggested. "My people have squashed the rebel movement. I'm certain you've noticed the lack of bodies being thrown in your path. In the past twenty-four hours there have been no reports of violence. Any others you discover will be those who choose to continue on their disobedient paths or incidents that occurred before my edict was issued."

She couldn't deny some truth in his words. Maybe this was her chance to confirm once and for all that Gabrielle's death had nothing to do with his world. "I have a problem with innocent victims being used for making points," Jess challenged.

"If you're referring to the unfortunate murder involving the wife of one of your detectives, the jury is still out on that one. I have found no one who wants to claim credit. You can rest assured that you will be the first to know if the culprit is uncovered in my organization. You will also find justice levied."

Surprised, she openly studied his face. "Why would you do that?" The MS-13 was the most ruthless gang on the planet. Why would the man who held a great many members on the West Coast in the palm of his hand offer to be supportive of local cops here in Alabama? She hoped Harper was hearing this, otherwise no one was ever going to believe her.

"I have a new vision," he said, clearly pleased that she was so startled by his offer. "I am a businessman, Chief Harris. The savage tactics of the past offer little advantage in the business world. There are many ways to maintain power."

Jess got it. He had allowed the ruthless tactics to get him where he needed to be and now he was done. Now he wanted to focus on drugs, guns, and such without all the fanfare of mass murders and the like. Well, wasn't that just the most interesting news? Give the man a medal. A Nobel Peace Prize or something. But his need to extend his business reach would never change the heinous traditions of the Mara Salvatrucha.

"You tell Agent Duvall that if he ensures my daughter receives immunity I will give him something immensely important to him. Something to which my wayward son Salvadore has no access."

"Does that include you?" Jess asked bluntly; might as well clarify his exact intent. "Because I'm under the impression that's what Agent Duvall and most of the federal, state, and local agencies between here and California really want."

Leonardo smirked. "I have something much more personal to his beloved bureau than that in mind."

Jess looked him straight in the eye. His statement could mean only one of two things. He either knew of plans to launch attacks against the bureau or he had someone on the inside. A *mole*. Anticipation sent a new kind of shiver up her spine. "I'm all ears, Mr. Lopez."

"I have many powerful and influential people in my operation. Some are deeply imbedded within his circle. This, I believe, will interest him greatly."

He could be bluffing. Jess ignored the way her pulse skipped a little more swiftly. "I'm afraid he'll need something more conclusive than innuendoes. Irrefutable evidence is the traditional requirement."

He leaned close to Jess. The air stalled in her lungs.

"You must trust me, *lucerito*, I have much evidence." Lopez stood. "You tell them for me, Chief Harris. Hector will know how to reach me. I will notify you if I find your killer among my people. You have my word."

Stunned but certain he would do exactly what he said, Jess watched Leonardo Lopez and his posse drive away.

She tugged her cell from her pocket and confirmed that the call to Harper was still connected. "Did you hear any of that, Sergeant?"

"Yes, ma'am. Where the hell are you? We haven't had time to triangulate your position."

"Marconi Park but I'll be at the office in about ten minutes. Let Duvall and Burnett know I need a meeting."

Jess ended the call and sat there for another couple minutes. Mostly because she still felt a little weak-kneed. She'd just had an up close and personal meeting with the most ruthless man on the West Coast.

Birmingham Police Department, 9:05 a.m.

"That's what he said," Jess reiterated. "Sergeant Harper can confirm every word."

"I can't believe he approached you out in the open like

that," Wesley argued. "And the suggestion that he has someone inside the bureau is ludicrous."

Between him and Burnett, they would have the carpet worn out in the chief of police's office before this meeting concluded.

"You think you're surprised." Jess scoffed. *Men.* The entire species had a way of delivering the most memorable understatements. "I was still in a state of near shock five minutes after he walked away."

Burnett shook his head. "This is exactly what I was worried about. You're all over the news, Jess. You need out of the limelight until this Lopez business is resolved."

Jess shot to her feet. "I have a murder case and a missing child. I will not step back from this case, so don't even ask me to."

"I wasn't planning to ask," Burnett warned, fury lighting in his eyes.

"Fine." Jess shrugged. "Take me off the case. You know I'll just continue to investigate on my own. Either way works for me."

"Calm down, both of you," Wesley fairly shouted. "We have to weigh every step. This is far bigger than any one of us or any one case."

Judging by the outrage on his face, Jess estimated that Burnett was on the verge of having smoke roil out of his ears. She didn't have time for territorial wars or politics. She had work to do. These two could go at each other without her around.

"Watch yourself, Duvall," Burnett warned, "you are a part of this meeting and our ongoing investigation at my pleasure. Push me and you're out of here."

So much for department-bureau relations.

"I did what Lopez asked me to do." She gathered her bag and smiled. "As far as I'm concerned, I'm done here. Have a nice morning, gentlemen."

Before either could demand she stay, she was out the door. Wesley had the details Lopez had given her. That was his problem. The only thing she wanted from Lopez was word about anyone in his organization who might know something about Gabrielle Grayson's murder.

Thankfully, Sheila, Burnett's secretary, was on the phone when Jess left his office, which prevented her being derailed for small talk. Jess gave the woman a wave and hurried out. In the lobby she got lucky again when she found Tara away from her desk.

By the time she made it down the corridor and to the stairwell door without being intercepted, Jess felt confident she might even reach her office before being waylaid.

The door opened before Jess could reach for it. Lori, purse hanging over her shoulder and keys in hand, skidded to a stop to prevent running into her.

"I got a call from the administrator at the New Life Rehabilitation Center. She wants to talk to us about Gabrielle Grayson. I was just coming to look for you."

This could be the break they needed. "Where's Harper?" Jess followed Lori back into the stairwell and down the first set of steps.

"He's in a meeting with the search team leader. Nothing new on Devon Chambers as of five minutes ago."

Renewed worry twisted in Jess's stomach. "And Cook?"

"He's following up with a guy who was partnered with Lieutenant Grayson while Sergeant Riley was out of commission after his accident."

Anticipation zinged Jess. The more leads they uncovered

the more likely they were to find answers about who killed Gabrielle Grayson and who might have taken Devon Chambers. The faster they got to the truth the higher the odds of finding that child alive.

Jess was glad to let Lori drive. After this morning's unexpected encounter with Lopez she was still a little shaky. She didn't like admitting anything scared her but she couldn't claim those few minutes hadn't rattled her just a little.

"I have a personal issue we need to talk about at some point," Lori announced as she guided her Mustang from the city parking garage and pointed it in the direction of New Life Rehabilitation Center.

"We have twenty minutes or so." Jess shifted in her seat until she was facing Lori. "What's going on?"

"I'm considering moving into Harper's place. Is that going to be an issue?"

Technically, yes, but Jess didn't want to lose either one. And she couldn't point to a single reason as far as their work record went to indicate their personal relationship was causing any difficulty.

"You need to keep it low key. The fewer who know, the better. As far as I'm concerned, as long as your private affairs don't impact your work, I'm fine with wherever you take your relationship."

How hypocritical would she be if she felt otherwise? She and Burnett had a thing. She wouldn't quite call it a relationship, but it was some undefined connection. Friends with benefits...sort of. A mental eye roll accompanied the idea. She still couldn't get used to thinking in those terms. But for now, there wasn't a better definition of what they shared.

"Tread carefully," Jess warned. "What you went through two weeks ago is still coloring your perception on life."

"Harper said the same thing."

At least one of them was keeping that in mind. "Just take it slow and you'll be fine." Both Lori and Harper were smart and levelheaded. They could make this work if that was what they really wanted. And if their relationship continued to progress, Jess would deal with the changes in her unit that progression would require.

A minute or two of silence followed. She and Lori were both at milestones in their lives. Lori with decisions about moving into her first serious relationship and Jess with the decision as to how she wanted to proceed with almost every aspect of her life. Her career was getting back on track. But the rest, well that was a whole other ball of wax.

At forty-two it was time to take a step back and seriously consider where she went from here. Though she was pretty damned happy with where her career had landed, what about marriage and children? A person could marry almost anytime but the decision as to whether or not she would have children in her life fell within a swiftly closing window.

She didn't want to ignore any one option and wake up one morning to realize it was too late.

God, had she just thought that?

"Can I ask you a question, Jess?"

Jess gladly dismissed the nagging doubts about her own life and turned back to Lori. "Why not?" She didn't need a preview to know it would be about Burnett. Certainly it would be personal, since Lori had chosen to use her first name.

"I've asked you this before," she hedged, "but do you think you and the chief will ever be able to be together as a couple again? I mean, really together? Like married?"

Married? "I honestly don't know." Jess hadn't even considered the possibility. "I've been married once and it wasn't anything like I thought it would be." That, however, had been as much her fault as Wesley's. "And Burnett's taken vows three times and failed. Maybe we're not the marrying kind."

"But you've never been married to each other. That could be the issue. Maybe the two of you belong together and nothing is ever going to be right until that happens."

Lori had been thinking on the subject way too much. "To be honest, I'm not sure we could live together without killing each other or ending up hating each other." And his mother would never accept her only son marrying Jess.

The idea of having Katherine Burnett to dinner on a regular basis was terrifying.

Lori sent her a sideways look. "It just seems like you belong together. Harper says the same thing."

Jess laughed. "You two don't have better things to do when you're together than to talk about Burnett and me?"

"We have lots of deep conversations these days."

"You should never stop doing that." That was the most important advice Jess could give. "Communication is so damned important." Jess wasn't sure she had realized just how important until very recently. "When all else fails, if you can talk about things then you always have a way to work out the worst of the problems that come your way."

The conversation died a natural death as Lori made the turn into the rehab center's parking lot. That hopeful anticipation of finding a new lead had Jess's heart pumping.

"The administrator's name is Pauline Allison. She replaced the one who retired last year. She's mid-forties," Lori went on, "and seems sharp. I'm hoping she's learned new information from her personnel interviews."

"We can also assume that one or more of those employees said something that Allison felt might assist in our investigation."

Jess and Lori exchanged a look before getting out of the car. "We could sure use a break about now," Lori suggested.

"No question," Jess agreed.

There were cases, like this one, where there was no place to go in the investigation. There was no one piece of evidence that gave them a definitive direction. No witness—that they could find—who could provide details that might point toward a suspect.

They basically had nothing that jumped out and said here you go.

This was the kind of case where a good cop had to shake the apple trees until the fruit started to fall. Otherwise they were going to be in for a long wait. Because apples rarely just fell at one's feet unless they were too ripe or full of worms and already half rotten.

11:00 a.m.

Pauline Allison had an office not much larger than a closet and enough files and paperwork to fill the National Archives. There were manila folders stacked from the floor to the ceiling in three of the four corners.

The administrator, a petite, pleasant woman, made

quick work of emptying out the two chairs in front of her desk and ushering Jess and Lori into them. Then she collapsed into her own as if the task had taken the last of the energy she had on reserve.

"You'll have to forgive the mess. We're in the midst of an unexpected State audit and I've been working twenty-hour days."

"I appreciate your taking the time out of your hectic schedule to help us with this investigation, Ms. Allison," Jess said.

"No problem." Allison unearthed a legal pad and then scrounged for her reading glasses. "What I have here is a list of three nurses who worked with Gabrielle"—she glanced over the rim of her glasses—"before my time here. Two of the three were reluctant to talk but one couldn't spill her guts fast enough. Bear in mind," she pointed out, "that she was written up twice by Mrs. Grayson while she served as the charge nurse on the drug side."

Needing clarification, Jess asked, "Drug side?"

"Our facility is divided into the drug side and the alcohol side."

Made sense. "Will we be able to interview this nurse today?" Jess broached, hopeful. "I know the request is short notice but this is a murder investigation and time is our enemy."

"I thought you might want to do that, so I asked her to come in this morning. She's waiting for you in the employee lounge." Allison pushed back her chair. "I'll show you the way."

The center was quite large and immaculate. Allison explained that the facility was both privately and state funded. Their services ranged from long-term inpatient care to twice-weekly counseling sessions for ongoing maintenance. They ranked in the top ten in the nation.

Beyond two layers of security, the employee lounge, like the rest of the facility, was state-of-the-art, clean, and welcoming.

"Netty Winters," Allison announced, "this is Deputy Chief Jess Harris and Detective Lori Wells. They'll be speaking with you about Mrs. Grayson." She turned to Jess. "Let me know if you need anything else. I'll be in my office."

When Ms. Allison had left the room, Jess and Lori joined the off-duty nurse at her table. "Ms. Winters," Jess began, "Detective Wells is going to read you your rights. Not because you're in any kind of trouble," she hastened to add, "but because we have an obligation to ensure you're informed before we begin this interview."

Winters couldn't be much over thirty. Tall and thin, she wore her black hair in a tight bun and apparently attempted to disguise her pale coloring with an extra helping of blush and eye shadow.

"Whatever you need to do," she said agreeably.

While Lori took care of the Miranda rights, Jess readied to take notes. She settled her eyeglasses in place and waited until Ms. Winters had indicated that she understood her rights and still wanted to speak with them.

"Ma'am, you worked with Gabrielle Grayson for how long?"

"Two years. She's probably the only reason I still have a job. And in today's economy that's saying something."

"She was your supervisor?"

"She was."

"Why do you say she's probably the only reason you still have a job?"

"I was fairly new to nursing back then. I was too busy trying to keep my social life up to par to do my job the way it needed to be done. She wrote me up twice for not paying attention and making dumb mistakes. That last time she sat me down and we had a come-to-Jesus talk. She made a believer out of me for sure. And she was right. I've had three raises since then and I'm real grateful to her for the way she set me on the right course."

Jess had actually expected the woman to have negative things to say about Gabrielle Grayson. She hoped this interview wasn't going to be a waste of time.

"Did you ever know Gabrielle to use any sort of prescription drugs?" Jess ventured.

"No way. That's one thing that made her so good at her job. She really hated drugs, even prescription ones that are so easily abused."

"During Gabrielle's time here were you aware of any trouble between her and any of the patients or the other staff members?"

"That's why I told Ms. Allison I wanted to talk to y'all," Winters explained. "There was one patient who gave her a real hard time. Made a lot of threats about what he would do to her when he had the chance."

"Do you remember this patient's name?" Tension rippled through Jess. More than forty-eight hours into the investigation, they needed a break. This could be it.

"Yeah, I do, 'cause he was a big flirt. His name was Johnny Trenton. He was real cute and cocky but he treated us all like we were worthless. I think maybe he has a thing against women."

Somehow Jess had expected she'd be hearing his name again. "Thank you, Ms. Winters. If you think of anything else at all, please call me." Jess passed her a card. "And please talk to the other nurses who knew Gabrielle. We need all the help we can get finding the person responsible for her murder."

Winters accepted Jess's card. "I'll do that. You know, Gabrielle had the biggest heart of any person I've ever met. Her work hadn't changed that."

"What do you mean?" Didn't it take people with really big hearts to be a part of the medical field? Sure as heck took a strong sense of justice to keep cops pounding the pavement every day.

"Most of us start out with a touch of the Florence Nightingale complex," Winters explained. "We love all our patients and we'd do anything in the world to save them. But time and dealing with illness and death kind of hardens us. It's not that we stop caring, but we learn to maintain some level of detachment to keep our sanity. Gabrielle didn't do that. She loved, in a chaste way of course, every patient. Even the ones who were mean spirited. She never gave up on anyone. Like I said, she changed my life. She was a saint."

There it was again. That word. It wasn't that Jess doubted the goodness of either Gabrielle or her husband, who was also touted by his colleagues as a saint. But somehow, somewhere, one or both of these good folks had encountered the exact opposite of goodness. Someone truly evil. Someone who knew Gabrielle Grayson well enough to want to stab her over and over.

Someone who took the time to write dozens of words in her blood while it was still warm.

Someone full of raging emotion.

They were scarcely out of the building when Jess's cell clanged.

Lily.

Jess couldn't risk ignoring the call. Her sister could have gotten test results and as terrified as Jess was to hear them... her sister needed her.

"Is everything okay?" Jess asked instead of bothering with a greeting.

"No," her sister sobbed, "everything's wrong."

Blood running cold, Jess braced herself. "What's happened? Did the doctor call?"

"He called Blake and me in to discuss my test results."

Dear God, she just needed to spit it out. "And?" Jess prompted.

More sobbing. Jess's heart thumped harder and harder. "Just tell me, Lil." Tears burned her eyes. *Please don't let it be that bad.*

"He said I'm depressed," Lil wailed. "That I'm just losing my mind, that's all. Getting old and probably about to go through the change." Lil groaned an agonizing sound. "How can I be forty-four years old and feel a hundred? How can I hurt all over? Forget every damned thing? And just be depressed?"

Jess waited through the tears. Mostly she waited for her own emotions to stabilize. She'd just zoomed from terrified and ready to cry to furious and ready to kick the crap out of something.

"Dr. Collins told you this?" she confirmed. It took every ounce of control she had to speak calmly. "The same Dr. Collins I used to see? Downtown?"

"Yes," came the pitiful response. "He prescribed an

antidepressant and wants me to get counseling. I don't understand. I've never been depressed in my life. This is so humiliating. I put my family through all this worry for nothing. I'm just pathetic!"

"Lil, you stop that, do you hear me?" Jess demanded. "You're going to be fine and we'll get this sorted out."

"I'm falling apart," Lil muttered.

"Sweetie, I have to go right now, but I'll call you tonight. Okay?"

It took another minute to get Lil reassured enough that Jess felt comfortable ending the call. She turned to her detective. "I need to see Dr. Carl Collins," Jess said. "His office is downtown." She gave Lori the address.

"Are you feeling ill?" Lori asked, visibly concerned.

"Oh yes," Jess assured her as she headed for the car. "I'm ill, all right. Ill as a hornet."

Twentieth Street South, 1:30 p.m.

One flash of her shield and the receptionist ushered Jess to Dr. Collins's private office. He was with a patient, so she had no choice but to wait a few minutes.

The last doctor's appointment she'd had in this office had been about twenty-four years ago. She'd just turned eighteen and she wanted to get on birth control. Things had been too crazy between her and Dan to continue to risk their self-control. Condoms were necessary but not one hundred percent reliable.

"Mercy." Jess sighed. Where had the time gone?

The door opened and she sat up a little straighter. Dr. Collins was short and pleasantly plump. Time had broadened his waist as well as the hairless path across the top of his head. The black-rimmed glasses looked exactly the same as the last time Jess saw him.

"I apologize for keeping you waiting." He hurried around his desk, his lab coat swishing. "Give me a minute," Collins said without looking at her. "I haven't had time for lunch." He dragged two protein bars from a desk drawer and offered one to Jess.

"No thank you, Doctor."

He ripped the wrapper off and bit into a bar. "Lordy me, there aren't enough hours in the day." He savored a swig from the bottle of flavored water on his desk. When he'd gotten down another bite of fortification he beamed a smile at her. "What can I do for the Birmingham PD and their newest deputy chief?"

"Actually, Dr. Collins, I'm here on a personal matter."

A frown claimed his face. "The last time I saw you as a patient, you were..."

Jess held her breath.

"...about to graduate high school and go off to Boston."

Relieved, Jess smiled again. "That's right."

"I've been watching you on the news!" He shook a finger in the air. "You've gone places, young lady. Built quite the career for yourself. Turned into a sophisticated lady. My, my." He gave her a nod of approval.

Before Jess could thank him, he launched into another sermon. "I was awfully proud to hear that you'd turned out so well." He laughed, the kind that shook his belly. "I had my doubts when you were young. I swear, you were the sassiest thing. Told anybody and everybody just what you thought."

"Well, Doctor," her face hurt with the effort of keeping her smile in place, "some things never change."

The frown was back. "I beg your pardon?"

"You talked to my sister, Lily, about her test results today."

He riffled through the files and notes on his desk. "Yes, yes, that's right, but I won't be able to discuss those results with you unless—"

"No need, Doctor," Jess assured him. "Lily has already passed along your professional opinion."

"I see." Collins gave her a knowing look. "You and Lily have put your heads together and decided that an old man like me doesn't know what he's talking about. Well, let me tell you a thing or two, missy"—he was shaking his finger again, this time at her—"your sister has the classic symptoms of what I like to call over-the-hill or empty-nest syndrome. She's hit that age, and you're right on her heels," he warned, "where this sort of thing is to be expected. You look in the mirror one day and realize you're getting older or, like your sister, the kids are suddenly gone and she doesn't know what to do with herself. Being a mother defined her and she's lost. There's no need to be embarrassed or in denial. It's part of being a woman."

Jess nodded. "I see," she echoed. So that was the way he intended to roll, was it? She loved it when a doctor decided what a woman was feeling was simply because she was a woman before eliminating any medical issues. Jess stood. "I'm sorry I wasted your time, Dr. Collins."

Smug in his assessment, he waved her off. "That's what I'm here for. My patients are my number-one priority."

Wasn't that reassuring? "How's your son doing these days? Kurt was, what, a year ahead of me in school?"

Understanding wiped that self-satisfied look off his

face. "He's fine, fine. Four kids. His wife is still teaching school and he's established one of Birmingham's top medical equipment providers. He's matured into quite the businessman."

Most likely because he flunked out of medical school. "I did a little checking on my way over here. Seems his love of hanging out at the bars downtown has matured into spending time at the country club on Saturday nights." Three times in the past two months he'd been pulled over and his wife called because he wasn't *feeling well.*

"What're you trying to say, Jessie Lee?" The doctor's friendly tone and nonchalant expression was long gone now.

"I'm saying I want you to run every test you can think of on my sister until you have exhausted your vast medical knowledge. And if you haven't figured out what the problem is by then, I want you to send her to someone who doesn't lump all women together and who doesn't assume that fatigue and achiness automatically means she's depressed."

Collins held up his hands. "Now you know I can't just run all sorts of tests. The insurance companies require justification for every test we run."

She flattened her palms on his desk and looked him dead in the eyes. "I'm sure you'll figure out that part. I expect you to call her and tell her that you've been thinking about her all afternoon and you want to do some other testing. Meanwhile, I'll talk to the manager at the country club and make sure he knows to call your daughter-in-law before Kurt gets behind the wheel. That way none of us have to go through any unpleasant business."

"I'll call her right now."

"Thank you, Dr. Collins. We'll just keep this little chat between us."

As Jess left his office she could hear him grumbling under his breath. Crusty old fart.

Lori was pacing the sidewalk outside when Jess exited the building. She quickly ended her call.

"Did you get things worked out?"

Jess grinned. "The doctor and I reached a mutually beneficial understanding."

Lori went for a smile but it fell short of her usual dazzler.

"Is something wrong?" Jess asked.

"Kids can be a pain in the ass."

"Sounds like you're speaking from experience." Jess headed for their parking spot. "And I happen to know you don't have any children. Something up with *your* sister?"

Lori exhaled a big breath. "We're picking up Chester after work tonight."

"Is that typically a problem?" Jess didn't need to tell Lori that her relationship with Harper was a package deal.

She threw her hands up. "I don't know. I've never spent any time with him."

Sounded like Lori and Harper had gotten the cart before the horse on this moving in together thing. "Take it slow," Jess advised. Before she could say more her cell clanged. She checked the screen. Burnett. Her instincts went on alert. Could be news on Devon. "Hold on, it's Burnett," she said to Lori. "Harris."

"I need you in my office now," Burnett announced.

Jess tried to analyze his tone. Not angry or annoyed. Worried, she decided. "What's up?" She consciously attempted to slow her heart rate, but that wasn't happening this side of the grave.

"You with Wells?"

"Yes, why?" The *thump, thump, thump* in her chest got louder, echoing in her ears.

"The reason the Taurus wouldn't start, Jess, was because someone had rigged an explosive to detonate upon ignition."

His words quaked through her. A *bomb*?

"Luckily," he went on, his voice a little high pitched, "whoever planted it got in a hurry or just didn't know what they were doing and screwed up the wiring. When you tried to start the engine, everything shorted out. Hell." He made a sound of frustration. "Just get here. Now, Jess. I don't want you on the street."

"Yeah... okay." Jess ended the call, a kind of fog draping over her.

"Did the chief have news?"

Jess nodded, or at least she thought she did. Her stomach felt a little queasy. "Someone tried to kill me, Lori." Her gaze collided with her friend's. "And the part that scares me is that I think it's one of us... a *cop*."

17

2:30 p.m.

I've initiated a separate investigation into this tampering," Burnett explained from his standing position behind his desk. The man hadn't been still since she walked into his office. "We will find out how this happened, Jess. You can count on that."

His face wasn't as red as it had been when she first arrived, but he was still markedly upset.

"Who's lead in the investigation?" Jess crossed her legs. She worked at keeping her foot from tapping. He wasn't the only one upset. She hated that she had let the fear slip so deeply under her skin, but there was no denying it.

"Harold's on top of it." Burnett loosened his tie. "He asked to take the lead." Fury visibly tightened his lips. "He's already grilling personnel in the car pool. The whole place is on lockdown."

Jess resisted the urge to ask why he didn't consider Deputy Chief Harold Black a suspect. But that would be her ego talking. She and Black had seriously butted heads over a case and likely would do the same in the future, but Harold Black was a loyal cop.

No use pretending she could keep the break-in to herself. If someone was this serious about taking her down, she couldn't afford to flirt with that particular denial. "There's something..."

He planted his hands on his hips and fixed that look on her—the look that warned she wasn't going to like whatever he said next. "Jess, it's time for you to admit this threat is serious. I want you off the streets. Period. Harold said he would step in and take the reins while you work in the background."

Not only did she not like that suggestion, she was not going to listen to another word, much less tell him about the break-in. How could she get her job done like this? She reached into her bag and pulled out her pad and pencil. While he watched, she wrote a short, sweet note, then passed it to him.

"Bullshit!" He crushed her resignation and tossed it across the room. "This is not a game, Jess. This is—"

Jess stowed her stuff and stood. "You can have someone follow me around and I'll concede to having Harper or Wells with me every minute on the job. But"—she held up a hand when he would have interrupted—"*but* if you push this idea that I have to duck and run for cover, I will resign."

The standoff lasted another five seconds. "You try to evade protection," he warned, "and I swear, I'll put you in protective custody."

He was forgetting a little thing called her civil rights. He was upset. She was upset. But this case—finding

Devon Chambers alive and nailing Gabrielle Grayson's killer—was more important than either of their egos.

"I will not attempt to evade my assigned protection." *Unless it's absolutely necessary.* "Can we move on now?"

He rubbed at his forehead as if a headache had started there. "Sure."

She resumed her seat and he finally settled into his. She gave him a rundown of what they'd learned from Netty Winters, the nurse who once worked with Gabrielle Grayson. "Wells and I are following up with Trenton as soon as I'm finished here."

"I want to know where you are and who you're with at all times."

Jess flashed him a fake smile. "Then you'd better make sure whoever's pulling surveillance knows to relay that information to you." She grabbed her stuff and stood. "I will let you know if there are any major developments."

Her cell clanged before Burnett could argue with her last word. She dug for it and checked the screen.

Leslie Chambers.

Worry got a good sharp jab into her gut. "Harris." To Burnett, she whispered, "It's Devon's sister."

He nodded his understanding.

"You have to help me," Leslie cried. "The people from Child Protective Services are here. They're asking about Devon. I don't know what to do."

"I'll be right there, Leslie. Tell them to wait."

Jess shoved her phone into her bag, anger sparking. Though she understood this was the way the system worked and whoever had showed up at Leslie's door was only doing their job, the timing made her mad as hell.

One way or another she would see that Leslie and Devon were not separated under any circumstances.

Assuming they found him alive...

4:05 p.m.

Jess waited until the introductions were out of the way and then she let the kindly looking woman named Selma Peterson from Child Protective Services have it. Politely, of course.

"Ms. Peterson, I appreciate and respect what you're doing. I'm certain your job is rarely pleasant or simple. Unfortunately I'm about to make things a lot more complicated. This young woman and her brother, who is currently missing, are persons of interest in an ongoing homicide case. Until that case is solved or I tell you otherwise, you have no authority to question her. So, with all due respect, I will need you to leave these premises and not return until I've instructed otherwise."

Ms. Peterson looked from Jess to her colleague, Heather Phipps, and back. "Frankly, Chief Harris, I'm speechless. In my career of twenty-four years I have never had an officer of the law speak to me in such a manner."

Jess gifted her with a patient smile. "Well, ma'am, I'm awful sorry if you took anything I said the wrong way, but, if you have any questions, my boss is Chief of Police Daniel Burnett. You can direct any questions you, your colleague here, or your supervisor have to him. You have a good day now."

The two women grumbled about rude cops and rules

all the way out the door. As soon as they were gone, Jess turned to Leslie. "I don't know what repercussions might come from that, so we're going to get you moved someplace else until this is over."

Leslie shook her head. "I can't go anywhere. If Devon comes back he won't know what to do."

"Leslie." Jess pulled her down to the sofa, since she looked as if she were about to drop. "We have your brother's psychologist and two other specialists working with our search commander. We have Devon's picture everywhere. We have an officer watching your home. If he comes back, we'll know it. My top priority at this moment is to ensure your safety as well as your peace of mind."

"I promise I'm fine." Her voice shook.

"Have you eaten today?"

She shrugged. "I don't know."

"How about I order your favorite pizza?" Lori suggested. "My treat."

Leslie looked from Jess to Lori and back. "Cheese is my favorite."

Lori smiled. "Done."

"Chief Harris," Leslie interrupted before Jess could resume, "do you have a brother or sister?"

Jess blinked. "Yes, I do. A sister." A sister who might be very sick. An ache twisted deep inside Jess.

"If this were your sister missing like this," Leslie said, her worried gaze searching Jess's, "would you leave?"

She had her there. "Okay, you win. Let's go over the rules again and I'll give you an update on the search."

Leslie grabbed her and hugged her. Startled, Jess wasn't sure how to respond at first. Then she just went with it and hugged the girl back.

Edgewater Condominiums, 5:30 p.m.

Johnny Trenton had managed to save up enough for a down payment on a low-end condo in Homewood. There was a pool and plenty of other folks his age. Just went to show that before the housing crash mortgage lenders would approve a loan for anyone, whatever their source of income.

Lori spotted Trenton lying on a chaise near the glistening pool. Jess could have gone the rest of her life without seeing the guy in a mankini and tanning oil. Why any woman would consider a self-serving player like him attractive she would never know.

Jess stared down at the glistening creep and wished she had saved the ice from the Pepsi she'd hit a drive-through for on the way here so she could cool him off before he scorched every female on the property.

"I'm sure you're enjoying the view," he said without opening his eyes, "but you're blocking my sun."

"We should step out of the way, Detective. We wouldn't want to block his sun."

Trenton's eyes popped open but he didn't bother getting up. "Chief Harris, what an unexpected pleasure."

He looked her up and down with that usual smirk he wore most likely when any breathing female was in his line of sight.

Evidently not wanting to play favorites, Trenton gave Lori the same appraisal. Lori rolled her eyes.

"Remember I said we might need to speak with you again?"

"Yes, ma'am. I surely do." He got up and stretched to ensure everyone around got a good look at his mostly naked body.

"Would you like to talk here or some place more private?" Jess asked.

"Come on up to my place." He grabbed his towel. "I think I might even have some lemonade in the fridge."

Like she would drink anything he had in his fridge if she were dying of thirst.

His condo was on the first floor with a slider leading to the pool. Not as bad as she'd expected. The décor was blasé but the place was spacious and relatively tidy.

When they had settled around the coffee table, Lori reminded him, "Mr. Trenton, your rights were explained to you when you were interviewed previously. Do you need me to read them again?"

He shook his head. "I have nothing to hide and as far as I know I don't need an attorney. So shoot." He smiled at Jess. "I'm ready for whatever you got."

"Mr. Trenton," Jess flipped through her notes just to make him nervous, "do you recall threatening Gabrielle Grayson when you were a patient at New Life Rehab Center three years ago?"

He flinched. "I do." He shook his head. "I was a genuine asshole to Gabrielle. But, like I told you, she wouldn't let me give up. She kept on urging me to hang in there even though I threatened her seven ways to Sunday. I called her every imaginable ugly name. But she never gave up. She's the reason I got clean and stayed that way."

"Why didn't you mention this when I questioned you on Monday?" Jess hated wasting her time. This investigation was far too important to cater to his massive ego.

"It's not the kind of thing I want to brag about. Besides, that was someone else. It wasn't the man you're sitting here talking to now. Gabrielle saved my life. There is no way in this world I would have done anything to harm her." He looked away then. "I pretend to be all nonchalant and like I don't care about anything but I care that she's gone. I hate like hell that some sick son of a bitch gangbanger did this to her." His jaw tightened with the fury Jess heard in his words. "I hope they kill each other until the fuckers are extinct."

Now there was a thought. Only, a gangbanger didn't kill Gabrielle.

"Mr. Trenton," Jess offered, "I'm going to go out on a limb here. I believe you when you say you would never have hurt Gabrielle. But I need you to think long and hard about your relationship with her." She had to be careful. She couldn't put words in his mouth. Yet she wanted desperately to get a break in this case. The only way that was going to happen was if someone who knew Gabrielle started talking. "Did you ever see or hear anyone do or say anything that might have developed into the motive for murder? Did she have a boyfriend? Did her husband have a girlfriend? Was anything going on that signaled trouble?"

His shoulders slumped. "Honest to God, I wish I knew something. But there's just nothing to know. Gabrielle's whole life revolved around that kid and her husband. She got frustrated sometimes, mainly I think, because she was used to working outside the home. But she was happy. Her husband was happy as far as I know. He wasn't usually around when I worked on the pool. He didn't like her associating with anyone like me. Can't say that I blame him. Most addicts who had it as bad as I did don't stay clean. But I had Gabrielle. There was no way I was going to fail."

"On Monday," Jess countered, "you said Gabrielle's husband wasn't taking care of her needs. That her child was driving her nuts. Which is it, Mr. Trenton? The woman you hold in such high regard is dead. Someone cut off her head and stabbed her body ten times. Imagine what she must have suffered." That wasn't true but he didn't know that. "Don't you want us to find the person who did this?"

Cocky, full-of-himself Johnny Trenton cried. Like a baby. Jess felt like a total buttwad.

Lori shrugged and grabbed a paper towel for him to dry his eyes.

"Okay," he mumbled, then sniffed. "I know I said Gabrielle was unhappy, but she wasn't. Not really." He looked at Jess with watery eyes. "Gabrielle loved her son more than life. She almost never complained. And she worshipped her husband. He could do no wrong in her eyes. She set the standard for being a wife and mother."

There it was. More proof of Gabrielle Grayson's sainthood.

How the hell was Jess supposed to solve a case when everything was so perfect?

Except for the fact that a woman was dead.

And a little boy was missing.

Outside, Jess dropped into the passenger seat of Lori's Mustang. It was hot as blazes and she was exhausted and disgusted and mad as hell. What jerk disliked her so much he would try to blow her up?

Lori started the car. "Wow. I feel like I just walked off the set of an episode of *Dr. Phil.*"

Jess laughed, sort of. She was too tired and overwhelmed to really laugh, but it was a start. She adjusted the air-conditioning vents. "So, her former coworkers and patients think Gabrielle walked on water. We know there is little or no likelihood this was a gang hit."

"Don't forget her neighbors," Lori added. "Everyone we talked to thought she was super mom. We got nothing but rave reviews."

Didn't add up. All those post mortem stab wounds spoke of the killer's rage. "This killer had to be someone who knew her. Hated her. Was envious of her. Or feared her somehow."

Their gazes locked. Lori spoke first. "All her friends are cops and cops' wives."

As unpopular as exploring that avenue would be with the whole department, they had no choice but to take this investigation right there. "Grayson's mother-in-law is home now. We need to nail down an interview with Sarah Riley. She has no more excuses."

"She's put me off every time I call," Lori complained.

"She and her husband are closer to the Graysons than anyone," Jess said, mostly to herself. "We need that interview." They needed a hell of a lot more than that. "We need whoever the hell was close enough to know Grayson's work schedule and *whoever* Gabrielle knew well enough to let into her house at that time of night.

"We need," she said, frustrated and tired, "to find whatever it is that prompted a motive strong enough to kill a woman and then mutilate her body."

Find the motive, find the killer.

9911 Conroy Road, 8:40 p.m.

Jess's new surveillance detail parked on the street right across from the drive to her place. When she pulled into the drive and shut off the engine of her Audi, her gaze automatically swept up to the top of the garage stairs. There was a man there. He seemed to be doing something to her door.

Good grief! Was she being burglarized?

What next?

She grabbed her Glock, opened her door very carefully, and eased out. The guy still hadn't moved. He had surely heard her car pull into the drive. How could he have missed her headlights?

Maybe he had a hearing problem. If so, he needed a new line of work.

Could be her landlord. But why didn't he turn to greet her? Why keep his back to her arrival? She surveyed the back of his house. Lights were on downstairs. He was up it seemed.

Moving cautiously, she made her way to the stairs and slowly started upward. When she was two steps from the landing, her weapon in hand but aimed downward, she cleared her throat in hopes of alerting the man to her presence.

He turned around, seeming startled. This was no young man. Sixty-five or seventy. Eyeglasses with very thick lenses. Thin gray hair. Had to be her landlord.

"Mr. Louis?"

"Chief Harris, I presume?" He passed a hammer to his left hand and offered his right for her to shake.

Jess shifted the Glock to her left hand and accepted his gesture. His grip was firm. Steady. "Yes, sir. That's me. Sorry about the gun. But I thought someone was breaking in."

He shook his head. "We don't ever have any trouble like that around here. It's quiet. Peaceful."

She could argue that point but she opted not to. Her problems had nothing to do with the neighborhood.

"I'm almost done here," he said. "I noticed when the locksmith was here that some of the trim around the door was loose." He pointed to the strips of painted wood around the frame. "I thought I'd tack them back into place and freshen the paint. So be careful, it's still a little wet."

That was when she noticed the bucket of white paint and well-used brush. She also noticed there was light. He'd taken care of the outdoor light on the landing.

"Thank you for taking such good care of me." She gestured back to her car. "I'll just get my stuff."

"I'll clean up and then I'll be out of your way. With this heat, I have to wait until the sun goes down for outside maintenance."

"Smart plan." She smiled before turning to hustle back down to her car. She grabbed her shopping bag and the Chinese takeout she'd picked up on the way home. By the time she reached the top of the stairs again, Mr. Louis had finished his work and was preparing to be on his way.

She waved the box. "I picked up Chinese. I always order far too much. Would you like to join me for my first meal in my new place?"

He shook his head. "I couldn't do that."

"Please. I'd love to have the company."

He kind of shuffled his feet and gave a vague nod.

"Great." She picked through the keys and unlocked the door. After the day she'd had she could use the distraction and she needed to get to know her landlord. She flipped on the interior light and walked in. "Feels way better in here." The heat index had neared another record today.

Thank goodness the air-conditioning was up to par in this place.

"I repaired the light." Louis pointed to the light outside her door, then flipped the necessary switch to turn it off then on.

"I can't thank you enough." She dumped the load in her arms on the table. "Maybe I'll get one of those automatic thingies that makes the light come on at dark. My schedule is so crazy I never know what time I'll get home."

He nodded, his gaze directed more at the floor than at her. "I can install a sensor for you."

"That'd be great. You can add the charge for the work onto my rent."

He shook his head. "No charge. That's part of being a good landlord."

He needed to spread that word around. "Well come on in. Have a seat." She gestured to the table. "I haven't had time to get a sofa yet."

Rather than take a seat, he waited a few feet away and watched as she spread the dinner on the counter. "Bottled water okay with you? I don't have any beer or wine." She wasn't much of a host.

"I don't drink alcohol."

Oops. She should have considered that possibility. Lil said he was at church every Sunday and though Lil drank wine, not all churchgoers approved of alcohol consumption. Jess checked the bag to ensure they'd included more than one set of chopsticks. Usually they did, since they assumed she was ordering for two or more.

What they didn't know wouldn't hurt them. She might go all day without eating but when she did, she made up for the missed meals.

"We can eat in here or sit on the steps. I'm planning to get a glider for the deck." She laughed. "Eventually."

The sound of a car door slamming outside had her guest turning toward the door neither of them had bothered to close.

"I should get back to the house." Louis backed up the two or three steps he had taken. "Let me know if you need anything else."

Before Jess could argue he had snagged his toolbox, rags, and paint can and hurried across the landing and headed down the steps. She walked outside to see that he got down the stairs in one piece at that speed and with both hands full. The new arrival was Wesley. And she looked a mess. Too late to do anything about that. She ordered her jittery nerves to settle down. It was only Wesley. He'd probably spoken to Lopez's people and had an update for her.

Wesley nodded and said hello as he and Mr. Louis passed. Louis didn't appear to say anything but maybe he spoke too softly for Jess to hear. He just kept going as fast as he could walk until he'd disappeared into his house.

Nice man but quite peculiar.

"I brought dinner." Wesley held up a bag that looked oddly familiar. "And wine." He held up a bottle next.

"The wine will get you in the door for sure. But I hope you have a corkscrew and glasses. Otherwise we're doomed to merely admire your taste in wine."

When he was inside they laughed over the idea that they had chosen the same fast-food restaurant. That was one of the things that had drawn her to Wesley. They thought so much alike, or so it had seemed.

Not only had he brought a corkscrew and wineglasses, both of which were housewarming gifts, he had brought a blanket, which he promptly spread on the floor for their dining experience.

Jess couldn't deny enjoying his company and the food. Not to mention the wine.

But she knew Wesley well enough to know that he wasn't here just for dinner and conversation.

"I'm leaving tomorrow."

"I see." She'd wondered when that would happen. There was little more he could do here.

"Leonardo Lopez returned to Los Angeles late this afternoon. Based on our conversation, I must admit there appears to be merit to his allegations of a mole in my organization." Wesley swirled the wine in his glass. "That's difficult for me to believe but it's my duty to explore those allegations."

"What does he want in return?" Jess cradled her second glass of wine. "He wants something, I'm certain." Lopez had mentioned wanting immunity for his daughter. Jess hoped he wouldn't win that negotiation.

"If his claims prove true," Wesley said with obvious reluctance, "he wants probation for his daughter. To keep this business out of the media, his wish may very well be granted."

Jess downed the rest of her wine, a stall tactic to prevent speaking before thinking. The wine didn't do a thing to slow down her building outrage. "You're telling me that his daughter's charges, which include kidnapping me, will likely be lessened to basically nothing if you can verify his claims." That stunk like three-day-old roadkill in the middle of August.

Wesley refilled her glass. "You're aware of the way these things work, Jess. You have to give to get."

Yes, she was all too aware. "Seems incredible that our own people can create this sort of a predicament. And we don't ever want to believe that evil can be working right alongside us. We walk around assuming the best of everyone until the knife is plunged into our back."

Like the idea that someone in the Birmingham Police Department had rigged a bomb in her borrowed car. She glanced at her door. Not to mention broke into her place and left that message.

Wesley hummed a sound of agreement. "That's the part of this job that gets to me the most. To know that one of us is capable of selling out to that kind of monster."

Jess knew better than to ask any questions. So far he hadn't mentioned the incident with the car. Her guess was Burnett hadn't shared. She didn't plan to either. "Just make sure Lopez gives you enough to get the bastard."

Wesley held up his glass. "To getting the bad guys."

"Hear, hear." Jess bumped his glass and took a long drink.

"I've realized many things the past few days, Jess."

She tangled her chopsticks in the lo mein. "Such as."

"I've missed you." When she looked up he was staring at her. "One day, when we have some time, we need to talk about that."

"Wesley." Her stomach knotted with the mix of emotions his words evoked. "I've missed you, too." It was the truth. She wasn't going to lie. She might never see him again. She had made a promise to herself not to take another moment for granted and she intended to keep that promise. "But I'm happy with my life here just as it is."

That part was the truth, too. She was happy. For the first time in a long while.

Silence lingered for a bit.

"It's Burnett, isn't it?" he asked at last.

She'd expected that one. "It's far more complicated than that." She couldn't explain to him what she didn't fully understand herself. "Burnett and I have a history that's difficult to define. My happiness at the moment is about a lot more than him."

A smile spread across Wesley's lips. She had always loved his smile.

"Good for you, Jess."

She cared for Wesley. Respected and admired him. His approval meant a lot to her. She hoped that, moving forward, they could be friends. Somehow after taking their vows they had lost that ability.

Dinner went by too fast. Jess enjoyed the meal and the conversation more than any they had shared as a married couple. When they'd cleaned up and she'd walked with him to the landing outside her door, a feeling of uncertainty and just a pinch of regret lingered.

"I'll be in touch."

"You'd better be." She hugged her arms around herself. She wished the feeling of uncertainty or restlessness would go away. Would she never see him again? Did she want to?

He leaned down, and for a fraction of a second she couldn't breathe. Wesley kissed her on the cheek and whispered, "If you ever change your mind you know how to find me."

And then he took his leave before she could say a word.

Jess watched him drive away and she wondered if their marriage had been her last chance at having the traditional life—the picket fence and the kids.

The need to talk to Dan rushed through her. Would they...could they ever have that? Maybe. She just didn't know. They'd made that deal about turning sixty but what if one or the other met someone else before then? That was one worry she just didn't have time for.

She downed the last of her wine. Besides, what did she need with traditional?

She had the unexpected, the unusual. Her gaze settled on the one window in her landlord's home that poured light into the darkness. Oh yes. She had the unexpected, the unusual, and the peculiar.

What else could a girl want?

Jess turned to go back inside and the lovely stemmed glass Wesley had brought as her housewarming gift slipped out of her hand. She crouched and caught it just before it hit and shattered on the wooden deck floor.

"Oh good grief." She was tired. Too tired to be entertaining. *And having three glasses of wine*. Glass firmly in hand, she prepared to push to her feet. Spots on the wood stopped her.

Jess reached down and touched the specks. Red and dried. Not paint. Mr. Louis had been using white paint. Had the spots been there and she just hadn't noticed? She thought of the bloody message that had been left for her on that photo.

What if her intruder had come back? The new locks had obviously kept him out but maybe he left her a message on the...door?

Jess glanced toward her landlord's house and then at the door to her rented space. Would he have thought cleaning up the mess was the proper thing to do? Without ever mentioning it to her? That was ridiculous.

"You're getting paranoid, Jess."

She went inside and closed the door, taking care to lock it. She washed her glass and placed it on the counter next to the others. Now what? She could better organize her new stock of dry and canned goods in the cabinets.

"Forget it!" She couldn't ignore the spots.

She dug around in the take-out containers and got one of the chopsticks. After washing it thoroughly, she went back out to her landing and scraped up a specimen of the red spot. There were evidence collection bags in her car, but if she went down to her car the cop doing her surveillance would report that to Burnett. He was already going to get an earful about Wesley's late-night visit.

She was going to hear about that. Especially if that chaste kiss was mentioned.

Really all she needed was something plastic and clean. After fishing around in her bag for a whole minute she found a Tampax. She removed the packaging and tucked her specimen inside. Might not be sterile but it was clean.

"That works." She stored the package in the zipper compartment of her bag and then dusted her hands together. First thing tomorrow morning she'd hit up Ricky Vernon at the lab for a favor.

Two brisk knocks on her door made her jump.

It was past ten o'clock. Who in the world...?

Jess stamped toward the door. "Burnett, if that's you checking up on me, I'm going to be..." She checked the window.

Sylvia Baron?

"What the hell?" Jess opened the door. "You have news on my vic?" The woman couldn't call with news on the case? Why the heck was she working so late anyway? Surely Burnett hadn't recruited her to check up on Jess, too.

Baron adopted an offended expression. "Hello to you, too, Harris." She thrust a large bag at Jess. "That's for you." She pushed her way inside and surveyed the space. "So this is your new place."

Jess closed and locked the door. "Sorry about the yelling." No way she missed Jess's tirade. "I was expecting to find Burnett at the door."

Baron turned to her, her eyebrows arched in skepticism. "Does Chief of Police Burnett make a habit of stopping by at this hour?"

Jess pretended to be mesmerized by the can opener beneath all the fancy yellow paper stuffed in the bag. "Thank you for the gift." She flashed a smile as she deposited the bag on the table. "Do *you* make it a habit of stopping by to have refreshments with your ex-husband's wife on the day she's murdered?"

Baron's gaze narrowed. "I told you she called me but we never had that meeting." Baron folded her arms over her chest and cranked up her haughty meter. "Did you forget to write it down?"

Jess ignored her dig. "Someone came to Gabrielle's house after eight o'clock Sunday night. Someone she knew." She matched Baron's stance. "If it wasn't you, then who?"

"How would I know? You're the hotshot cop, why haven't you figured it out?"

Again, Jess ignored her potshot. "You want coffee?" The woman was here, they might as well accomplish something.

"It's not instant, is it?" Baron sent a suspect glance toward Jess's new coffeemaker.

Jess rolled her eyes. "No." She gave her nifty carousel a spin. "What's your pleasure?"

Coffee blends selected and cups brewed, they moved to the steps. It was far too nice to stay cooped up inside, especially with no sofa. The oppressive heat had subsided, taking the worst of the humidity with it.

"We're not dealing with a gangbanger," Baron said what they both already knew after a lengthy silence. "Burnett tells me there's still nothing in her background that would suggest an enemy out for revenge."

"It's not the husband," Jess said. She wasn't even going to pretend to believe otherwise.

Baron turned and stared at her profile.

"I know she called you and was worried about him, but I think it's about something he was involved in. I just have to find out what that something is."

Baron made a rather rude harrumphing sound. "Larry Grayson is all about work. That's what he does. That's all he does."

Was that resentment she heard in the assistant coroner's voice? "Then it has to be related to his work. Whatever it was," Jess argued. "Gabrielle was scared and needed someone to talk to. Maybe she called you because she thought you had experienced the same problem when you were married to him."

Baron shrugged. "I considered that possibility."

Another patch of silence elapsed between them. Someone had to say something. "Everyone she knew loved her," Jess said. "Doesn't look like she had any enemies."

"I know," Baron admitted. "Clearly she was the saint everyone says she was."

More of what sounded like resentment dripped from

her voice. Jess turned to her. "That doesn't lessen who you are." As soon as the words were out of her mouth, Jess regretted having said them. She and Sylvia Baron weren't friends. They barely knew each other and Jess wasn't sure she even liked the woman. She was reasonably certain the woman didn't like her.

"I know that, too." Baron's hands started to shake and she set her coffee cup on the step between her feet so she could clasp them together. "I just keep thinking that if I had made time for her...she would still be alive." She turned to Jess. "I was wrong to do that, you know. And she's dead." Tears slipped down her cheeks. "And maybe that little boy, too. I stood by and did nothing and now..."

God knew Jess had never been a hugger. Never. But this lady needed a hug and somehow they were alike in ways that Jess wanted to deny and, for whatever the reason, some force of nature had ensured their paths crossed at this time in their lives. Jess put down her cup and patted Sylvia Baron on the back, tried to think of something clever and comforting to say. Baron's shoulders shook and Jess had to hug her. There was no denying the instinct.

The embrace lasted all of three seconds before, as if they'd both taken a big mental step back at the same time, they drew apart.

Jess cleared her throat.

Baron swiped gingerly at her eyes. "Well, that was awkward."

"We all have our moments."

They talked a while longer. Around midnight Baron decided it was time to go home.

"Wait." Jess's gaze dropped to the wooden deck. "I

need a favor." What were friends for if not to help each other out?

While Baron grumbled, Jess dashed inside and retrieved the specimen from the spots on her floorboards. She offered it to the assistant coroner. "Can you tell me if that's paint or blood or what?"

Baron took the Tampax packaging between two fingers as if she feared contamination. "Seriously?"

"I didn't have any plastic bags so I tore the packaging off a *new* one." Jess pointed to the couple of spots on the floorboards in front of her door. "Paint or what?"

"I'll take it home and package it properly and then run the necessary tests in the morning."

"I appreciate that." The weight of the day suddenly crashed down and Jess couldn't remember when she had been this tired.

Baron sniffed the specimen, then frowned. "But I can tell you right now that it's not paint."

Deep inside, where her guest couldn't see, Jess trembled just a little.

"It's blood."

18

Caldwell Avenue, Thursday, August 5, 9:01 a.m.

Sarah Riley perched on her worn sofa, her hands twisted with worry, her back ramrod straight.

Jess and Harper had arrived at her town house half an hour ago, but since Sarah was at home alone with two children, an eight-month-old and a fifteen-month-old, she'd had to get the babies situated before she could talk. During that time Jess had studied the framed photos around the living room. She'd also come to realize several things about Sarah. Her home, though not exactly filled with top-of-the-line furnishings, was absolutely spotless. Even with two babies there was not a speck of visible dust or a smudge anywhere to be found.

"I appreciate you making time for us," Jess said. "Your interview was the last one on my list of close friends and family members." She gave her a broad smile. "I'm so glad you have a few minutes now."

Sarah nodded, the move stiff. "With taking care of little Gary and the girls and helping Larry with the memorial arrangements... it's been hard. But Gabrielle's mother is here now and she's caring for Gary at her house."

The memorial service was at five today. Jess intended to be there. "Lieutenant Grayson is fortunate to have a good friend like you."

A brief smile touched Sarah's lips. "I've scheduled professional cleaners to get started on the cleanup at Larry's house since the scene was released." She diverted her gaze from Jess's. "Jack and I thought it was the least we could do. Someone who knows the family should be there overseeing."

Sarah Riley had wide gray eyes and dark hair. She wasn't as big as a minute and hardly seemed old enough to be a nurse and a mother twice over. She was also very nervous. Maintaining eye contact was a problem for her. She wrung her hands repeatedly. Smoothed the skirt of her dress every time she seemed to realize she was wringing her hands. A woman married to a cop, a detective at that, should know the drill when it came to times like this.

"Your husband works all the time," Jess empathized. "It's a miracle you have a minute to yourself." She glanced at the younger woman's nicely manicured nails. Her hair was styled. Makeup perfect. And the sundress she wore fit well, showed off her small curves, and was really quite flattering.

Sarah stretched her lips into a smile that was as fake as any Jess had seen. "Jack likes me to have a spa day every other week. He says I deserve to look and feel nice. It makes him happy, too. He's always looking out for me, making sure the children and I have everything we need."

"You have a thoughtful husband. He works hard to take care of his family."

Sarah nodded, but she looked away again, stared at her hands. Maybe not such a nice husband, Jess decided.

"I imagine with him gone so much," Jess said, fishing, "that you have to take care of all the shopping and oversee the maintenance around here as well."

"That's my job. It wouldn't be right for him to work all those hours and then come home to more work." She shook her head adamantly. "He gives me his lists and I take care of it."

Jess thought as much. Time to move on. Making Sarah Riley suspicious wasn't on today's agenda. "You and Gabrielle were close friends?"

"Very close friends," Sarah asserted. "We started out working together and the next thing we knew we were having babies together." She blinked at tears that looked genuine. "I can't believe she's gone. Losing her has left a huge hole in my world."

"I understand," Jess said gently. "You and your husband had lunch with the Graysons on Sunday, is that right?"

Sarah nodded. "We did that a couple of times a month. Sometimes we would host the cookout. Other times they would."

"Did you hear from Gabrielle that night?"

Sarah moved her head side to side in a no, then abruptly stopped. "I take that back. I called her a couple of times. At lunch we talked about taking a vacation together next spring. I couldn't remember the dates she mentioned so I gave her a call. *Two* times."

"Have you taken a vacation together before?"

"Several times. We enjoy—enjoyed—a lot of the same leisure activities. We both loved the beach and finding restaurants we've never been to before. And with the children, we usually kept it simple."

"Were you aware of any problems between Gabrielle and her husband?"

Sarah's jaw dropped as if she found the question shocking. "No way. Wherever you got that idea, it is completely untrue. Those two were crazy in love. They couldn't have had any big issues. I would've known. For sure."

Jess cleared her throat. "I hate to be a bother, but may I have a glass of water?"

Sarah blinked, startled by the unexpected change in topic. "Sure."

She stood, the move slow and stiff as if she were sore. She walked to the kitchen and Jess went right behind her. Sarah pretended not to pay attention to her following but Jess spotted her having a look from the corner of her eye. She really was quite nervous and visibly stiff. Had she hurt her back lifting and running after not two but three kids?

Like the living room, the kitchen sparkled. Jess was reasonably sure she'd never encountered a kitchen this clean. Not one where two kids lived anyway. She watched as Sarah reached into a cupboard and retrieved a glass. The glasses in the cupboard were stored in perfect rows. OCD for sure.

Sarah filled the glass from the tap. "Here you go."

"Thank you." Jess sipped it slowly, using the time to note all she could about the way this couple lived. "You have a lovely home."

"Thank you."

"Have you lived here long?"

"Five years." Sarah looked around the room. "We bought this town house when Jack was promoted to detective."

Jess gifted her with a smile. "What a celebration that must have been. A promotion and a new home, too."

This time the woman's smile looked real. "It was, yes."

Jess set her glass on the counter. "Thank you so much, Sarah."

Sarah immediately picked up the glass, emptied the remainder of the water, and placed it in the dishwasher. Then she rinsed the sink.

This time Jess led the way to the living room, but she didn't sit down.

Taking that cue, Harper joined Jess near the door.

"One last question, Sarah."

"Anything," Sarah said, her voice almost giddy. "Ask me anything, Chief Harris."

"Were you aware of Gabrielle taking any drugs? Oxy-Contin, for example?"

The woman's jaw dropped a second time. "Where in the world are you getting these hateful ideas? Gabrielle Grayson would hardly take an antibiotic much less something like that!"

"There was a large amount found in her tox screen, Sarah. The facts don't lie," Jess challenged.

"There has to be a mistake." Her arms went over her chest and her head was moving side to side in firm denial. She almost looked angry. "That's impossible."

"The drug came from somewhere. Do you know if anyone in her family or any of her friends used that drug? Maybe someone gave it to her because she hurt herself somehow. Maybe she picked up the baby the wrong way and hurt her back?"

"I don't know anyone who uses that drug and neither did Gabrielle."

Oh yes. The lady was angry. "Not since your days working at New Life, right?"

"I have to feed the baby now." Sarah resurrected that fake smile and all other emotion vanished from her face. "Thank you for all you're doing to find Gabrielle's killer. We won't sleep at night until this horrible tragedy is put to rest."

Jess handed her a card. "I appreciate your taking the time to talk to us, Sarah. If you think of anything else you believe might help, please let us know. We're closing in on a suspect and we want to nail him but good."

Sarah's eyes widened in surprise. "That's great. I've been asking Jack and watching the news, but I hadn't heard you were so close to solving the case."

Jess nodded. "It's only a matter of time before we take him down."

Sarah stared at her, her disbelief as evident as if it had been written across her forehead in blood like the foul words that had been written on Gabrielle's. Then she seemed to jerk back to the here and now and opened the door to usher them out.

Jess waited until they were in Harper's SUV before saying a word.

Harper beat her to the punch. "Now that was a Stepford wife if I've ever seen one." He shook his head. "As hard as she tried to cover it up, it showed on her face. She alternated between being scared to death of giving the wrong answer and spewing what she'd been brainwashed to say."

"Did you notice that nice save when I asked her if she

spoke to Gabrielle that night?" Jess had seen the realization in her expression when the idea that phone records had likely been subpoenaed hit her. She'd recovered like a pro. "She specified that she had spoken to her *two* times after eight o'clock. God, we need those phone records." Jess hated that these things sometimes took so long.

"I saw how she was moving. Like she was in pain. You think that bastard beats her?"

"I think that's a very strong possibility." Whatever was going on in their relationship, it was off balance. There was something deeply wrong in that house. Jess could feel it.

"But that doesn't make him a killer," Harper noted with audible regret.

"That's true, Sergeant." A man who would abuse his wife and children was the lowest of the low in Jess's opinion. She wanted to shake the woman and demand why she would put up with such treatment. But she knew the answer without asking. Most often a twisted bond formed between the abused and the abuser. That kind of narcissistic bond was difficult to sever. Sometimes it ended only when one or the other was dead... *until death do us part.*

"But," Jess told her detective, a scenario forming quickly, "it does open up a whole new avenue of motive that may have set the stage for murder."

"How do you mean?"

"With a bond like that, anything that threatens it would be swiftly stamped out."

She didn't know the ins and outs of where this was going just yet, but Jack and Sarah Riley had just moved to the top of Jess's suspect list.

"Let's see if we can find anything in police reports or medical records that prove Jack Riley is abusing his wife." That was another avenue they could explore with Sarah's former coworkers—the same coworkers they were already questioning about Gabrielle.

"Yes, ma'am. But police reports are doubtful. He wouldn't have made sergeant if anything like that was on his record."

"Unless," Jess tossed back, "she claimed some unknown perp did the beating."

Abusers and victims that deeply entrenched in their bond knew how to work the system.

"Good point." Harper pulled his cell phone from his jacket pocket and checked the screen. "Dispatch." He glanced at Jess before answering with, "Harper."

Holy crap... what now?

Harper listened for five, six, seven seconds. "Chief Harris and I are en route."

As he tucked his phone away, Jess asked the question she feared the most. "Is it Devon?"

"No. Two adult vics. One male, one female."

If they had gotten the call, there was some sort of readily distinguishable similarity or connection to the Grayson case.

Just when Jess thought she knew where this investigation was headed, someone had to go and toss another body or two into the mix.

Norwood, 11:38 a.m.

"Both victims were dead prior to the decapitations and the stabbings." Sergeant Harper indicated the blood, skull fragments, and brain matter sprayed across the dingy wall beyond where the man and woman lay supine on the floor. "Ligature marks on the wrists indicate they were restrained at some point."

Jess stepped closer to the couple. "It appears they were forced onto their knees, facing the wall, and took a bullet to the back of the head. At some point after that they were dragged over here"—she gestured to where they lay—"cut loose from their restraints, positioned with their arms spread wide and their legs together, just as Gabrielle Grayson was posed."

"Only this time"—Harper crouched down and indicated the area of the neck where the heads were once attached—"the heads were sawed off with a bit more precision."

"Or maybe just a sharper saw," Jess suggested. Her stomach spasmed in revulsion.

"Definitely sharper," Harper agreed. "I counted twelve stab wounds on each vic. The pattern is random."

Twelve, not ten like Gabrielle. "It's a miracle they were found before they dissolved into DNA soup." Christ what a mess. It was all she could do to take a breath.

The house had gone into foreclosure and was now owned by the bank. The windows were broken and the paint inside and out was peeling. The yard was overgrown. Like several others in the area, the house had sat abandoned and neglected for months.

But not today. The smell of disuse and emptiness had been replaced by the pungent odor of human decomposition. There was no electricity and no air-conditioning. Even the evidence techs had had to take a break from the smell. The first officers on the scene hadn't come back inside since discovering the bodies.

"First officer on the scene"—Harper pushed to his feet and checked the notes he'd made on his phone—"said the old man who lives next door—the one who called it in, Pete Hall—identified the vics as Angel Flores and Javier Villa. He says they showed up here about two months ago and have been squatting in the house since. He's pretty sure they were selling drugs. Not that he bought any," Harper pointed out with a skeptical glance at Jess, "but he feels confident that's how they made a living. He hadn't seen or heard from either of them since last weekend and he thought they'd cut out without saying good-bye until he noticed the smell coming from the house."

Jess was pretty sure the old man had been a regular customer and that was how he knew the names of these victims. "Let's hope they've been printed somewhere or dental records exist, because I don't imagine even the next of kin could identify them now." A good portion of both victims' faces were missing. "Maybe the ME will find some identifying marks other than the tattoos."

Leonardo Lopez had insisted he did not believe his people were involved with Gabrielle Grayson's murder. Yet here they were with a similar scene on their hands and both vics were sporting the typical MS-13 tatts. Various forms of the number thirteen, the name Mara Salvatrucha, teardrops, and one Jess hadn't seen before, 666. Just lovely.

"Have Officer Cook run the names the neighbor gave us and see what he comes up with," Jess told Harper.

"Yes, ma'am."

She crouched down to get a closer look at the bodies. She shielded her nose with a gloved hand, for all the good it would do. "These two have been dead at least a couple of days." In this heat decomp had accelerated. She studied the damaged tissue around the neck where the head had been severed from the body. First the woman's, then the man's. "The beheading was done considerably later. A day at least."

"Stab wounds, too," Harper said.

The decapitation and stabbings had resulted in little blood loss. The victims' hearts had ceased to pump blood well before those final acts. Jess considered the one word, *RAGE*, written in blood on the wall at the other end of the small room. Their perp had avoided the blood, bone, and tissue pattern that resulted from the shootings. Why would he care and where were all the other written comments that had been present at Gabrielle's murder scene?

"Another element similar to the Grayson murder," Harper suggested, noting her attention on the wall.

Jess pushed to her feet. "Except this time there's just the one word. And the decapitations are much cleaner."

"Do we have some sort of fledgling ritual killer on our hands?"

Jess wasn't ready to go there. "I don't think so. The victims are far too different." It wasn't impossible but it was far less probable. She surveyed the small space. Four rooms. All of which were empty save for a mattress and scattered clothes and rotting food.

"How did the perp enter the premises, Sergeant?"

She and Harper had come in through the front door. There had been no sign of forced entry there. Of course there was always the chance the victims had known the killer and allowed him inside.

"The back door. Follow me."

Harper had been busy while she studied the victims.

She trailed him through each of the rooms. There wasn't much of a hall. Mostly a small spot where the four rooms converged. The one with the tiny closet she assumed was a bedroom. A tiny bathroom, the living room—where the bodies had been found—and then a kitchen. In the kitchen, the back door had been kicked in. Muddy shoe prints suggested that the breaking and entering had occurred closer to Monday than today. It hadn't rained since early Sunday night and there sure as hell wasn't a damp rut around here to be found.

"Two distinct sets of shoe prints," Harper indicated the imprints on the worn linoleum. He positioned his right foot alongside one of the muddy outlines. "One set's about a size ten, the other smaller, a nine maybe."

"Gabrielle's killer was careful not to leave behind that kind of evidence." She and Harper exchanged a knowing look.

At the counter Jess had a look at the papers lying there. Documents that announced the bank had repossessed the property. Neatly printed property detail sheets for the Realtors who came through. No business cards though. Typically when a Realtor showed a house, they left their business card for the listing Realtor. Certainly the house hadn't been shown since the couple in the other room took up residence.

Jess picked up a copy of the property detail sheet to take with her and roaches scurried across the counter.

Shouting at the front door drew her attention in that direction.

"Sounds like the ME's here," Harper said.

Dr. Sylvia Baron's voice boomed again. "What're you waiting for? The second coming? We have an oven in here. The sooner you've done your job, the sooner we can salvage these victims before they ooze through the cracks in the floor."

Apparently the evidence techs had loitered outside a little too long to suit her. This was the kind of scene no one relished dissecting.

"We certainly don't want to keep her waiting." She and Jess had reached a kind of wary alliance. After last night's bonding moment they might even be friends...sort of. Be that as it may, the law was the law. Dr. Baron might run things at the coroner's office and, as the ME of record on a case, she had jurisdiction over the body, but she didn't run Jess's crime scenes.

"Good morning, Dr. Baron." Jess tacked on a smile in spite of the urge to wrinkle her face and gag as the full impact of the smell hit her all over again. The smell was so much less strong in the kitchen.

"Chief Harris." Baron surveyed the bodies. "Do we have a copycat or is this the same perp from Gabrielle Grayson's murder?"

"Considering these victims were executed gang-style and have been dead for more than forty-eight hours, I highly doubt it. If you'll notice, the decapitations and stabbings occurred far more recently. I think someone wants us to believe it's related, but my money's on no connection whatsoever."

Baron turned up her gloved hands. "Well, excuse the hell out of me. I don't know why I bothered to show up since you have all the answers."

Jess laughed. "But you're the expert. I'm only speculating." She gestured to the bodies. "They're all yours."

"Thank you, Chief. And by the way," she said, prompting Jess to lean closer. "Not human. Animal. Feline to be exact."

Jess gave her a nod. "Thanks. I owe you one." The spots on her deck were the same type of blood used to leave that message on the Grayson photo. The only question was, were the blood droplets from the night the message was left inside her apartment or was this from a new message? One her landlord had covered up?

Why would he do that? It was time she had a long talk with Mr. Louis.

When Baron started ordering the evidence techs around again, Jess snagged Harper's arm and ushered him outside. "Get hold of Hector Debarros for me. Tell him I need to speak to Leonardo Lopez."

"Yes, ma'am."

An assistant from the coroner's office hurried from the van to the house with trace sheets and body bags. *Good luck with that*, Jess thought.

News crews waited at the corner of the block.

Jess considered the location. There wasn't much she didn't know about this city. Not so far from here was historic Norwood, where the homes were architecturally pleasing and the residents had the means to keep them that way. The residents over there, her gaze followed the street in that direction, pretended their neighbors only a few blocks away weren't murdered on a regular basis and that crime wasn't the only game around. If forced to drive along these blocks they overlooked the dilapidated homes, defunct businesses, and abandoned structures decorated with graffiti. As long as it wasn't on *their* block, it wasn't real.

Her lungs still cramping from the odor inside, Jess

turned to the house once more. Whoever attempted to make this resemble the Grayson murder had failed miserably.

Jess blinked when Captain Ted Allen rounded the west corner of the house. He'd been busy interviewing neighbors when she arrived. Now he was headed her way. She braced for an unpleasant encounter.

Allen was a little older than her, a year or two maybe. He had the tall, lean build of a runner. His dark hair was close cropped in a military style. He wore dark glasses, which concealed the color of his eyes. But there was no mistaking the set of his jaw. He was in no way glad to see her.

"Chief Harris."

"Captain Allen."

"What we have here," he said, getting to the point, "is a gang hit on interlopers. The two vics you got inside were likely trying to start up their own little business in the wrong territory. Whoever showed up and mutilated the bodies afterward has nothing to do with that."

He started to turn away. "How can you be so sure, Captain?"

"Because"—he turned back to her, impatience and dislike emanating from his every pore—"I have informants who report this stuff to me. Those two were taken out late Monday by two MS-13 members in Salvadore Lopez's clique. They were protecting their territory. The vics were shot once in the back of the head. That's what MS-13 does to interlopers."

Jess crossed her arms over her chest. "And you didn't report this double homicide? I know you and your joint task force with the bureau and the DEA have this grand plan, but I just don't get the way you sit back and let these guys get away with murder."

Allen laughed. “Frankly, I could care less what you get or don’t get.”

“Apparently you’re not alone on that one, Captain, considering someone has been sending me some rather firm messages.”

He backed off, held his hands up stop-sign fashion. “Work the gang world long enough, Chief, and you’ll learn to be grateful for two things. One is to bide your time and choose your battles so you take down the biggest fish. The other is to appreciate when they take each other off the street.” He gestured to the rundown house. “That’s two less dope dealers in there. Color me thankful to whoever took ’em out.”

Jess gave a little chuckle. “I suppose you’re right. You have to be there to appreciate that sentiment. Kind of like an inside joke.”

“Just telling it the way it is, Chief.”

“Who else knew this hit had taken place?”

“My informant and the lead members of my task force. Now, if you’ll excuse me—”

“There’s no way Lieutenant Grayson could have known?”

Allen stepped closer to her. Jess stood her ground. Maybe he thought the move was intimidating. He’d have to bring a better game than that.

“I don’t like the way you do things, Harris,” he said for her ears only. “Course that doesn’t mean a thing since you and Chief Burnett are such good *friends*. But, be advised, you don’t have a lot of friends in the department as it is. You start accusing good men like Grayson of murdering his own wife, you’re going to lose what few you do have.”

Jess studied his face, the part she could see around the

glasses. His body language told her he liked playing the role of tough guy. Probably got off on it. Either way, Jess wasn't going to apologize for doing her job. "And what about Riley? Is he one of the good guys?"

"Riley is a damned good cop," Allen all but growled. "He's just a little gung ho. Typical adrenaline junkie. Gets a little too proactive. He's one of those who would run in before getting the go signal. But that doesn't make him a bad cop. Anything else?"

"I appreciate your observations, Captain. I'm certain this won't be the last time we'll run into each other in the line of duty."

"I can always hope."

He walked away, every arrogant stride making her angrier. But there wasn't a damned thing she could do about those who decided she'd gotten her position because she was *friends* with Burnett. There was also nothing she could do about the kind of attitude that would find murder acceptable under any circumstances.

Jess stilled. And yet she dreamed of killing Eric Spears with her own two hands almost every day. Maybe she was no better than Allen. Did it matter that the two vics inside this rundown house were nowhere near the kind of monsters Spears was? Was murder ever justified?

The roar of an engine and squealing tires drew her attention to the street. The SUV barreling up the block she recognized as belonging to Lieutenant Grayson. The vehicle rocked to a stop at the curb. He climbed from behind the wheel and his partner emerged from the passenger side.

Things were about to get interesting.

Harper appeared at her side. They exchanged a look and Jess had to admit she was glad he was here.

"You gonna do this?" Harper asked. "Or am I?"

"I think I can handle it, Sergeant." She focused on the two men striding her way. "But I appreciate the backup."

The man's wife had been murdered; for that reason Jess disliked the need to be firm. But finding Gabrielle's murderer was far more important than appeasing him.

"Lieutenant," she said, holding up both hands, "you cannot be here." She glanced at his partner, who had no excuse for not heading off this situation. "You either, Sergeant Riley. Now take your partner home and cool off."

"I just want to know if the same person who murdered my wife did this," Grayson demanded. "That's all I want. Just tell me the truth, Chief."

"I can't answer that question, Lieutenant." He knew better than to ask such a thing. She'd barely begun her investigation into these murders. The scene was still being documented and analyzed for evidence. His ex-wife was in there doing her thing.

"You've been talking to her coworkers," Grayson said. "Looking into our personal lives as if you think Gabrielle did something to deserve this." His eyes pleaded with Jess. "I need to know who did this."

"What the hell?" Riley roared.

Jess followed his gaze and found Dr. Baron at the door instructing her assistant on the removal of the bodies.

Riley stormed right up to the front door. Thank God he had the good sense not to charge into the scene. "What the hell are you doing here?"

Baron didn't spare him so much as a glance. "Since you're not visually impaired, Sergeant, I'm certain the answer to that question is glaringly clear. Do not get in my way."

"You're the reason we don't have any answers about Gabrielle!" Riley stabbed a finger at Sylvia. "You want this to drag out and hurt him."

Grayson joined the shouting match.

"Sergeant Harper."

"Yes, ma'am."

"I'd like you to escort those two gentlemen outside the perimeter of my crime scene."

"My pleasure, Chief."

"If either one resists, you are to arrest one or both."

As Harper closed in on the two irate detectives, Grayson said something to Riley and the younger man stormed off. He didn't dodge the opportunity to send a drop-dead look in Jess's direction. She held that threatening glare until he'd shut himself up in his partner's SUV. If half of what she suspected proved true, he was going to be falling off that high horse of his.

Grayson was next. Harper was right behind him. Rather than heading to his SUV, Grayson headed straight for Jess.

"I hope you know what you're doing, Harris. You're letting that woman influence your assessment of this case and I swear to God I will take legal action." He struggled to regain his composure. His face was beet red, his nostrils flaring. "My wife scarcely took an aspirin much less a pain killer. If she"—he sent a furious glare in the ME's direction—"screwed up that toxicology..." He shook his head, didn't finish the statement.

Enough was enough. "Lieutenant, those two homicide victims are *not* related to you or to Dr. Baron. There is no ethical reason she should be removed from this particular investigation." He started to argue, but Jess cut him off. “She’s here to do her job and these victims deserve the best we have to offer, the same as your wife does. Dr. Leeds handled her case personally. You just go ahead and file whatever complaints you feel inclined to file. What you think of me or your ex-wife or what she thinks about you is irrelevant to me. I will conduct this investigation to the best of my ability.”

The fury started to recede. Agony haunted his eyes. “How am I supposed to trust what you say, Chief Harris? Monday afternoon both you and Chief Burnett promised to keep me up to speed on my wife’s case and just this morning I had to hear that the boy next door had gone missing and that you believe his disappearance is related to my wife’s murder!”

“We’re still talking to several of your neighbors, Lieutenant,” Jess hedged. “The fact that he’s gone missing right next door to where the murder occurred may or may not be connected.” She wasn’t ready for his partner to know that yet and if Grayson knew it, so would Riley.

Grayson dropped his head. “God almighty, the nightmare never ends.”

“Was Devon Chambers a regular visitor at your home?” She’d wanted to ask him about that.

“My wife said he watched her and the baby in the backyard. When she’d wave he’d move away from the window. To my knowledge he never came over.”

“Sir, you stated that you and Gabrielle didn’t have any problems.”

Anger tightened his features again. “I told you the truth.”

“In the interviews I’ve conducted, I learned that Gabrielle called a friend the day before she died and said she needed to talk about a problem that involved *you*." Jess braced for his retaliation.

The agony was back. His shoulders fell as if he no longer possessed the strength to hold them straight. "If you have anything else to say to me, call my attorney."

He returned to his vehicle and drove away. His departure lacked the fanfare of squealing tires and the roaring engine of his arrival. Devastation was leading Grayson. His partner didn't have that kind of excuse.

"Methinks he doth protest too much," she murmured.

Baron joined Jess on the overgrown lawn. "I'd estimate the victims have been dead approximately three days. The stab wounds and beheading were carried out postmortem, as you know. Maybe twenty-four to thirty-six hours later. Determining that timeline is somewhat more difficult outside a lab setting."

Time of death backed up what Allen had heard via his informants. "Thank you, Dr. Baron."

"I can give you more tomorrow or the next day but that's the way it looks."

"Just so you know, Grayson is threatening to take action against us both." Jess wasn't really worried about his threats. That was Burnett's problem. But, somewhere deep inside, the idea of how many enemies she had made here already nagged at her. And one of those enemies wanted her dead.

"I heard."

"I understand there's bad blood between you and the lieutenant," Jess ventured, "but what's the deal with you and Riley?"

"I never liked him." She pursed her lips and seemed to think a moment before she continued. "He was assigned to work with Larry just over five years ago and from day one I had a bad feeling about him. I don't trust him."

"I've found no reason he'd want Gabrielle dead," Jess said bluntly. "On the other hand, he seems to have oodles of simmering motives where you're concerned. If you turn up murdered, I'll consider him first."

"That would be a wise first step." She sighed. "He strikes me as the kind of man who would do anything to get ahead. Larry doesn't see it because his own ego blinds him. Riley pretends to worship him. What man doesn't want his very own fan club following him around, even if it does have only one member?"

"I think the lieutenant has a little more than one fan," Jess countered.

"But Riley is different. He treats Larry as if he's a god. Even his wife treats him as if he's some big hero."

"Was there ever a problem between you and Sarah Riley?"

"We hardly knew each other. They didn't come around when Larry was married to me. It wasn't until the last few months of our marriage that he began to drop by their home. I was too busy to notice. The next thing I knew they'd found him a new wife. One who fit into their intimate little circle."

"You believe Riley and his wife purposely tried to break up your marriage?"

Baron frowned. "Possibly. The part that bothers me most is that Larry knew who I was when we married. We dated for two years. Suddenly, that final year of our marriage, it was as if I was a stranger to him. He saw all the things he had once admired in me as shortcomings. Then he found the perfect wife."

"She admired and adored him the same as his partner and his wife, is that right?" That old familiar anticipation started pumping.

"One who couldn't wait to bear his children." Baron looked away. "Gabrielle was everything I wasn't. Patient, doting, submissive. She made him feel like the king of the world." She laughed. "He actually said that to me. I wish I could hate her for it, but I never could. Not really. And God knows I tried."

"That's the difference between you and the person who murdered Gabrielle." Jess met Baron's expectant gaze. "Gabrielle's killer hated her. Hated her so completely that even after she was dead, it wasn't enough."

19

1:50 p.m.

Sarah stared at the rear entrance of the floral shop only a few steps away. But she couldn't get out of the car until he said what he had to say. She was trapped like a child awaiting punishment. She didn't deserve any better after what she'd done.

She'd made a mistake and he was disappointed. She'd let that Chief Harris in their house.

Coming to buy flowers was the only way they could escape the preparations for the service to talk. Jack had driven around behind the shop and parked between the delivery vans so they could have some privacy.

"You fucked up, Sarah."

She thought about lying but he always found out everything. "I didn't have a choice."

He laughed long and loud. She hated that sound. It grated on her nerves so badly. He never laughed and meant it. Whenever he made that obnoxious sound it was either to intimidate or to humiliate. That's what he was best at.

"We wouldn't be in this situation if you hadn't fucked up in the first place."

He wasn't screaming like he usually did. But there was no mistaking how enraged he was. She'd failed him. Failed their union. Failed their children.

"I tried to fix it." The urge to cry welled in her throat but that would only make him more angry. He hated weakness. "I swear I did."

"You wore gloves? Shoe covers?"

She nodded. "I was very careful." Except for the bottle. Damn it. She had touched the bottle after taking off the gloves. She hadn't meant to but little Gary had started crying again and she'd known he needed more milk if there was any hope of him settling down for the night.

But he'd already had a bottle full.

That was when she knew someone was in the house. So she'd pretended to leave and waited.

It was the kid from next door! The worry and fear twisted in her belly. He'd been hiding in the baby's closet, which meant he'd probably seen her.

"Why was the boy hanging around the house?"

"I guess he heard the baby crying and came to see if he was okay."

"It's that retarded kid, isn't it?"

"He's not retarded. He's autistic." Please let him focus on the kid and not on her. *Please, please.*

"Can he tell that cop bitch he saw you?"

She thought about that for a second. She'd seen him staring out his bedroom windows before. Gabrielle always said he never talked the once or twice he came over. He just showed up in her backyard and watched her and the baby for a while without ever saying a word.

But that didn't mean he couldn't repeat exactly what he saw and heard if he chose.

"That's possible, I guess. But it was dark." Her heart started that painful thumping.

"Then he might not be able to ID you."

She licked her trembling lips. "I hope not."

He grabbed her by the hair and jerked her face toward his. "If he does, you're fucked. You know that, right? I won't save you."

"I know," she whimpered.

"We have to make sure this kid goes away. Permanently."

Maybe there was still a chance she could make this right. She swallowed back the lump of fear in her throat. "I understand. I've taken the first steps toward protecting our family."

"Is that right?"

She nodded, hope that he would see how smart she was blooming in her chest.

"If you fuck up again, they'll nail you for this. Do you have any idea what they'll do to you in prison? You'll never see the babies again. And I'll find me another woman. One who's smart and sexy and who doesn't fuck shit up!"

"I won't mess up," she promised, her heart pounding. *What if she already had?*

"Do it after the service," he ordered. "That bitch Harris is getting too close." He grabbed Sarah by the hair and pulled her face to his. "Remember, even if the police don't discover your fuckups, I know all your secrets. You mess this up and we're done."

That was the part that scared her the most.

20

Maple Road, First United Methodist Church, 5:00 p.m.

They barely got through the doors of the church before the service began. There was standing room only and she and Burnett were way at the back.

Jess left him gaping after her as she eased through the crowd until she was closer to the front. To Grayson and what was left of his family. She needed to see who surrounded him and how they reacted as the service played out.

Burnett stayed put at the back, no doubt appalled at her behavior.

Anyone in the church who knew her wouldn't be shocked. Anyone who didn't, well, what they thought didn't really matter.

The pews were lined with uniformed officers. Though the service was not for an officer, many had chosen to pay their respects dressed in their honor uniform. The choir loft filled with robed members was a spectacular sight.

Lawrence Grayson had certainly ensured a proper send-off for his wife.

Sergeant Jack Riley and his wife, Sarah, sat in the front pew with Grayson and his mother-in-law. But it was Sarah Riley who held Grayson's baby. Made sense, Jess supposed. If the child started to cry she could easily step out of the sanctuary. Grayson and his mother-in-law could remain focused on the somber event and their final moments with Gabrielle.

All in the sanctuary who weren't already standing rose to their feet, hymnals in hand, as a fervent rendition of "Amazing Grace" filled the room. Most knew the words or at least part of them. Jess knew the chorus and that was about it.

Church hadn't really been a part of her life since she was a kid.

She considered the young woman next to Sergeant Riley. Sarah expertly balanced the baby and the hymnal. Sarah was three years younger than Gabrielle had been; her two children were obviously with a sitter or relative since they weren't in attendance. While Jess watched, Riley put his arm around his wife's shoulder and leaned down and kissed her temple.

The two made a lovely couple. But there was something not so lovely and happy beneath the facade the Rileys showed the world. There was an ugliness that grew from control and rigidity and demands. Sarah Riley lived to please her husband. Maybe Jess was reading too much into what she'd learned and seen so far, but she couldn't let it go.

She had called the victim twice the night of the murder. Why? If she or she and her husband had committed this heinous murder what was the motive? Why would they kill a woman they seemed to adore?

Why was Gabrielle Grayson dead? What was the motive behind the act that took her life?

Until they had that answer, all the supposition and scenarios in the world wouldn't solve this case.

Jess's attention turned to the front of the church, where mountains of flower arrangements surrounded the ornate ivory coffin. Two large peace lilies anchored each side of the coffin. Jess shuddered at the memory of the last peace lily she'd seen. Eric Spears had sent it to Burnett's hospital room. Jess resisted the impulse to check her cell just to see if he'd sent her a text. She hadn't gotten anything else from him since the *pleasant dreams* message. He did love to play games. He'd rattled her. She couldn't deny it.

The cloying scent of the flowers reminded her of another event she'd just as soon forget. Her parents' funeral. There had been two large peace lilies that day, too.

Jess exiled the memories. She had a job to do here.

Two of Gabrielle's close friends who had flown in from Nashville spoke about what a beautiful and loving person she was. One went on to assure those listening that God had needed another angel in heaven and Gabrielle had gone to fill that glorious position.

Jess thought of what Devon had said about an angel taking the mommy. The only problem with that theory was that whoever killed Gabrielle Grayson didn't live in heaven. In fact, Jess was relatively sure, he would never so much as see heaven.

For another thirty minutes Jess watched the people gathered around Lawrence Grayson. Not one of them looked uncomfortable or out of place. None were missing.

Had one of these people killed Gabrielle? Was that very person going to be sharing their condolences with Grayson? Offering to help any way they could? That was the traditional thing to do down here, the offering of help part.

The baby grew restless and Sarah hurried out of the sanctuary with the baby in her arms and a bottle in her hand.

Several sets of fingerprints had been on that bottle found in the baby's crib. Gabrielle's and her baby's, of course. Devon's, his had been confirmed after he went missing, and one unknown.

Jess's gut was telling her that Gabrielle's killer not only knew her but was a cop. Her money was on Riley. Yet there was no match for the remaining set of prints. All BPD cops were in the database.

When the sanctuary had emptied, Jess caught up with Burnett once more. She was anxious to get out of here and back to work.

"You okay?" she asked.

Burnett was staring at her kind of funny. She instinctively reached up and swiped her cheek for any offending smudges.

He shrugged. "I was just thinking about how short life really is."

Jess knew he was thinking about finding that bomb in the Taurus. She looked out over the now empty pews, beyond the choir loft, and to the enormous wall of stained glass. Lil went to a church like this. The thought that she could be really sick and Jess might find herself at a service like this again in the near future suddenly made her knees feel a little wobbly.

"It really is." She swallowed at the lump of emotion now clogging her throat. Lily had been all upbeat last night when they talked. Dr. Collins had decided he wanted to run more tests and that maybe she wasn't just depressed.

Time to put the past hour and thoughts of illness and death out of her head. That idea should have had her laughing out loud. Death was a big part of her job.

She dug for her cell and checked for any missed calls. One from Lori. As Jess followed Burnett to his SUV, she put through a call to Lori.

"You learn something new?" she asked as soon as Lori answered.

"I got a call from one of Gabrielle's former coworkers. She wants to talk. This is one of the two who insisted they had nothing worth telling."

Jess snapped her seat belt into place. "When can we see her?"

"Right now."

"Meet me outside BPD."

"Will do."

Jess ended the call and turned to Burnett. "Another one of Gabrielle's coworkers wants to talk." She felt almost breathless with hope. Maybe this time, they would learn something beyond what a saint Gabrielle was.

"Keep me posted on the results. We need this one closed, Jess. The whole department wants this killer found."

"No one wants that more than me," Jess reminded him.

He hesitated a moment, then said, "So Wesley left today."

She had known that was coming. "He did."

"Dropped by for a visit last night, I hear."

"He did," Jess repeated.

"And?" Burnett sent her a look.

"We ate Chinese. We drank wine and we talked."

"He wants you back, doesn't he?"

Jess considered how best to answer that one. "He wants me to keep in touch."

"I knew it!" Burnett slammed the steering wheel with the heel of his hand. "I knew it from the moment he said your name that first night. He's still hung up on you."

It would be nice to say she wasn't getting any glee out of this but that would be a lie. "Who knows?"

Burnett whipped his fancy Mercedes into the nearest parking lot. He jammed the gear shift into park and turned to Jess. "Are you still hung up on him?" he demanded. "Just tell me the truth, Jess. If that's how you feel... I'll understand."

The set of his jaw told her he was mad as hell but the hurt in his eyes was about uncertainty and no small amount of desperation. "I am *not* still hung up on Wesley. I fully intend to keep in touch because it's the right thing to do. But I don't want to be with him."

The relief on Burnett's face, in his eyes, was almost her undoing. "Okay."

He faced forward once more, shifted into drive, and eased back onto the highway.

They rode in silence. She felt a little off balance and she was pretty sure he did too. He'd said a mouthful. Jess reached out and took his hand. He glanced at her and she smiled.

One step at a time.

Bessemer, 6:55 p.m.

Rochelle Arnold's home was in a comfortable neighborhood. She had three children, all boys under the age of ten, who were busy in the backyard attempting to dismantle the new tree fort their father had built for them. Jess felt confident that if the father wasn't home soon he would find a pile of lumber and a bucket of nails for all his hard work designing and constructing the elaborate structure.

"We appreciate you taking the time out of your busy schedule to see us, Mrs. Arnold."

"When the administrator first mentioned that the cops were asking questions about Gabrielle, I sort of blew it off." She pushed her brown hair behind her ears as if she were accustomed to wearing it out of the way. "I didn't want to speak badly of anyone. But then the rumors starting floating around about how she died and that there was still no real suspects and I felt guilty for not speaking up."

Jess's fingers tightened on her pencil. "We are very glad you decided to talk to us."

"If I'm speaking ill of anyone and I'm wrong," she went on, "I hope the Lord will forgive me."

Jess nodded when what she really wanted to do was tell her to get on with it.

"Until she decided to become a stay at home mom, I worked with Gabrielle. She was my supervisor. There were four of us who were pretty good pals. Took breaks together when we could. Even shopped and lunched together occasionally. Especially around the holidays. There was Gabrielle, Netty Winters, Sarah Riley, and me."

"Sounds like you were close," Jess nudged.

"We covered for each other when things came up. If I needed to be off to take one of the boys to the doctor, one of them would take my shift and then I'd take theirs.

It made life a lot simpler and the paper pushers like the administrator always appreciate our working things out so they don't have to.

"Anyway, two years ago last month Gabrielle learned from one of the patients who was a recovering opiate addict that Sarah had asked him repeatedly about his drug connection. Sometimes recovering addicts will say things like that because they're desperate."

"Was an investigation conducted into his accusation?" Jess asked, anticipation sending her pulse into high gear.

"Gabrielle asked Sarah about it and she laughed it off, so Gabrielle dismissed the whole business."

Jess wanted to ask more specific questions but she held her tongue and let the woman talk.

"A few weeks later," Rochelle went on, "there was another incident. It was family visitation day and one of the patients had gotten his younger brother to slip him a few OCs without his parents finding out. When the pills went missing he lost it. He had to be sedated, but he insisted over and over that Sarah had stolen his OC."

"OC meaning OxyContin," Jess confirmed.

Rochelle nodded. "The coincidences were adding up to a situation Gabrielle couldn't overlook so she confronted Sarah. We were all tore up about it. Sarah cried and claimed she had hurt her back and that she'd just needed a couple to get through it. But Gabrielle didn't believe her. She insisted Sarah have a drug test." Rochelle snorted. "She did and it was clean. No OC. Sarah admitted then that the drugs were for her husband. He was still recovering from an old accident and she said the doctor was skimping on his pain meds."

"Sarah wasn't charged or dismissed?" Jess asked,

startled that she'd not found this in the background research conducted on Sarah Riley.

"Gabrielle felt sorry for her. She knew how pushy Sarah's husband could be, so she made a deal with Sarah. Sarah would resign and Gabrielle wouldn't put anything about the incident in her personnel file. Sarah pleaded with her not to tell their husbands. Jack would lose his job and they'd be homeless. Not to mention he would kill her if he found out she'd told anyone about getting him prescription meds."

"Sarah was really that terrified of her husband?" Maybe this woman could confirm the abuse.

Rochelle laughed but there was nothing amusing about the sound. "Oh yeah. She didn't talk about it much but I picked up on it."

The woman's assumptions weren't proof but her statement backed up Jess's instincts. "What did Gabrielle do about Sarah's request?"

"Gabrielle agreed not to tell as long as Sarah made sure Jack started following the doctor's orders instead of his own selfish needs."

"We have random drug tests for just that sort of problem," Jess said. She was aware there were ways around almost any test but she couldn't see the guy getting away with it for more than two years.

"He was in an accident," Rochelle suggested. "All he has to do is keep a script for the occasional pain killer of his choice and he's covered if he gets hit with a test. Addicts do it all the time. They explain away a heavy concentration with the excuse that the night before had been a rough one for pain and they'd doubled up on the dose. People walk around believing that if a doctor prescribes it that it must be okay. They don't realize they're killing themselves and endangering others."

"Did this incident change Gabrielle and Sarah's friendship?"

Rochelle shook her head. "No way. Their husbands were partners. And Gabrielle felt like Sarah was the sister she never had. The two were closer than the rest of us. Sarah and Jack introduced her to the man she married. The father of her child. There was a strong connection."

"Do you believe Sarah did as Gabrielle asked and urged her husband to get help?"

Rochelle shrugged. "I sure hope so. Can you imagine your partner having a drug problem you didn't know about when you're depending on him to provide your backup? A partner like that could get you killed."

And suddenly, as if lightning had struck right out of a clear blue sky, Jess understood they had one possible, immensely disturbing motive.

What she was about to ask could be construed as leading the witness, but Jess wanted this woman's opinion based on her work in the field. "Mrs. Arnold, based on your experience working with recovering addicts, what steps would have been necessary for Sarah's husband to have gotten clean of his addiction to pain meds?"

"It's a tough drug to beat and, depending on how much he was taking, it could be extremely dangerous to stop cold turkey. The best results are seen in those who commit to rehab. At least thirty days followed by long-term counseling. He would need to carry a card indicating he had an opiate addiction. It takes work."

"Would his partner not be able to see there was a problem? After all, he's a cop. We know the signs to look for."

"You may know all kinds of signs and symptoms," Rochelle agreed, "but you might not necessarily see what's right in front of you. Some people have serious addictions and their family and coworkers never know. The desperation that accompanies needing something that badly and having to jump through hoops to get it and hide it from the world will make a person do things they would never ever do otherwise."

Slowly but surely the pieces started to fall into place. "Did you ever know of Gabrielle using drugs herself?"

Arnold laughed, the real thing this time. "You're kidding, right?" She gave a firm shake of her head. "Gabrielle was the most anti-drug person you will ever meet. She lost a brother to drugs when he was in high school. She hardly took an aspirin when she had a headache. No way she'd touch anything like that."

After thanking the lady, Jess couldn't get out of the house fast enough.

"Harper told me what an asshole Riley is," Lori said as they climbed into her Mustang.

"We need to get a tail on Riley." Jess's cell clanged. As if he'd heard her request, it was Harper. "Harris."

"Chief, we got the phone records. Gabrielle made a call to Dr. Baron on Saturday afternoon, just like she said. On Sunday, Gabrielle made one call and received two calls shortly after her husband returned to duty that night. All three were Sarah Riley."

"That corroborates what Sarah told us." Didn't make Jess feel any better. Maybe the two had been talking about vacations.

"There was another, much later," Harper said. "Gabrielle also made another call at eleven o'clock that night."

Jess frowned. "Wait. That can't be right." Time of death was estimated at somewhere between nine and midnight. It was possible, she supposed, but that was stretching it. "Who did she call at eleven?"

"Jack Riley."

A jolt of adrenaline slammed Jess. "You and Cook trade out shifts. I want one of you watching Riley twenty-four/seven." Now they were getting somewhere.

"Yes, ma'am."

"Anything new on the search for Devon?" she asked before he could end the call. Jess knew there wasn't. Harper or Cook would have called. But she couldn't help hoping.

"A few more false sightings, but nothing else."

"Thanks, Sergeant. Keep me posted on who's got Riley under surveillance."

Following this lead wouldn't win her any friends in the department, but she knew in her bones they'd just been given a motive for Gabrielle's murder.

"Where we headed now?" Lori asked.

"To the home of Sarah and Jack Riley. I have a few more questions for Sarah."

"The shit's going to hit the fan as soon as we cross that line."

"Yeah, well, I do have a reputation to maintain."

21

The light was back.

It was real bright.

It hurt Devon's eyes.

He was so hungry. The angel had given him a drink and some bites of sandwich last time the light came. But that was a long time ago.

His belly growled as the light got closer. He knew he should be scared but he was too tired.

He didn't know how long he'd been in this dark place but it felt like a real long time.

Leslie had probably quit looking for him by now. She was prob'ly sad.

He'd heard the kids in the house crying again. And the man and woman yelling at each other. Once when he woke up he thought he heard the blond lady cop talking but he prob'ly dreamed it.

The angel put the light down on the ground by Devon's feet. He heard a tearing sound. More tape, he was pretty sure. He blinked. Tried so see but his eyes wouldn't work good. The light made them hurt. More of that yucky tape was stuck to his face. This time over his eyes.

He didn't like it but he couldn't say anything. He was pretty sure it wouldn't matter anyway.

The angel was pulling at his arms. Dragging him. Where were they going? Was the angel taking him home?

Maybe he was going to heaven. Tears made his eyes sting. He didn't want to go . . . he wanted his sister.

Devon went inside himself.

22

Caldwell Avenue, 8:30 p.m.

Lori rapped on the town house door again.

Even at this hour Jess felt as if she were melting, especially in this borrowed black dress. She'd ignored four calls from Burnett. He hadn't left any voice mails, which meant nothing was wrong. He just wanted to know where the hell she was and what she was doing. Oh yes, and when she would be home.

Apparently her assigned tail had lost them. It wasn't on purpose. But there was no time to waste.

Speaking of wasting time, Jess did the knocking this time. "Maybe they went to a wake or something for family and close friends that we weren't invited to."

"Or dinner," Lori suggested.

"What's that?" Jess teased.

"Something we've both missed this evening."

Jess tried to recall if she'd had lunch.

The door to the left of their position on the sidewalk opened.

Jess prepared to apologize for all the loud banging when the old man derailed her by blatantly sizing her up in her too tight, too short black sheath. She'd had to borrow this dress from Lori. That had become a habit lately.

"I'm Deputy Chief Jess Harris," she announced, drawing the man's attention from her legs to her face, "and this is Detective Lori Wells. We're here to speak with Sarah Riley."

"Garland Haines. Lived here for fifteen years. Been neighbors with the Rileys for five of those years. They're not home," he groused. "If they were, you'd hear 'em yelling at each other," he rambled on. "Trust me, they're not home."

"Thank you." Jess gave him a smile. "We'll just be on our way then."

"Another thing," he added, "if they were home all that banging would've had both their brats screaming at the tops of their lungs."

What a friendly neighbor. "I guess it's a good thing they're not home then."

"Most of the time I don't care. I'm watching TV or whatever and I can't hear 'em. But what gets me riled up is when the bawling starts in the middle of the night. And she don't do nothing about it. What kind of mother does that?"

The last nabbed her attention. "Does that happen often?"

"If it happens once it's too often," he griped. "Like this weekend. That youngest one of hers started bellowing around ten and by ten thirty the other one was squalling, too. I banged on her door like you did just now but she didn't answer. I checked the street and her car was gone. She'd done gone off and left those two babies in the house alone. She's done it before. I told her if it happened again I was calling the police. So I called her husband. He's a cop after all and they're his brats. He guaranteed it wouldn't happen again and it ain't happened since."

"Mr. Haines, can you recall what night that was?" The adrenaline was already charging through Jess's veins.

"It was Sunday night. I know 'cause I went to a church supper with my sister. I was watching the ten o'clock news when the squalling started. Is that certain enough for you? I missed nearly all of it banging on that damned door and calling her husband."

"Thank you, Mr. Haines. We're sorry to have bothered you."

"When you're an old man who lives alone," he called out as they walked away, "you get used to being bothered. Every damned thing bothers you."

When they were loaded in the Mustang, Jess said, "I need to go back to the church."

First United Methodist Church, 9:49 p.m.

While they waited for the minister to arrive and unlock the door, Jess paced in front of the main entrance. She had spoken to Burnett and given their location. He was not happy that she'd avoided his first four calls.

Lori had checked with Harper. He hadn't located Sarah Riley, but her husband was on duty with the GTF.

"It's official, by the way," Lori said, drawing Jess from her musings.

"I'm sorry, what was that?"

"It's official," she repeated. "I'm moving into Harper's place this weekend. Even if his son hates me."

Jess winced. "I take it last night didn't go so well." The last she heard Lori and Harper were picking up his son after work.

"He wouldn't talk to me or even look at me." She groaned. "All he wanted to do was stay in his dad's arms. It was just awful."

"Give him time. When he warms up to you he'll want to be in your arms all the time. Then you'll have something to groan about."

"I don't know." She shook her head. "Maybe." She leaned against the wall next to the front entrance of the church. "I realized watching those boys this afternoon that having boys in the house is way different from having girls."

Jess laughed. "My sister says boys and girls are as different as daylight and dark. Be patient. It'll work out if you give it time. Time is the key." To most things, Jess reminded herself.

"At least there's only one kid I have to make like me," Lori interjected.

"Until you decide to have one or two of your own," Jess pointed out.

A car rolled into the parking lot.

"Saved by the minister," Lori said with a laugh.

"Notice I'm not laughing," Jess said.

"Not to worry, Chief," Lori promised, "I have no plans like that for a long, long time."

"Mmm-hmm." Not more than two weeks ago Jess had heard something similar about moving in with Harper.

The minister hustled up the steps to the front entrance of the church, keys in hand. "I apologize for keeping you ladies waiting. I was all the way across town."

"Not a problem, sir. We appreciate you coming on short notice."

He pushed the door inward and motioned for them to go inside. "Might I ask why you needed to come back?" He turned on the overhead lights as they entered. "Did you leave something at the service?"

"I just need to see about something..." Jess hurried along the aisle until she reached the spot where she had stood during the service.

"Here we go." She moved into the row where the Graysons and the Rileys had sat during the service.

On the pew right where Sarah had left it was the hymnal she had used.

Jess retrieved the largest evidence bag she carried. With a gloved hand she placed the song book in the bag, careful to touch only the very edges of the cover.

"You won't mind if I borrow this, will you?" she asked the minister.

He looked confused but then shook his head. "Of course. Keep it as long as necessary." He chuckled nervously. "Just remember where it came from."

"Oh I will, sir. You can rest assured."

Jess thanked him again and then hurried to Lori's Mustang.

"The lab?" she asked.

"The lab," Jess confirmed.

If Sarah Riley had been in the Grayson home the night Gabrielle was murdered there was only one possibility that they had discovered so far for placing any person, besides Gabrielle and Devon, there. The unidentified set of prints on the bottle. Those same unknown prints had been found on the handle of the milk jug in the fridge.

And if they could prove Sarah was in the house that night, was her husband helping to cover for her as she had covered for him when she lost her job over the OxyContin?

Jess thought about the seemingly loving couple she had watched in the church today. With two kids, it couldn't be easy surviving on one income. And with a drug problem to boot, how were they managing to hold it together? Their neighbor had mentioned the two yelling at each other. He insinuated it was a routine business.

But did a volatile relationship or a drug addiction lead to murder?

Could Sarah Riley be Devon Chambers's angel? Or was she just doing what she always did and protecting the devil himself?

23

Conroy Road, 11:50 p.m.

It had been a hell of a long day. Dan was beat. Why couldn't Jess have rented a first-floor apartment? When he reached the landing outside the door of her new garage apartment he found her sitting in the darkness on a vintage patio glider. She wore that used-to-be-pink, one-size-fits-all cotton robe Wells had given her and her hair had obviously air-dried after her bath. He liked the way it curled and twirled when it dried naturally. Made him want to run his fingers through the silky strands.

In the moonlight she looked soft and cozy sitting there cradling a glass of red wine. His mouth watered with the desire to taste hers. But that would have to wait. He would respect her wishes about keeping work and *them* separate. As hard as that proved every single day.

"You got any more of that?" he asked hopefully.

She hitched her head toward the door. "On the counter. Help yourself."

Dan went inside and found the bottle of pinot noir. He searched the cupboards until he found another wineglass. After pouring himself a nice serving he returned to the deck and sat down next to Jess.

"I'm envious." God, she smelled good. Like fresh lavender and natural vanilla. "You've shed your deputy chief clothes and gotten comfortable. I haven't even made it home yet." He needed a shower and a shave.

"Where've you been all night?" She sipped her wine. Seemed content to stare off into the darkness as if she had no desire to talk and have him or anything else disturb her moment of relaxation.

"I had a charity fund-raiser for the historic foundation."

"Ah, one of Katherine's pet projects."

His mother had served on Birmingham's historic foundation for nearly three decades. Dan helped out when he could. It made his mother happy and let his dad off the hook once in a while. There was a limit to how many times a retired man could be forced to wear a monkey suit again. His father had worn a jacket and tie to work every day for as long as Dan could remember. He'd retired just last year. He deserved his freedom from the three-piece ensemble.

"They do a lot of good work."

Jess made a noncommittal sound. She and his mother would never see eye to eye on the sun rising in the east, much less anything else.

"I like my new landlord," she said. "I came home at ten and he was still out there working in his flower beds. Making the place look pretty. Last night when he was working on my door I mentioned in passing that I wanted a glider on the deck and, voilà, I came home this evening and here it is. He left a note saying it had been gathering dust in the garage."

"What a guy," Dan agreed. "You'll have to make him a fruitcake for Christmas."

"I might buy him one," Jess tossed back. "If I made him one he'd hate me."

A comfortable silence drifted between them for a bit.

"The other prints on the baby's bottle belong to Sarah Riley."

Dan shifted so that he faced her. "Is that right?"

"It is." She had another swallow of her wine. "She'll try to say she probably touched the bottle when the two families had lunch together that day but I'm not letting her off that easily."

Jess had brought him up to speed on Sarah Riley's undocumented work troubles as well as her neighbor's complaints about her children crying in the middle of the night Sunday. A whole hell of a lot of circumstantial evidence but not enough to charge her with anything beyond child endangerment.

"What's your plan?" He tasted the wine. Made a sound of approval. "Nice choice."

"It's a housewarming gift to myself. The glasses are from Wesley."

Dan scrutinized the stemmed glass he held. "I guess I'm behind. I haven't gotten you a present yet."

"Don't worry." She finished off her glass. "I'm making a list. It's the least you can do after I maxed out my MasterCard at your friend's shop."

"My mother's friend."

"Oh yeah. How could I forget?" She sighed. "My plan. Well, the more direct path would be to wrangle a confession out of Sarah Riley, but that's not going to happen because I'm not sure she killed Gabrielle Grayson. More likely she's been protecting her husband. For years."

"And how did you come to those conclusions?" He pointed to her glass. "Refill?"

She passed it him. "Yes."

"Hold that thought."

Back in the kitchen he added a generous portion to Jess's glass and splashed a little more in his own. Before rejoining her outside, he shed his jacket and tie. Enough of the monkey suit today for him too.

"You were saying," he prompted as he settled beside her once more and she took her glass.

"I can't see her holding Gabrielle's body still and sawing off her head." Jess shuddered "I mean, could she possibly have the stomach to do the job? Sawing off a head is no easy task. Not with a handsaw, and that's what we believe was used."

"Good point." Damn. The idea that one of his cops could be responsible for this... or even covering for someone else was unthinkable.

"I wish I'd had more opportunity to observe Sarah. Maybe I can shake her up tomorrow. See a more unguarded side. I'm interviewing her at nine downtown. You might want to be around."

"Which of the husbands do you believe did it? Hers or Gabrielle's?" He couldn't believe he'd just asked that question.

"Not Gabrielle's. The lieutenant has no idea who did this. He's in shock or denial or both. The avalanche is coming, he can feel it but he can't figure out from which direction it's barreling his way. He's waiting for me to show him. That's what people who don't want to see do. They wait for someone else to show them and then the someone else gets blamed."

As unfair as it was, she was right about that.

"What about the two victims from Norwood?"

"Territorial killings. Low-level drug distributors who set up shop in the wrong territory. Our perp in the Grayson case used them to try to throw us off his scent. He somehow learned about the hit. Allen admitted that he knew about it days ago. You know damn well how the grapevine works. Our perp hears about it, cuts off their heads, and does a little scene staging and we're supposed to believe Gabrielle's case is connected to that one. Just another gang hit. The problem is, he failed to set up a proper motive. He should've known better. He's a cop." She savored another swallow of wine.

"You're pretty certain it's Sergeant Riley." It wasn't a question. "Before you go public with this, you need to be absolutely certain, Jess. Everyone in the department is watching you right now, waiting to see where your loyalties lie. Do this right and you'll be a hero. Make a mistake and... well you know. The whole department will want to see you pay."

She made a derisive sound. "I'm damned certain it's him. But I have no real evidence. No motive I can confirm. I can't even place him at the scene that night. But I know he did it. Maybe his wife helped him. They did it to protect his secret drug addiction. But I can't prove it."

"So what's your plan?"

"I'll make him and his wife believe that I have a witness who can identify the killer and that I'm about to make an arrest. Force one or both to react."

"What's the bait you're planning on using?"

"My witness, of course."

"But you don't have a witness."

"Riley doesn't know that. For all he knows we found Devon and Devon saw everything. Unless Riley and his wife took Devon," she qualified. "If that's the case, they still can't be sure I don't have someone else who saw something. That's the thing about an emotion-based act of murder. You just can't think clearly enough to cover all your bases at that pivotal moment."

"True."

Silence settled between them again. Dan allowed enough time to pass to back up the point he was about to make.

"Notice I didn't ask what role you planned to play in this operation." She'd been on his back about the whole overprotective business. He really was trying to lighten up. It wasn't going as well as he'd hoped. The idea that she would be dead right now if that Taurus had started twisted in his gut.

"You didn't ask," Jess agreed, "but you were thinking about it."

"Was not."

"Yes you were."

"Maybe I was just a little."

"My job is to plant the seeds of fear and doubt in the interview with Sarah and then we'll wait and watch for the reaction."

"As long as Harper or Wells is with you at all times," he reminded her.

She made an agreeable sound.

"You mentioned Allen having prior knowledge of that double homicide. Is he a suspect, too?"

"Nah, he's just a jerk. He hates my guts and wants me gone."

"He told you he hates your guts?"

"In a roundabout way."

Dan would be talking to that cocky SOB. Whatever his beef with Jess, Allen had better learn how to respect his superiors—all his superiors. Or else.

"I imagine when word gets around that I'm trying to pin a murder rap on one of BPD's finest I'll have a lot more fans like him." Jess turned to Dan. "You sure you didn't see all this coming and you hired me to be the ax man? Lopez said we had some bad cops."

"You're friends with Lopez now?" Dan shook his head. "You have a knack for attracting some very strange people, Jess."

"Evidently I do. I was hoping I'd hear from him again about these latest vics."

Dan couldn't say he hoped for the same. "As much as I despise the idea of having that kind of cop in my department, if you're right about Riley," Dan promised, "he's going down. What others think is irrelevant." The fury built to a full blaze inside him. "Riley won't get off easy because he's a cop. I'll see that he goes all the way down."

"It helps to know you've got my back on this one."

"Jess." He reached out, caressed her cheek. "I'll always have your back."

It was all he could do not to kiss her. She didn't turn away or try to evade his touch. But she had asked him not to go there until the case was done.

For her, he could wait.

He dropped his hand away. "You and Sylvia seem to be hitting it off."

"She's not so bad. She just likes making everyone think she is."

"That's Sylvia." He finished his wine.

"One of these days you'll have to tell me about your marriage to her sister. Feels like there's a story there."

"One of these days," he promised. "Speaking of sisters, how's Lil?"

"The doctor's doing more tests. I spoke to her tonight and she sounds tired. So not like herself. I'm really worried, Dan. This could be bad."

"Lily is a very strong woman. Just like you. She'll get through this." He wished he knew something more original to say but what he said was true. Frankly he didn't know any one stronger than Jess and Lily.

"Tomorrow is going to be a long one," Jess murmured, almost too softly for him to hear.

He worried that she was more right than she knew.

Putting a fellow cop's head on the chopping block was a bold, unpopular move.

Dan would lay odds on Jess's instincts every time.

Her cell rang. She fished it out of her pocket and checked the screen. She sat up. The glider swung askew. "Leslie, is everything all right?"

The Chambers girl? Tension cranked up inside him.

"We'll be right there."

Jess ended the call and shot to her feet. "It's Devon."

Ice trickled in his veins. "Has he been found?" *God almighty let him be alive.*

"He just showed up at the door of his own house."

24

Whispering Stream Drive, Friday,
August 6, 1:30 a.m.

Devon Chambers was dirty and he had tape burns around his mouth, his wrists, and his ankles. He was starving and possibly a little dehydrated, but otherwise he appeared to be fine.

At the moment he was at the kitchen table gobbling down a second bowl of his favorite cereal and milk. Jess and Leslie stood at the far end of the room in the doorway leading to the living room.

"That was the first thing he said to me," Leslie said without taking her eyes off her brother. *"Fruity Pebbles, please."* She swiped at a lone tear. "I was so glad to see him I just grabbed him up and hugged him to death." She turned to Jess. "Then I called you."

The boy had sneaked through the fence that separated the Grayson property from his own yard and then he'd climbed up the trellis and into his room. The officer on surveillance duty out front never spotted him. Devon had stealth down to a science.

"He told you that the angel put him under the dead mommy's house?" Jess kept her voice down for fear of spooking him. "And that he kept pulling and tugging until he got the tape loose on his hands and that's how he freed himself?"

Leslie nodded. "He said he'd been trying to get loose since the angel took him." She shrugged. "Maybe it took all this time to get the tape loose enough."

Possible. "But he couldn't tell you where he'd been before the angel moved him to the Graysons' home?"

"Under the screaming mommy's house was all he could tell me."

Jess mulled over the answer. "You think he'll talk to me now?"

"Maybe I can ask him stuff and you can listen," Leslie suggested.

That would work. "I'll make you a list."

While Devon finished his cereal, Jess quickly scribbled a list of questions for the boy.

Leslie placed a small can of potted meat and crackers next to her brother's empty bowl. "I thought you might like this, too."

"Yummy!" He snapped the lid off the can of meat and, using the crackers like dipping chips, had a bite.

Leslie made a face at Jess. "He loves the stuff."

Jess sat down at the other end of the table. Devon paused in his eating, but he didn't look at her. Leslie picked up the list Jess had made and sat down close to her brother.

"Devon, when you were under the screaming mommy's

house, did you hear any other people? Like a daddy or kids?"

Devon licked a cracker and nodded. "A mean daddy. Two crying kids."

Leslie stole a glance at Jess. "Did the angel give you any food or water while you were there?"

He nodded again. "Sometimes."

"Did you see the angel?"

"The light was shining in my eyes. I couldn't see nothing."

Shit! Jess needed to add a question. She couldn't exactly write it down and pass it to Leslie without risking Devon shutting down. It was a miracle he'd spoken at all in front of her.

Leslie's cell phone lay on the table. Maybe there was a way. Jess retrieved her phone and sent Leslie a text with the next question.

The girl's phone signaled she had received the text and Leslie checked the screen. She set the phone aside and asked the questions. "What kind of kids were crying, Dev? Boys or girls?"

He shrugged.

Leslie waited a second then asked, "Big kids or little kids?"

He ate the last cracker and turned to his sister. "Baby kids."

Adrenaline had Jess's heart thundering in her ears. Sounded like the Riley family to her. Their neighbor had said they screamed at each other all the time and that the kids cried frequently.

"What kind of light shined in your face, Dev?"

He frowned. "A flashlight, silly. Like I keep in my secret hiding place. Angels have flashlights, too."

Leslie had told Jess that his secret hiding place was under the house. He'd been trying to get away from the angel so he'd hidden under his house. That, Jess presumed, had given this so-called angel, who she suspected was either Sarah or Jack Riley, the idea for hiding him under the floor of their own home. It was the perfect solution until one or both decided what to do with him. Killing a child likely wasn't as palatable as having murdered a grown woman. Case in point, they'd left the Grayson baby sleeping in his crib the night they murdered and mutilated his mother.

"This angel wasn't too smart."

Jess's attention snapped back to Devon.

"What do you mean, Devon?" Leslie asked.

"The angel put me under the wrong house." He made a face. "*This* is my house."

Jess had a bad feeling the angel had hoped Devon would die under the Graysons' house. The Rileys weren't fools. They knew Jess was on to them. Clearly they'd moved Devon to prevent his being found under their own home. With Gabrielle's murder still too fresh, Lieutenant Grayson would be in no hurry to move back into his home. There was no telling when anyone would have gone under the floor over there for any reason. If Devon hadn't worked his way loose while he still had the strength, he would have fallen victim to their evil plan.

Leslie glanced at the list Jess had made once more. "How did you know this was an angel? Did you see wings?"

Devon shook his head. "No silly! I smelled the flowers. Angels smell like flowers."

"Who told you that, Devon?" Leslie asked, going down the list.

"My teacher told me. When our mommy went to

heaven. He said people gave flowers to her because heaven smells like flowers and that way the angels knew where to find her."

Leslie looked to Jess again. She didn't know what else to say or do. She'd asked all the questions.

Jess could see how he'd made the leap. If heaven smelled like flowers, then the angels who lived there were bound to smell like flowers, too. Harper's comment about the shampoo in the Graysons' shower...Gardenias... elbowed its way into her thoughts. Even though they hadn't gotten any clear prints off the bottle, they knew the killer had washed off in the shower since some of Gabrielle's blood had been found in the drain. If the killer used the shampoo that might be why Devon smelled flowers while he was hiding in the closet in the baby's room.

"I don't want that angel to come to get me again."

Fear made his voice sound smaller. The happy-go-lucky little boy was gone now. Devon was scared. He had a right to be scared; he'd been traumatized.

"Why would the angel come back again?" Jess heard herself ask.

Devon blinked. Stared at her. She held her breath. Prayed he wouldn't go into his shell.

He held up his arm. "I got the angel scratch. I think that's bad."

Going for broke, Jess dug around in her bag and retrieved her shield. She slid it down the table toward Devon. "You keep this with you at all times, Devon, and the angel won't bother you."

Hesitant at first, he reached out and picked up the shield. He studied it closely, then he looked at Jess. "You sure that'll work?"

"Absolutely," Jess promised. "You can clip it on your shirt"—she tugged at the collar of her blouse—"right there."

Leslie helped her brother clip the shield on the neck of his T-shirt.

"Now. The angel will know you're untouchable."

Devon frowned, then he held up his arm. "What about this?"

Jess beamed a smile at him. "If you and your sister will come with me, I can take you to see a doctor who knows all about angel scratches."

Cooper Green, 2:58 a.m.

Dan thought he had seen it all.

Obviously he had been wrong.

Jess and Sylvia were smiling and fussing over the kid as if they had been doing that sort of thing their whole lives. Two women who swore they didn't have time for children.

He watched Jess smile as Devon drew pictures of what he saw that night. Sylvia had attended to his scratches and checked him over thoroughly. The kid was safe and that was what mattered. He hadn't given them much to go on. The angel smelled like flowers. Jess had connected the idea to the shampoo she'd had logged into evidence.

Jess glanced at Dan and he straightened away from the door frame. As she and Sylvia started his way, leaving Leslie to entertain Devon, Dan stepped out into the corridor.

Sylvia closed the door to the exam room.

"Leslie's going to help Devon change into clean clothes," Jess explained.

"I'll test samples of the dirt and other trace elements on his clothes," Sylvia picked up where Jess left off. "If he was held in the Rileys' crawlspace you might be able to use those test results for confirmation."

"I sent a text to Cook," Jess went from there. "He's arranging for an evidence tech to accompany him to the Grayson home, where they'll attempt to find the tape Devon removed when he freed himself."

The so-called angel had felt confident taking the kid there, since the crime scene had been released. Bastard.

Leslie opened the door. "We're ready in here."

Sylvia looked from Dan to Jess. "I'm going to get on those tests."

"Thank you, Dr. Baron," Jess said.

Sylvia nodded and disappeared into the exam room.

Those two had made friends, Dan decided. "Where's Harper?"

"I've got him watching the Rileys." She glanced at Devon and his sister. "We need these two tucked away in a safe place until this is over."

"Agreed." Dan dug for his phone. "I'll make the arrangements. We'll drop them off and then I'm taking you home."

Jess sagged against the wall. "You won't get any argument from me."

25

Conroy Road, 7:30 a.m.

Two hours of sleep had hardly been worth the trouble. Jess lugged her bag onto her shoulder and descended the stairs. Two cups of dark roast had not done the trick. She still felt hungover. She glanced at her landlord's house as she shuffled to her car. He hadn't complained about her random comings and goings so far. She hoped he continued to be a good sport about it.

She held up her keys and started to punch the fob to unlock the Audi. The driver's side door—her door—was ajar. Moving with caution, Jess eased closer. The door had definitely been opened.

"Well, damn."

She backed up a few steps just in case and put in a call to Lori for a ride. Then she called Burnett to have whoever was working the investigation into the Taurus tampering to come pick up her Audi.

This shit was getting old.

BPD, 9:05 a.m.

"I appreciate you coming in this morning, Mrs. Riley," Jess said. "I hope you didn't have any trouble finding a sitter for your children."

"They're with my mother and father. They love going to visit their grandparents."

Thank God. "Let's get started then. You stated that the last time you saw Gabrielle alive was on Sunday when you and your husband had lunch with her and her husband, is that correct?"

"Yes."

Sarah Riley was as calm as a cucumber and her husband was furious she was being questioned again. Burnett had sequestered Sergeant Riley and his superior, Deputy Chief Waters, to the conference room. Harper had sent Jess a text since she'd entered the interview room to let her know that Lieutenant Grayson had arrived to show his support for the Rileys.

"You may find some of these questions repetitive," Jess warned, "but it's important that we're thorough."

Sarah Riley nodded her understanding.

"Did Gabrielle appear to be worried about anything or anxious in any way?"

"Not at all."

Sarah really was a petite woman. Maybe five two and ninety or so pounds. Far too small to physically control a woman Gabrielle's size unless the OxyContin had already kicked in, and even then handling her dead weight wouldn't be easy for someone Sarah's size.

This morning she was calm and poised. Where was the

cowering, beaten-down housewife who feared her husband? Today she wasn't even nervous.

Abuse victims often covered for their abusers. Fear that no one else would love them or that there would be even more severe repercussions was often the motive. But sometimes the victim enjoyed the cycle of fighting and making up. Could Sarah Riley be one of those? Was she protecting that bond?

Maybe.

"And when you spoke later that evening? No indication that anything was wrong?"

"Our conversations were short but she sounded just fine."

"You and Gabrielle were very close," Jess went on. "You knew each other well. You stated that you even took vacations together."

"Yes." Sarah carefully resisted adding any other details. She answered only the question Jess asked.

Her husband had coached her well.

"You met on the job when you were both nurses at the New Life Rehabilitation Center."

"Yes."

Jess flipped through her notes. "You harassed patients for their drug connections and even went so far as to steal some drugs, isn't that right?"

Sarah blinked and her expression closed. "I don't know what you're talking about."

"Really." Jess made a surprised sound and pretended to reread some of her notes. "I have statements from several of your coworkers that suggests otherwise."

That deer trapped in the headlights look abruptly vanished and determination took its place. "They were jealous of my relationship with Gabrielle. You can't believe what they say. If those accusations were true Gabrielle would have written me up and I would have been fired and charged with a crime."

"So Gabrielle didn't tell you that you had to resign?"

"I resigned after my first daughter was born because I really wanted to be home with her."

"I see." Jess jotted a few words on her notepad. "So the notations Gabrielle made in your personnel file about suspected drug abuse were untrue."

Fury lit in Sarah's eyes. "I have no idea what you're talking about. Gabrielle was my friend. She would never have made up lies like that."

"Maybe I misread the notes. I've read so much about you and your husband that it's just all running together." Jess shook her head. "Does your husband still have a problem with OxyContin? I noted where the drug was found in several of the required drug tests here at BPD."

"What're you talking about? My husband doesn't have a problem with drugs or anything else. Why are you saying these things?"

Jess decided to take a chance. She leaned across the table. "I know what you did, Sarah. We found your prints. Your neighbor told us about you leaving the kids at home alone on Sunday and the timing just happens to coincide with the timing of Gabrielle's murder. You were there, Sarah. I know you were. Gabrielle didn't call Jack at eleven that night, you did. Using her phone. Did you tell him there was a problem? What did he do, Sarah? Something you're afraid to tell me? I'm prepared to give you until four o'clock today to get your story straight but after that, the deal is off the table. You'll be picked up and charged with first-degree murder."

Confusion and fear claimed her features. "What deal? I don't know what you're talking about. Gabrielle never called my husband! I was at Gabrielle's house all the time. Of course you found my fingerprints there. And yes, I left the house Sunday night. Jack and I had a big fight on the phone so I went to see him. Ask anyone on shift with him that night, they saw him come out to my car but we never left the street. We just sat there in the dark and talked. Anyone on duty could have looked out the window and seen the car."

There was a new revelation. No matter, Jess shook her head. "Save yourself, Sarah, so you can be there for your children. Otherwise you'll go down with him."

"I think I want a lawyer now." Fury twisted the woman's face.

Jess closed her notepad and set her pencil aside. "I understand. You're afraid." Jess pushed to her feet. "But keep in mind that we have a witness, Sarah. He saw everything."

With that Jess headed for the door.

"Wait."

Victory roared through Jess's veins. She turned back to the woman who could help them nail Gabrielle's killer.

"You're wrong," she said, to Jess's surprise. "Jack would never hurt anyone that way. He loves me and he loves our children too much. He worships Larry and thought the world of Gabrielle. You're wrong, Chief Harris." Sarah picked up her purse. "You should be ashamed of yourself for trying to ruin an innocent man's life. A *cop's* life and career."

Stunned at the about-face, Jess opened the door and let her go. "Just remember," she said as Sarah walked past her, "you have until four o'clock today before I take my witness and the evidence we have to the DA. After that I can't help you."

Sarah walked out.

Damn it. Harper was right. The woman acted like some weird Stepford wife.

Burnett joined her in the hall. He'd watched the interview from the viewing room. "I've sent a cruiser to keep an eye on the grandparents and the children."

"I was just about to set that up myself."

"Chief Harris."

Jess turned to find Lieutenant Grayson striding her way. Judging by the outrage on his face and in his posture she was in for a battle. "Lieutenant."

Grayson acknowledged Dan. "Chief Burnett."

Burnett shook his head. "Lieutenant, it would be in your best interest if you stayed clear of this mess."

Jess spoke before Grayson could. "Let him have his say. There are a few things I need to clear up with him."

"All right." Burnett turned to Grayson. "Don't make me regret that decision."

"I don't know what the hell you're thinking, but Jack and Sarah Riley are friends of my family. I wouldn't have gotten through the past few days without their support. How dare you make them feel like suspects!"

"They are suspects, Lieutenant." Jess wasn't going to sugarcoat this for the man. Not anymore. She'd given him some time to grieve, but right now he needed a wake-up call. "Your wife discovered Sarah was stealing OxyContin on the job two years ago. She swept it under the rug to protect Sarah for the same reason you're standing by them now. That was her first mistake. Continuing to trust a woman who would steal drugs to support her husband's habit was her second."

Jess took a second to calm the outrage now rushing through her. "Those two so-called friends of the family know what happened to your wife, Lieutenant. I would suggest you be more careful who you trust. Particularly who you trust with your baby son's life."

He shook his head. "I don't believe you."

"Believe what you will, but you work with Jack every day. You haven't seen any sign of drug abuse? You don't feel the odd tension between him and his wife? Snap out of that denial you're in and look closer."

"I know what your problem is." He stabbed a finger at Jess. "You can't solve this case so you're using my partner as a scapegoat."

Jess ignored the accusation. "Did your partner's wife show up at your surveillance location on Sunday night before midnight?"

Confusion furrowed his brow. "What? Wait. Yes. She and Jack had a fight. He sat out there in the car with her for probably half an hour before he came back in. They're young, they still have stupid arguments."

"And nothing about that incident seemed amiss? It's happened before?"

He hesitated. "Well, no...I mean she's dropped by before but never for an extended time in the middle of the night like that. What the hell difference does it make? That alone should tell you Jack couldn't have killed Gabrielle. He was right there with me the whole shift."

Except for when he was in the car with Sarah. "Think long and hard, Lieutenant," Jess urged. "You've already allowed blind trust to cost you your wife. Will you allow it to cost you your son, too?"

11:30 a.m.

In Burnett's office, Jess set her phone to speaker so he could hear the update from Harper.

"I followed the Rileys to Sarah's parents' house. They picked up their children and then drove to their town house and, judging by the frantic gestures in the vehicle, they argued the whole way. Jack was mad as hell when he got out of the car. He kicked it a couple of times before storming into the house."

"Did Sarah get out of the car then?" Jess was beginning to have second thoughts about her. She hadn't reacted the way Jess had expected at all. She had given the woman the perfect opportunity to get free of the twisted situation with her husband and she'd walked away.

What if Jess were wrong? What if Sarah wasn't a victim? Grayson had confirmed that she had come to their surveillance location that night. Though Jack had sat in the car with her, the two had not left the scene.

Damn. Damn. Damn.

But a spouse showing up at a stakeout like that was way, way outside protocol. The kind of action that would get a cop written up. And what were they fighting about that night?

No, Jess decided, she wasn't wrong.

But what about the children? Now they were caught in the middle of this precarious situation. Damn it.

"She and the children went inside as well."

"Stay on them, Sergeant."

"Yes, ma'am."

Jess ended the call and plopped into a chair in front of Burnett's desk. "We didn't get the confession I'd hoped for," she admitted, "but we've got them worried and in a reactive state."

"They have four hours to make a move," Burnett reminded her. "If one or both were involved in Gabrielle's murder, there will be a reaction."

"That's what I'm counting on."

Lori was at the safe house with Leslie and Devon. Jess wanted this over for their sakes as well. Devon needed his routine back. They needed to feel safe in their own home again.

"Chief Waters has placed Riley on administrative leave until this is cleared up."

Jess shook her head. "Why is it when something like this happens, no one seems to have noticed all the signs leading up to it? How could Larry Grayson not know Sarah was being abused or that Jack was hooked on painkillers? Has our entire society become so oblivious that we don't see anything we don't want to?"

Burnett got up and came around to her side of his desk to sit beside her.

Uh-oh. "You got news on the Audi?"

He nodded. "Someone jimmied the lock, but the car is clean. The perp either changed his mind or got interrupted. Nothing else in the car was touched. They lifted prints and we'll be running those. I'm having the Audi delivered to the parking garage this afternoon."

"Looks like my landlord was wrong." Jess shook her head. There was no such thing as a safe neighborhood these days.

"Wrong about what?"

"That break-ins and stuff like that didn't happen in his neighborhood."

"Jess," Burnett said in that voice that warned she had better listen up, "someone is trying to hurt you. It's not a random act. Don't even think about wrapping yourself in the denial you keep throwing in everyone else's faces. Until we find the source of this threat, you won't be safe."

God, she was so tired. Tired and frustrated…and scared. "I know."

He pulled her out of her seat and into his arms. She let him. She needed to feel the strength of his arms right now.

No more denial.

3:00 p.m.

Jess checked her cell again.

"Eat," Burnett ordered. "You can't function on no sleep and nothing but coffee."

She picked at the fries. Tara, Burnett's receptionist, had gone out for burgers and fries. Jess appreciated the gesture but she had no appetite. Besides, she'd had her fill of burgers and fries this week.

If this plan didn't work, they were back at square one. There was no other evidence. Devon wouldn't be able to return to his normal life.

And Gabrielle Grayson's killer would continue to get away with murder.

Burnett had refused to let her out of his sight since he got the report back on the Audi. She was a prisoner. She couldn't even do her job. Admittedly the investigation was kind of in a holding pattern right now. But she would like to be out there doing something!

"Jess," Burnett scolded.

She stuffed a fry into her mouth and chewed.

Her cell clanged. She jumped, almost choked. *Harper.* Thank God!

"Harper, what's going on?" She had her phone on speaker so she wouldn't have to repeat the news to Burnett.

"Chief, we have a problem."

Tension coiled tighter. "What's going on?"

"About twenty minutes ago Mr. Haines went over to the Rileys' door and started pounding. Eventually I got out of my car and asked what was going on. He said the babies were crying and no one was coming to the door. I heard the crying too and after identifying myself, I kicked in the door..."

Jess braced for bad news. She had pushed too hard. If Sarah was dead...or, dear God, if the children were hurt...

"Jack Riley is dead. Two stab wounds to the chest. I've called dispatch. The kids are okay. But, Chief, Sarah Riley is gone."

"How the hell did that happen?"

"The back door was unlocked. I'm assuming she took off on foot."

"See if you can get ahold of the grandparents to come take custody of the kids," Jess directed. "Burnett and I are on the way."

When she ended the call Burnett was already on the horn ordering backup.

Jess considered this newest turn of events. Whatever

twisted bond had existed between Jack Riley and his wife...it was broken now and she was a loose cannon. Sarah Riley had gone over the edge. There was no telling what she was capable of in the state of rage that had no doubt risen inside her.

Jess and Burnett had just reached his SUV when her cell rang again. She expected it to be Harper but it wasn't. "Harris."

"Chief Harris, this is Larry Grayson."

His voice sounded strange. Cold, distant, full of terror. "Yes, Lieutenant. What can I do for you?"

"Sarah is here at my home and she would like to see you. *Only you.* She says it's time you knew the truth."

Equal parts anticipation and worry detonated in her veins. "Lieutenant, is she armed?"

"Yes." He made a sound, almost a whimper. "She has Jack's service weapon and she has my son. Please... please help us."

Shady Creek Circle, 4:15 p.m.

"All you have to do is say the word and we're coming in," Burnett reminded her.

Like she needed to hear that again. Jess was wearing a wire and a vest. She had a backup piece in a thigh holster under her skirt. She had on the vest under her jacket. They had set up a command post in the Chamberses's home. SWAT was in position.

They'd thrown this together in fifty minutes. No matter how well prepared they were, Sarah was playing it smart. All the blinds in the Grayson home were closed.

There was no view into the house. Sarah had shown up at Grayson's mother-in-law's home and taken the baby. The mother-in-law had immediately called the lieutenant who had gone to his minister for a counseling session. No sooner than the lieutenant had gotten into his car, Sarah had called him with her demands.

"I should get in there. It's been an hour." Jess had given herself some leeway by telling Grayson that she was nearly an hour away.

Unless Sarah had gone completely around the bend she likely wouldn't buy that story but so far he hadn't called demanding to know when Jess would arrive.

Burnett took her by the shoulders. "Don't try to be a hero, Jess. Do the best you can. That's all anyone can expect."

"That's the plan."

He held on to her a second longer. She held her breath, worried he would hug her with all the others watching. Finally he released her and she breathed easy again.

Jess gave him a nod before climbing into her Audi. She drove down to the end of the block and parked in front of the Grayson home. The crime scene tape was gone. Looked as if they had taken it down a little too soon.

SWAT had taken positions all around the home.

Jess rang the bell so those inside would know she had arrived, wherever they were in the house.

Grayson opened the door. His face was ashen. But he was alone.

"Where is she?"

He swallowed with visible effort. "In the nursery with Gary."

"Go," Jess instructed. "Leave. I will take care of this. You have my word."

"I can't do that. My son—"

Jess moved past him and into the house. "Go." Why the hell didn't he listen to her?

He closed the door. "This way."

She worked at calming herself. She supposed she couldn't fault him for not wanting to leave his son. Jess followed him to the nursery. Sarah sat in the rocking chair, baby Gary in her arms, the .40 cal weapon belonging to her dead husband in her hand.

"Hello, Sarah." Jess moistened her lips. "I'm here. Why don't we let Larry take the baby so we can talk woman to woman?"

Sarah glared at Jess. "I am not as naïve as I look." To Larry she said, "Get out of here. We have to talk in private."

He looked to Jess and she nodded. With obvious reluctance, he left the room.

"Close the door," Sarah called after him.

Jess heard the latch click behind her.

"What would you like to talk about, Sarah?"

"You need to know what really happened. It wasn't like you think. Gabrielle left us no choice."

Jess kept her hands at her side and held very still. The baby was sleeping and the weapon was in Sarah's right hand. For now that was good, but everything could change in a single heartbeat. "Why don't you tell me what happened."

Jess had an idea of how things had gone. Sarah had been trying to protect her abusive husband. She would have done anything to protect that insanely twisted bond. Things got out of control...Riley went into a rage and Gabrielle was dead.

Somehow Jess had to make sure there wasn't a second act to this tragedy.

"She found out Jack was still using the OC. The idiot dropped one in her goddamned bathroom when we were here for lunch Sunday and he was so fucked up he couldn't find it. Well, she did. She called me that night after Larry came by to tuck in the baby. She'd gone in the bathroom to take a shower and saw the damned thing. I came over and begged her not to tell. She wouldn't listen." Sarah shrugged. "She wouldn't listen to reason so I did what Jack told me to do. I put OC in her drink, but she just sipped at it. She didn't drink enough fast enough." Sarah shook her head, her lips tight with fury. "She didn't do anything right."

Jess waited out her silence, the thickness of it making breathing difficult. Judging by the changing expressions on Sarah's face she was remembering that night.

"She always thought she was better than me. Smarter. A better wife and mother. I never could do anything as well as she did. She was a better nurse, wife, mother... everything!"

"Sounds like she wasn't a very good friend," Jess offered.

Sarah made a face. "She was the kind of friend who loved surrounding herself with those she could feel superior to. She wanted to humiliate us. She wanted to tell us what she was going to do before she did it. And this time she was going to ruin us." Sarah made a scoffing sound. "How dare she suggest that Jack might get her husband killed! Jack was the best partner Larry ever had. He said so a dozen times!"

"Did the two of you argue?"

Sarah nodded. "She just kept arguing and not drinking her wine. Jack's plan wasn't going to work! How could the stupid bitch OD if she didn't drink it?"

Jess's respiration hitched at the news. She watched the frantic woman's arms tighten around the baby, adding another layer of tension. The child started to squirm and fret. Jess needed to do something. "She forced you to do it. She left you no choice."

Sarah's face went blank as she stared at Jess. Her hold on the baby relaxed a bit. "She did. I couldn't take it anymore." A smile stretched across her face. "Then the OC started to kick in. Not enough to send her into respiratory arrest, but enough to make her weak and clumsy. She accused me of poisoning her!" Sarah laughed. "I just watched her get more confused and frantic."

"She got a taste of how you felt," Jess suggested.

Sarah nodded. "Then she tried to call for help. She shouldn't have done that. I knocked her down and she just kept trying to get up. I held her down. It was easy. She was all weak and uncoordinated. Her tongue was thick from the drug when she warned that I was going to jail." Sarah shrugged. "She kept on and on and then I put my fingers around her throat and I choked her. I choked her until she shut up."

Dear God. It wasn't Jack...it was her.

"For a long time I just sat there looking at her. It was storming and I watched the light flash on and off over her body." Sarah blinked repeatedly as if coming out of a trance. "Then Jack called and said I'd better go home and check on the kids. So I turned out the lights and went home."

Jess held herself steady when deep inside fury was twisting like a hurricane. She needed just one more thing. "But you had to go back."

"Jack made me. When I got the kids settled I sneaked out to see him and he went ballistic. He told me what I had to do to make sure no one ever knew it was me who shut her up."

"So you went back and did what he told you."

"It took a while but I got her head cut off. Like he said. I had to do it in the dark, but the lightning helped. Then I wrote the words he told me to write. He was mad when I told him about the knife...but I decided that Gabrielle deserved that. I stabbed her ten times. For all the times I could remember her making me feel beneath her. Then I called him and told him it was done. I had to use her phone. The battery was dead on mine."

"I guess you got her blood on your hands."

She visibly shuddered. "It was all over me. I took a shower and checked on the baby. That's when I knew someone was in the house." Fury tightened her lips. "The little shit."

"This isn't your fault," Jess lied. "You're suffering from all his years of abuse. You did what you thought you had to do. This is Jack's fault. Any decent lawyer will recognize post-traumatic stress disorder."

Sarah seemed to snap out of her coma, and her gaze connected with Jess's. "Everything would have been fine if that retard hadn't gotten in the way. And you." She turned the barrel of the weapon toward Jess. "You took everything from me. We had the perfect family until Gabrielle and you stole it from me." She got up. The baby sighed and stretched. She walked straight up to Jess, the weapon steady in her hand. "You caused this."

"Wait, Sarah," Jess urged. "I should've told you already, but Jack isn't dead. When your neighbor heard the girls crying he called the police. I heard over the scanner on the way over here that the police had kicked in the door and found Jack hanging on by a thread. He's in surgery but he's going to be okay. We should get to the hospital so you can be with him when he wakes up. You can still be a family."

Her face twisted in fury. "Don't try to fool me! I'm a nurse. He was dead."

"You have my word," Jess promised. "Call the hospital if you don't believe me."

Sarah hesitated, seemed to weigh her claim. "If you're lying," she threatened, "I'll kill you and the baby. I have nothing else to lose."

"You want to go in my car?" Jess asked. "I didn't see yours."

"I went down the alley behind my house and called a taxi to pick me up. I knew that cop was watching my house. I'm not as stupid as Jack said."

"We should hurry," Jess suggested. "You don't want Jack to wake up and be alone."

Sarah started forward.

Jess made a worried face. "They won't let the baby in the hospital. And if we run into trouble the baby will only slow us down."

Sarah smirked. "Give it up. They're not going to shoot at me as long as I have the baby. I am not leaving him."

"But you have me now. You just keep that gun pointed at me and no one is going to bother you. I'm a deputy chief. I'm way more important than that baby."

"Maybe you're right." Sarah pressed the barrel of the weapon against Jess's forehead. "Take him."

Jess scooped the sleeping boy into her arms. He squirmed a little but quickly settled. Jess's heart skipped into an erratic rhythm.

"Put him in his crib."

The weapon jammed against the back of her skull, Jess

walked over to the baby's bed and carefully placed him there, then covered him with his blanket.

"Let's go," Sarah ordered. "You drive."

Jess walked out of the bedroom and turned to her right. At the end of the hall were the steps down to the entry level. Her heart stumbled when she got a fleeting glimpse of Burnett hovering to the left at the bottom of the stairs. She hoped he wasn't going to do anything that would get them both killed.

There was just one thing Jess could do.

As she reached the third step from the bottom, she pitched forward as if she had stumbled and hit the floor.

Sarah screamed at her to get up.

Burnett swung around the corner and slammed her in the head with a lamp base.

The weapon discharged.

Jess rolled and jumped to her feet, her fingers snatching the .38 from her thigh holster.

Sarah was down and Burnett was cuffing her. She bucked and screamed at him.

SWAT swarmed into the house.

Jess rushed to the baby's room and scooped up the fretting child. "It's okay, sweetie," she cooed. "Let's go find your daddy."

She turned to find Burnett in the doorway. The tender expression on his face tore at her heart.

She arched a skeptical eyebrow. "Don't get any ideas. I'm just doing my job."

"You did good, Chief."

"I know." Jess scooted out the door past him. "I always do."

26

Whispering Stream Lane, 8:00 p.m.

Devon sat crossed-legged on the living room floor, his favorite show on the TV.

Leslie smiled at Jess. "I can't believe it's really over."

Jess patted her arm. "You and Devon were instrumental in helping us solve this case."

The girl's eyes widened. "We were?"

"Absolutely," Jess assured her. "I don't want you to worry about Child Services or work or anything but being happy. You deserve it."

"That won't be so easy." Leslie sighed. "I missed all these days and I got fired from my job. I have to find a new one soon."

"No you don't." Those silly old emotions Jess hated dealing with rose like a big old tidal wave. She absolutely refused to cry. "Dr. Baron is going to pay for yours and Devon's schooling. She's also offered you an intern position at the coroner's office—in the file room, of course—

around your class schedule so you can be home in the evenings with Devon. No more working at night away from your brother."

Leslie wasn't so successful holding back her tears. "I don't know what to say."

Jess smiled. "*And*, Lieutenant Grayson is so thankful to Devon for checking on his wife and child that awful night that he and some of his friends in the South Precinct are going to start working on your house to get it back in shape."

Leslie threw her arms around Jess and hugged her tight. Jess hugged her back. She might turn into a hugger after all.

Tugging on her jacket had Jess pulling away to look down at Devon. "Did we leave you out?"

He made a face and shook his head. Leslie laughed. "He's not much of a hugger."

A boy after her own heart, Jess mused.

Devon offered her a drawing. "For you."

Jess smiled. "What an artist you are, Devon." The drawing had a stick figure lady with yellow hair standing in the sunshine. At her feet sat a big black purse and a silver badge-shaped object. There were large buildings in the background, maybe to signify Birmingham. "I'm hanging this in my office. But first"—she pointed to the bottom right-hand corner—"can you sign it for me? All artists sign their work."

Devon took the picture and ran back to where his crayons waited.

"Thank you, Chief Harris."

Jess turned to Leslie. She hadn't really done anything. It was Baron and Grayson who were doing all the wonderful things for these kids.

"You're our angel."

Lakefront Trail, Bessemer, 9:30 p.m.

By the time Jess reached her sister's house, an unmarked car still tracking her every move, she was way past burned out.

Lily was sitting on the porch swing waiting for her.

Jess climbed the steps and joined her. "Where is everybody?"

"I made them go to the movies." Lily smiled. "They've all been so worried about me they've been hovering. I needed a break. The kids leave next week, they needed some fun time with their dad."

"You want me to fix us a cup of tea or something?"

Lily shook her head. "You go ahead. I'm good."

"In that case," Jess snuggled closer to her, "I'm good, too."

"I went for some more tests today."

"When will you hear something?"

"Next week, I hope."

Jess put an arm around her sister and pulled her close. "You listen to me, Lily. Whatever this is, we'll get through it. You hear me?"

Lil nodded. "I know. I'm glad you're home, Jess."

Hells bells. The tears started to flow and there was no stopping them. "I'm never leaving you again. I promise."

They held each other and sobbed softly for a long while. Then they both sucked it up and went inside to play a game of Scrabble. Lily had always beaten her at the game. But Jess didn't care. It was being here, with her sister, that counted.

"I love you, Jess."

"Love you, too."

27

Parkridge Drive, Homewood, Saturday, August 7, 9:00 a.m.

Chet worried that Lori would be disappointed in his place. She'd never been here before. It was nothing fancy. One of the houses they called mid-century modern. Built in the fifties, with big windows and sharp angles. Only two bedrooms with a small yard, but it was affordable and the neighborhood was kid friendly. For him that was the most important part.

"Nice place," she said as she climbed out of the rented truck. Her gaze connected with his and she gave him a nod of approval.

A load lightened from his shoulders. "I'm glad you like it."

She surveyed the block again, then his home. "I like it a lot." She grabbed him by the hand. "Show me inside."

His pulse skipping with happiness, he led her to the door or maybe she led him. He turned the key in the lock and opened the door. "After you."

She walked in and he held his breath. The living area was one big space. Family room, kitchen, and dining room all neatly laid out beneath a vaulted ceiling complete with a couple of cool wood beams. Beyond the open space was a short hallway with two bedrooms and a bathroom. The larger of the two bedrooms had an en suite bath but it was kind of small.

"The hardwood floors are beautiful."

"The floors and ceiling sold me on the place," he confessed.

She walked around the room and checked out his big, comfy sofa and the other furnishings he'd painstakingly selected. Who knew that shopping for furniture could be so difficult?

"You did good on the furnishings." She sank into the big faux leather sectional he'd gotten at a big box store for a steal. "Nice."

He offered his hand. "Come on. I'll show you the bedrooms."

At the door of the first, smaller bedroom, she smiled. "Chester's room is cute."

Chet had gone to a lot of trouble to give his son a room he'd feel at home in. "It's small but he likes it."

"Who wouldn't?" She checked out the decorating, which was a stroll down Sesame Street with all the props, like Oscar the Grouch's trash can that served as a storage place for toys.

She turned to Chet. "You did really good."

"There's one last room to see." He took her hand again.

Before they entered the master bedroom, she peeked into the hall bath. "Kind of guyish but it's cool."

"I thought Chester and I could share that bath so you'd have your own private space."

Her smile widened. "Thank you. A girl needs her own space."

As soon as she'd told him she would move in, he'd rushed to Bed Bath & Beyond and bought all new bedding. And the curtains. He'd tried hard to capture a little feminine elegance while not completely diminishing his manhood.

He hadn't had time to repaint the walls but the pale green and tan stripes of the bedding worked with the sand colored walls. There was also a tiny lavender stripe in the bedding. The clerk who'd helped him assured Chet that tiny little line of feminine color would make all the difference. She'd suggested he buy sheets in that color as well.

"Wow." Lori plopped on the bed to try out the mattress. "You do have a feminine side."

His smile vanished. "The bedding is new. I picked it out with you in mind." No need to mention the clerk who'd helped or the fact that his previous bedding had been camouflage. He did not have a feminine side. "I'm a guy, all the way."

She grabbed his hand and pulled him onto the bed with her. "You want to prove that, big guy?"

She leaned forward and kissed his throat at the vee of his shirt.

"What about all your stuff in the truck?" They'd rented a truck to move her belongings rather than borrowing one from a friend. That way there was no need to explain. They had decided to keep this move low profile. The goal was to avoid feeding the rumor mill in the department by borrowing a truck.

"It can wait." Lori teased his lips.

"But we have to pick up Chester in an hour."

Her face fell and she pushed off the bed and walked to the window.

Chet sighed. He had worried that this was going to be a problem after the way Chester behaved the other night. He got to his feet and went to stand behind her. "We'll make this work."

"He hates me, Chet. He really does."

The pain in her voice was like a knife stabbing deep into his gut. "He just has to get used to you. To *us*."

She turned around to face him, her eyes watery with worry. "Are you sure? Maybe I'm just not mom material and he senses that."

Chet laughed softly. "You are the most amazing woman in the world and I swear to you that my son will learn to love you just as much as I do."

Lori nodded. "Okay."

"Does that mean you haven't changed your mind?"

She laughed, the real McCoy. "Give me five minutes and I'll let you decide for yourself."

28

10:00 a.m.

This was the first time Jess had had the opportunity to have a real look around the yard of her new place. Technically it wasn't her yard, but she got the benefit of the picturesque view without the physical labor involved with upkeep. Louis certainly had his hands full with maintenance. The man had endless flower beds. Some raised stone beds. Brick ones. And lots of different sizes, shapes, and colors of flowerpots.

Despite the heat already building and with a glass of iced tea in hand, she strolled. The sweats and tee and flip-flops made for the perfect Saturday morning attire. There was no one to impress and no need for a place to carry her weapon. Her case was closed and she was ready for a nice weekend break.

Jess paused at the most recent flower bed she'd noticed Louis working on into the late evening hours the other night. Seemed a little late in the summer to be planting, but then what did she know? She had no green thumb. Maybe she would ask Lily, just out of curiosity. The way the bed was mounded reminded her of a grave. She shuddered. Just went to show she spent too much time around bodies. Jess crouched down and plucked loose the little plastic tag stuck in the ground to see the type of plants he'd selected. Lantana. Plant in full sun.

"That tells me absolutely nothing." She tucked the tag back into place.

"They love the sun and the heat."

Startled, Jess pushed to her feet. "Good morning." She gave herself a mental pop against the forehead. "I was just admiring your lovely gardens."

"This spot was looking a little lonesome for company."

He smiled at her. Jess was pretty sure he didn't do that often. "You have an amazing talent for bringing an outside landscape to life."

"Not so much talent as time on my hands." He surveyed his work. "You run out of things to do and well… you know what the Bible says about that."

"Idle hands are the devil's tools." It had been a long time since she'd gone to church but she remembered the basics.

"That says it all, doesn't it?"

"I guess it does." Jess kicked herself for not having done this already. "Thank you so much for the glider. I love it. I really do."

"As I said, it was gathering dust in the garage." He waved his arm wide. "What is mine is yours, to quote Shakespeare."

With that he turned and disappeared back into his home.

"What is yours is mine," she finished the quote. What a peculiar man.

Jess climbed the steps and returned to her little haven. Maybe today she'd go in search of a couple of side chairs and a sofa. Birmingham had plenty of neat thrift stores. She didn't dare invite Lily. If she even mentioned she needed furniture her sister would have the whole church rushing over to donate to the cause.

Her apartment was cool inside and it smelled like the fresh blossoms candle she had lit. It hadn't taken her five minutes to do a little straightening up. She didn't have enough stuff to make a mess yet.

Her cell chirped at her and she walked to the table to check it. Voice mail. She tapped the screen. Not a number she recognized. Just the same, she hit play.

A woman cleared her throat. "Jessie Lee, this is your… aunt Wanda."

Anger stirred instantly at the sound of the woman's voice.

"I've done some thinking and you're right about needing some family history. So I made a list of everything I know about our folks. I'll mail it to you if you want. Or you can come by and pick it up. I don't know where you live but I could bring it to the police department I guess. Just…let me know…ah…bye."

Jess played the voice mail again. She started to delete it but decided not to. She needed whatever she could get from the woman for Lily.

Her cell clanged. Jess jumped. "Damn it!"

She stared at the screen. Another number she didn't recognize. "Harris."

"Chief Harris, this is Hector Debarros."

Jess tensed. "Mr. Debarros, hello. Do you have a

message from Mr. Lopez?" Hearing from him at this point about the Norwood victims was pretty much a moot point but she wasn't about to say as much.

"The two executions were carried out by rebels against our clique. They have been taken care of."

She supposed, like Captain Allen said, that saved the taxpayers the cost of an investigation and a trial. Not to mention housing in whatever jail the perps ended up in. But that view was wrong.

"Mr. Lopez also said that I should tell you that the problem you had in the BPD has resolved itself. You are no longer in danger from that source. He believes you have yourself an *angel de la guarda*."

Another wave of tension rippled through her. "What does that mean, Mr. Debarros?"

"You need not worry, Chief Harris, you have a guardian angel."

The call ended.

Jess stared at the phone. She stamped her foot. "What is with all this angel talk?" Frustrated, she tossed her phone into her bag and grabbed her keys. "Shopping is what I need."

If she found a sofa she'd have to call Harper. Unless the store provided delivery. She laughed at herself. She'd never heard of thrift stores providing delivery services but who knew.

Maybe she could rent one of those trucks by the hour from the Home Depot. Couldn't be that different from driving a car. Then again, she'd still need Harper's strong back.

Or Dan's.

She'd figure it out.

She opened the door and instantly jumped back.

"I was just about to knock."

Daniel Burnett stood in her doorway. "You can't call before you show up at my door?" What was it with men these days? They thought women were just moping around the house waiting for them to appear?

"I had to drop off a couple of antiques in the neighborhood from the silent auction the other night. I thought I'd stop by and see if you wanted to have an early lunch."

"You making deliveries in that fancy Mercedes of yours?"

He shook his head. "I'm using my dad's truck."

"Your dad has a truck?"

"Ford F150. Crew cab. 3.7 liter V-6. Flex fuel," he bragged, though she had no idea what all that meant.

"Yes," she enthused. "Lunch would be awesome. You don't mind helping me run a few errands, do you?"

His gaze narrowed with suspicion. "What kind of errands?"

"I need a few things." She smiled. "I promised to make you dinner here tonight. I'll make it extra special."

"Is that a bribe?"

She nodded. "Absolutely."

He came inside, forcing her to back up a step, and closed the door behind him. "Give me a little preview and I might be persuaded."

She dropped her bag to the floor and reached for the buttons of his shirt. "I'll take my time undoing every one of these buttons." She kept going until she'd reached the one that disappeared into the waistband of his jeans. "Sorry I can't get to that one." She gave him a wicked look. "Unless I do this." She tugged the button at his waistband loose. The sound of his fly lowering made him groan. She pulled his shirt loose and finished the unbuttoning.

"Then," she flattened her palms on his chest. He shivered. "I'll explore all this delicious territory." She smoothed her palms over his chest, down his rib cage, her heart ached at the feel of the scar Eric Spears had left him with. She banished thoughts of that bastard. This was hers and Dan's time. No one else mattered. He was breathing heavily. The idea that he was so ready for more had her burning up. A fire for him had been smoldering deep inside her all week. "But I'm a little greedy so that will never be enough."

She pushed his jeans and briefs down his thighs. "Hmm." Her fingers wrapped around him. He shuddered.

Just to torture him, she backed up a step and kicked off the flip-flops, slid her sweats and panties down her thighs, leaving them in a puddle on the floor as she reclaimed the space between them.

She leaned against him. "Then..."

"Then," he echoed as he grabbed her up and twisted around until her back was against the door. "I'd do what I've been dying to do all week."

Her body melted against the hard planes of his. "And what's that?"

He pressed into her, filling her slowly and completely. "Make love to you." He kissed her nose. "Again." He kissed her chin. "And again."

Her hips moved against his, pressing him deeper. She moaned with pleasure. "Good answer."

Her phone chirped, signaling she'd received a text, but she didn't care. All she wanted right now was *all* of Dan.

It was so good to be home.

A high school graduation party ends in a death.

More than a decade later, an invitation to a special class reunion is sent.

And so begins a series of murders that will test Deputy Chief Jess Harris as a chilling game of retribution is set in motion…

Please turn this page for a preview of

Revenge

Revenge... its delight is murder, and its end is despair.
—Johann Christoph Friedrich von Schiller

1

9911 Conroy Road, August 9, 10:45 p.m.

The room went as black as a tomb.

"Oh, shoot." Jess Harris heaved a beleaguered sigh. She tossed the now useless hair dryer onto the bed. This was the second night in a row the power had gone out on her. "One of the perks of living in a historic—aka *old*—home," she muttered.

Reaching forward into the darkness to prevent any collisions, she shuffled across the room. She hadn't been here a week, and small as the place was, she still didn't know it by heart. In her defense, she was hardly ever home. A cop's life was rarely calm or routine.

Where the hell had she left that flashlight her landlord had given her? By the kitchen sink? On the table? Wait... she squinted—tried her best to see as her eyes focused to the darkness—maybe she'd stuck it out of the way on top of the fridge. One of these days she had to get organized.

Deciding the vintage appliance was the most likely

place she felt her way there and ran her hand as far back and over the top as she could reach. A smile of triumph slid across her lips as her fingers closed around the plastic flashlight.

She nudged the switch with her thumb and a beam of light cut through the blackness. Some of the tension bunching her shoulders ebbed. "Hallelujah."

Now what?

At this hour chances were Mr. Louis, her landlord, was in bed. It wasn't as if she really needed the lights back on since she'd planned to hit the sack herself as soon as her hair was dry. Jess ran a hand through the still-damp ringlets. But, she did have food in the fridge that needed to be kept cold. Besides, this was the second time that breaker had gotten thrown by her hair dryer. According to Mr. Louis that wasn't supposed to happen. He'd promised to call an electrician today. She'd gotten home late so there'd been no opportunity to ask him if the problem was fixed.

"Obviously not," she muttered as she tapped her thigh with the flashlight sending its beam back and forth over the wood floor. "Well, hell." No use standing around here putting off the inevitable.

There was just no way around it. She'd have to go down to the garage and take care of the breaker herself. Resetting the damned thing wasn't a big deal. Not really. After getting Dan out the door last night, she'd hurried through a shower and switched on her hair dryer and *poof* the lights had gone out—just like tonight. Thankfully her landlord had still been puttering around in his kitchen then so she'd knocked on his door.

He'd explained that her apartment and the garage were on a subpanel, which also clarified why there was no service disruption in the main house when her lights went out. Inside the garage last night, she'd carefully watched him reset the breaker and even remembered which one it was. Fourth from the top.

"Easy as pie." Jess shoved her cell phone into the pocket of her worn-comfortable robe and strode to the door. She could do this without bothering her elderly landlord.

On the deck outside her door, she verified that Mr. Louis's house was indeed dark before descending the stairs. She hoped the side door of the garage wasn't locked. That could be a problem. Damn it. She hadn't thought that far ahead. People generally locked all doors at night. Then she'd have no choice but to bang on his door.

"Don't borrow trouble, Jess."

At the garage's side door the knob turned without resistance and she was in. Thank the Lord. She roved the flashlight's beam over the cavernous space to get her bearings. Smelled like wood shavings and vaguely of oil. Last night she hadn't really noticed. She'd been too focused on how to get the power back on in her place. This go-around her curiosity got the better of her.

There was just one vehicle in the garage, a classic, black Cadillac Eldorado. That she had spotted last night. The car fit the man, she decided. The thought of Mr. Louis and his horn-rimmed glasses behind the wheel of that big, formidable-looking automobile reminded her of a character straight out of *The Sopranos*. Like the money man or the bookie.

The exposed stone walls were lined with shelves on three sides, all were neatly organized with cans of paint and tools. The brush lying across the top of a can of white paint had her remembering and wondering about her landlord's sudden decision to freshen the door to her apartment the other evening. She should ask him about that. Not that it really mattered to the homicide case she had just closed at this point but he needed to understand that in her line of work sometimes trouble followed her home. And if some jerk decided to leave her a personal message it was essential that she see it—all of it, no matter how unpleasant—before it was whitewashed.

The sooner she made that point clear to him the better. Maybe tomorrow when she spoke to him about the electrician.

Jess padded across the rough concrete floor and settled the light on the gray metal door of the breaker box. She opened it and sure enough breaker number four from the top had jumped into the off position. Might not technically be considered off but it was off as far as Jess was concerned.

"So you don't like my hair dryer, is that it?" She reached up and snapped the breaker into the on position. She watched for a moment to ensure it wasn't going to repeat its unruly behavior. When the breaker remained in the proper position she closed the door to the box and turned to go. She stubbed the toes of her left foot and cringed.

"Damn, damn, damn!" She hopped on one foot while she stretched the injured toes. Aiming her flashlight at the offending object, she glared at the large wooden box. Looked like a homemade toolbox. Something else she hadn't noticed last night. Tucked against the wall it really wasn't in the way. She just hadn't been paying attention to what she was doing. She would definitely pay attention next time. Her aching toes curled in agony.

Something on the floor had her looking twice at the space just left of the box. The floor was a little uneven and not smooth at all. Looked as if it had been poured in sections in different decades. But the small round object that had snagged her attention glittered in the light...silver. Jess leaned down and picked it up. A ring. Not just a ring...a *wedding band.*

She couldn't read the inscription since her glasses were upstairs. The ring made her think of the one she had stopped wearing recently, only this one was larger, a man's maybe, and hers had been gold—

The garage filled with flickering lights.

Her breath stalled somewhere in the vicinity of her throat and she squinted at the flood of harsh fluorescent glare.

"Is there a problem, Chief Harris?"

Mr. Louis waited at the door she'd entered and left standing wide open maybe two minutes ago.

Uh oh. Busted. So much for not pestering the man. It was a wonder he hadn't barged in toting a twenty-gauge. Jess shoved her hand, along with the ring, into her robe pocket. "Just that breaker again." She smiled, knowing damned well she must look as guilty as sin. "I should've known better than to use my hair dryer until I checked with you. I hope I didn't disturb you." She gestured to the breaker box. "I thought I could take care of it myself this time. It's so late and all." She clicked off the flashlight and tried to analyze his face. He didn't exactly look annoyed. Maybe frustrated or unsettled.

"The electrician will be here in the morning." His lips shifted into a smile, banishing the hard-to-read expression he'd been wearing. "I apologize for the inconvenience."

"No trouble." Truth was she felt like a nosy Nellie. This man had kindly offered his garage apartment when she had no other place to go—besides her sister's and that was just not doable for a whole cast of reasons—and here she was treating her gracious landlord as if he were a suspect. Dan's paranoia about her renting from a stranger was evidently rubbing off on her. No, that wasn't fair. She couldn't really blame it on Dan. She'd always overanalyzed people and situations. She walked straight up to her landlord and held out the ring. "I found this on the floor."

He accepted the band, turned it over in the light. "Oh, thank you. I'd wondered where it had gotten off to."

She wasn't about to ask the questions pinging at her and have him recognizing that she really was nosy in addition to a pain in the butt with her comings and goings at all hours of the night and day. A certain level of nosiness came naturally after twenty years in the business of criminal investigation but he might not understand or appreciate that undeniable and sometimes bothersome fact.

Before she could apologize again for the trouble he said, "You have company."

Her cheeks flushed. Surely Dan hadn't come back. He'd taken her to dinner earlier this evening and they'd discussed the ongoing investigation into the bomb that had been planted in the police vehicle she'd used last week. Knowing him he'd returned with one more reason she should be wearing full body armor at all times and that she should never be spotted in public without at least two armed bodyguards.

The man took *overprotective* to a whole new level.

Not to mention, it was Monday and they were having enough difficulty already leaving their personal relationship with the weekend. That was the deal they had made when she had accepted this position. During the workweek he was the chief of police and she was one of his deputies. No exceptions.

She'd been back a month and that rule had gotten broken with tonight's dinner and dessert which had included getting naked afterward and it was *Monday*, for Christ's sake.

God, she had to get this mess that was her personal life in some sort of order.

Starting right now, she promised herself silently. If Dan was at her door to check on her yet again, she was going to give him hell. Until there was reason to believe otherwise, she felt confident the threats aimed at her last week had been buried along with the cop they'd discovered had been involved with the murder of his partner's wife.

One way or another she was going to get the message through to Dan that she could take care of herself.

"Sorry again," she said to Louis. "I'm sure you weren't expecting all this middle of the night activity when you offered to rent the apartment to me."

"Your presence keeps life interesting, Chief Harris." With that he stepped aside for her to exit the garage.

"You should call me Jess," she suggested. It was silly for them to be so formal considering she was living on his property.

He ducked his head in one of those shy nods she'd come to associate with the older gentleman. "Of course, and you should call me George."

"Well, George, thank you and good night." Jess gave him a nod as she walked past him.

"Good night, Jess," he called after her.

She almost paused and turned around at the way he said her name. Familiar almost, like they'd known each other for a long time. Instead she left the garage and checked the driveway. He was right about her having company, but thank God it wasn't Dan.

A white sedan she didn't recognize sat in the drive behind her Audi. The slightest inkling of trepidation trickled through her veins as she rounded the rear corner of the garage and peered up at the top of the stairs leading to her apartment. The light outside her door illuminated a woman who knocked firmly, most likely not for the first time. She wore khaki slacks and a matching blouse. Her gray hair was tucked into a neat bun. Her bearing looked vaguely familiar. As Jess watched, the woman reached up and knocked again.

"Hello," Jess called as she started up the stairs.

Her visitor turned toward the sound of her voice, and recognition jarred Jess.

"Ms. Frances?" Of all people... "Is that really you?"

Frances Wallace had been Jess's ninth-grade English teacher. She was unquestionably the only reason Jess hadn't quit school the day she turned sixteen. What in the world was she doing here? Jess hadn't seen her in ages. She hated to admit it but she hadn't even been sure the woman was still alive.

Yet, here she was.

"The one and only," Frances confessed. "I've been following the news about you since you returned to Birmingham," Frances announced as Jess climbed the final step. She looked Jess up and down, then gave a nod of approval despite her unkempt appearance. "You always did do things with panache, young lady."

It had also been ages since anyone had called Jess a young lady. She liked the sound of that. "I had an excellent teacher."

Frances Wallace was a genuine character. No one got anything over on her and she did everything—including her teaching—exactly the way she wanted, the rules be damned. Everyone loved her—even the ones who didn't want to, when she ignored their edicts.

For one long moment Jess got so caught up in the memories she lost all sense of decorum. "Come in, Ms. Frances. Please."

She opened the door and ushered her former teacher inside. "Have a seat." She gestured to the new-old sofa she'd discovered at a thrift store on Saturday. "Would you like coffee?" She should have had wine to offer, but she and Dan had finished it off before getting naked. A flush of embarrassment went through her at the idea of even thinking about that in front of Ms. Frances.

Her former teacher took a moment to survey the apartment. Jess felt that same flush rise in her cheeks as her gaze lit on the tousled sheets of the bed.

"I'm still getting organized—"

Frances turned to Jess then, and the unabashed fear on her face stole the rest of what Jess was about to say.

Without a word of explanation Frances drew her into a fierce hug. "I need your help, Jess," she whispered with the same ferocity as her embrace. "I think I'm about to be charged with murder."

THE DISH

Where Authors Give You the Inside Scoop

♥ ♥ ♥ ♥ ♥ ♥ ♥ ♥ ♥ ♥ ♥ ♥ ♥ ♥ ♥

From the desk of Debra Webb

Dear Reader,

It's very exciting to be back again this month with RAGE, the fourth installment of the Faces of Evil series.

Writing a series can be a challenge. There are many threads related to the plots and the characters that have to be kept in line and moving forward (sometimes the characters like to go off on paths of their own!). Former Special Agent Jess Harris and Birmingham Chief of Police Dan Burnett have their hands full as usual. Murder hits close to home in this story and takes us to the next level of evil: rage. We've explored obsession, impulse, and power already and there are many more to come. The face of evil is rarely easy to spot. But Jess and Dan won't rest until they solve the case and ensure the folks of Birmingham are safe.

While I was writing this story, a new character joined the cast. I wasn't expecting a new character to appear on the page and demand some special attention, but Dr. Sylvia Baron, Jefferson County associate coroner, has a mind of her own. She stepped onto the page in her designer stilettos and her elegant business attire and told me exactly what she wanted to do. From hello Jess and Sylvia butt heads. The two keep Dan on his toes!

I hope you'll stop by www.thefacesofevil.com and visit

with me. There's a weekly briefing each Friday where I talk about what's going on in my world and with the characters as I write the next story. You can sign up as a person of interest and you might just end up a suspect!

Enjoy the story and be sure to look for *Revenge* coming in July and *Ruthless* in August!

Happy reading!

Debra Webb

♥ ♥ ♥ ♥ ♥ ♥ ♥ ♥ ♥ ♥ ♥ ♥ ♥ ♥ ♥

From the desk of Roxanne St. Claire

I packed a lot of emotional themes and intense subjects into my writer's beach bag when I penned BAREFOOT IN THE SUN, from faith and trust to life-threatening illness and life-altering secrets. The Happily Ever After is hard-won and bittersweet, but that seems to come with the Barefoot Bay territory. The heroine, Zoe Tamarin, has to overcome a tendency to run away when life goes south, and the hero, Oliver Bradbury, must learn that, despite his talents as a doctor, he can't fix everything. During their reunion romance, Zoe and Oliver grow to understand the power of a promise, the joy of a second chance, and the awesome truths told by Mother Nature.

But this is Barefoot Bay, so it can't be all heartache and healing!

In lighter moments, Oliver and Zoe play. They kiss (a lot), they laugh (this is Zoe!), they swim (some might call it skinny dipping), and occasionally Zoe whips out her deck of cards for a rockin' round of Egyptian Rat Screws (ERS).

I've mentioned Zoe's penchant for ERS in other books, and readers have written to ask about the card game. Many want to know the origin of the name, which, I have to admit, is a complete mystery to me, as the game has nothing to do with Egypt, rodents, or hardware of any kind. The secret of the name is one of many aspects of the game that reminds me of Zoe...a character who reveals in the opening scene of BAREFOOT IN THE SUN that she's not the person everyone believes she is.

Like the woman who loves to play it, Egyptian Rat Screws is fast-paced, intense, and not for the faint of heart, but I promise a good time. So grab a deck, a partner, and your most colorful curses, and I'll teach you the two-person version. ERS can also be played with more people, but I find one-on-one is the most intense...like any good romance, right?

The object of the game is simple: The winner ends up holding the whole deck. Of course, play can easily be transformed into something even wilder, such as Strip Rat Screws (Oliver's favorite) or Drinking Rat Screws, a game our four best friends, Tessa, Lacey, Jocelyn, and Zoe, played a few times in college.

Before playing, the players face each other across a table and choose who goes first. Player One is selected arbitrarily—closest birthday, rock-paper-scissors, or the ever popular "least hormonal." Leading off is no advantage, so save your voice for more important arguments, because there will be many. Each player gets twenty-six well-shuffled cards and *may not look at them.*

To begin, Player One flips the first card face-up on the

table. If this card is a 2 through 10, Player Two puts her first card on top of the card on the table. Again, if that card is a number card, Player Two goes again.

The action begins when either player puts down a Jack, Queen, King, or Ace. When a face card is revealed, the other player must try to "beat" it by placing another face card of equal or higher value on top of it. Depending on the face card Player One has put down, Player Two has only a certain number of tries to beat it: one for a Jack, two for a Queen, three for a King, and four for an Ace.

If Player Two can't beat the face card in her allotted number of tries, Player One gets all the cards on the table. ("Strip" ERS losers would shed one article of clothing; drinkers, take a gulp.)

If Player Two lays down another face card in her allotted tries, then Player One has the same number of tries to beat that card. (If more than two players are in the game, just keep moving around the table.) It's not uncommon for the pile to grow to five or even ten cards, which results in a constant shift of power as each play becomes more and more valuable.

That's it. Oh, except for the slap rule. And I don't mean each other. When two of the same card is laid on the pile consecutively, the first player to notice can "slap" the pile and gets to keep all the cards in it. This is why it is very important that a player lays down his or her card without looking at it.

In the case of a simultaneous slap, whoever is on the bottom gets the pile. (Hint: Remove rings and clip nails; there can be blood!)

When I step back and look at the many aspects of Zoe's character, it's no surprise ERS is her favorite card game. In many ways, this riotous game is much like Zoe herself: hilarious, unpredictable, fast, wild, addictive, and irresistible fun. Enjoy!

From the desk of Nina Rowan

Dear Reader,

"I want to write about Victorian robots," Fanciful Nina said as she ate another chocolate bon-bon.

"Huh?" Serious Nina looked up from alphabetizing the spice rack. "You're writing a historical romance. Not a paranormal. Not steampunk."

"But look at this," Fanciful Nina persisted, clicking on the website of the Franklin Institute. "Here's a robot…okay, an automaton, to use the historically correct term, called the Draughtsman-Writer. It was an actual invention by the eighteenth-century Swiss engineer Henri Maillardet, and it can produce four drawings and three poems in both French *and* English. Look, you can watch a video of it! How cool is that?"

"You can't just write about something because it's cool." Serious Nina arranged the paprika, parsley, and peppercorn bottles. "You have to have a reason."

"Coolness *is* a reason."

"Coolness is a reason for a teenager to wear earcuffs. You are writing a historical romance novel. You need much more than coolness as a basis for your story. You need intense conflict, sexual attraction, danger, and agonizing goals that tear your characters apart before they overcome all obstacles and live happily ever after."

"But—"

Serious Nina frowned. "Focus and figure it out. Conflict. Emotions. Anguish. Happy ending. No robots."

"Okay, there's a war going on, right?" Fanciful Nina pushed aside her bon-bons and hauled out her research books. "Rich with possibilities for conflict and emotion. Did you know that in 1854, scientist Charles Wheatstone invented a machine that transmitted messages in cipher? It drew the attention of Baron Playfair, who thought encoded messages would be useful during the Crimean War, and they submitted the machine to the British Foreign Office. How cool is..."

"No," Serious Nina said firmly. "No cool."

"How *interesting* is that?" Fanciful Nina amended.

"May I remind you that you're writing about Sebastian Hall?" Serious Nina put a bottle of rosemary before the sage. "Sebastian is a musician, a free spirit, a gregarious, talented fellow who loves to perform and enjoy himself. He doesn't care about robots or cipher machines. His brother Darius, on the other hand..."

"But what if Sebastian has to care about a cipher machine?" Fanciful Nina reached for another bon-bon. "What if something happens that makes him lose his fun-loving attitude? Omigod, what if something happens that makes him lose his *career*?"

Serious Nina blinked. "You would make Sebastian lose his career?"

"You're the one who said 'anguish.' What if his right hand is permanently injured?"

"But... but Sebastian is so dreamy. So devilishly handsome. Why would you do that to him?"

"So that he's forced to find a new purpose." Fanciful Nina jumped up and started pacing. "What if Sebastian has to stop focusing on himself for once in his life in order to help someone who needs him? Like his brother? Or Clara? Or his brother *and* Clara?"

"Well..."

Fanciful Nina clapped her hands. "What if Darius knows something is wrong? Being a mechanical-minded fellow, he's seeking secret plans for a machine that could be used in wartime. And because encoding machines and automata often have similar mechanisms, the plans are hidden in the Museum of Automata where Clara lives. So Sebastian has to approach Clara because he promised to help Darius, only he can't tell her what he needs. And he doesn't yet know that Clara has a desperate, heart-wrenching goal of her own. And Sebastian is the only person who can help her attain it!"

Fanciful Nina raised her arms in victory. "Conflict. Anguish. Strong goals. Very hot, sexy attraction. I'll figure out the happy ending later."

Serious Nina was silent. She picked at the label of a turmeric bottle.

"What?" Fanciful Nina frowned. "It's good."

"But does Sebastian *have* to lose his career?"

"He'll find his way back to music," Fanciful Nina said reassuringly. "I promise."

"With Clara."

"Of course! Their love is so powerful that they create a

new and exhilarating future together. With lots of steamy lovemaking."

Serious Nina put the turmeric bottle back into place on the rack.

"Okay," she finally agreed. "That's cool."

Happy Reading!

Nina Rowan

From the desk of Jane Graves

Dear Reader,

Our cat, Isabel, is a rescue kitty. She had it rough her first few years, but after living with her foster mom for several months, she was ready to be adopted. She was so sweet and engaging in spite of what had happened to her that we bonded instantly. Her foster mom was delighted that I was a writer, which meant someone was home all day every day to cater to Isabel's every whim. As she put it, "She hit the jackpot!"

As an animal lover, I'm always on the lookout for romance novels that feature pets. So when I was deciding what to write next, I wanted to include pets in a big way. Then I read a popular legend that revolves around pets—the Legend of the Rainbow Bridge—and I knew I'd found the basis for my new series. According to the legend, there's a spirit world tied to earth, inhabited by beloved pets who've passed to the other side. With all earthly age and disease erased, they wait in this transitional paradise for their human companions to join them. After a joyful reunion, together they cross the Rainbow Bridge to heaven.

From there, I created Rainbow Valley, a small town deep in the Texas Hill Country, which is considered to be the home of the mythical Rainbow Bridge and bills itself as the most pet-friendly town in America. The first book, COWBOY TAKE ME AWAY, revolves around the Rainbow Valley Animal Shelter, a place where animals like Isabel get a second chance to find a loving home.

As I write this, Isabel is asleep in my lap. She weighs approximately a thousand pounds these days and makes my legs fall asleep, but how can I tell her to move? We're here to make her life better than the life she knew before. I don't know if the legend is true or not. But I do know that the spirit of the legend—that of enduring love—couldn't be more appropriate for a romance novel. And I like the idea that someday, when I leave this world, she just might be waiting for me at the Rainbow Bridge.

I hope you enjoy COWBOY TAKE ME AWAY!

Happy reading!

Jane Graves

janegraves.com
Facebook.com
Twitter@janegraves

Indian, Soldier, and Settler

Experiences in the Struggle for the American West

Robert M. Utley

Jefferson National Expansion
Historical Association, Inc.
11 N. 4th Street, St. Louis, Missouri 63102

International Standard Book Number: 0-931056-01-2
Library of Congress Catalog Card Number: 77-18408
Printed in the United States of America

Design: Massimo Vignelli

Contents

Foreword

When I was a boy we played "cowboys and Indians" out in the orchard. In our version it was always best to be a cowboy, since then you always won and didn't have to fall down so much from being shot by an infallible six (or ten or seventeen!) shooter. Television was new and I'm not sure where our stereotypes came from, but we certainly knew that the cowboys (or settlers or cavalry) were noble, and the Indians were bad. The pendulum has swung since, and just a few years ago a common image was of the noble Indian, incapable of lying, being crushed by men who were barbarians in all but technology.

Perhaps such gross oversimplifications are inevitable when the most common source of our "knowledge" of the past is the one hour TV show, or small paperbacks, which must pack a vivid adventure into as small a space as possible. But the stereotypes are wrong. They do grave injustice to the remarkable people who won the American West, and to the equally remarkable people who resisted that winning. Their story does not need such distortion or embellishment. This book proves that all it needs is a careful, articulate historian to tell the story as it was. Robert Utley is one of today's foremost scholars on the frontier army and the Indian wars. He is a founder and past president of the Western History Association, was the Chief Historian of the National Park Service, and now is the Deputy Executive Director of the President's Advisory Council on Historic Preservation. Other books by him include **The Last Days of the Sioux Nation, Frontiersmen in Blue** *and* **Frontier Regulars** *(which together form a major history of the frontier army), and he is co-author with Wilcomb Washburn of The American Heritage* **History of the Indian Wars.**

For this book, part of **The Gateway Series** *on America's westward expansion being issued by the Jefferson National Expansion Historical Association, Mr. Utley has chosen an interesting device. Rather than generalizing about Indians, soldiers, and settlers, he has chosen an actual individual from each group, not a hero or leader, and tells us that person's experience. This is not* *fiction: these are documented case histories. Using his sources carefully, Utley reconstructs the experiences these people of the frontier had, as well as what they knew or thought they knew. For their attitudes were formed both by their experiences, and by what they had heard. Dread can feed on words as well as experience. It was easy for an Indian who had heard of the Sand Creek Massacre, or a settler who had heard of the Sioux uprising in Minnesota, to develop fear-filled anger no matter what his own experience had been.*

It is the gift of the historian to put flesh on the bare bones of the past. He reads sentences in dusty documents and resurrects from them the passions of lives now ended. Through Mr. Utley's lucid text we taste events now a century old. We begin to understand how experiences different from ours molded attitudes different from ours; and we fathom a little more of our own past.

Dan Murphy

Opposite:
Dewey Horn Cloud, survivor of Little Bighorn and Wounded Knee. Courtesy South Dakota State Historical Society

"Fifth Infantry Bugler." Bronze by Rudolph Torrini in the Museum of Westward Expansion, St. Louis. Photo by Joseph Matthews

Catherine German. Photo taken after her capture by Indians and rescue, 1875. From Grace Meredith, *Girl Captives of the Cheyennes* (Los Angeles, 1927). Courtesy Missouri Historical Society

Prologue

On a bleak December day in 1890 the long struggle between white man and red for mastery of the North American continent ended violently and tragically on the banks of Wounded Knee Creek, in South Dakota. In the narrow valley, edged by pine-dappled ridges that gave the Sioux reservation its name, the tipis of Big Foot's band of Miniconjou Sioux clustered compactly, while nearby stood the precise ranks of A-tents of the Seventh Cavalry. From a dominating hilltop four Hotchkiss rapid-fire cannon pointed at the Indian camp. On this fateful morning, heavy with coming storm, the mounting conflict between the white officials and the Sioux over the ominous teachings and rituals of the Ghost Dance religion reached a new pitch of suspicion and misunderstanding. No one, red or white, expected or intended a fight. But when the cavalry chief demanded that Big Foot's people give up their guns, tensions boiled over. Savage, bloody fighting engulfed soldiers and Sioux in a holocaust that fired Indians everywhere with an outrage that would burn fiercely for generations.

It is hardly surprising that an experience such as Wounded Knee would so decisively shape the way that Indians then and now looked upon their white conquerors, and upon the process by which the conquest was accomplished. That view, indeed, is widely shared today by whites as well as Indians. No longer is the frontier movement viewed in such scenes as grim-faced pioneers in covered wagons trekking westward to carve a civilization out of the wilderness; warriors with feathered bonnets on fleet ponies sweeping down on corralled wagons and circling in attempted massacre; cavalry charging with bugles sounding, banners whipping, and sabers flashing to put the Indians to rout and save the day. Most people recognize images like these as misleading if not altogether false.

But equally misleading are the darker images that have been substituted: pioneers who were grasping ravagers of the land and oppressors of the natives, soldiers who were brutes rampaging about the West taking fiendish delight in slaughtering Indian women and children, Indians ennobled in the mold of James Fenimore Cooper's *The Last of the Mohicans.*

History is rarely this simple because life is rarely this simple. There are few genuine heroes or villains in real life, merely people who are sometimes heroic, sometimes villainous, but most of the time simply human. Such were the forebears of today's white Americans who advanced the frontier across the continent, and such were the forebears of today's red Americans who were so tragically the victims. They belonged to different cultures and hence looked at the world from different attitudes and beliefs. They were of another time, with values and assumptions entirely plausible for that time. But they were still, for the most part, decent, ordinary human beings. Historical forces over which they had little control brought them into conflict and wrote one of the blackest chapters of United States history.

One way of seeking a balanced understanding of this chapter of history is to look at it through the eyes and experiences of some of the principal actors in the drama—not the brass-buttoned generals or the frock-coated politicians or the befeathered chieftains, but the ordinary, almost anonymous people who more decisively charted the course of history. Dewey Horn Cloud represents the Indian, Bugler William Drown the soldier, and Catherine German and her sisters the settler. Their stories are not typical because most Indians, soldiers, and settlers did not experience such violence and tragedy. Although untypical, their experiences were nevertheless common enough to mold the way each group saw the others and to afford a glimpse of the historical ambiguities that marked the conquest of the frontier. They thus reveal much about the process by which the Indian lost his land, his freedom, and ultimately his way of life.

Indian

Previous Page: *Battle of the Little Bighorn ("Custer's Last Stand"). An Indian view of a great victory, drawn five years after the event by Red Horse, a Sioux chief who took part in it. Fourteen year old Dewey Horn Cloud fought in this engagement.* Photo by Henry B. Beville. Courtesy Smithsonian Institution: National Anthropological Archives

Among Big Foot's followers at Wounded Knee was the family of Horn Cloud, a man of stature and a counselor to the chief. Horn Cloud's sons, bowing to the insistence of government officials that Indians answer to white-man names, were carried on the reservation rolls as Dewey, Joseph, Sherman, and William. As a youth of fourteen Dewey (he would later take the name of Dewey Beard) had ridden on the fringes of the mass of exultant Sioux warriors that had crushed General Custer and his troopers on the Little Bighorn. Now he was twenty-six years old, husband to Wears Eagle, father of an infant daughter, Wet Feet, yet not wholly purged by a decade of deadening reservation life of his warrior instincts and skills.

When the fighting erupted Dewey was standing in the council square where Big Foot, prostrated by pneumonia, directed the surrender of the guns. Soldier and Indian fought face to face and hand to hand, and many died. Dewey caught the glint of brass buttons through the smoke of crashing rifles and carbines. He seized a carbine from a soldier. They struggled, Dewey stabbing wildly with his knife as the soldier screamed and tried to get a strangle hold on Dewey's wind pipe. Finally Dewey got on top and plunged his knife repeatedly into his opponent's kidney.

With the dead soldier's carbine Dewey bolted through the cordon of troops. A bullet hit him in the shoulder and knocked him down. A soldier pointed his carbine and pulled the trigger, but the hammer snapped on an empty chamber. Dewey aimed at the soldier, but his hammer snapped too. Foolishly the two snapped their weapons at each other until Dewey pulled himself to his feet and ran again. He met another soldier, who tried to get around him, but Dewey loaded his carbine and shot him.

Dewey slid down the slope of a deep, broad ravine. It was filled with Indians. Soldiers stood on both edges, firing down. Another bullet smashed his thigh, dropping him again. Cartridges piled in front of him, he sat methodically loading and firing at the bluecoats above until his carbine jammed. He discarded it, and began a painful ascent of the ravine.

From an old man Dewey obtained another carbine. He and two men charged some soldiers on the flat above, but he retreated when his comrades were killed. Back in the ravine he confronted an army Indian scout. Both fired and missed.

After resting briefly Dewey continued up the ravine. It was a scene of horror, roiling with smoke and dust, deadly with flying bullets, and littered with dead and dying people. Mothers hugged the banks clawing out shelters in which to place their infants. Dewey came on his own mother, badly wounded, holding a soldier's pistol. "My son," she said, "pass by me, I am going to fall down now." Another bullet struck her and she fell.

From another old man Dewey got a fully loaded Winchester repeating rifle to replace his single-shot army carbine. Farther up the ravine he found his brother William leaning against the bank, blood running from a hole in his chest. White Lance, Dewey's closest friend, tumbled down the bank. He was wounded too. Dewey and White Lance carried William up the ravine.

The pocket in the ravine at Wounded Knee where Dewey Horn Cloud fought on 29 December 1890. The modern church (approximately where the Hotchkiss guns were) is now gone, burned in the "Second Wounded Knee" in 1973. Photo by George Grant: National Park Service

At a point where the ravine turned sharply, forming a pocket, the three men and several others crawled to the brow. From the hill to their front the Hotchkiss cannons raked the Indian camp, shredding the tipis and mangling everyone who remained in them. Dewey and his friends began shooting at the soldiers working the cannons. In return the artillerymen threw back a deluge of shot and shell. Bullets and shrapnel snapped through clouds of smoke and dust. Explosions churned up the earth and caved in the banks. Dewey saw a shell punch a six-inch hole in a man's stomach. People sang death songs.

Led by an officer on horseback some soldiers pushed one of the cannon toward the ravine pocket, firing as they came. Dewey shot one of the soldiers and the others paused to drag him to safety. Then Dewey knocked the officer from his horse and stopped the advance. A bullet furrowed the ground in front of Dewey's face, throwing dirt in his eyes and blinding him. He slid back down the bank.

Now regaining his strength and sight, Dewey left White Lance and William and proceeded up the ravine, searching for his wife. He ran into a squad of soldiers coming down it, and dodging their bullets he scrambled out of the ravine and raced across the brown prairie to the chance safety of a small party of Oglala Sioux who had come out from the Pine Ridge Agency to investigate the shooting. At this moment Dewey's brother Joseph rode up on a pony. He said all the Horn Clouds had been killed and he was going

The day after at Wounded Knee; Photo by G. E. Trager: courtesy National Archives

Opposite: *Those Indian dead not gathered immediately by relatives were buried in a mass grave on 1 January 1891. The dead included Dewey Horn Cloud's father, mother, wife, and two brothers. His infant daughter died later.* Photo by G. E. Trager: Jefferson National Expansion Memorial

Dewey Horn Cloud in early 1950s. Courtesy South Dakota State Historical Society

back to be killed too. Dewey dissuaded him, and together the brothers rode away from the battlefield.

Though twice wounded, Dewey had lived through a slaughter that had swept away at least 153 men, women, and children of Big Foot's band of 350 and maimed another 50 or more. His own family had indeed been all but annihilated: his father, sitting next to Big Foot, struck down in the first burst of fire, his mother killed in the ravine, Sherman and William both slain, Wears Eagle found dead with the tiny Wet Feet nursing at a bloody bullet-punctured breast. Three months later the infant died—from swallowing too much blood, Dewey believed. Of the Horn Clouds only Dewey and Joseph survived.

For another sixty-five years Dewey Horn Cloud lived out his life quietly on the Pine Ridge Reservation. Finally, after three wars beyond the oceans in which Sioux youth fought as U.S. soldiers, he came to be venerated as the last Sioux veteran of the Little Big Horn. But far more than the triumphant fight with General Custer, it was Wounded Knee that seared Dewey's memory to the day of his death, at ninety-one, in 1955.

"Review of the Cavalry at Pine Ridge." In 1890 Frederic Remington was at the height of his powers and popularity. As a correspondent for Harper's Weekly *he was visiting the army at Pine Ridge and sent back articles and the sketches on these and the following pages.* Reproduced from Harold McCracken, *The Remington Book* (Garden City, 1966). Courtesy Harold McCracken

FREDERIC REMINGTON

"Infantrymen Digging Trenches at Pine Ridge"

"Merry Christmas in a Sibley Tepee." A few days before the conflict. "Sibley tepees" were official army tents, designed by Henry Sibley, patterned after the Plains Indian tepees.

"Watching the Hostiles from the Bluffs." Lt. Edward W. Casey, a friend of Remington, is holding field glasses; Remington has drawn himself in on Casey's left. Casey was killed shortly after Wounded Knee.

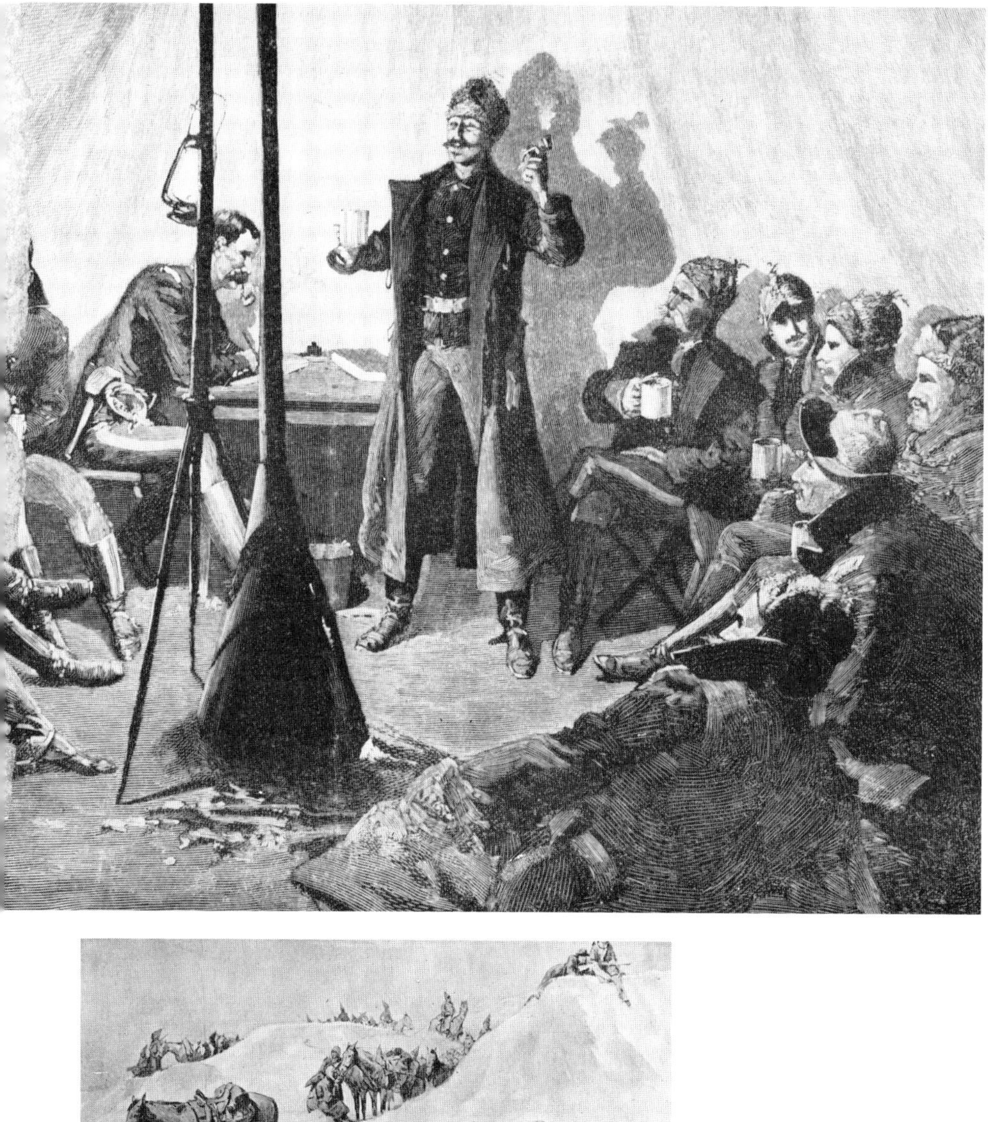

"Opening of the Fight at Wounded Knee." This was the face-to-face situation that produced such high casualties. Having started just a few moments before during an attempt to confiscate Indian weapons, the incident by now is out of control.

"The Wounding of Lt. Hawthorne." Lt. Harry L. Hawthorne, in charge of two of the Hotchkiss guns, was wounded by the counterfire from Dewey Horn Cloud and his friends in the pocket of the ravine.

It was not solely the horror of Wounded Knee that shaped the way Dewey and his tribesmen looked upon white people. Dewey lived at a time when the Sioux were thrust upon the bridge the whites tried to build between the old Indian world and the alien new world of their conquerors. The bridge—the reservation system—had failed to carry the Sioux all the way across, but rather had left them suspended in a cultural purgatory between the two worlds. To Dewey's generation fell the lot to contrast the satisfactions of the old life with the wretchedness of the new.

The old was rich and satisfying indeed—or so they remembered it with nostalgia after it was lost. The plains had teemed with deer, antelope, elk, and buffalo. Game animals, especially the buffalo, supplied an incredible array of life's needs. From the buffalo alone came meat for food, skins and robes for clothing, shelter, containers and other utensils, and bones for tools and implements. Following the great herds that darkened the plains by the millions, the tribesmen evolved a way of life profoundly influenced by the bounty and the seasonal habits of the huge lumbering beasts.

They were a handsome, proud, and strong people, these plainsmen, and they have provided the stereotypical image evoked today by the word "Indian": tall, lithe, sinewy, bronze-skinned; with high cheek bones, acquiline nose, low forehead, thick, wide mouth, dark, expressive eyes; clad in dressed skins ornamented with bead- and quill-work of enduring artistic merit; weapons and braided, jet-black hair fluttering with eagle feathers; skilled horsemen and bowmen; masters of war and hunt. They lived close to the land, venerated it mystically as "Mother Earth," and utterly failed to understand how it could be sold. They practiced a religion ordered by the wonders of nature and that rewarded each communicant with a highly personal brand of "power" to carry him along the pathways of life. They cherished individual freedom and independence and embraced a democracy that bordered on anarchy.

Above all they were creatures of war. "When we were young all we thought about was going to war with some other nation," recalled Encouraging Bear, an intimate of the legendary Crazy Horse; "all tried to get their names up the highest, and whoever did so

"Buffalo Hunt Under the Wolf-skin Mask" by George Catlin. The rich world as the Indian remembered it. Catlin went up the Missouri in 1832, and was among the first to paint the almost-undisturbed West. To capture this scene he himself crawled under such a wolf-skin. Courtesy Smithsonian Institution: National Collection of Fine Arts

The Indian lived in a spirit-filled world, and celebrated it in rich pageantry. This is Pehriska-Ruhpa, or "Two Ravens," in the costume of the Dog Dance, as painted by the young Swiss artist Charles Bodmer who saw him on the upper Missouri in 1833. Courtesy Lyle S. and Aileen E. Woodcock, St. Louis, Missouri

"Warpath." The Indian found his greatest glory in war, long before the white man came. Painted by Alfred Jacob Miller who visited the western tribes in 1837. Courtesy The Boatmen's Bank, St. Louis, Missouri

"All our people now were settling down in square gray houses, scattered here and there across the hungry land..." A home on the Rosebud Reservation in the early 1900s. Courtesy J. A. Anderson Collection, Nebraska State Historical Society

was the principal man of the nation.'' They fought over hunting grounds, or to defend themselves against the raids of others, or to gain plunder, but above all they fought for personal recognition. The greatest honors the tribe could bestow were for achievements in war, and almost from infancy the warrior values were inculcated and the warrior skills honed to perfection. They fought mainly against other tribes—the Sioux and Northern Cheyennes, for example, against the Crows, Shoshonis, and Pawnees. But increasingly they also fought with the ''Wasichus,'' the white-skinned people who invaded their homeland in mounting numbers in the middle of the nineteenth century.

''As I think back upon those days,'' reminisced Wooden Leg, a Northern Cheyenne whose tribe roamed with the Sioux, ''it seems that no people in the world ever were any richer than we were.'' It was a life they loved while they lived it and mourned when they lost it. The Comanche Ten Bears hinted at the reverence all the tribes of the Great Plains felt toward it when he told government commissioners in 1867: ''I was born where there were no enclosures, and where everything drew a free breath. I want to die there and not within walls.''

''Plains Indian Bowman on a Running Horse'' by Titian Peale. Peale caught the spirit of the Plains Indian as the artist on Major Stephen H. Long's expedition across the plains in 1819. Courtesy American Philosophical Society Library, Philadelphia

The new life the Wasichus clamped on Dewey Horn Cloud and his people after their conquest stood in stark and dispiriting contrast to the old free life of the plains. ''All our people now were settling down in square gray houses, scattered here and there across the hungry land,'' explained Black Elk, ''and around them the Wasichus had drawn a line to keep them in.'' Agents of the Great Father took charge. ''I don't want a white man over me,'' protested Sitting Bull. ''I don't want an agent.'' But even the mighty chief who had wiped out Custer had to accept an agent. Inside the lines the agents tried to dress the Indians in white-man clothes and make them into farmers and Christians. The old customs and values lost their meaning in the new setting, or were ridiculed or even suppressed by the agent's Indian police and judges. Warriors and huntsmen could not make war or hunt buffalo, which vanished anyway before the heavy rifles of white hide-hunters. Climate and soil and the instincts of a nomadic people conspired against the crops. Government dole, always inadequate, substituted. Hunger and disease stalked the gray

The frozen body of Chief Big Foot, leader of the Sioux at Wounded Knee. A severe blizzard followed the massacre. Courtesy Smithsonian Institution: Bureau of American Ethnology

cabins. Cultural breakdown pressed the people ever deeper into despair.

This sudden and devastating passage from one world to another gave rise to the Ghost Dance religion. It assured the Indians that a Messiah would come, deliver them from their present oppressors, and restore the world they once knew. So the Hotchkiss guns that littered the flats beside Wounded Knee Creek with the torn bodies of Big Foot's followers shattered more than flesh. "I can see that something else died there in the bloody mud," mused Black Elk, "and was buried in the blizzard. A people's dream died there. It was a beautiful dream."

An Indian need not have been a victim of Wounded Knee, or even be a Sioux, to taste its bitterness and to pass it on from generation to generation. All the Indians of the West had their Wounded Knee, however bloody or bloodless, that brought an end to the old order and signaled the beginning of the new. With variations of time, place, and detail, the experience of Dewey Horn Cloud and his people was repeated all over the West in the four decades after 1850.

The tribes fought valiantly against the overwhelming numbers and technology of the white men, but it was hopeless. One reason for this was that they never could unite on any significant scale in the common defense, because in truth they were not one people, but many. There were similarities between tribes, to be sure, but there were basic differences too. Unlike the plainsmen, for example, the Apaches of the southwestern mountains and deserts preferred to travel on foot rather than horseback, tended scattered corn patches, and lived in brush "wickiups" instead of skin tipis. Their neighbors, the proud Navajos, also raised corn, and fruit too, herded sheep and goats, lived in log-and-mud "hogans," and like the plains people rarely went anywhere except by horse. The Pacific Northwest tribes followed a pattern of life ordered by the seasonal cycles of the salmon and edible roots such as the camas. Whatever the similarities and differences, however, most tellingly the tribes looked upon themselves as different—as Cheyenne and Ute and Nez Perce and Paiute and Modoc rather than as Indian—and they reserved their deepest antipathies and most savage warfare for one another rather than for the white invader. One after another the tribes fell before the relentless advance of the frontier.

American Indians never were "a" culture, and separate tribes had widely different customs. Upper: *Plains Indian culture was revolutionized by the horse.* U.S. Army Signal Corps photo: Courtesy National Archives

Center: *Apaches by their brush "wickiup."* U.S. Army Signal Corps photo: Courtesy National Archives

Left: *Northwest coast Indian salmon fishing.* Photo by Edward Curtis: Courtesy National Historical Society

Opposite:
(1) *Keintpoos, or "Captain Jack," Modoc leader who first tried to cooperate with whites, then led his people in the Modoc War.* Courtesy Smithsonian Institution: National Collection of Fine Arts

(2) *Satanta, or "White Bear," a leading warrior of the Kiowa, active in the Red River War (1874-75).* Courtesy Smithsonian Institution: National Collection of Fine Arts

(3) *Hin-mah-too-yah-let-kekt, or "Chief Joseph," a skilled diplomat and leader of the Nez Perce. Although others did most of the military leadership on the famous flight of the Nez Perce to Canada, it was Joseph who caught the public's eye.* Courtesy Smithsonian Institution: National Collection of Fine Arts

Not military defeat alone, nor even chiefly, overwhelmed them, or accounted for their bitterness. The Wounded Knees stood for more than just the clashes with the bluecoats. They stood as symbols of a process. First came the white pioneers to scare off or kill the game, cut the timber in the stream bottoms, graze off the grass of meadow and prairie, and even rip open the breast of Mother Earth. Then came commissioners to buy the land. Bewildering councils that Indians never learned to understand or cope with left them divided among themselves and puzzling over a piece of paper that recorded their agreement to part with their land. Most knew, without quite knowing how, that they had been victimized. "We did not give our country to you," declared Sitting Bull; "you stole it."

Somewhere in this process the provocation became too great to bear, and a leader fired his people to fight. Usually it was after the white pressures on land and food resources had become so intense as to prompt at least part of a tribe to sign a treaty and accept a reservation. Most of the big Indian wars were actually breakouts from a reservation rather than resistance to going to one. Wounded Knee occurred almost a decade after the last Sioux had surrendered. Names of patriot chiefs who valued their birthright more than life leap from the annals of tribal warfare: Sitting Bull and Crazy Horse of the Sioux, Little Mountain and Satanta of the Kiowas, Kamiakin of the Yakimas, Captain Jack of the Modocs, Chief Joseph of the Nez Perces, Manuelito of the Navajos, Mangas Coloradas and Cochise, Victorio and Geronimo of the Apaches. Always revolt brought soldiers to exact harsh retribution, and to scar the memories of the victims with scenes such as Dewey Horn Cloud carried from Wounded Knee.

The tribes of the Columbia Basin never forgot the havoc wrought by the bluecoats' cannon and new long-range rifles at Four Lakes and Spokane Plain in 1858. And they never forgot the big-framed soldier-chief who marched grimly through their country plucking men he thought guilty of crime from their lodges and carrying them off in chains or, for fifteen, summarily hanging them from the nearest stout tree-limb.

The Eastern Sioux scarcely forgot the vengeance provoked by their uprising in Minnesota. Defeated by soldiers at Wood Lake, many surrendered only to be

1

2

3

4

5

6

(4) *Tatanka Iyotake, or "Sitting Bull," great chief, warrior, and holy man of the Teton Sioux. His total commitment to the Sioux way of life inevitably pitted him against the whites. He is most famous for his part in the Battle of the Little Big Horn, although there he made medicine rather than actually fighting.* Courtesy National Archives

(5) *Victorio, Chiricahua Apache leader. A master military strategist. When his people were removed to a totally unsuitable reservation he led a three year resistance.* Courtesy Arizona Historical Society

(6) *Goyakla, or "Geronimo," Apache leader and medicine man. Perhaps the army's most famous foe—and perhaps he deserved it. After the death of his family set Geronimo's direction, he eluded all forces for almost a decade. When finally he surrendered (the last Indian formally to do so) there were forty-two companies of American infantry and cavalry, and four thousand Mexican soldiers, pursuing him and his band of fifty or so.* Courtesy Smithsonian Institution: National Collection of Fine Arts

Indians could recall a multitude of incidents to justify fear and resentment of their conquerors.

Upper: *Following an uprising in Minnesota brought on by starving conditions and a corrupt Indian agent, thirty-eight Santee Sioux were hanged simultaneously on 26 December 1862. This painting is part of a series on rollers—called a "panorama" then—painted shortly after the event by John Stevens. Others are reproduced on pp. 62-63.* Courtesy Minnesota Historical Society

Center: *"Attack at Dawn," oil by Charles Schreyvogel. On numerous occasion—the Sand Creek Massacre in 1864, Black Kettle's village on the Washita in 1868, to name but two—sleeping villages that thought they were secure and even at peace suddenly found themselves under attack.* Courtesy Thomas Gilcrease Institute of American History and Art, Tulsa, Oklahoma

Lower: *Navajos under guard at Bosque Redondo, the barren reservation they were banished to in 1864-68.* Courtesy National Archives

hurried through a bewildering series of "trials" that left 303 sentenced to die. The Great Father in Washington, a kindly bearded man, took time from the white people's war among themselves to save most of the convicted Indians, but thirty-eight died on the gallows on a frosty December day in 1862.

More horrifying even than Wounded Knee, Sand Creek inflamed Indians everywhere as word of the deeds of the Colorado militia and their fanatical preacher-colonel sped from tribe to tribe in 1864-65. Black Kettle's people had supposed themselves under military protection when the soldiers stormed among their tipis and perpetrated an orgy of blood-letting that knew no bounds of age or sex or barbarity. "All manner of depredations were inflicted," testified a mixed-blood scout; "they were scalped, their brains knocked out; the men used their knives, ripped open women, clubbed little children, knocked them in the head with their guns, beat their brains out, mutilated their bodies in every sense of the word." Sand Creek hung over military-Indian relations for years afterward. "Have you never heard of Sand Creek?" Tall Bull demanded of General Hancock in 1867. "Your soldiers look just like those who butchered the women and children there."

The tribal memory of the Navajos will always bear, as a central fact of their history, the four-year ordeal of "Bosque Redondo," the "round grove of trees" near Fort Sumner, New Mexico, that gave its name to the reservation where they passed the terrible exile of 1864-68. Bosque Redondo began with the tragic "Long Walk" in which soldiers herded more than two thousand people, the first of eight thousand, across two hundred miles of desert and plain to the barren, sickly bottoms of the Pecos River. Two hundred perished on the way, and many more died of disease and despair at Bosque Redondo. Crops would not grow there, and Kiowas and Comanches raided the Navajo herds. But above all the people mourned their lost homeland. With the expense of their upkeep soaring, the Great Father at last admitted defeat and let them go back to their beloved homes. "Nahondzod," the Navajos still call this period, "The Fearing Time."

Most tribes could recount similar tribulations at the hands of the soldiers—Kiowas, Comanches, and Apaches imprisonment in the ancient fortresses of far-off, sickly Florida; Modocs the hanging of Captain Jack and other chiefs; Nez Perces the tragic fighting retreat across mountain and plain to defeat heartbreakingly near their goal of Canadian sanctuary; Cheyennes shot down defenseless in the snow during a desperate break from a starving, freezing confinement designed to make them go back to a hated exile in the south.

The white people who destroyed the game and timber and grass and broke open the prairie sod did not wear blue coats. Nor did the top-hatted, black-suited officials who talked the Indians out of their land. Nor did the agents and farmers and school teachers and Christian missionaries who tore apart the old life without being able to substitute a satisfactory new life. But for Dewey Horn Cloud it was the bluecoats whose bullets struck down his wife and daughter and father and mother and brothers, and for the Dewey Horn Clouds of the American West and their descendants it was the bluecoats who came to personify all the forces, immediate and remote, that had spelled their doom.

Makhpiya-Luta, or "Red Cloud," in old age. Once he led the ferocious and successful resistance of the Sioux to the Bozeman Trail; here old, blind, a leader of a defeated and fragmented people. Photo by Edward Curtis: Courtesy Library of Congress

Soldier

Previous page: *A young trooper poses for photographer J.C.H. Grabill of Deadwood, S.D., about 1892.* Courtesy Library of Congress

Below: *"Writing Home," Frederic Remington.* Courtesy Harold McCracken

"I commenced the day this morning by being orderly bugler for the commanding officer, and at half-past eight in the morning attended guard-mounting, and immediately after saddled up and rode two miles, and assisted in digging a grave; returned at half-past twelve, and started again at one with the funeral procession, after which was marched home, dressed myself for evening parade, marched back again to the corral or stable, assisted in flogging a deserter, came home, ate supper, and here I am scratching it down in the old journal. Some people surmise that a soldier's life is a lazy one, but soldiers themselves think otherwise."

So passed another routine day, 1 February 1854, in the military life of bugler William D. Drown. Of dark complexion and slight build, bugler Drown was a first-rate horse soldier. He was not, however, typical of his bunkies of the First United States Dragoons—if indeed any could be said to typify that diverse lot of men who made up the frontier army. At thirty-two Drown was older than most and nearing the close of his third five-year enlistment. He was also a combat veteran: in the Mexican War he had fought under General Winfield Scott from Vera Cruz to Mexico City, helped storm Chapultapec Castle, and taken a wound at Molino del Rey. Before signing up in the regulars in 1840 Drown had been a printer in his New Hampshire home town, which may explain why, again unlike his comrades, he had an eye for the telling detail and the literary ability to commit it to paper.

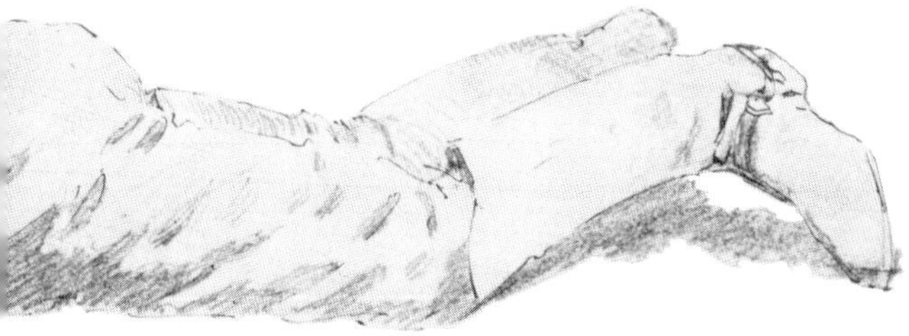

Unlike most frontier soldiers, bugler Drown's Indian service brought him not only the usual monotony of garrison life and the fatigue and discomfort of long futile marches in search of an invisible enemy; it brought him as well the danger and zest of combat. This came as the climax to one of those rare pursuits of Indian raiders that actually ended in a fight.

The pursuit began in the New Mexican capital of Santa Fe on a crisp January day in 1855, when the first sergeant ordered Drown to sound "Boots and Saddles." A dozen Mescalero Apaches had fallen on a ranch south of town while most of the men were absent and had raped the women, killed two herders, and ridden off with seventy-five horses and mules. Behind Lieutenant Samuel D. Sturgis, Drown and seventeen other dragoons and six men from the ranch took up the trail. Three days and 175 miles later the patrol came up with the marauders.

The Indians were spied leading the stolen herd from a pine grove. Despite bitter cold, the dragoons removed their greatcoats and gauntlets and placed them on the snow-spotted ground. At a distance of one hundred yards they drew up in attack formation. Suddenly seeing their danger, the Apaches began to shout and gesticulate in a bid for a peace talk, but as Drown observed, "that was not what we were sent there for."

Drown records what happened then: "The Lieutenant said, 'Well, men, I do not understand one word they are saying; haul off and let them have it, and look out for yourselves.' The words were no sooner out of his mouth than bang! bang! bang! rang the musketoons and pistols, and the Indians began to jump and dance around like so many awkward crows. . . . They at last began making towards the wood, and then was our last chance at them. Our hands were so cold that we could not reload our pieces, and, as soon as the shots that were in them were exhausted, were forced to draw our sabers and make a desperate charge, to prevent them from entering the wood."

With slashing sabers and blazing pistols the soldiers galloped into the midst of the Indians. Drown singled out a big warrior about to fire an arrow at another charging dragoon, took aim, and dropped him with a pistol ball in the thigh. The Indian rose and stumbled toward the woods. Drown fired again and missed, but a comrade brought the Indian down with a musketoon shot.

"I had already fired five shots from my pistol, and consequently had but one more left. I saw another Indian making for the woods with no one after him, and I thought I could do no better with my last shot than to give him the loan of it. I at once gave 'Old Boston' the spur, and started after him." Riding past the warrior he had already shot, "the first thing I knew—bang! went his gun, and the ball entered my right shoulder near the centre. The ball passed clear through and came out the front, just touching the bone. I thought the fellow would die anyway without further assistance, and kept up the chase."

"I got up to about fifteen yards of the man I was after, and, he being straight in front of me, I raised my pistol and brought it down on a level for him, and was just ready to pull the trigger when I found my hand kept falling, and that I had not sufficient strength in my arm to hold up the pistol, and was forced to return it to the holster and ride out [to] one side." Corporal Katon then took on this Apache, who ran at him with a long lance. Katon parried with his saber, deflecting the lance into the breast of his horse. The Indian tried to dodge beneath the horse to escape the saber, "but Katon was too quick for him, and took off nearly all one side of his head, just as he was in the act of stooping, and thus finished his mutton."

"I looked around to see how my particular friend was getting on, and what should he be doing but upon his feet again and loading his gun. I was not able to finish him myself, but there was another man now at hand"—one of the civilians—"who gave him a shot from a sharp-shooting rifle, which dropped him to rise no more."

Sturgis's sudden, aggressive assault had smashed the marauders. His little command had killed three Apaches, badly wounded four more, and recovered all the stock. Three of his own men were down with wounds. The operation was uncharacteristic because most never brought the quarry to bay. For those that did, however, it typified dozens of such actions of the Indian wars: short, sharp, bloody, and of no special significance for the large issues of war and peace.

The return march was a painful ordeal for the wounded Drown. "I never was so cold in my life, although every man who had a spare blanket had it around me and the other two wounded men." As a slight recompense, however, he carried with him a trophy of the fight: "One of my comrades came up to me and made me a present of the scalp-lock of the Indian who shot me, which I am going to keep as long as possible, as I do not wish to forget my particular friends."

Drown's almost flippant tone reveals a daredevil temperament and a somewhat casual attitude toward what in reality was a deadly business. However inconsequential the stakes for the big picture, they were portentous indeed for the participants, as the fate of Private Patrick Rooney showed. An arrow had buried itself two and a half inches in his skull just above the right ear. The shaft had broken off, leaving an eighth of an inch of the point exposed. One man tried to pull it out with his teeth. Another tried to cut it out with a bowie knife. Finally the company saddler succeeded with a pair of pliers. Alive but unconscious, Rooney was draped over the saddle of his horse and packed eighty miles to the nearest settlement. He died two weeks later in the Santa Fe hospital.

Bugler Drown's personal legacy consists of a few fragments of his graphic diary published in an 1875 book and yellowing official documents that record enlistments and discharges in the United States and Confederate armies and the sad efforts of a rheumatic old man to obtain a large enough pension to live out the last of his eighty-eight years in quiet dignity. Most of his comrades left even less by which to be individually remembered. Their role in history was thus composite, institutional. They were the anonymous blue-clad frontiersmen of the little regular army that opened the way for the civilization of the American West. Or at least so they saw themselves.

"Fight for Water," Charles Schreyvogel. Courtesy Thomas Gilcrease Institute of American History and Art, Tulsa, Oklahoma

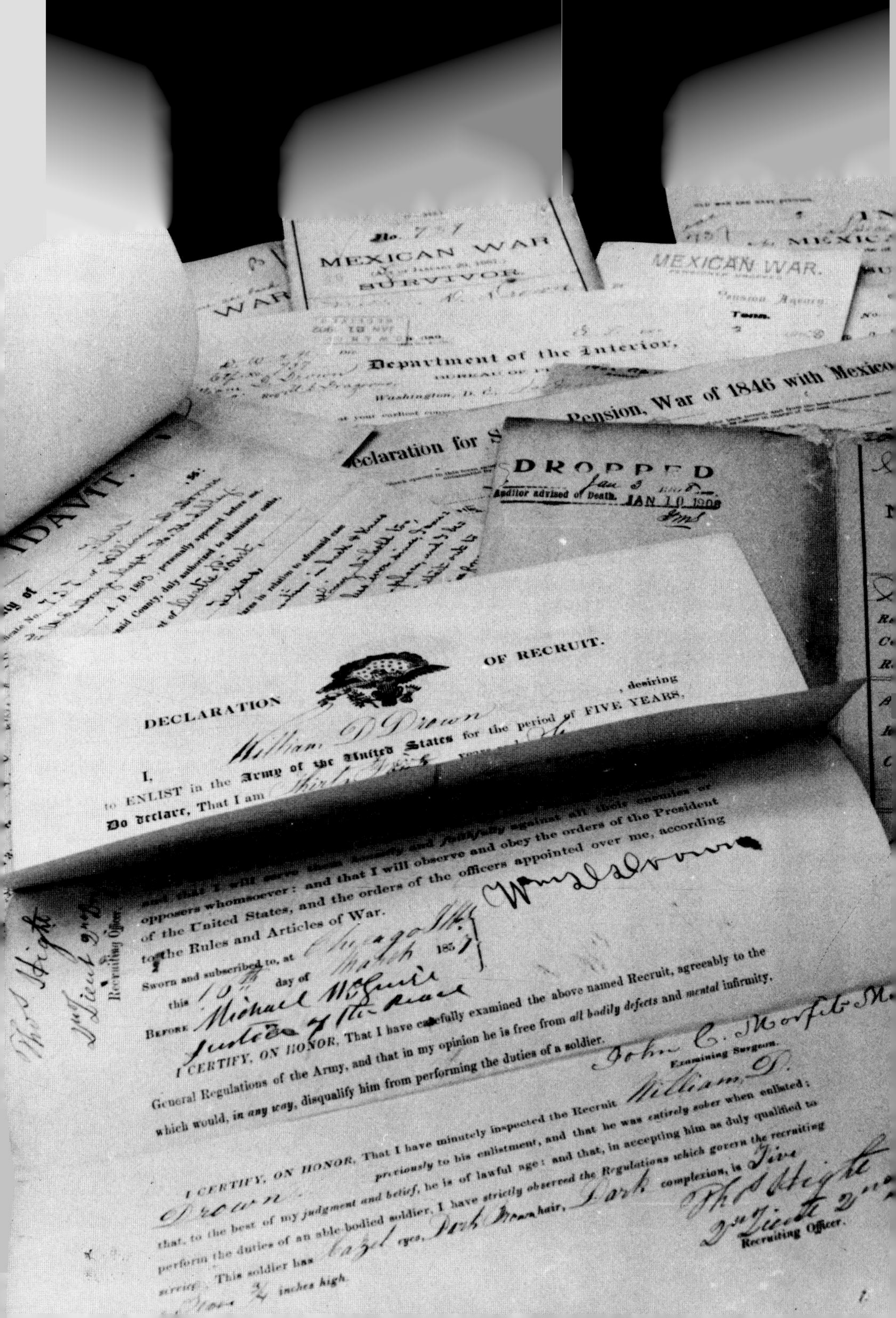
MEXICAN WAR
SURVIVOR
MEXICAN WAR.
Department of the Interior,
Washington, D. C.
Pension, War of 1846 with Mexico
DROPPED
Auditor advised of Death. JAN 10 1908
AFFIDAVIT.
DECLARATION OF RECRUIT.
I, William D. Brown, desiring to ENLIST in the Army of the United States for the period of FIVE YEARS,
Do declare, That I am
opposers whomsoever: and that I will observe and obey the orders of the President of the United States, and the orders of the officers appointed over me, according to the Rules and Articles of War.
Sworn and subscribed to, at
day of
Before
I CERTIFY, ON HONOR, That I have carefully examined the above named Recruit, agreeably to the General Regulations of the Army, and that in my opinion he is free from all bodily defects and mental infirmity, which would, in any way, disqualify him from performing the duties of a soldier.
Examining Surgeon.
I CERTIFY, ON HONOR, That I have minutely inspected the Recruit previously to his enlistment, and that he was entirely sober when enlisted; that, to the best of my judgment and belief, he is of lawful age; and that, in accepting him as duly qualified to perform the duties of an able-bodied soldier, I have strictly observed the Regulations which govern the recruiting service. This soldier has eyes, hair, complexion, is inches high.
Recruiting Officer.

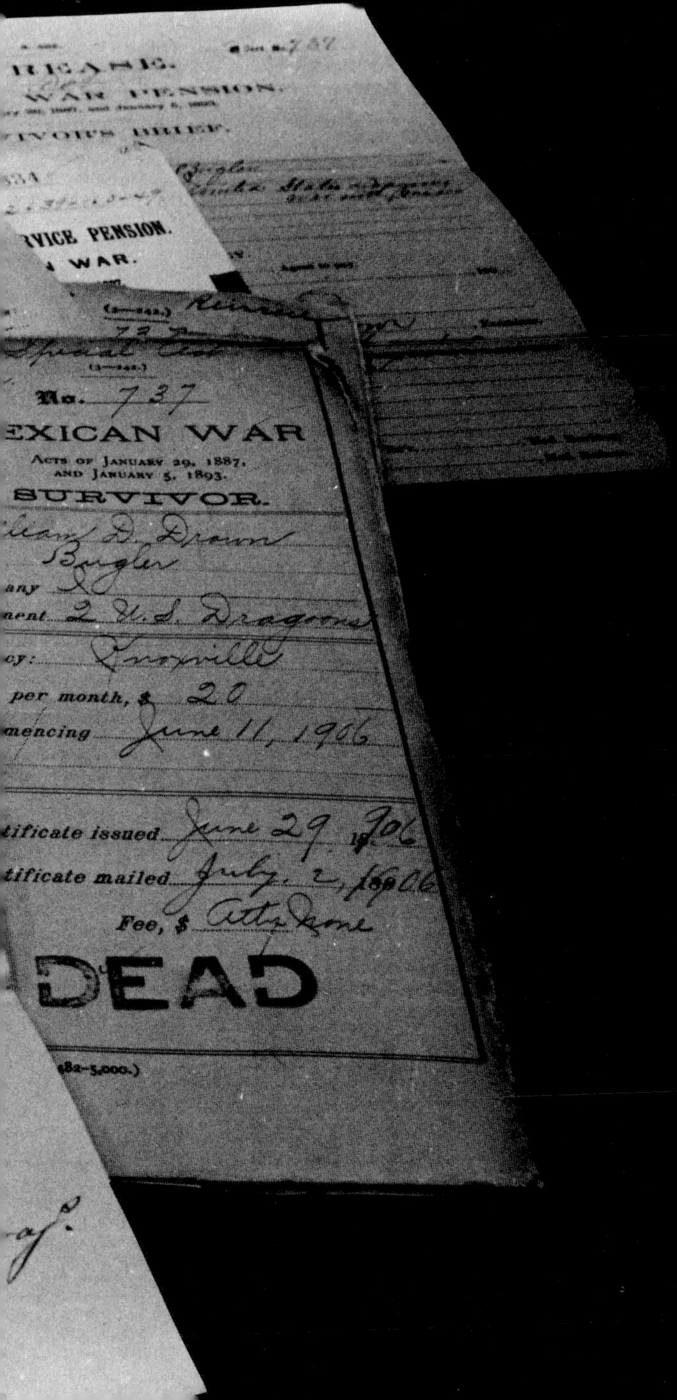

The everyday lives of the men of the frontier army, their boredom, occasional fright, joys—all that a life is made of— today come to this; documents in the National Archives. These are the papers relating to William D. Drown, sometime printer, soldier for the U.S. in the War with Mexico, bugler in the frontier army during the Indian Wars, soldier for the Confederacy in the Civil War, and subject of this chapter. Photo by William Clark: Courtesy National Archives

"Breaking Through the Lines," Charles Schreyvogel.
Courtesy Thomas Gilcrease Institute of American History and Art, Tulsa, Oklahoma

Upper: *One view of the infantry: Dressed for inspection.* Courtesy Fort Laramie National Historic Site

Center: *"A Beautiful Fight Ensued." Another view: Off-duty frontier army life drawn for* Harper's Monthly *by Frederic Remington.* Courtesy Harold McCracken

Lower: *Army life rarely was glamorous. Here soldiers are cutting wood at Ford Grant, Arizona, 18 May 1885.* Courtesy Arizona Historical Society

Frontier soldiers were every type of humanity and from every walk of life. "In my company," wrote a cavalryman, "we have one printer, one telegraph operator, two lawyers, three professors of languages, one harness maker, four cooks and bakers, two blacksmiths, one jeweler, three school teachers, also farmers, lumbermen, peddlers, railroad men and day laborers." There were romantic youths seeking adventure, Bowery toughs, ruined professionals, fugitives from justice or a nagging wife, jilted lovers, criminals, drunks, and even, after the Civil War, former Confederate soldiers. Half were foreign born, mainly Irish, German, and English. As a veteran of three European wars and the French Foreign Legion put it, arriving in New York at the height of the Panic of 1873, "it was either the soup house, starve, or the recruiting depot." All in all, recalled an old soldier, "The Regular Army was a tough bunch in those days."

"Glittering misery," an officer's wife labeled frontier military life. The men paraded in blue and gold under snapping banners and plumed helmets. But, as an officer observed, they "use the shovel more frequently than the rifle and saber." "Government workhouses," they called the little forts scattered around the West. Discipline was rigid and punishments severe, the social gulf between enlisted men and officers wide and unbridgeable. Hard labor, occasional field expeditions, and whiskey—"the curse of the service"—relieved but little the monotony and boredom. In return the army paid them thirteen dollars a month, clothed them in a uniform of heavy blue wool even in the desert, lodged them in crowded, badly ventilated, unsanitary barracks, and fed them bacon, beef, and beans. "The poor privates are perfect slaves," concluded an army wife. "I do pity them from the bottom of my heart."

For all their flaws the poor privates achieved a surprising professionalism, and they could make light of their slavery in verse after verse of rollicking song that bespoke their esprit de corps:

Oh the drums would roll, upon my soul,
This is the style we'd go,
Forty miles a day, on beans and hay,
In the Regular Army O.

They served officers who were also professionals, but also dulled by the low pay, slow promotion, and frontier discomforts of the peacetime army. "Most of the commanding officers were petty tyrants," a general remembered of his early years in the West, who "had been in command of small posts so long that their habits and minds had narrowed down to their surroundings." On the frontier, observed another, an officer "learned all there was to know about commanding forty dragoons, and forgot everything else."

The soldiers looked on their Indian foes with an ambivalence uncharacteristic of the civilian population of the West. On the one hand, with the civilians, they subscribed to that tired old saying, already a cliche by the 1870s, about the only good Indian. A cavalry recruit at an Indian agency on the upper Missouri overheard it in an exchange between a young officer and the regimental commander, the same Sturgis who two decades earlier had led Bugler Drown's memorable charge: "There are a good many Indians here, Colonel," observed the lieutenant. "The *good Indians,*" replied Sturgis, pointing to a hillside cemetery where Sioux dead, according to custom, lay on elevated platforms, "are up there on those poles." To soldiers full of stories and even some direct observation of torture, mutilation, and atrocity—Sturgis had just lost a son at the Little Bighorn—it was easy to believe that the only good Indian was a dead Indian.

On the other hand, unlike the civilians, the soldiers often could understand the Indian side of the question. Indians might be, as one trooper saw them, "a dirty, thieving lot . . . the worse beggars I ever saw," but they were also the victims of the white man's greed, double-dealing, and provocation. "We thought they were not getting an even break—and they weren't," declared a cavalry sergeant about the Apaches. "The soldiers did not hold hard feelings about the Indians. I could always make friends with them, when they were treated right." Most of the regulars held corrupt or incompetent Indian agents responsible for Indian hostilities, and they never understood the government's Indian policy. "It certainly seems foolish," wrote a company commander, "to fight Indians with one hand, and to make presents and give them arms with the other."

But the soldiers followed orders. They fought the Indians when ordered, guarded them against vengeful whites when ordered, and coexisted with them amicably in times of peace when ordered.

The warfare was the worst kind—guerilla warfare against an unseen foe. "In a campaign against Indians, the front is all around, and the rear is nowhere," commented an officer. Sometimes it resulted in combat. In an Indian fight, as bugler Drown and his comrades discovered, the consequences could be painful and even deadly if you stopped an arrow or bullet, and with many tribes if your body fell to the enemy it was certain to be scalped and fearfully mutilated. More often a campaign was simply a grueling physical ordeal unrecompensed by decisive action. "We traveled through the country," wrote an officer to his mother, "broke down our men, killed our horses, and returned as ignorant of the whereabouts of Mr. Sanico"—a Comanche chief—"as when we started."

Although most operations were small-unit affairs such as Drown chronicled, there were some big battles too. The nation recoiled in horror and outrage in 1866 when Sioux wiped out Captain William J. Fetterman's command at Fort Phil Kearny and, a decade later, when General Custer rode to the Little Bighorn and immortality. More than two hundred troopers perished with Custer, but from the disaster sprang a legend to be nourished and treasured for generations. Often the army won: at Four Lakes, Spokane Plain, Whitestone Hill, Killdeer Mountain, and Bear Paw Mountain superior numbers and firepower proved decisive; and in such operations as the Red River campaigns of 1874-75 simple perseverence so harassed and wore out the foe as to bring victory without significant combat.

"I shall fight no more forever," Chief Joseph declared as he laid his rifle at the feet of General Miles in 1877. Although rarely so poignantly, one after another tribal leaders enacted surrender rituals in which they acknowledged the futility of continued resistance. Three weeks after Wounded Knee Kicking Bear yielded his rifle to this same General Miles. Wounded Knee was the last major Indian fight in the United States. In that same year of 1890 the Census Bureau could no longer trace a frontier of settlement on the map of the American West. Understandably the Bugler Drowns of the regular army believed that they more than any others had made that possible.

However exaggerated history would pronounce their self-appraisal, the frontier soldiers did play a

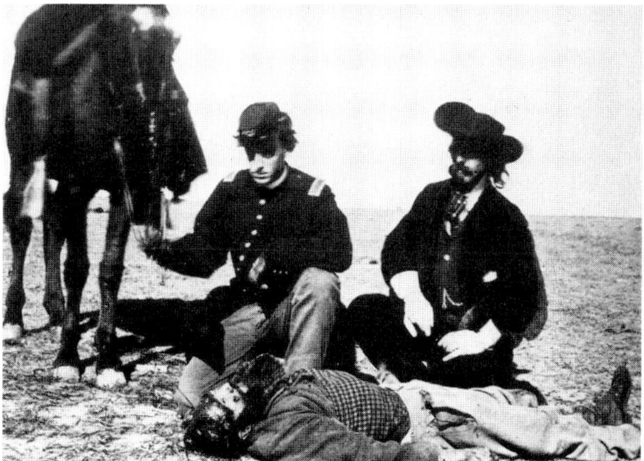

"Chief Joseph Surrenders" after the heroic Nez Perce attempt to reach sanctuary in Canada. Painting by Olaf Seltzer. Courtesy William Gilcrease Institute of American History and Art, Tulsa, Oklahoma

Ralph Morrison, hunter, scalped by Indians near Fort Dodge, Kansas in the late 1860s, as he was found by an army officer. Indians fiercely resented the commercial buffalo hunters. Photo by William Soule: Courtesy Smithsonian Institution

Detail from "A Cavalryman's Breakfast on the Plains," painted by Frederic Remington in 1890. Courtesy Amon Carter Museum, Fort Worth

prominent role in the opening of the West. They helped to explore and map its vast expanse of mountain, desert, and plain. They built roads and strung telegraph lines. They stood guard over railroads and stagecoaches. They erected and garrisoned farflung forts that attracted pioneer settlements, then gave them protection and markets. The flag and the uniform brought the illusion and sometimes the reality of order and security to civilization's raw edge. And throughout the regulars fought the wars that, if not conquests complete in themselves, were a final blow that accomplished the Indian's inevitable collapse.

LAST CHANCE
OR BUST

Settler

Previous page: *"A Doubtful Visitor" by Charles M. Russell.* Courtesy Thomas Gilcrease Institute of American History and Art, Tulsa, Oklahoma

John German's westward migration consumed four years. A Georgian with a large family, he had returned from the Civil War wasted in health by the ravages of a Union prison camp to find his farm cleaned out by guerrilla bands. Five years of toil yielded enough capital to head west in search of restored health in Colorado's high, dry climate. His trek began in 1870 and was three times interrupted by homesteading pauses in Missouri and Kansas, but at last, in August 1874, the long journey entered its final stage. A covered wagon drawn by a team of oxen bore the family belongings, while chickens rode in a coop strapped to the end gate. The family walked. There were John and Lydia and their seven children: Rebecca Jane, twenty; Stephen, eighteen; Catherine, seventeen; Joanna, fifteen; Sophia, twelve; Julia, seven; and Addie, five. A milk cow and two calves ambled in the rear, tethered to the wagon by a long rope. In the golden autumn dusk of 10 September 1874 the Germans made camp beside a dry stream amid the high rolling plains of western Kansas. Tomorrow they would reach Fort Wallace. The Colorado boundary lay less than a day's journey beyond.

John German had heard vague rumors about Indian hostilities, but he did not know that a full-scale war had burst over the southern plains. Even then army patrols laced the Staked Plains of Texas, to the south, in pursuit of rebelling Cheyennes, Kiowas, and Comanches. Medicine Water's Cheyenne band had slipped out of the military net and ridden north to raid the Kansas travel routes. A party of seventeen warriors and two women from this group discovered the Germans breaking camp on the morning of September 11.

The high-pitched war cry announced the presence of the Cheyennes as they dashed among the Germans. Stephen, rounding up the cattle with Catherine a short distance away, shouted "Indians! Indians!" With his muzzle-loading rifle he ran behind a ridge but was pursued and slain. An arrow hit Catherine in the thigh. A big Indian threw himself from his mount, jerked the arrow out, kicked her several times, and threw her on the pony. At the wagon Rebecca Jane had seized an axe to defend herself against an assailant, but another warrior shot and killed her. John German, who had been scouting the road ahead, dashed back with his old muzzle-loader but was shot down before he could fire it. Lydia screamed and ran toward him. An Indian grabbed her. "Oh, let me get to father!" she exclaimed. "Let me get to father!" With a tomahawk the Indian split open her skull.

The remaining sisters had been corralled at the wagon. The raiders singled out Catherine and Joanna and carried on an animated discussion. Finally they removed the bonnet of each. Joanna had long hair, Catherine short. A warrior shot Joanna and claimed her scalp. As the four surviving sisters watched, the Indians scalped the other victims who had long hair and plundered the wagon. Little Addie cried. A Cheyenne aimed his rifle at her, but one of the Indian women intervened to save the child. At length the war party threw the captives on the backs of ponies and rode away. "We were so shocked and stunned that we could scarcely realize what had happened," Catherine later recalled of that terrible night, after a grueling ride in drenching rain. "I could not think, and only saw over and over the dead bodies of my parents, sisters and brother. I heard again the awful outcries of the Indians and their victims."

Sophia and Catherine German as they appeared at the time of their capture by Indians, 1875. From Grace Meredith, *Girl Captives of the Cheyennes* (Los Angeles, 1927). Courtesy Missouri Historical Society

To the anguish of this memory, intensified by the sight of the family's scalps fluttering from rifle barrels, the Indians added punishing physical demands. They traveled rapidly, to evade the army columns that seemed everywhere. The sisters had to keep up or be left behind, perhaps even shot. The two youngest girls, Julia and Addie, were in fact abandoned; they wandered for days on the plains, living off berries and the scattered grain and cracker crumbs of old military campsites, until once more seized by the wandering Cheyennes. The rain and sleet of autumn turned to snow, ice, and the bitter cold of a plains winter. The Indian women forced the captives to chop wood and carry water. The men tormented them: they threw Catherine in an icy pond to see if she would drown and held a rifle to her head while laughingly snapping the hammer on an empty chamber. Hunger made the ordeal worse, for the girls could not get used to the almost raw buffalo meat the Indians gave them. Passed from family to family and band to band, they lost touch with one another.

Gradually they adjusted to the harsh new life. Their skin darkened and hardened and they donned Indian clothes. They became members of Indian families and experienced acts of kindness and expressions of affection from their owners. They learned to eat the strange food and even to speak enough of the strange language to communicate in a rudimentary way.

But the labor never lightened, the memory of slaughter never dimmed, the exhausting flight from the bluecoats never slackened, and always the terror lurked close by. Two of Sophia's masters used her for sexual pleasure. When Catherine came into the possession of Long Back, he admitted young men to her blanket in exchange for ponies and other property, and his wife forced her from the tipi to obtain wood and water when as many as six young men were waiting to rape her. "It would be too sad a story were I to tell of all we endured that winter," she later wrote.

Julia and Addie were with Gray Beard's band on McClellan Creek, Texas, on 8 November 1874, when shots rang out and the village boiled with commotion. "Suddenly the lodge I was in went down and was dragged away from me," wrote Julia. "I was terrified and hid under a large buffalo robe. The next I knew—two soldiers uncovered me and tried to have me stand up but apparently I was too weak so they made a seat for me to ride on their guns. Thus, the soldiers carried me from the ravine to a wagon where I saw sister Addie."

Gray Beard's village had fallen before an extraordinary surprise attack by troops under Lieutenant Frank D. Baldwin, who had been escorting a string of twenty-three empty supply wagons. Discovering the Cheyennes, he had formed his cavalry, then hastily mounted his infantry in the wagons and shucked back the canvas covers. With rifles and pistols blazing, wagon soldiers and horse soldiers stormed into the village and chased the startled Indians across twelve miles of prairie. As soldiers searched the village, they spied a lone Indian, mounted, taking aim at the buffalo robe under which Julia had crept. A trooper's carbine dropped the warrior before he could carry out his intent. Addie, weak and emaciated, was found in a tipi trying to kindle a fire. The soldiers tenderly bore the sisters to Fort Leavenworth. "Their story of woe and suffering is simply too horrible to describe," wrote General Miles. "They were almost naked and nearly starved."

As the long cold winter wore away, Catherine and Sophia despaired of rescue. The bands they lived with ranged far to the west, sometimes even into New Mexico, in a ceaseless effort to keep clear of the soldiers.

Stone Calf, chief of the band holding Catherine, favored surrender while some terms might still be exacted from the army. Gray Beard, who since McClellan Creek had come into possession of Sophia, stood firm against giving up.

Peace emissaries came from the soldier chiefs to urge surrender. They were Indians who had themselves already given up. One day in late winter such an emissary, a Kiowa Indian, arrived in Stone Calf's camp. He handed Catherine a little packet. She unwrapped it and joyfully beheld a photograph of Julia and Addie. On the back of the picture was a message:

Fort Sill, I.T.
Jan. 21st, 1875.

To the Misses Germain.

These Germain sisters are well and are now with their friends. Do not be discouraged, efforts are being made for your benefit.

Nelson A. Miles,
Col. and Bvt. Maj. Gen.
U.S. Army

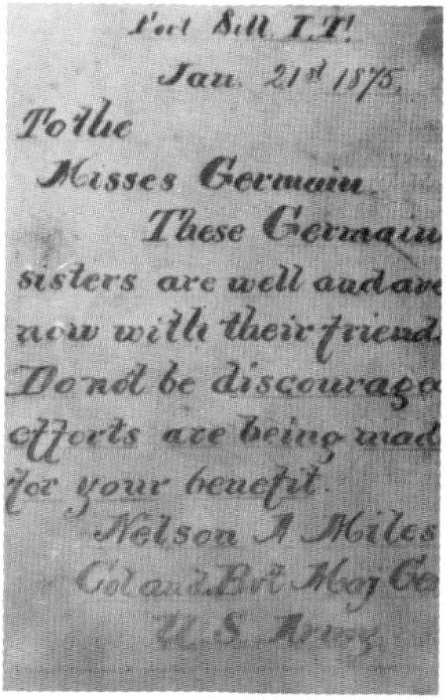

Fort Sill I.T.
Jan. 21st 1875.
To the
Misses Germain.
These Germain
sisters are well and are
now with their friend
Dont be discourage
efforts are being mad
for your benefit.
Nelson A. Miles
Col and Bvt Maj Ge
U.S. Army

The picture and note by which Catherine and Sophia German learned that their sisters were still alive. From Grace Meredith, *Girl Captives of the Cheyennes* (Los Angeles, 1927). Courtesy Missouri Historical Society

The Red River War was drawing to a close. It had begun the previous summer when Kiowas, Comanches, and Cheyennes, angered by the slaughter of the buffalo and the tribulations of reservation life, had broken loose and bolted for the Staked Plains to the west of their reservations. Military columns had campaigned relentlessly ever since, prevailing at last more by sheer persistence that wore down and discouraged the fugitives than by decisive battles. Hope of liberating the German sisters had spurred the troops to special exertions, for their captivity had become known when a patrol from Fort Wallace discovered the murdered family. Near the scene they found a worn Bible, with the names and birthdates of all the children. Signs told that four had been carried away as prisoners, and throughout the winter an occasional report from surrendering Indians confirmed that they still lived. One after another, from autumn to spring, the rebellious bands came in and gave up. At last even Stone Calf and Gray Beard could hold out no longer.

At dusk on 1 March 1875 an army ambulance bore Catherine and Sophia into the military camp at the

The West developed so rapidly that the German sisters lived to see an era when memories of Indian capture seemed incredibly remote. Upper: *Addie and Sophia.* Lower: *Catherine and Julia.* From Grace Meredith, *Girl Captives of the Cheyennes* (Los Angeles, 1927). Courtesy Missouri Historical Society

Cheyenne and Arapaho Agency, Indian Territory. Soldiers lined both sides of the road, cheering and waving their caps in welcome. "We cried and cried for joy," Catherine wrote. " 'Safe at last! Safe at last!' were the words that repeated themselves in my mind."

The tragedy of the Germans struck horror throughout the nation and kindled sympathy for the survivors. The girls identified some of the murderers from among the surrendered Cheyennes, and they were packed off to imprisonment in Florida. General Miles assumed the legal guardianship of the three minor sisters. Congress had appropriated $2,500 each for Julia and Addie, to be taken from treaty annuities due the Cheyennes, and after four years or urging by Miles made similar provision for Catherine and Sophia. With this aid, the girls obtained educations, ultimately married, and lived out long and unadventurous family lives. The last of the sisters, Julia, died in California at the age of ninety-eight in 1959.

The specter of women and children being captured by Indians, rare though the actual event may have been, lay near the surface of each pioneer's mind. As both a cause and result of this constant fear "the capture" was a common theme in nineteenth century art, illustrated in the portfolio on this and the following pages.

Above: *In 1811 the Hudson's Bay Company attempted to plant an agricultural colony in Indian hunting lands along the Red River of the North. Peter Rindisbacher was a seventeen year old boy in a Swiss family of settlers in that colony when in 1823 Sisseton Sioux murdered David Tully, a near-by Scots settler. Rindisbacher painted this and other early Minnesota scenes.* Courtesy West Point Military Academy Museum

"An Osage Scalp Dance" by John Mix Stanley, painted about 1845. Stanley traveled widely in the West painting Indians and frontier scenes, though this stylized picture does not represent any specific incident. Courtesy Smithsonian Institution: National Collection of Fine Art

"Captured by Indians." Missouri painter George Caleb Bingham painted this scene in 1848. Bingham knew well the frontier fears and attitudes, but it is not known if this picture is related to any particular incident. Courtesy St. Louis Art Museum

The most famous kidnapping in all the westward movement was that of Daniel Boone's daughter, Jemima, in Kentucky, followed by her dramatic rescue by Boone and others. Charles Wimar painted "The Abduction of Daniel Boone's Daughter by the Indians" in 1853. Courtesy Washington University Gallery of Art, St. Louis

The tragedy of the German family was scarcely typical of the pioneer experience. Few westering Americans ever saw a hostile Indian, and of these, only an infinitesimal handful suffered Indian atrocities. However rare, nonetheless, the danger of captivity or death and mutilation was an ever present part of the pioneer experience. From colonial times to the passing of the frontier, captivity and atrocity narratives abounded in the nation's literature, and their real-enough horrors found magnification in the sensational fiction of the "penny-dreadfuls." Every westward migrant lived with the knowledge that he courted the fate of John German and his hapless family.

During their brief residence in Kansas, John and Lydia German would have read newspaper accounts of the afflictions visited on the exposed settlements of the Republican and Solomon rivers, where Indian raids felled dozens of citizens and threw others into brutal captivity. Kansans knew of the butchery of Mrs. Clara Blinn and her two-year-old son, captives in Black Kettle's Cheyenne village when General Custer attacked it on the Washita in 1868. They knew of Mrs. Morgan and Miss White, beaten and terrorized by Medicine Arrow's Cheyennes but spared Mrs. Blinn's fate when liberated by Custer the following spring. And they knew of Mrs. Alderdice and Mrs. Weichell, prisoners in Tall Bull's village at Summit Springs, Colorado, when General Carr attacked in July 1869—both shot, although the former recovered.

For virtually every Indian war in which the Indians saw themselves as outrageously victimized, whites could point to provocations that seemed just as outrageous. On the eve of the Columbia Basin warfare of the middle 1850s, Indian Agent A. J. Bolon went among the tribes on a peace mission. Three Indians, professing friendship, joined and traveled with him. Around a nighttime campfire one, a huge powerful man, suddenly pinned Bolon's arms while another calmly pushed his head back and slit his throat. After the battles of Spokane Plain and Four Lakes, few whites thought that Colonel George Wright's summary execution of people capable of such treachery was excessive. The Minnesota uprising that for thirty-eight Sioux ended on the scaffold began with the slaughter of hundreds of settlers amid unrivaled scenes of barbarism—children nailed to cabin doors and swung back and forth until dead, women and young girls raped by a dozen or more braves before being put to death, a pregnant woman ripped open and her unborn child nailed to a tree, whole families trapped in flaming cabins and cremated. And the heartrending "Long Walk" of the Navajos to exile at Bosque Redondo followed on two centuries of butchery, burning, and pillaging of the Rio Grande settlements. To white pioneers, such savagery justified any extremity of retaliation.

Under any circumstances cultural differences would have made Indians and whites quite incomprehensible to each other and encouraged in each an unflattering view of the other. In addition, however, for settlers everywhere in the West ordeals such as suffered by the Germans and the white victims of the Minnesota uprising gave form to an ugly stereotype of the Indian. In this stereotype all Indians were treacherous wild beasts driven by blood-lust and the impulse to plunder. In a single editorial in 1866, for example, a Nebraska newsman characterized Indians as "red savages," "barbarian monsters," "blood-washed animals," and "heartless creatures. . . destitute of all promptings of human nature" and bent upon the gratification of "a heathenish pleasure."

Refugees from the Minnesota Sioux uprising of 1862, resting during their flight to Fort Ridgely. Photo taken by J. E. Whitney, a member of the group. Courtesy Library of Congress

Nineteenth-century America's obsession with its "manifest destiny" reinforced the stereotype. This heady doctrine, which pictured the nation's destiny in continental proportions and gave divine sanction to westward expansion, commanded Americans in stirring Old Testament stanzas to overspread the wilderness, subdue it, and make it blossom. Indians thus interfered with the God-given rights and Biblical injunctions. They did not take gold from the mountains, nor graze cattle or sheep on the boundless grasslands, nor harvest the great stands of timber, nor plant the prairies to wheat; indeed, they did not even believe that land could be bought and sold.

Thus self-interest fortified the "red devil" image. If Indians could be seen as a subhuman species, deserving no more consideration than wild animals, how much easier to justify the seizure of their territory or even their extinction. They could not be made human, much less civilized, and they stood in the way of progress. "Sickly sentimentalists" in the East might promote schemes for civilizing the Indians, but westerners cried for the same treatment a rancher would accord a pack of scavenging wolves. "Many

The Minnesota Sioux Uprising of 1862 was one of the most costly in the history of the West. Certainly over four hundred settlers and soldiers were killed, possibly as many as eight hundred. The uprising erupted as a result of the dealing of a corrupt Indian agent, and raged for a whole summer. In the end thirty-eight Indians were hanged (see p. 26). Immediately thereafter John Stevens, a Minnesota artist, painted a multi-paneled scroll which, mounted on rollers, travelled as an illustrated story of the tragedy in those pre-television days. The panels depict reportedly true incidents of the uprising.

1. *The raiders bypass a farmer considered friendly.* 2. *The Tom Ireland family, Mrs. Ireland's infant still attempting to nurse.* 3. *Julia Smith attempted to shield her mother, and reportedly both were slain by the same bullet.* 4. *A mother compelled to watch her daughter's torture.* Courtesy Minnesota Historical Society

1

2

4

plans have been tried to produce peace on the border,'' editorialized a Kansas journalist in 1869, ''but one alternative remains—EXTERMINATION.''

A nation that had freed the slaves could not bring itself to exterminate the Indians, and the eastern insistence that Indians, however degraded, were indeed human and could be civilized ultimately prevailed over western attitudes. But even easterners could not deny the acts of barbarism that gave the Indian his reputation, or sanction his possession of rich natural resources that begged for exploitation. And so he must stand aside or be crushed as overpowering numbers of miners, stockmen, farmers, and entrepeneurs of every stripe heeded the call to conquer the wilderness and make it blossom.

3

Frederic Remington

(Previous Page) *"Twilight of the Indian" by Frederic Remington. A square house and a circular house... a black horse and a white horse... and a warrior plowing.* Courtesy Harold McCracken

Dewey Horn Cloud, William Drown, and Catherine German all saw the clash of red and white in the American West through lenses colored by their own culture and their own personal perceptions and experiences. It is not remarkable that the images were very different.

White people had robbed Dewey of his birthright, emptied his way of life of much that gave it meaning and vitality, and finally wiped out his family in a nightmare of flying bullets and bursting cannon shells. He could scarcely be expected to look kindly on his conquerors. He could not know the cultural imperatives that powered their restless advance and insatiably exploitive instinct. He could not have understood the humanitarian impulse that underlay their efforts to confer on their red brothers the blessings of education, Christianity, and agricultural self sufficiency. He would not have appreciated the academic distinction between a plotted massacre and a tragic armed clash that just happened.

Nor could Catherine German reasonably be expected to understand why Medicine Water's warriors butchered her mother and father and brother and sisters. With the social sciences yet in their infancy, even the learned men of the time had only the dimmest understanding of the intricate workings of culture. Neither would Catherine ever have comprehended why a rich empire should be left to the undisturbed possession of a scattered population that made so little apparent use of it, why an energetic and ingenious race should not heed the divine command to conquer the land and make it yield up its bounty.

Sharing Catherine's culture, William Drown would have shared many of her attitudes and perspectives. He would not have understood why Indians behaved as they did. Not for a moment would he have conceded that Indians should be allowed to interfere with the settlement and exploitation of the West. Yet as a professional soldier—and an uncommonly thoughtful one at that—he probably could reconcile the necessity of conquest with sympathy for the victims and understanding of their grievances. But intermittent flashes of compassion would not have modified his performance as a soldier, or spared trapped Apache raiders from his pistol and saber.

All three, so far as they thought about it at all, would have given too much credit for the conquest to the soldier—Dewey because soldiers gunned down his family, Catherine because soldiers rescued her from terror-filled captivity, and Drown himself because of self-esteem and the conventional wisdom of his time. But military conquest is too simple an explanation. Far more than the Bugler Drowns, the John Germans conquered the Indians.

By thousands and then millions these anonymous pioneers rolled westward from the Mississippi, settling in the mountains, overspreading the plains, and even venturing into the deserts. Instead of ranging lightly across the land like the Indians, they planted roots that bound them firmly to the land. They demanded that their government remove the Indians, obstacles to permanent settlement, by persuasion or force, and their government quite predictably responded.

Yet governmental action was not the decisive ingredient in the process either. At each critical step along the way the Indians found the territory effectively held by the settlers expanding, and the game and other resources essential to their own way of life diminishing. Acquiescence in the government's demands seemed the only reasonable course. When reason did not prevail, soldiers came to provide the extra pressure needed to make reason prevail.

It was not a sudden, cataclysmic process, although from the Mississippi to the Pacific it occurred in less than half a century. Rather it was a piecemeal process in which the Indians found themselves confined to ever shrinking ranges and finally to scattered reservations that in turn shrank bit by bit. This sequence insured that not until they had fallen wholly under the control of their conquerors would they fully perceive the enormity of the ethnic disaster that had befallen them. Thus, even had the tribes been able to unite and offer effective resistance, never was there a point at which the vision of the future came into sharp enough focus to prompt a truly determined stand. At last, like Dewey and his tribesmen, they could only reflect with bewilderment and despair on what they had lost and how they had lost it.

Dewey Horn Cloud, William Drown, and Catherine German were bit players in a historical drama featuring a cast of millions. They acted their parts with fidelity to their time and place and culture. In that spirit they must be understood. In that spirit, and that spirit only, may they be judged.

Traveler's Guide

The encounter between the expanding United States and the native Americans happened in many places, at many times. Sometimes it was peaceful, as the two cultures puzzled over each other at trading posts and military forts; other times the encounters were tragic, as they fought over land that both sides wanted, or at some spot where mere chance brought warring factions together. Today many of those places are very developed, perhaps even cities, and have lost their "feel." But the history of the American West is so recent that in other cases the "place where it happened" is virtually unchanged or else well-restored. There with a little imagination today's visitor can taste the past.

In watching millions of visitors come to national parks, we have discovered that those who have invested a small amount of effort learning the story behind a particular place always seem to enjoy their visit the most. And of course, there are many more worthy spots than just those listed here. For the traveler who is not in a hurry a few questions at parks and at local historical societies and museums will often lead to unexpected and rewarding side trips.

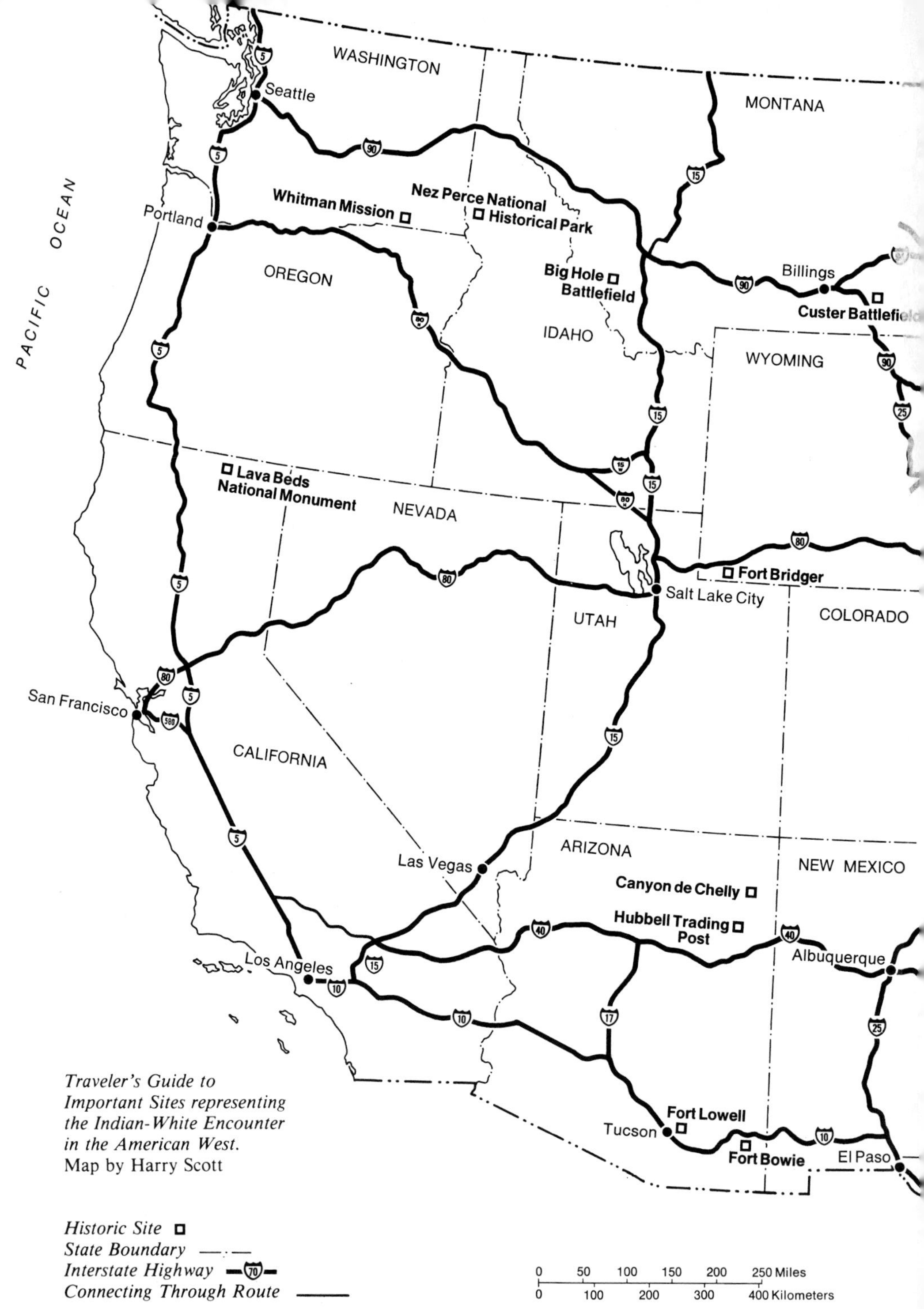

Traveler's Guide to Important Sites representing the Indian-White Encounter in the American West.
Map by Harry Scott

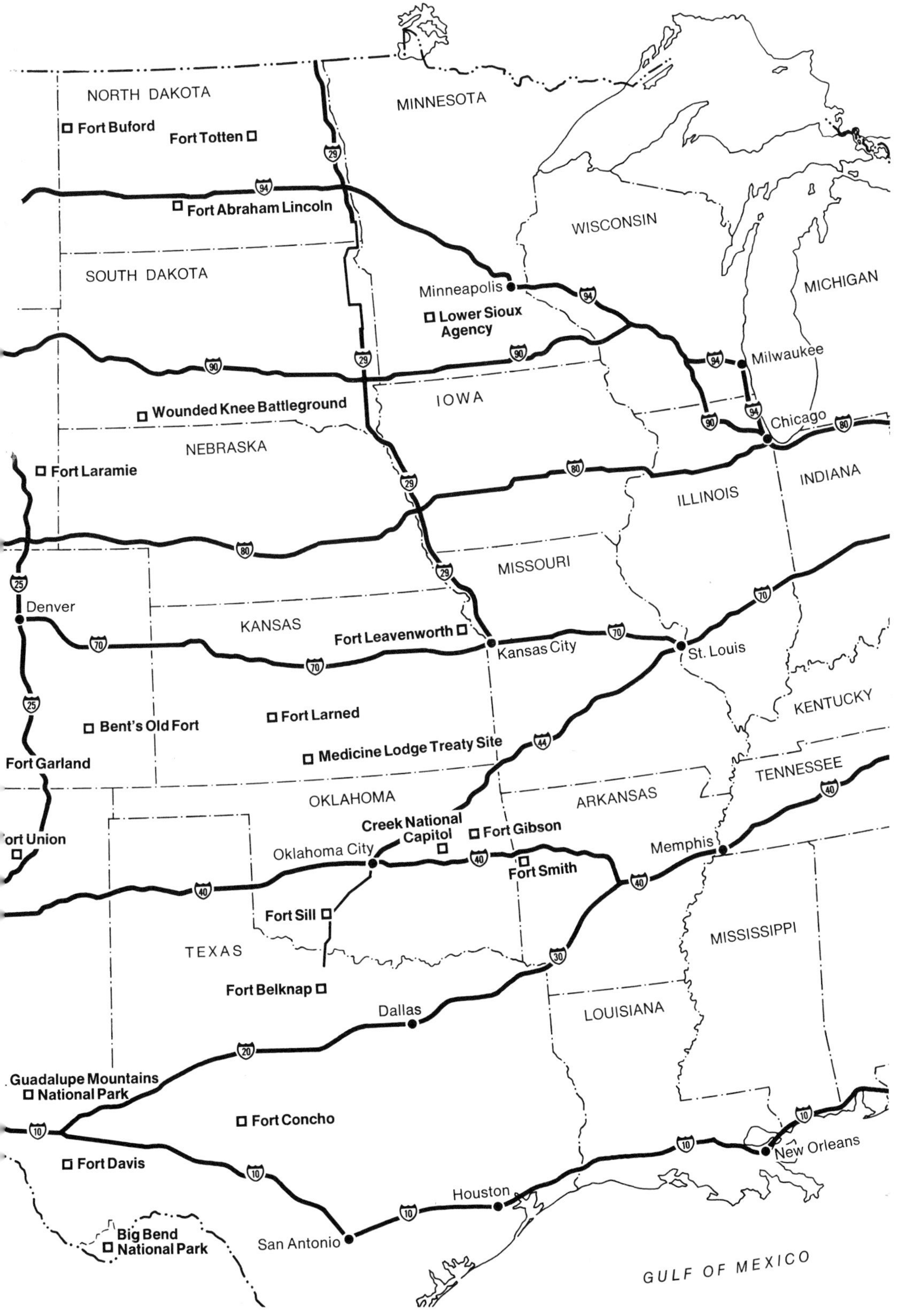
NORTH DAKOTA
Fort Buford
Fort Totten
MINNESOTA
29
94
Fort Abraham Lincoln
WISCONSIN
MICHIGAN
SOUTH DAKOTA
Minneapolis
Lower Sioux Agency
94
Milwaukee
90
29
90
94
IOWA
Wounded Knee Battleground
90
94
Chicago
80
NEBRASKA
Fort Laramie
80
INDIANA
29
ILLINOIS
80
MISSOURI
29
25
Denver
70
KANSAS
Fort Leavenworth
Kansas City
70
St. Louis
70
70
25
Fort Larned
Bent's Old Fort
KENTUCKY
Medicine Lodge Treaty Site
44
Fort Garland
TENNESSEE
OKLAHOMA
ARKANSAS
40
Creek National Capitol
Fort Gibson
Fort Union
Memphis
Oklahoma City
40
Fort Smith
40
40
Fort Sill
MISSISSIPPI
TEXAS
30
Fort Belknap
LOUISIANA
Dallas
20
Guadalupe Mountains National Park
Fort Concho
10
10
10
New Orleans
Fort Davis
10
Houston
10
Big Bend National Park
San Antonio
GULF OF MEXICO

Bent's Old Fort (near LaJunta, Colorado)

In the 1830s and 1840s Bent's Old Fort was the central point of contact on the southern Plains between American traders and the Plains Indians. From this massive adobe structure on the north bank of the Arkansas River, on the Mountain Branch of the Santa Fe Trail, William and Charles Bent and Ceran St. Vrain presided over a farflung trading empire that involved Indians, mountain men, traders, the military, and the famed "commerce of the prairies" that developed over the Santa Fe Trail between Missouri and Mexican New Mexico. The fortunes of the partnership declined after the Mexican War. In 1849 the fort blew up under mysterious circumstances, possibly blown up by William Bent himself, who then moved downstream to try his hand, unsuccessfully, in another location. The ruins of the old fort melted into the earth.

In the 1950s the Colorado Historical Society excavated the site and exposed the foundations. Further excavations by the National Park Service in the mid-1960s led to a complete reconstruction of the fort in its original dimensions and appearance, where costumed personnel go about the daily tasks of a century ago. Here the visitor can get an idea of a fort not as an old building, but as it was when it was new and thriving. Operated by the National Park Service.

Big Bend National Park (Southern Texas)

Embracing a wild tangle of mountains, desert, and canyons nestled in the Big Bend of the Rio Grande, this park is noted for historical values as well as natural and scenic. The "Great Comanche War Trail," connecting the Great Plains with the Mexican provinces, crossed the Rio Grande in the park. Generations of Kiowa and Comanche warriors rode over it to launch raids against the Mexican frontier settlements until at last confined to reservations in 1874-75. Also, Apaches lived in the Chisos Mountains of the Big Bend, depredating along the stage road between San Antonio and El Paso and skirmishing with troops from Fort Davis. This wild and remote corner of Texas remains virtually unchanged in appearance from the years of the Indian wars.

Big Hole Battlefield (near Wisdom, Montana)

This park preserves the site of the Battle of Big Hole, one of the series of engagements between U.S. troops and the fleeing Nez Perce under Chief Joseph and other leaders. Colonel John Gibbon attacked the sleeping Indian camp at dawn on 9 August 1877, and inflicted severe casualties before a vigorous counterattack drove him back and allowed the Nez Perces to escape. Operated by the National Park Service.

Canyon de Chelly (near Chinle, Arizona)

Established for the magnificence of its scenery and the significance of its prehistoric Indian ruins, Canyon de Chelly is also notable as the scene of climactic events in the conquest of the Navajo Indians by the U.S. Army. Colonel Christopher C. ("Kit") Carson's invasion of this bastion of Navajo defenses in the winter of 1863-64 was a final blow that convinced most of the tribe to surrender. Some eight thousand people, three-fourths of the tribe, participated in the tragic "Long Walk" across New Mexico to Bosque Redondo (see p. 25). In 1868, after four years of exile, they were allowed to return to their homeland. Navajo hogans and fields still spot the sandy canyon floor, shadowed by awesome red sandstone cliffs rising as high as one thousand feet. Operated by the National Park Service.

Creek National Capitol (Okmulgee, Oklahoma)

During the 1820s the United States attempted a policy of moving some of the eastern Indian tribes to land west of the Mississippi, where presumably they could remain undisturbed. The Creek Nation was one of those so moved, partly voluntarily, partly by force. There is no way to describe this dislocation as a good thing: for all the tribes it was jarring and destructive. But more than any other group the Creeks did a remarkable job in making the best of a bad situation. After many trying years they organized into the Muskogee Nation in 1867, and adopted a written constitution similar to that of the United States. They functioned well in their self-government, and rapidly assumed a position of leadership among other tribes. This lasted until 1906, when Oklahoma became a state.

The Creek Nation Capitol building, 100 years

old in 1978, is administered by the Creek Indian Memorial Association. It now houses a museum of Creek history. (Sketch by Kountoupis)

Custer Battlefield (near Hardin, Montana)

Here on 25 June 1876, in the Battle of the Little Bighorn, a large force of Sioux and Cheyenne warriors under Sitting Bull, Gall, Crazy Horse, and including young Dewey Horn Cloud (see p. 8), overwhelmed General Custer's Seventh Cavalry in one of the most complete defeats in American military history. The park consists of the ridge on which Custer and some 225 men were slain in the famous "last stand," and the bluffs four miles up the Little Bighorn River where Major Marcus A. Reno and the rest of the regiment held out for two days until help arrived.

White headstones mark where Custer's troops fell and a monument stands over their mass grave. A museum interprets the history of this most dramatic of all Indian battles. Operated by the National Park Service.

Fort Abraham Lincoln (near Mandan, North Dakota)

One of the major forts on the northern frontier. General Custer commanded this post for three years. From here he led the expedition into the Black Hills in 1874 that confirmed the existence of gold there, which led to a flood of miners trespassing into the territory. During the Indian resistance that resulted Custer again marched from here, this time to disaster and immortality at the Little Bighorn. Troops from here also participated in the survey of the Yellowstone country in 1873, and in the pursuit of Chief Joseph and the Nez Perce in 1877.

The park includes the fort site, some restored buildings, restored Mandan Indian earth lodges, and a museum. A North Dakota State Park.

Visitors may also want to include ***Fort Rice,*** *25 miles south. Fort Rice was the base for several major expeditions against the Indians, including against the Sioux involved in the Minnesota uprising mentioned in this book (pp. 62-63). Also several army explorations organized here. The site is now a North Dakota State Historic Site, with foundations marked and two restored blockhouses.*

Fort Belknap (near Newcastle, Texas)

When the United States acquired Texas in 1845, the U.S. Army acquired the responsibility for protecting the settlements from Kiowa and Comanche raids. Fort Belknap was part of this effort, and as the fort nearest the Indian territories, was in the thick of the fighting. There was enough success that in 1854 it was decided to establish two Indian reservations near the fort. Under a remarkably humane and far-sighted Indian agent, Robert Neighbors, the reservations seemed to be doing well. But area settlers bitterly resented the Indians' presence, and mob action eventually forced abandonment of the reservations, and Neighbors himself was killed. This, along with recurrent water problems, brought about abandonment of the fort in 1859.

The partially restored fort, and museum, is administered by Young County with help from the Fort Belknap Historical Society.

Fort Bowie (near Bowie, Arizona)

Located in forbidding Apache Pass, a landmark on a principal overland emigrant and stagecoach route, Fort Bowie played a significant role in the wars with the Chiricahua Apaches. Here in 1861, even before the fort was established, Lieutenant George N. Bascom faced Cochise in the dramatic confrontation that set off a quarter-century of bloody hostilities between these Indians and the white invaders. General James H. Carleton, leading a Federal army eastward in 1862 to head off the Confederate invasion of New Mexico, founded Fort Bowie to guard his line of communication with California. Thereafter until the final surrender of Geronimo the post was the base for scouts, patrols and major offensives against the Apaches. Most notably it served as headquarters and base of operations for General George Crook and his successor Nelson A. Miles in the campaigns deep into Mexico that brought about the surrender of Geronimo and his band. From the Fort Bowie parade ground in September 1886 Geronimo and his people were started on their journey to Florida and imprisonment.

Near Fort Bowie is ***Chiricahua National Monument.*** *While no specific Indian encounters* took place within the park, its complex, forbidding (and beautiful) terrain is typical of where the Apaches lived, hunted and fought. Also nearby in the Dragoon Mountains is **Cochise's Stronghold,** the home grounds of that famous Apache leader.

Fort Bowie and Chiricahua National Monument are operated by the National Park Service; Cochise's Stronghold by the U.S. Forest Service.

Fort Bridger (near town of Fort Bridger, Wyoming)

Although never the base for any major military expeditions, this fort nevertheless represents the many facets of the army in the West. It was involved in the protection of stage routes, the transcontinental telegraph line, emigrants, miners, and railroad workers, and was a Pony Express station.

Many structures remain, some reconstructed and some as ruins. There is a museum. A Wyoming State Historical Park.

Fort Buford (near Buford, North Dakota)

Created in 1866 near the confluence of the Yellowstone and Missouri rivers. This was the midst of hostile (Sioux) territory, and for the next four years the fort was under virtual siege, with Indians attacking work parties sent out to cut hay or get supplies. The fort figured prominently in the northern campaigns of the '70s and '80s. When chiefs Crow King, Gall, Sitting Bull, and their followers, who had annihilated Custer's command at the Little Bighorn, finally were worn down and forced to surrender they did so here at Fort Buford. Throughout the spring and summer of 1881 they straggled in, hungry and tired, until about thirteen hundred had surrendered, including the great medicine man Sitting Bull himself. The post was abandoned in 1895.

The site preserves some original building remains, and there is a museum. A North Dakota State Historical Site.

Fort Concho (San Angelo, Texas)

Fort Concho was built immediately after the Civil War, and was the center of a line of forts separating the settlements from Indian territory. Strategically placed astride the Goodnight-Loving

Cattle Trail and the Southern Transcontinental Trail, for more than a decade it was involved in virtually all central Texas Indian fighting, culminating in the campaign against Victorio in 1879-80. The fort was abandoned in 1889.

The fort is now owned by the city of San Angelo, and operated by the Fort Concho Museum Board. There are numerous well restored and maintained buildings, and a museum. (1880 photo courtesy Fort Concho Museum)

Fort Davis (near town of Fort Davis, Texas)

Picturesquely located in the Davis Mountains of western Texas, Fort Davis affords one of the most complete views of the typical frontier Indian wars fort. It was established in 1854 to guard the San Antonio-El Paso Road, and played a conspicuous part in hostilities with the Apaches for almost thirty years. The fort was involved in the army's remarkable experiment in the use of camels for desert transportation. After the Civil War black troops operating from Fort Davis achieved a notable record in the Indian campaigns. With the death of Victorio in 1880 the menace to west Texas ended, and the post was abandoned in 1891.

Fort Davis has been partially restored. Two barracks, sixteen officers' quarters, a hospital, a commissary, and assorted other buildings, mostly in ruins, may be seen today. There is a museum. During summer months an extensive living history program includes tours through a refurnished officer's quarters, kitchen, and commissary. A cavalry soldier rides daily, and there are demonstrations of adobe making, life in field camps, and frontier army medical care. Operated by the National Park Service.

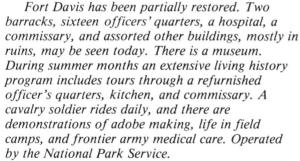

Fort Garland (near town of Fort Garland, Colorado)

During the Civil War Fort Garland was an active Northern post. After the war the legendary mountain man and guide "Kit" Carson commanded the post, and was active in settling problems between the Ute Indians and settlers in the San Luis Valley.

There are numerous restored and refurnished buildings, and a museum. A Colorado State Historical Monument.

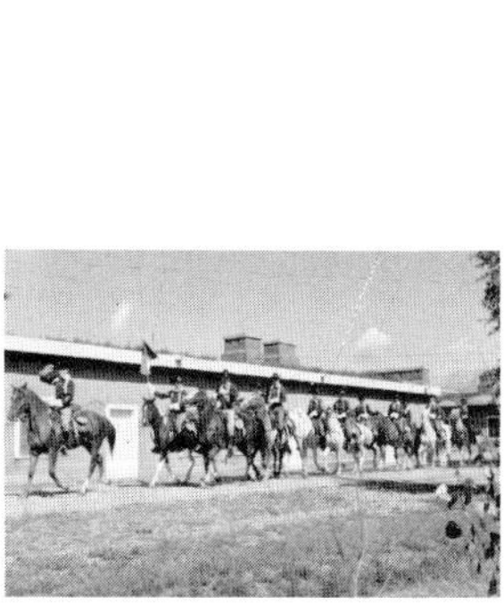

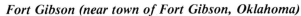

Fort Gibson (near town of Fort Gibson, Oklahoma)

Fort Gibson was unusual in that it was established (1824) largely to keep peace between Indians, rather than between Indians and whites. Eastern Indians, pressured by the expanding United States, were filtering west of the Mississippi and encountering the Indians already entrenched there. The problem increased in the 1830s and 1840s when official policy removed the Five Civilized Tribes from the Southeast to what was imagined to be the "Permanent Indian Frontier." But the nation's expansion refused to stop, and the "permanent" frontier disintegrated.

All the original ruins have disappeared, but faithful reconstructions recall the fort's active days. Operated by the Oklahoma Department of Tourism and Recreation. (Photo courtesy Dub West)

Fort Laramie (near town of Fort Laramie, Wyoming)

From 1834 until 1890 Fort Laramie was a center of trade, transportation, warfare, and diplomacy on the northern Plains. Its long and varied history epitomizes successive stages of the westward movement. First a fur-trading post, then a way station on the Oregon-California Trail, it became a military installation in 1849. For the next 41 years it was the most important post in the warfare between the U.S. Army and the Sioux and Cheyennes to the north. Many buildings and ruins survive to illustrate the successive stages of Fort Laramie's development; several buildings are fully restored and refurnished. There is an extensive living history program. Operated by the National Park Service.

Fort Larned (near Larned, Kansas)

Erected in 1859 to guard the Santa Fe Trail, Fort Larned figured prominently in the wars of the 1860s with the Cheyennes, Arapahos, Kiowas, and Comanches, both as a base for military operations and as a center for peace efforts. With the conquest of the southern Plains Indians in 1874-75 and the coming of the railroad, the post lost its importance and was abandoned in 1878.

Today stone barracks, officers' quarters, and storehouses face a parade ground to recapture the picture of a typical frontier military post. Remains of the Santa Fe Trail may be seen nearby.

Operated by the National Park Service. A few miles east is Pawnee Rock, a famous landmark of the trail and now a Kansas State Park.

Fort Leavenworth (near town of Fort Leavenworth, Kansas)

One of the most important forts of the American West. Founded in 1827 at the edge of the Great Plains and where the Missouri River swings to the north, it was therefore the jumping off place for virtually all major expeditions. From here army units left to explore the West; to protect fur brigades; to escort civilians on the Santa Fe Trail and the Oregon-California Trail; and on military expeditions, including the Army of the West that occupied New Mexico and California during the War with Mexico, and numerous forays against the Indians. Many councils with the Indians were held here.

Fort Leavenworth still is an active U.S. Army post, with historic areas and a museum open to the public.

Fort Lowell (near Tucson, Arizona)

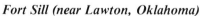

Fort Lowell was established in 1873, replacing an earlier supply depot in nearby Tucson. The fort was active during the '70s and '80s both as a supply depot and as a base for military excursions, especially in the Geronimo campaign. Later, after the Indian wars but before abandonment, it was considered "good duty" — a good place to be stationed, with Tucson nearby.

There are impressive adobe ruins, and the reconstructed Commandant's Quarters house a museum. A Pima County Park, with the museum operated by the Arizona Historical Society.

Fort Sill (near Lawton, Oklahoma)

Immediately after its establishment in 1869 Fort Sill was one of the sites of a well-meaning but unsuccessful experiment in Indian relations. President Grant, responding to public outcry over the mutual cruelties of the Indian wars, directed that church men be used as Indian agents, and Fort Sill was one of the places where this was tried with the Kiowas and Comanches. For various reasons it did not work, and often the Indians fled the

strangeness of farming to return to raiding.

With the failure of the experiment Fort Sill became a major base for the resumption of the Indian campaigns, especially the Red River War (1874-75) which ended in defeat for the southern Plains Indians. Many of the patrols looking for the German sisters, as related in this book, were sent from here. Later, in 1894, many Apaches were returned from their Florida exile and settled at Fort Sill. Geronimo lived out his days here (pictured is the Geronimo Guardhouse) and is buried at the fort, along with chiefs Satank, Satanta, and Quanah Parker.

Many historic buildings remain, and there is a museum that covers the Indian wars era and many other military matters as well. Fort Sill is an active army post, with the historic portion open to the public.

Fort Smith (at town of Fort Smith, Arkansas)

Established in 1817 at the junction of the Arkansas and Poteau rivers, Fort Smith was intended to protect the settlers, control the Indians, and foster the fur trade as America's westward movement resumed after the War of 1812. It became one of a chain of posts extending from Minnesota to Louisiana that defined the "Permanent Indian Frontier," a line beyond which, policy makers hoped, all Indians might be concentrated and left undisturbed by a white migration that would surely stop at the edge of the "Great American Desert." But the advance continued and the territorial acquisitions of the Mexican War doomed the concept. Fort Smith was a base for exploring expeditions and the projection of the military frontier to the Great Plains and Texas. Later it became the seat of justice for the lawless Indian Territory beyond Arkansas' western boundary, made famous from 1875 to 1896 by the justice of the federal court and its most famous judge, Isaac C. Parker.

Surviving today are the site and archeological remains of the stockaded first fort (1817-38), the enlarged second fort (1838-71), and the building that housed the federal district court (1872-89). Judge Parker's courtroom has been restored. Operated by the National Park Service.

Fort Totten (near town of Fort Totten, North Dakota)

While no major events of the Indian wars took place here, Fort Totten is interesting for being almost totally preserved as it was built a century ago. It was established in 1867 to protect the overland route through the Dakota Territory. When that need passed it became an Indian boarding school until 1960.

Still on the Fort Totten Indian Reservation, the fort itself is now a North Dakota State Historic Park, and has a museum.

Fort Union (near Watrous, New Mexico)

Fort Union was built in 1851 near the junction of the Mountain and Cimarron branches of the Santa Fe Trail. For the next four decades it was one of the largest and most important installations in the Southwest, providing a base for campaigns against Apaches, Utes, Navajos, Kiowas, and Comanches. The fort included a major quartermaster depot and arsenal, where supplies and equipment that had just been hauled over the Santa Fe Trail were re-distributed to other southwestern forts, and its active hospital was the first one available after the long trek from Missouri.

Today the eroded ruins stand starkly against the vast prairie, and trail ruts are visible nearby. A museum and living history programs interpret Fort Union's long and colorful history. Operated by the National Park Service.

Guadalupe Mountains National Park (in Texas, south of Carlsbad, New Mexico)

The peaks and canyons of this dry, rugged country were the homeland of the Mescalero Apaches during the period of America's westward expansion. In the late 1860s and the 1870s troops from Fort Davis and other posts scouted and campaigned in the Guadalupes and occasionally skirmished with the elusive quarry. Little altered by modern intrusions, the mountains still evoke images of Apache warfare, like that described in the William Drown section of this book. At the foot of Guadalupe Peak remains may be seen of the Pine Spring stage station (pictured) of the Butterfield Overland Mail, and a military subpost of Fort Davis.

Hubbell Trading Post (near Ganado, Arizona)

Since the first arrival of Europeans on this continent Indian trade has played a key part in intercultural relations. Through traders the Indians acquired the implements and other goods—including the gun—that transformed their material culture. At the trader's they also learned much about the alien ways of the white people. Hubbell Trading Post graphically illustrates the activities and influence of one kind of trader, the reservation trader who operated from a fixed post under government license. John Lorenzo Hubbell traded from this post with the Navajos from 1878 until his death in 1930.

The visitor may view, little changed from Hubbell's time, the wareroom, storeroom, office, and rug room as well as the sprawling adobe hacienda in which the Hubbells lived, all given vivid meaning by continued use as an active trading post. Operated by the National Park Service.

Lava Beds National Monument (near Tulelake, California)

Established as a national monument chiefly for its geological and scientific value, Lava Beds is also significant as the principal battleground of the Modoc War of 1872-73. In a twisted, almost impregnable volcanic fortress that came to be known as Captain Jack's Stronghold, a handful of Modocs held off a sizable force of U.S. soldiers for six months. Included in the park are the sites of the base camp from which the military operations were conducted, the peace conference where on Good Friday of 1873 the Modoc leader Captain Jack shot and killed General Edward R.S. Canby, and the Thomas-Wright disaster where Modocs ambushed and badly mauled an army column. Operated by the National Park Service.

Lower Sioux Agency (near Redwood Falls, Minnesota)

In the summer of 1862 the Minnesota River Valley witnessed one of the bloodiest uprisings in United States history (pp. 62-63). Under Chief Little Crow the Sioux raided farms, the town of New Ulm, and even Fort Ridgely itself. At least five hundred settlers and soldiers lost their lives during the initial uprising and the six weeks of fighting that followed, before the temporary Indian coalition broke up under military pressure. Besides mass imprisonments, there was a mass hanging of thirty-eight Indians at Mankato (page 26).

At the Lower Sioux Agency the Minnesota Historical Society has prepared exhibits telling the overall story of the uprising. ***Fort Ridgely,*** *also with exhibits, is about twenty miles away, and the interested visitor can receive directions to other sites related to the tragedy.*

Medicine Lodge Treaty Site (near town of Medicine Lodge, Kansas)

This site represents one of the milestone attempts at moving Anglo-Indian relations from war to negotiation. In 1867 Congress, wearied of war both for its mutual cruelties and for its indecisiveness, created a Peace Commission to negotiate with the Plains tribes. It was an immense gathering: about five thousand Indians of various tribes were encamped, and the Peace Commission wagon caravan was over two miles long. They met in a natural ampitheater near where two creeks merge, on land the Indians already held sacred. Over the next ten days treaties were worked out with the various tribes, granting them reservations in return for their promise not to oppose further United States expansion and development. Intentions may have been good on both sides, but the pressures in both cultures doomed the attempt. War returned to the prairies within a year.

A park now includes the natural ampitheater, and overlooks the Indians' campground. At five-year intervals a pageant recreates the great treaty council. Operated by the Medicine Lodge Peace Treaty Association. (Reenactment photo courtesy R. D. Noland: Barber County Index)

Nez Perce National Historical Park, Idaho

This park was created to interpret the prehistory, history, and culture of the Nez Perce Indians; missionary efforts among them; the Lewis and Clark Expedition; the invasion of white fur traders, miners, and settlers; and the Nez Perce War of 1877. The park consists of twenty-three units scattered over Idaho. Of particular note are

Spalding, site of the Lapwai Mission of Henry and Eliza Spalding from 1838 to 1847; Fort Lapwai, now headquarters of the Nez Perce Reservation; and the White Bird Battlefield (pictured) where the warriors of Joseph, White Bird, and other chiefs defeated a cavalry command in the first engagement of the Nez Perce War of 1877 which ended only after a thousand-mile fighting trek across the Rocky Mountains almost to the Canadian boundary. Operated jointly by the National Park Service and other state and local agencies.

Whitman Mission (near Walla Walla, Washington)

Marcus and Narcissa Whitman founded the Waiilatpu Mission in 1836. Here they attempted to minister to the neighboring Cayuse Indians while also aiding emigrants on the Oregon Trail. In 1847 disaffected Indians killed the Whitmans and most of the other mission staff, thus ending the mission and firing up hostilities between the Indians and white settlers, which eventually led to a series of wars in the Northwest.

The park preserves the foundation remains of the mission buildings, a restored irrigation ditch, millpond, an orchard, the "Great Grave" of the massacre victims, a monument honoring the Whitmans, and has a museum. Operated by the National Park Service.

Wounded Knee Battleground (near Pine Ridge, South Dakota)

The tragic events of Wounded Knee, of Dewey Horncloud and of his people, are described in the opening chapter of this book. Pictured is the ravine Dewey fought from.

The site of the battle is on the Pine Ridge Indian Reservation. It is open to the public. There are markers, and nearby is the cemetery with the mass grave of the Indians who died that day, including Dewey Horncloud's parents, his wife, and two brothers.